"Crafted with great cunning and flair which makes for a wild and electrifying read."
—Ann Coombs, futurist and best-selling author

"A terrific tale, fast paced and gripping to the end."
—Mike Harcourt, author and former Premier of British Columbia

"A band of 12th Century characters fan out across southern England, Europe and the Holy Land unravelling a mystery about lost birthright, power and magic. Full of twists, turns and incidents and vivid descriptions of the violence and lawlessness of medieval life and of the medieval landscape; a thought provoking read."
—Island Tides, newspaper

"… A good story well told. Moves along with speed and clarity, and with such vivid imagery and dramatic action that the reader becomes excited and possessed, as are the book's characters themselves."
—Robin Skelton, poet, author of *Fires of the Kindred*

THE ANCIENT BLOODLINES TRILOGY

BOOK ONE
THE POWER IN THE DARK

BOOK TWO
SHADOW OF THE SWORDS

BOOK THREE
KEEPER OF THE GRAIL

THE ANCIENT BLOODLINES TRILOGY
BOOK THREE

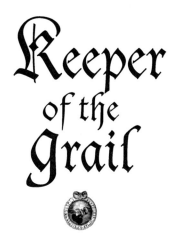

Keeper
of the
grail

BARRY MATHIAS

Agio
PUBLISHING HOUSE

PUBLISHING HOUSE

151 Howe Street, Victoria BC Canada V8V 4K5

For information and bulk orders, please contact
info@agiopublishing.com *or go to*
www.agiopublishing.com
Visit this book's website at www.barrymathias.com *and*
ancientbloodlinestrilogy.com

ISBN 978-1-897435-1-15-1 (trade paperback)

10 9 8 7 6 5 4 3 2 1

DEDICATION

This is dedicated to Clare,
my soul mate and best friend,
who helped me, in so many ways,
to complete this book, and the other two of the trilogy.

ACKNOWLEDGEMENTS

I am grateful to my family for their encouragement and help through the long gestation of this story. My particular thanks to my younger daughter, Natasha Smith, artist and printmaker of Nelson, B.C. (www.natashasmith. net) whose artwork has added immeasurably to this trilogy. I am grateful to Carol Stewart for her perceptive comments, and to other friends who gave me enthusiastic support.

I thank Bruce and Marsha Batchelor of Agio Publishing House, who have enabled me to reach a wider readership, and whose expertise has been invaluable.

KEEPER OF THE GRAIL

THE HOLY LAND

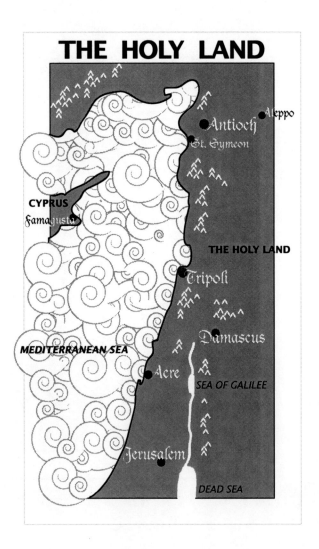

CYPRUS

Famagusta

Aleppo

Antioch

St. Symeon

THE HOLY LAND

Tripoli

Damascus

MEDITERRANEAN SEA

Acre

SEA OF GALILEE

Jerusalem

DEAD SEA

PROLOGUE

South of Antioch 1116

IN THE EARLY AFTERNOON, as the great battle reached its climax, the earthquake struck. Until that point it had been uncertain which army would prevail. The Moslem forces had appeared unexpectedly on the high plateau, and the Crusaders' heavy cavalry barely had time to assemble in enough numbers to stem the rapid advance of their enemy. Because of the cavalry's heroic charge, hundreds of the foot soldiers and archers had been able to complete a hasty march up the steep hill, getting into their formations mere moments before the enemy's major onslaught began.

At the same time, Moslem light cavalry had attacked the supply column in the valley below the high plateau. Only a few soldiers and camp followers had been left to defend the wagons, and after a brief and bloody fight, the surviving defenders were compelled to retreat, unable to withstand the ferocious assault by greatly superior forces. If it had not been for a tall, stocky sergeant, who had maintained the discipline in a small section of soldiers, it was doubtful if any would have survived. In a defensive formation, they had retreated up the hill towards the large red wooden cross, close to where the rest of the Crusader forces were assembled. A keen eye would have noticed the sergeant guarded a beautiful young woman.

On the rocky plateau, amid dust and clouds of arrows, the

soldiers clashed in deadly earnest. The two separate armies of the Crusaders lacked the cohesion that a single command would have achieved, but their heavy cavalry had eventually regained the advantage until a powerful Moslem charge, led by a huge warrior dressed in black and with flowing red hair, had shattered the Crusader lines. When the defeat of the Crusaders seemed likely, the red-headed warrior had fled the battle followed by a knight on a black horse. Moments later, the earthquake struck, and each side had retreated in disarray.

CHAPTER 1

NEWS OF THE BATTLE reached Antioch in the late evening. Disjointed accounts, brought by weary and frightened men, confirmed that a large force of Moslems had attacked the two Crusader armies on the second day of their march to Tripoli. At the crucial point in the fighting, when the result hung in the balance, a powerful earthquake had struck and the surviving soldiers on both sides had fled the field of battle. Neither of the armies had claimed victory and the losses were unknown.

In the great hall of the Knights of the Order large candles flickered on a broad table. The night was cold under a clear sky, but the High Lord was unaware as he assessed the latest report of the battle. He stared at the youth in front of him with conflicting emotions.

"You are certain that Lord Longsword is dead?" He pushed back his shoulder length blond hair, bleached almost white by the sun, and tilted up his aquiline nose.

"Yes, my lord." The young squire lowered his eyes, missing the gleam of triumph that passed across the thin face of Sir Raoul de Warron. "Sir Stephen de Bois was also killed. Both of the nobles died opposing a cavalry charge led by a huge warrior on a black horse."

"He killed them both?" The squire nodded. "Tell me about his sword."

The youth looked up quickly, eyes wide in his exhausted face. "My lord, you know about the sword?" He continued as though he was speaking to himself. "It was the worst of nightmares. The sword gleamed blue in the dusty haze of the battle, and killed all those who stood against it. Their leader was like a monster from

Hell. He dispatched Lord Longsword, and cut down Sir Stephen de Bois almost immediately afterwards. When all seemed lost, the enemy leader suddenly quit the field."

"Why did he do that?" Sir Raoul interrupted.

"I know not, my Lord." The squire appeared close to tears. "Some say he was pursued by a knight on a black horse. It makes no sense, my Lord." There was a waver in his voice. "We were almost defeated and then the giant rode away, and his troops began to fall back. When it looked as if we might win the day, the ground began to shake, and the earth split, and everyone ran for his life. The dead and injured were left; there were so many of them...." A shuddering spasm shook him, and he sank to his knees holding his face in his hands.

"You've done well, Andrew." Sir Raoul stood up, placing his hand on the youth's shoulder. "Your parents will be proud of you." He raised him up gently, and put his arm round the young man's shoulder. "Just one more question, Andrew: Did you see what happened to the young woman whom our Order was escorting?"

"Mistress Gwen, my Lord?" He shook his head. "She was with the supply wagons when I last saw her. That was before the fighting started."

The High Lord patted Andrew solicitously on the back. He steered him towards the door. "You have done well, now get some rest." Sir Raoul returned to his large, oak chair.

As he did so a tall knight strode out from behind a screened area. He was a thickset man with powerful shoulders and long hair, the colour of jet. A prominent nose dominated the broad clean-shaven face, but the thick lips could not hide the cruelty etched on his mouth.

"You heard all of that, Raymond?"

"Yes." Raymond de Wulfric looked disdainfully at the door. "His report was much like the others: fair news and foul." He gazed out of the window at the darkened streets of Antioch. "We are rid of the fanatical Longsword, and of his ambitious henchman, Stephen de Bois, but we appear to have lost the jewel in the crown."

"Perhaps. But there is no confirmation of her death, for which we can give thanks. It's early days." Sir Raoul sat back in his chair.

"I have persuaded Maurice de Maron, our illustrious governor, to send out a recovery force to bring back the injured and dispose of the bodies of our fallen friends. I want you, with some others of our Order, to accompany it and make your own investigations. Your task is to find the Maid and secure her safe return to this city." Sir Raoul examined his long, tapering fingers. "You noticed the youth gave yet another report of a knight on a black horse who followed the giant off the field of battle?"

"It must be him." Raymond de Wulfric's dark eyes glazed over as he stared out. "The one who calls himself John or Giles Plantard, and whom we know as Gilles de Plantard?" He curled his lip. "The self-styled Keeper of the Grail."

"He has the sign of power on his right hand."

"Anyone can have a tattoo."

"Yes, perhaps." Sir Raoul de Warron chewed thoughtfully on his lower lip. "I understand this Gilles de Plantard was riding with the forces of the young Lord Ralph d'Escosse, who was sent by our noble King Henry to keep an eye on us." He gave a humourless laugh. "We can blame the late Lord Longsword for igniting the King's interest in our Order."

Sir Raymond de Wulfric raised his black eyebrows in surprise. "Is there any report of d'Escosse's death?"

"Not so far. But, it would serve our purposes if he were found dead, or even severely injured. That way we could combine our two forces, with the King paying half. It would also allow us free movement, especially now that Longsword is dead."

"I truly believe the man was mad." Raymond began to pace about on the rich carpets that covered the stone floor. "Ambition, power and overwhelming pride were his downfall."

An ironic smile appeared on Raoul's thin face. "Of course, we are not guilty of any of those things!"

Raymond whirled round, his eyes flashing with anger. "We are not fanatical zealots, like Longsword. His belief in the Swords of Power! His desire to capture Aleppo and Damascus! He really believed that merely having the Maid was enough to guarantee his victory over the Moslem hordes."

"I would not dismiss the Swords of Power as the imaginings

of a crazed zealot. You've heard the reports. They all mentioned a sword that glowed with a blue light and cut down all who opposed it. Neither you nor I have been involved in a battle where they were used. We disregard their existence at our peril."

"Magic swords! Do you really believe in magic swords?" Raymond stared at the High Lord in disbelief. "These are the stories old women tell to scare their grandchildren." He approached the table, towering over Raoul. "Now, the reports of the giant warrior I can accept. He is obviously immensely strong, and an excellent fighter. He may be our most dangerous enemy, yet he is but a man with a fine sword. Nothing more!" He slammed down his clenched fist on the polished table.

Raoul stared unblinking at the angry man in front of him. "I did not use the word magic. Like you, I associate the word with childish stories. But, I have lived long enough to know that there are things I do not understand. This country is full of secrets," he raised a hand towards the window, "and events happen out there that I cannot explain. Before you came out here and saw a camel, you would have thought it a childish tale if I had described a large creature with a hump on its back that lived in the desert and could go for days without water."

Raymond sank into a chair. "That's different. We're talking about magic swords, not strange creatures."

"No, Raymond, we are talking about Swords of Power. To call them magical is to make them seem unbelievable and lessens their danger. If it helps you to believe in them, think of the Swords in terms of power, not magic. I have received first hand reports of this giant and his Swords. At one time we owned one of them."

"What?" Raymond de Wulfric's mouth sagged.

"Let me tell you the story." Raoul poured wine into two silver goblets, passing one across the table. "When we captured Jerusalem in 1099, one of our Order, a knight called Sir Maurice de Ridefort, took possession of one of these swords. He described it as the most beautiful and the most dangerous weapon he had ever seen."

Raymond made a derisive sound, but Raoul appeared not to notice.

"In our writings there are references to such a sword, of which only our most senior members are aware. It was thought possible that one, or both, of these swords, which have been lost for centuries, might be found near the Temple Mount. During the chaos and the slaughter following the capture of the city, such a sword was found. Sir Maurice claimed that anyone who tried to use it, died by it. Somehow, he smuggled the sword back to England together with two small children. One of those children was Mistress Gwen."

Raoul stopped to take a long drink. Raymond sat unmoving, his eyes fixed on Raoul's.

"To protect her from our enemies, he left her in the safe-keeping of a trusted blacksmith in a small village in Wessex. Sir Maurice also left him the sword with strict orders not to use it except in the protection of the child. Three years ago after almost twelve years, our enemies discovered Gwen's whereabouts. She was about seventeen by that time and, while defending her we lost the sword. The Order believes the Giant captured it and now he has both of them."

"My father knew Sir Maurice de Rideford," Raymond sipped his wine, deep in thought. "If these swords are so powerful, why has the Giant and his Moslem hordes not recaptured the Holy Land?"

"There are many things we don't understand. But I have had reports that he is unpopular with the Moslem leaders, as they believe he is only interested in his own plans. It would seem that regaining the two Swords of Power and capturing the Maid are his priorities. He has greater ambitions than merely defeating our armies."

"Greater ambitions?"

"The Moslem leaders believe the Giant seeks the overthrow of all Christianity throughout Europe."

"Hah!" Raymond almost choked on his wine. "And you believe this senseless drivel? Why, if he is seeking world domination and possesses magic swords, did he abandon the battle yesterday when victory was seemingly so close?"

Raoul poured himself more wine, and slowly swirled it round in his goblet. "Why indeed? Perhaps it had something to do with the enigmatic John, our Gilles de Plantard. Perhaps he is special after all. Perhaps he can control the Swords of Power."

"Are we to believe that de Plantard was the other child that Sir Maurice de Rideford took to England?" It was clear that Raymond was struggling to keep his anger under control.

"It is most likely, but we can't be certain. The boy was placed with an order of nuns, after he was injured in the head. We investigated his bloodline, but before we came to any conclusions he disappeared."

"How convenient," Raymond sneered.

"Not at all. He literally vanished. We heard nothing more of him for more than twelve years. Then, according to Sir Richard de Godfroi—."

"—Another fanatic, who I'm told died fighting the Giant near Christchurch?"

"He was a fine knight in his younger days. He was quite clear in his report, however, that Mistress Gwen was captured by a huge warrior near her village in 1113, and was rescued by a youth called John, who also answered to the name of Giles Plantard. Apparently, this John claimed he had killed the Giant's identical twin and owned, for a short time, one of the two Swords of Power, before losing it to the second Giant. Recently, as you know, he has reappeared, dressed and armed as a knight and in the company of the young Lord Ralph d'Escosse. He seems to have become well trained in warfare."

Raymond flexed his thick fingers and took in a deep breath. "And you believe this? This…," he struggled to control himself, "this fantasy: magic swords, identical twins, unidentifiable youths, and world domination by a giant who has red hair and leads a Moslem army!"

He moved towards the window and looked up at the stars. "The Maid, I can believe in. We are certain of her bloodline, and we know she will further our cause. But Lord Longsword and Sir Richard de Godfroi were fanatics who believed in anything that suited their own demented view of the world. I cannot take their reports seriously."

The High Lord looked steadily at the angry knight. "Raymond, you are new to the higher ranks of the Order and you have only recently come to this strange land. There is still much you have to learn. I value your friendship and your courage in battle, and so I would urge you, as a friend, to keep an open mind. The Giant exists and it is possible he once had a twin brother. Certainly, it would explain how he was often seen in two places at once. The Swords exist and are dangerous in his hands. Accept that, if nothing else. We are still unsure who this de Plantard really is, but for the moment our concern is for the Maid, whom we know as Mistress Gwen. Her safety is paramount. This could be the most important moment in the life of the Order." He stood up and placed a hand on Raymond's shoulder. "Find her, my friend."

"I will, Raoul. If she's alive, I'll find her." He nodded his head.

"The relief force leaves at first light." The High Lord clasped hands with Raymond de Wulfric. "May God go with you on this most important quest." His face clouded. "If she is dead, all our planning and preparations have been in vain."

As he left the building Raymond ignored the guards' salute and walked confidently down a major street towards the square in which his officers had requisitioned a luxurious house. It had once belonged to a wealthy trader and now provided comfortable lodgings for a least ten knights and their retinue. His mind was focused on his recent interview with Sir Raoul de Warron and he took little notice of the dark alleys on either side of the street. He was a strong man in the prime of his life. He wore a long, white surcoat over a chain mail suit, and a long dagger hung from his tooled leather belt. His mailed hood rested across his broad shoulders revealing a thick shock of black, wavy hair. Confident in his ability to defeat any adversary, he had left his heavy long sword with his squire, who, even at that late hour, was polishing it, fearful of his master's anger.

Raymond stopped a short distance from the square and stared up at the myriad of stars in the cloudless sky. "She can't have died," he whispered. "It's not possible." He stuck out his lower lip. "I'll find her, wherever she is. That is my pledge."

A sudden cry from a dark alley behind him interrupted his

thoughts. It was the voice of a young man, cursing in French, and if not for the sound of clashing swords, Raymond might have thought it was a game. Never had he heard a serious fighter yell: "Damned heathens! I'll teach you manners!" He drew his dagger and turned towards the noise of the fight.

· · ·

SIR VERNON DE KARI was a young knight with little experience of life. He was courteous, well tutored, and always exhibited a wild enthusiasm for anything that seemed adventurous. He had gained a belief, solely through reading, in the romance of travel and the noble chivalry of war. His perpetual bright-eyed optimism combined with his thoughtless behaviour had frequently enraged his elderly father. Being the youngest of a large family, and having little likelihood of inheriting the de Kari's substantial wealth, he had finally persuaded his father to allow him to join the Crusader army in the Holy Land.

"You may as well break your stupid neck fighting the Infidel, as risking life and limb in my forests." Lord Richard de Kari shook his head, as though disagreeing with his own decision. Only his wife was aware, despite of her husband's angry outbursts, that Vernon was his favourite son. "Just make sure you equip yourself in a suitable manner. Remember you're my son."

Eventually, he arrived in Antioch with a fine suit of armour, bright chain mail, and some of the best horses in the city. His father had provided an armourer, a squire, a bevy of servants and ten men-at-arms, all with fine accoutrements, and Vernon's triumphant entry into the city caused a flurry of interest. When he presented himself to the well-fed Lord Maurice de Maron, the Governor was more impressed with the ten soldiers than with the young knight, who seemed unbelievably naïve. De Maron thought it wise, however, to appoint Vernon to his staff, as wealthy young knights were few and far between.

Shortly after his appointment, the armies from Cyprus arrived and Lord Maurice had been heavily involved in the negotiations leading to the departure of the armies towards Tripoli. Lord Maurice had refused to contribute any soldiers. In spite of Vernon's excited requests, the Governor had forbidden him to join the armies when they departed. As a consequence, three days later he was still alive but aching for action.

"Would you like me to join the relief force tomorrow, my Lord?" Sir Vernon tried to make it sound a casual request, and one of no importance. Although physically fit, he did not possess the huge muscular bulk common to most Crusader knights; he had only recently taken to shaving. In all respects he looked of noble birth, but lacked the authority and the brutality of his fellow knights. The governor was unimpressed.

Maurice de Maron lifted his tired eyes from the parchment he was reading. The verbal reports were still coming in, but thankfully he had received a competent, unemotional document from d'Escosse, which had enabled him to grasp what had really happened. He damned Longsword and cursed the Order. If it were not for them he would have had an army strong enough to lead an assault on Aleppo. Now, it would appear that hundreds of lives had been lost, and for nothing. He frowned at the young man in front of him.

"Do you want to go?"

"Yes, my Lord. I have little experience of this country, and the sooner I acquaint myself with its wonders and its difficulties, the sooner I will be a useful member of your entourage."

"Wonders!" Lord Maurice almost choked. "This is a Hellish place, and it's hard to believe that God chose this hot, dry, fly-infested country as the birthplace for his Son." He rubbed a hand over his brow. "Never use the word difficulties. It is far too polite. Say acute problems, dire predicaments, heathen blasphemies and foul incidents, and you might sound as if you are referring to this particular part of the world's most pestilent domain. Further more, I do not have an entourage! You make me sound like the owner of a brothel."

"Yes, Sir. I quite understand."

"No, you don't! Which is why I am agreeing to your request." He glared at the young knight in front of him and wondered if, as a young man, he had ever been so gauche and naïve. "It will not be enjoyable. Do not expect to see any wonders. You will have to control recalcitrant soldiers who do not wish to march; it will be a journey of unending heat and flies during the day and bone-wrenching cold at night. You and the other officers will be responsible for ensuring that the numerous bodies are identified where possible, and burnt. The smell will be appalling. You must also arrange for the wounded to be safely conveyed back to this city, and you must exert your authority over the surviving elements of a dispirited army and ensure they all return. Sir William de Bracy is in charge. Report to him now. Any questions?"

Sir Vernon blew out his cheeks and immediately wished he hadn't. "Um, no, my Lord." He was about to turn away when he remembered there was something he did need to ask. "My Lord?"

"Yes?" Lord Maurice was already turning back to his report.

"What about the Knights of the Order?"

"What about them?"

Sir Vernon de Kari felt he was back home with his ancient, authoritarian tutor. "I wondered what I should do if the knights... a knight... of that Order disagreed with my... um, orders from you?"

"You will decapitate him! What else did you imagine?" Lord Maurice glanced up and experienced a fleeting moment of sympathy, when he saw the alarm in the young man's face. He stood up and stretched his arms almost hiding a yawn. "No, Sir Vernon, do not fear. Your question was reasonable."

He poured himself some wine, taking a deep draught. "I want you to observe these Knights of the Order. Report back to me if their behaviour is strange in any way." He frowned. "They seem to place a lot of importance on a young woman who was travelling with their part of the army. Find out if she survived the battle, and if she did, inquire if she is prepared to continue with them. I would be pleased to offer her an alternative guardianship. Understand?"

"Yes, Sir. Thank you, my Lord," he paused, "for putting your trust in me."

Lord Maurice de Maron turned away and waved a dismissive hand, as Sir Vernon bowed his way out of the room, smiling delightedly.

A few minutes later, as he strode purposefully from the Governor's house, Vernon felt he was finally on the verge of the great adventure that he craved. It was the chance to prove himself a man and fight the Infidel for the glory of God, civilization, and a certain pretty young woman on his father's estate. In his shining mailed hauberk and his new white surcoat with its red cross, he was conscious of how heroic he looked. It would have surprised him if he had known that the Governor considered him an object of ridicule. He rested his right hand on the hilt of his sword; he was ready to take on the world.

Vernon turned into an alley. It was a dark fetid passageway, with high, windowless walls on both sides, and only the occasional unmarked doorway. He remembered it would lead to the square where his temporary accommodation was situated. He strode quickly along, his left hand on the handle of his sword, the scabbard occasionally knocking against his leg. Consumed with his dreams of glory, it did not occur to him that there could be any danger within the city. After all, Antioch had been in Crusader hands for many years. He believed the enemy forces were somewhere out in the desert, where he would eventually confront them. It did not concern him, therefore, when three large shadows appeared at the end of the alley; their dark shapes silhouetted by the lights in the square, their headdresses confirming them as Arabs. Only the sound of the running feet behind alerted him to his predicament.

He quickly drew his sword and backed into a shadowy doorway. "Stop!" he yelled in French, his voice sounding unnaturally high. "Stop! I command you!"

The two figures behind him were closing fast; the three at the other end were also racing towards him, but were further away. Vernon raised his sword and prepared to defend himself. He swiftly parried the first curved blade, knocking the weapon from the attacker. In a flowing movement he sidestepped the second opponent and was able to swing round, landing a powerful blow with the pommel of his sword into the man's back. The potential assassin collapsed, crashing into the first man who was frantically trying to regain his lost sword. There was enough light for Vernon to see that his attackers wore body armour and carried quality weapons. They were not mere cutpurses, but fighting men.

"Damned heathens!" he yelled. "I'll teach you manners!" His blood was racing, and he felt outraged that he should be attacked. He did not fear these unknown assailants even though they outnumbered him. This was what he had trained for, and his mind was working quickly.

Vernon realized he was now facing all of his enemies. With a quick glance behind to confirm there were no more, he positioned himself in the middle of the narrow alley, gripping his sword, two-handed, in front of him. There was a moment of silence as the three new fighters stopped a few paces beyond his sword. The one in the middle, who appeared to be the leader of the gang, gave some muttered orders in a harsh, grating voice. The second attacker lay unmoving on the ground. The first had taken up the sword of his fallen accomplice and stood next to the leader. The four men began to advance slowly in a line, filling the width of the alley.

"Damned heathens!" Vernon yelled again. "Prepare to meet your God!" In spite of the impending onslaught, Vernon still had a momentary feeling of satisfaction in the sound of his words. It was a noble speech.

The silent attackers moved a step forward. Instead of retreating backwards Vernon leaped towards them, bringing his sword up in a sweep towards the man furthest on his left, then cutting the blade back towards the right across the line of advancing fighters at chest level. The man on the left jumped back, but the original attacker in the middle, perhaps keen to impress the leader, lunged forward attempting a shoulder high slash with his curved blade, but was too late to avoid the returning long sword. Vernon felt a slight jarring in his arms as his sword sliced into the attacker's arm. With a howl of pain the man staggered sideways, upsetting the balance of his leader next to him. Vernon sprang back and prepared himself for the next attack. The man on the right moved quickly, attempting to get under the young knight's sword, while the man on the left advanced more slowly, a long knife in his outstretched hand. As if by agreement the leader sprang forward with a manic scream, slashing wildly at Vernon's head with his curved sword, forcing him back. The other two fighters glided in from each side. Almost overwhelmed, de Kari resorted to huge sweeps of his long sword in a figure of eight, concentrating on keeping out of reach of the deadly weapons that confronted him. He was conscious, however, of losing the initiative. For the first time in his life he began to worry.

Then it all changed. The leader in the middle suddenly paused: his body arched forward and his sword dropped to the ground. Vernon was in the act of moving backwards towards his left to counter the advance of the man with the long knife, when he became aware he was undefended on his right. He forced the knife back with a thrust of his long sword and, with panic in his eyes, swung to his right, fearing he was too late to fend off the advancing swordsman. But the expected sword thrust did not materialize; he was amazed to see the attacker drop to the ground in front of a very large man in Crusader uniform, wielding a bloody dagger. De Kari turned quickly back to face the man with the long knife, only to see him sprinting away down the alley, into the light of the square beyond.

Vernon staggered back against the wall. His arms were aching; he was breathing heavily and he felt utterly exhausted. Around him, the attacker with the amputated arm was moaning and the one Vernon had clubbed with his sword was attempting to crawl away.

The tall knight casually wiped his dagger on the clothes of one of the corpses. "I am Sir Raymond de Wulfric." It was an arrogant voice that spoke of accustomed power, and huge self-confidence.

"I'm Sir Vernon de Kari," he gasped. He ran his tongue over his dry lips. "Thank you." He bent forward with one hand on his hip, the other holding the sword. He straightened up, taking in a deep breath. "Phew. That was close." After a moment's consideration, he added: "Not too close, you understand. I was just beginning to get the upper hand." He gave a modest laugh. "But thanks, anyway."

Sir Raymond frowned at the young, undersized knight in front of him. By the dim light he could see he had aristocratic features;

his refined voice indicated a wealthy background. Although obviously stupid, the youth had fought bravely, so he refrained from the angry retort he was about to give. Without comment, de Wulfric stalked away down the alley. He paused when he caught up with the injured Arab, who was still dragging himself painfully along the ground in the direction of the lighted square. Reaching down, he effortlessly lifted the man up by one shoulder. The Arab cried out and was quickly silenced as the knight hit him with his mailed glove. Sir Raymond strode out of the alley and across the square in the direction of the headquarters building, dragging the unconscious man by his wrist.

After a short pause, when he had regained his breath, Vernon examined the bodies. It was the first time in his life he had been involved in mortal combat, and the shock of the fighting was beginning to affect him. Sir Raymond had dispatched two of the Arabs with a remarkable display of efficiency and detachment. The third man, with the amputated arm, had stopped moaning and appeared to have died from loss of blood. Vernon examined him carefully, almost willing him to be alive, but there was no pulse in this throat.

He was in the company of three corpses, and it was unsettling. Although he had hunted large animals all his life, nobody he knew had ever died. In fact, he had never seen a dead body before. In the dim light, he was unable to discern clearly the features of the stranger who had tried to kill him, and whom he had killed. He tried to remind himself that his reason for coming to the Holy Land was to kill infidels. He was trained for this. Yet, somehow, he did not feel any pride or satisfaction in his accomplishment. It had been a messy, savage affair, lacking in any nobility; without Sir Raymond de Wulfric, it would have been his body lying unrecognized and besmirched in this foul alley.

He bent down and picked up one of the curved swords. He weighed it thoughtfully in his right hand. Looking about, he walked down to the square in search of a patrol; he had still to report to Sir William de Bracy. In his left hand he carried the long sword, resting on his shoulder, and in his other he carried the curved sword of his enemy; one seemed to balance the other.

CHAPTER 2

GWEN'S FIRST AWARENESS WAS of water flowing over her face. It was cool and reassuring. She drank gratefully when a strong arm raised her throbbing head and placed a water bottle to her parched lips. Her mind groped back into the fog of previous events. She was aware of sounds: the moaning and crying of injured people; but there was no clashing of iron against iron, which told her the fighting was over. She could feel a warm breeze blowing against her face and ruffling her torn tunic, and she tried to imagine what she would see when she raised her eyelids. A gentle voice spoke her name, and she opened her eyes.

Ralph d'Escosse was staring down at her, urging her to wake up. He was not wearing his helmet, and his long, golden hair framed the most wonderful blue eyes. Perhaps it was not Ralph, but the face of an angel? The words echoed in her mind. She closed her eyes, secure in the protection of the strong arm that supported her. If she were dead it was very pleasant, and if it was Ralph and not an angel, that meant she was alive and all would be well. She was sinking into a warm darkness, when the voice called her back. "Gwen, can you hear me?" She focused on his face: it was Ralph. He did not appear to be in a hurry; his voice and manner showed concern rather than panic. "Gwen, can you her me? Tell me how you feel. Do you recognize me?"

She nodded her head. On her left arm she could feel the weight of the silver bracelet; it was something tangible. Her mouth felt sore and full of grit, and she tried to clear her throat. Ralph lifted her head and gently placed the water bottle to her lips. Gwen tried to grasp it with her right arm, but she felt physically weak and mentally exhausted. She drank gratefully. "Thank you,

Ralph," she murmured, then closed her eyes and drifted back into unconsciousness.

It was dusk when she awoke, that brief moment in the Holy Land before darkness suddenly descends. She realized many hours had passed, and although she felt stronger her head ached; she tentatively felt the bandage across her forehead. A warm cloak covered her and the temperature of the air had fallen. As her vision cleared, she saw Ralph sitting on a nearby rock in conversation with Martin. A small fire crackled in front of them and neither had noticed her recovery.

Gwen closed her eyes, feeling the need to prepare herself for the emotional demands she knew would soon be made on her. She wanted to discover who had won the battle and was relieved both Ralph and Martin had survived. She remembered the earthquake, the fall of the huge cross, and her uncanny memory of the owl. She thought of John, and a cold fear gripped her. Where was he? Why was he not here? The possibility of his death was so overwhelming she screwed up her eyes, trying in vain to prevent the tears coursing down her face. She lay perfectly still, determined to get some control over her emotions, unwilling to have John's death announced to her before she had prepared herself. As she fought down the hysteria, her mind began to focus on the conversations of the two men. It was Martin's voice she heard first.

"M'Lord, I still reckons if the earthquake hadn't come, we'd 'ave won the day."

"I don't agree, Sergeant, we were very close to being defeated. The monster had already killed some of our best knights, including Longsword and de Bois, and if he had not unexpectedly left the field of battle, I would not be alive and neither, I suspect, would you."

"It looked bad at one time, m'lord," Martin agreed. "I were trying to fight me way back to the Cross when that shaking began. I 'ad with me a good body of men, and I reckons we would 'ave caught the main part of the enemy between us and your cavalry."

"Perhaps." Ralph sounded unconvinced. "The point is, I was able to lead the counter charge only because the enemy had lost heart after the departure of their leader."

"Why did he leave the battle, d'ye think?"

"I think it had to do with John." Ralph clicked his tongue. "I've had a lifetime of military training, but in the end it meant nothing when opposed to a creature employing the black arts. Without John and his strange power, I'm certain the fiend would have won the day."

"John, was it?" There was a resigned sound in Martin's voice. "I understand you know him?"

"Aye, Sir, but I don't think 'e knows I'm here."

"A friend of yours?"

There was a pause. "We both knows Mistress Gwen." He breathed out loudly. "My name be Martin."

There was another long interval, during which Gwen could identify the groans of wounded people, the whinnying of horses, the crackling of fires, and the distant hubbub of many men in conversation. The aroma of cooking floated past her nostrils. She raised her eyelids a fraction: it was almost dark and she could see the outlines of Martin and Ralph in the flickering light from the small fire, which, fanned by a light breeze, flared up in front of them. They were both staring into the flames; each lost in his thoughts.

"You're Martin. Of course! You're the one John talked about," Ralph said at last. "I should have realized." He sounded tired.

"John talked about me, m'Lord?"

"Oh yes, Martin. John told me all about you. He said you were responsible for rescuing Gwen from the enemy on the beach near Christchurch." He threw some fuel on the fire. "We think the diabolical creature who tried to abduct Gwen in England, is the same one who led the attack today."

"I never knew 'im well." Martin drank from a leather bag. "John, I means. I met 'im for the first time during that final battle on the beach, about two years ago. Afterwards, we was put up at the castle. Two weeks it were. We never said much to each other. John be always friendly. But it were just, 'e and me didn't have much in common."

Gwen forced herself to breathe deeply. They were talking about John as though he was dead. She wanted to cry out, "Tell me the truth! Is he dead?" But she did not have the energy. The words were too painful. Better not to know. She sought refuge in sleep, but the conversation drew her back.

Martin gave another deep sigh. "We both 'ad our eye on Gwen, you see, m'Lord."

"Did she know?"

"I reckons so. But it weren't like it seems now." Nothing was said for a while, then Martin continued. "When I first meets 'er, she be just a girl who wanted to find 'er father. I decided to help 'er, ye see… 'cause I wanted to get away from the mill for a bit, and 'cause she were good looking. I gets to know 'er, and she weren't like no other girl I'd met," he paused. "She be different."

"I know what you mean. Go on."

"Well, m'Lord, we travels a bit together, and during the battle at Potters Crossing, we gets separated, and she takes up with John, who 'ad rescued her from them foreign soldiers. An' later when I catches up with 'er in Christchurch, I knows then I weren't part of things no more. Them knights thought she be special, an' I could tell Gwen fancied John." Martin relapsed into silence.

"How strange," Ralph mused, "that your three paths should cross again, and in this God-forsaken place."

"I reckons it be Gwen. She be the reason, m'Lord." He cleared his throat. "'Course, things be changed a bit. What with 'er being a lady now, and educated an' all. Now John, 'e be an officer, and you 'is friend be a lord. Everything's different."

"After what happened today, Martin, we talk as friends. I'm Ralph d'Escosse." He held out his hand, and Martin, after a brief hesitation, shook it awkwardly. "Call me Ralph when we're away from the men. You needn't feel ill at ease. Once again, you've been responsible for saving Gwen's life." Ralph gave his familiar, enthusiastic laugh. He slapped Martin on the back. "I can think of no stronger bond for our friendship."

Martin cleared his throat again. "It were nothing, m'Lord, um… Ralph. It were all over when you rides up. There weren't much fighting after the earthquake. I be just standing guard really."

"There was chaos when I reached the Cross. Most of the Moslems were running away, but some still wanted to plunder.

I saw you in action as I galloped up." There was a warm tone in Ralph's voice. "I should have known you were not just any sergeant when I saw the way you carried Gwen to safety."

"It were nothin'." He sounded uncomfortable, and took another drink.

Gwen closed her eyes, swallowing hard trying to keep her emotions under control. She was so grateful to have friends like Martin and Ralph, yet it was John's voice she wanted to hear. Her mind cleared. Surely, if John were dead, Ralph would not be laughing?

The thought prompted her memory of her servant, Barbara, who had died so suddenly when the supply train had been attacked. The horror of those terrifying moments flooded in. Gwen let out a wild scream as she relived the nightmare, seeing the spear plunging into Barbara's body: her gaping mouth, the look of incomprehension, and the cry....

"It's all right, Gwen. It's all right now. You have nothing to fear." Ralph was kneeling beside her, cradling her head in his arm. By the firelight she could see Martin crouched down on her other side.

"Is he dead?" she wailed. "Tell me! Is John dead?" She raised herself on her elbow, her distraught face staring into Ralph's.

His tired eyes changed from concern to understanding. He forced a gentle smile. "Gwen, don't distress yourself. John is well. He'll be back soon."

Gwen's eyes widened, and she turned openmouthed towards Martin. As she did so, Ralph flashed him a warning glance.

"Is he really alive. Oh, Martin, is he really alive?"

"That be what I 'eard," Martin nodded encouragingly. He stood up clumsily. "I'll just get ye something to drink."

"Gwen, it's all right. John will be back soon. You can sleep now. He can tell you everything when he returns. Sleep now." Ralph lowered her onto her makeshift bed.

By the time Martin returned with some wine, she was oblivious to her surroundings. She slept with her head slightly to the left, a small smile enhancing her beauty. Ralph covered her carefully with the cloak, and he and Martin gazed down at her for a long time. Eventually, they walked silently back to the fire. Martin threw some dried horse dung onto the embers and pretended to busy himself.

Ralph stood apart, running his index finger up and down the bridge of his nose. The fire picked up, and soon aromatic smoke curled upwards, occasionally buffeted by a light breeze. Overhead, the stars shone brightly in the dark sky. "I had to tell her John was safe, Martin. She's not well enough to be given the truth."

"What be the truth then?" Martin whispered, glancing towards Gwen.

"I've no idea." Ralph drew his sword and showed it to Martin. "This was his. He gave it to me after the giant had disarmed me."

Martin took the sword and examined it carefully.

"Then," Ralph continued, "with only a shield and a dagger, he galloped away in search of that accursed devil, who seems to have unnatural powers on his side. The giant has a sword like no other. De Bois claimed there were two of them, and both in the hands of the enemy." He looked up at the stars. "Yet, still he was unable to win the day, which may mean even with his Swords of Power, he is vulnerable. I believe John holds the key to our success."

"Do ye reckon John'll get back safely, then?"

"I pray he will, Martin, or we could all be in grave danger, apart from losing a good friend." Ralph shrugged his shoulders, as though off-loading a heavy burden. "This sword," he said, returning it to its scabbard, "John calls it Tegwen's Gift."

"Oh?" Martin turned and looked at Gwen; she was sleeping peacefully.

"It was given to him by a remarkable Welsh woman called Tegwen. She had the sword made for her by her father, and she gave it to John so he could continue his part in a complicated series of events which I am, only now, beginning to comprehend."

Martin did not understand what Ralph was talking about, but he did grasp the fact that John had another woman in his life. "Is she a beautiful woman?"

Ralph laughed, and stretched his arms luxuriously. "She is the second most beautiful woman in the world."

Although he wanted to ask the obvious question, Martin felt

it was not his place to inquire. But maybe John's relationship with this woman called Tegwen was the reason he had not been spending much time with Gwen. On the journey from Antioch, Martin had kept close to Gwen's wagon, and had noticed that John often remained at the front of the column. A warm glow spread through him. He knew he had no chance of being more than just a friend to Gwen, but at least John was no longer a competitor for her favours. He rubbed his rough hand down his face, removing a stupid smile that was creasing his grimy features. "Good to know women like 'er," he said ambiguously.

They sat down and shared the remains of a bag of wine. "Tomorrow, the relief column should arrive." Ralph yawned. "When we've finished this wine, Martin, we'll take it in turns to do a final check of the men to make sure the sentries are still awake. I want one of us to remain with Gwen at all times."

"Yes, m'Lord." Martin looked apologetic. "I best gets used to calling ye that again, I reckons." He stood up awkwardly. "I'll do the first check." He gazed down at Gwen, who slept peacefully, her bandaged forehead surrounded by a swirl of black hair. As he marched off, he whispered, "Sleep well, Gwenny, I be keeping an eye on ye. Don't ye worry about nothin'."

Ralph sat motionless, staring into the fire. It had been a bad day, yet it might have been worse. Gwen could have died or been captured by the enemy. He shook his head; he did not want to think about it. After the earthquake, he had managed to gather together a large body of men, no longer an army, but at least with some semblance of order. Under his supervision they had been able to salvage some of the damaged wagons and organize the care of many of the injured. There had been a series of minor skirmishes after the battle, as soldiers on both sides had wanted to plunder each other's dead. But the majority of the enemy forces had fled, taking with them only those injured men who could travel.

Eventually, the deaths of Lord Longsword and Sir Stephen de Bois had been confirmed, and a group of junior members of the Knights of the Order had appropriated some of the few surviving horses, and had raced back towards Antioch. Their departure had threatened to unnerve the soldiers, and it was only by force of will that Ralph had mustered the survivors of his own army and, helped by his sergeant, the indestructible Little, had once again stamped his authority on the dispirited men. With discipline restored, and light fading, he had dispatched a small body of the remaining cavalry to gallop back to Antioch with the news. "Arrange for a relief column," he ordered a senior knight, "and provide the governor, Sir Maurice de Maron, with accurate details of the battle before any of the deserters arrive back in the city and spread panic."

In the meantime, there were the dead to bury; but little was achieved before darkness fell.

"Nothing more I can do but wait and hope the morrow brings good news," he murmured sadly, and turned to look at Gwen. Even with her injuries, she was lovely. He crept closer to her and knelt down, his eyes tracing the contours of her face: her closed eyes, her well-defined nose, and her generous mouth. It was a face that even in repose, and with a dirty bandage across her forehead, was astonishingly beautiful. The cloak rose and fell gently around the curve of her body, and he was aware of a feeling that seemed strangely out of place in such bizarre circumstances: a strong desire to hold her, to kiss her soft skin, to tell her he… Ralph shook his head. This was madness. He stood up and walked slowly back to the fire, his breathing was irregular, and he was shocked by his aroused emotions.

To the south and east of him the plateau was dotted with the lights of numerous camp fires, but no shadows moved around them, and the hum of chatter of the earlier evening, and even the groans of the injured, had died away. Most were asleep, or too exhausted to stir. The darkness was lonely, and he felt overcome with wretchedness and self-pity.

He drew out his sword. "Tegwen's Gift," he said, "but a gift to John, not to me." He knew he was looking for excuses. Tegwen was his lover, but she was far away, and Gwen with her beauty and vulnerability had aroused in him both desire and guilt. Replacing the sword, he threw back his head, his eyes searching the heavens; he had generated enormous energy during the day, experienced horror and almost died, and perhaps he had lost his best friend.

Now he needed the soft embrace of a woman to smooth away the empty feeling of failure and despair. He sat down and reached for the wine.

"John," he said, staring up at the stars, "come back safely tomorrow, my friend. Come back safely."

As Ralph sat staring at the dimming fire, an owl glided low over his head but he failed to notice it. Even if he had, it would not have meant anything to him. But Gwen, wrapped up in her dreams and her fatigue, smiled.

CHAPTER 3

A FTER A LONG NIGHT, the briefest of dawns gave way to the return of the heat. The copper sun erupted from behind distant mountains, illuminating the horror of the battlefield. Around the high plateau the dead lay in pitiful heaps where the fighting had been fiercest, and as sad, lone corpses in those areas where individual conflicts had been resolved. The vultures had descended to feed on the dead horses, but the corpses of the soldiers were, as yet, mainly untouched. As the light thickened the injured soldiers groped their way across the rocky ground in search of water, or lay calling for help as the wild animals, scenting blood, drew closer.

From the north, groups of able-bodied soldiers moved slowly among the injured, giving small amounts of water to those who were able to drink, and helping to organize the walking wounded. Behind them lurched the few surviving wagons into which the seriously wounded were loaded. A large, powerful sergeant was using a combination of encouragement and threats to force the walking injured to abandon the despair that gripped them.

"Come on now, ye can help yourself. Don't just lie there. Do ye want to be food for them birds?" He shook the shoulder of a young English archer, who had wrapped a bloody bandage around his left leg and sat hunched in a fevered stupor. "I know who ye be, young Rob. Come on now, snap out of it. I'll help ye to your feet."

"Leave me alone, Sergeant Martin. I'm hurting, damn ye."

Ignoring the groans of pain, Martin picked up Rob and made him stand on his good leg. "Give 'im your shoulder," he ordered a sweating soldier. "Take 'im back to the main group, and then come and tell me how things be."

He turned towards a party of soldiers who were shuffling behind a distant wagon. "How much space ye got left in there?" he yelled.

"Not much, Sergeant!" One of them shouted back. "Don't matter though. I reckon few of them are goin' to survive anyways."

"Ye wouldn't say that if it be your brother, or your father out there," Martin said. He glared at the soldiers. "Ye do the best ye can, understand?"

The soldiers looked askance at each other and after a mumbled agreement, continued wearily across the stony, broken ground. Far behind them, already indistinct in the heat haze other teams of men were piling corpses in heaps.

"Well done, Martin. You're doing a good job." Sir Ralph d'Escosse rode up slowly on a tired horse. "The relief column should be here soon. Not much longer."

"Let's 'ope so, Sir. Let's 'ope them infidels don't get 'ere first," Martin answered. He would like to have called him Ralph, as a friend, but he knew that was over now, and whatever confidences they had shared last night in the darkness had been swept aside with the cruel light of day. They might love the same woman, but Ralph was a lord and he was a mere sergeant. "Mistress Gwen, is she…?"

"Gwen's fine, Martin," Ralph smiled encouragingly. "She's sitting up and taking notice. The wound to her head seems to be superficial." He noticed the worried frown on Martin's face. "I've left a guard of trusted men around her. She'll be quite safe for the moment."

"Well, that's good then," Martin wiped the dust from his face, and took a swig from his water bottle. "Ye don't reckon them infidels will come back?"

"No. Not without their leader. I haven't seen any able bodied enemy soldiers today. I think they've fled back to their villages." In spite of his begrimed face, his torn and soiled tunic and his obvious fatigue, Sir Ralph d'Escosse was still an impressive figure as he sat easily on his horse and surveyed the treeless landscape. "Check for any more survivors, then get the men back to the camp. The relief column can deal with the rest of the dead." He wiped his arm across his forehead. "I think these men have had enough." He turned his horse towards the distant makeshift camp and moved slowly away. "I know I have," he muttered under his breath. Overhead the sky was thick with vultures, and on the ground, out of sight of the officers, looters searched for anything of value.

• • •

THE RELIEF COLUMN ARRIVED in the late afternoon, when the worst of the heat was over. There was frantic activity while the dead officers were identified and, along with the common soldiers, were burned in huge fires. The injured were gathered together, and where possible were given some medical care, while fresh food and drink was distributed to the survivors. It was impossible for the arriving forces to grasp the full magnitude of the disaster, and Sir Vernon de Kari was overwhelmed. "It's all so awful," he muttered, holding a cloth to his mouth and nose.

Sir Vernon was shorter than most, but like all knights possessed the powerful shoulders and thick neck of a young man trained to fight. He considered himself good looking, and could never understand why he had been relatively unsuccessful with women. As the youngest in a large family he had envied his brothers who seemed to have no problems in social matters, and although better educated than them, he had an uncanny knack of saying the wrong thing and appearing awkward and gauche. Throughout his childhood he had always been in trouble and rarely comprehended the stupidity of his actions, which was why his brothers nicknamed him 'Dunnit', a recognition of the family complaint: "He's done it again."

Behind him sat his squire, Philip de Gortz, only a year or two younger than Vernon, but already taller and heavier. He was a fine musician and was considered by many young women to be a handsome youth. Next to him sat Giles, Vernon's armourer, a stocky countryman, who had been appointed by Lord de Kari to keep a close eye on his daredevil son. He was an experienced campaigner and although twice the age of his young lord, was physically fit and well versed in the use of arms. For the past five years Giles had tutored the young man in all aspects of warfare, and often boasted: "Young Lord Vernon's the best fighter in the area." But after a few drinks, he would add: "'Don't matter 'ow good he be with a sword and a knife, he's bound to do something stupid."

Vernon closed his eyes for a moment, trying to shut out the scene. Around him men groaned and screamed in pain, as medics changed their makeshift bandages and made necessary amputations. A foul smell drifted from the huge pyres, and dead horses and broken wagons littered the area. A large wooden cross, painted red, lay on its side. Near it, a deep rent in the earth bore testament to the violence of the earthquake, and pieces of armour were scattered around, some half buried in the broken rock. Everywhere there were smoking campfires, with small clusters of men, some with bandages, just sitting and staring silently into the flames. There was plenty of activity around the food wagons, and horsemen were rushing about the site taking messages between hastily erected tents, some located at a considerable distance from others. Sergeants were shouting orders and the blare of trumpets added to the noise and apparent confusion, as hundreds of men were slowly identified, assessed and reorganized.

"You get used to it," an older knight remarked, as he stopped his horse next to Vernon's. "Most battles are like this: hours of preparation, a short time of intense excitement, and, if you are lucky enough to survive, a long and unpleasant clearing up."

Vernon glanced at the man, and nodded wearily. "Not much glory then?"

The knight gave an ironic snort. "Glory! That's not a word we often use. You must be new out here?"

"I arrived two weeks ago."

"I hope you live long enough to understand." The knight turned to face him. "Out here, things are not what they seem to be."

In his full mail suit and body armour, and with his helmet covering much of his face, Vernon's youth and size were concealed and he was aware of a polite deference in the knight's speech. The quality of De Kari's horse, armour and weapons, and those carried by Philip, his squire, and Giles, his armourer, indicated to others that he was a knight of some substance and he was grateful for the camouflage. Nothing in the past twenty-four hours had measured up to his expectations, and he felt vulnerable and exhausted.

The knight adjusted his helmet. "I would not look for glory if you wish to survive." He nodded his head and kicked his horse into a canter.

Vernon watched him disappear in a cloud of dust. In a short while it would be dark, and he knew he should find the tents that had been erected for his commander, Sir William de Bracy, and the other officers. There was little for him to do, and he realized his inexperience was immediately apparent to seasoned soldiers whenever he tried to give an order. He blew out his cheeks and wiped the sweat from his eyes. "Philip! You and Giles get something to eat. Find me in the morning."

"What about ye armour, Sir?" Giles queried.

"Don't worry about it. Get some rest."

His two servants exchanged glances, and turned their horses towards the wagons, as Vernon cantered off towards the nearest tents.

"Not his usual self, is 'e?" Giles said.

Philip shrugged his shoulders. "Not much to joke about, is there?"

"Well, I 'ope he don't lose that armour, that's all. Ye know what he be like."

Philip smiled. "You're his armourer, not his wet nurse. Come on, we need some food and something to drink."

• • •

VERNON HANDED HIS HORSE to a soldier in charge of the security and feeding of the animals, and wandered towards a large tent where other knights were congregating. Soldiers were assisting the knights with the removal of their armour, and most were relinquishing their swords; he did the same. He acknowledged a sentry at the entrance to the tent and went inside. An assortment of food was displayed on an improvised table, and servants were carving roasted birds and goat meat. The knights helped themselves to the meat and to olives, dates, cheese and hard, dark bread. While some sat on benches, the majority stood with their meat in one hand and their goblet in the other. There was plenty of wine and some of the knights were already in their cups, their voices loud and raucous.

"You weren't here!" A tall knight exclaimed. He had a lurid gash on his cheek. "You didn't see the Giant. He was invincible, I'm telling you." His voice was slurred. "The demon killed Lord Longsword, Sir Stephen de Bois, and many other knights. They didn't have a chance." The knight staggered slightly, spilling his wine. "Whether you believe it or not, I'm telling you his sword glowed blue." He stared angrily around the tent. A small group of his supporters, their red eyes sunken in their flushed faces, clearly identifying them as survivors of the battle, chorused their agreement.

"Then why did he suddenly leave the field if he was so invincible?" One young man asked. His bright chain mail and clean tunic indicated he was one of the relief columns. "Why aren't you all dead?"

"I don't know why he stopped fighting. But I saw him." The tall knight paused, aware that most of the others in the tent were listening to him. "The Giant was in black armour, and he was single-handedly destroying the cream of our cavalry when he suddenly turned and galloped back through his army." He took a deep draught of wine and pointed at a knight with long blond hair. "He was attacking you at the time. I saw him destroy your shield and then he stopped. You know what happened." All heads turned towards Ralph d'Escosse. "You tell them what happened."

Ralph had been standing alone, discouraging company, wrapped up in his own thoughts. He was eating steadily and drinking little, aware of his exhaustion and knowing a few cups would unman him. His mind was focused on the problem of what to do with Gwen. If John returned, the three of them could return to Antioch and decide how best to fulfil their mission on behalf of King Henry. Their orders had been to observe the Knights of the Order. But was the Order still of any importance with Longsword and Stephen both dead? Would the three of them still have to journey to Jerusalem? He chewed meditatively on a slice of goat.

Supposing John did not return, what then? Were they to

consider him dead? If so, Ralph wondered if he could return to England with Gwen. If King Henry was convinced that the Order was of no further importance then perhaps he would forgive the d'Escosse family, and Gwen might, in time, forget John… He shook his head; he must not go there. He sighed and a passing knight patted him on his back in a brotherly fashion. "More wine, my friend. That's the answer."

Ralph nodded his agreement and turned away. He knew that Gwen was, somehow, important to the Order and that she had been under the protection of Sir Stephen de Bois and Lord Longsword. But with their deaths would other members of the Order try to take charge of her again? He would not allow it. Whether or not John returned, Gwen would not be forced to return to the guardianship of such men, unless she wished it.

As he made his decision he was aware of being the focus of attention. He looked around at the sea of curious faces, recognizing only a few and wondering what he had missed.

"Tell them about the Giant," the tall knight repeated loudly. "You were the only one to survive direct combat with him."

"Perhaps I was," Ralph said quietly. He tried to clear his mind and focus on the question. In a short well-organized speech he described the phase in the battle when the two Knights of the Order had been killed, and when the Giant had destroyed Ralph's sword and battered down his shield. "At that point, when he could have killed me, he turned his horse and galloped away." Ralph took a sip of his wine.

"But why?" demanded a chorus of voices.

Ralph shrugged his shoulders. He could not tell them that John, his great friend, was possessed with strange powers. As he did not understand the situation himself, how could he possibly try to explain it to this group of worldly knights, many of whom were drunk? He decided to resort to facetiousness: "Maybe, he doesn't like fighting handsome young men with blond hair."

There was a roar of laughter and Ralph turned away, determined to leave the tent before others thought to question him.

"Sir Ralph d'Escosse, you have not mentioned your friend, Gilles de Plantard."

Ralph stopped. Barring his way was a tall, thickset knight, with a small dark cross on the shoulder of his tunic, identifying him as an important officer of the Order.

Although Ralph was above average height, the knight was a hands-breadth taller. Their eyes locked and Ralph instinctively knew he was in the presence of a very dangerous man. "And you are?" He gave the slightest of bows.

"Sir Raymond de Wulfric." The knight inclined his head. "Tell me about Gilles de Plantard."

"What about him?"

"He was near to you in the battle. When the Giant fled, your friend de Plantard was seen to follow him after giving you his sword." Sir Raymond smiled, and his cruel mouth formed a thick straight line. "Why did he pursue this dangerous warrior without his sword? And where is Gilles de Plantard now?"

"I have no idea, Sir Raymond." Ralph gave a small bow. "I, also, would like the answers to those questions." He handed his goblet to a servant and headed towards the exit.

Raymond's cold eyes followed him as Ralph strode out of the tent. He gestured to a servant, "I want to know where he is billeted. Get someone to follow him." The servant nodded and scurried away, as the tent erupted with animated conversation.

Outside, the air was cool and the stars were bright in a clear sky. A half moon provided some illumination around the sprawling camp, and small fires and a collection of torches flared in a light breeze. The sentry by the doorway came to attention with a clash of metal as his sword beat against his shield. Ralph acknowledged him, and the soldier relaxed, pleased to have been noticed. After picking up his sword from the makeshift armoury, and returning it thoughtfully to his scabbard, Ralph turned to his left and began to walk back towards a distant tent where Gwen was being safely guarded by Martin and a small platoon of English soldiers.

He had walked only a short distance, when he heard the clash of metal behind him as the sentry came to attention once again.

Without hesitating, Ralph darted behind the nearest tent and stood motionless in the shadows, his white tunic and light hair blending with the bleached tent. He did not have to wait long as a small figure hurried past. The figure stopped and seemed to be unsure which direction to take.

"'Looking for someone?" Ralph asked, his voice barely above a whisper.

The figure spun round and his hand went to an empty scabbard. There was a gasp of frustration, followed by a muttered curse. "Who's there?"

"Why are you following me?"

"Sir Ralph?" There was obvious relief in the voice. "I'm Sir Vernon de Kari."

"Yes?" There was a hint of ridicule in Ralph's response.

"I wanted to warn you. I think you could be in danger."

"From whom?"

Sir Vernon was unsettled by the reaction to his statement. He had imagined this young knight would have been impressed with his chivalrous deed, and recognized him immediately as an honourable fellow. Instead, he could detect suspicion in his voice. Quickly, he continued with his message. "I was in the tent when you described your battle with the Giant. When you left, the knight who challenged you when you were leaving, sent a servant to have you followed." Vernon paused, waiting for a reaction. "Afterwards, he turned to another knight and said he believed you were hiding someone he called 'Mistress Gwen'."

"Why have you come to tell me this?"

Vernon cleared his throat. This was not the reception he had hoped for. "I'm new out here," he blew out his cheeks. "I don't know what's going on most of the time, but I can tell when one person is honourable, and when another can't be trusted."

"Do you know Sir Raymond de Wulfric?"

"Hardly at all," Vernon said. "I mean, he did save my life when I was attacked in an alley in Antioch." He paused, and could feel his face going red. "That sounds odd, I know, but I still don't trust him." His voice trailed off. He was about to develop his explanation, when he felt Ralph place a finger to his mouth, and indicate with his other hand for Vernon to move behind him.

Almost immediately, Vernon heard the sound of people approaching and he moved quietly behind Ralph, imitating his alert posture. In the gloom he could see two men hurry past. He remained still, hardly breathing, until Ralph relaxed. "It looks like you were telling the truth. Well done!"

Sir Vernon glowed. Nobody had said an encouraging word to him since he had left his father's estate, and even then it had only been the pretty young wench his father would never allow him to marry. "What will we do now?" he asked, feeling emboldened by the compliment. "Just say the word, and I'm your man." In Vernon's mind this was a fine speech, smacking of knightly virtue, and he was unaware that Ralph was clenching his teeth together.

After a pause, Ralph placed his hand on the smaller man's shoulder. "I thank you for your warning. I'm sure we'll meet again, Sir Vernon." He patted Vernon twice on the back, and walked quickly away in the opposite direction of the two spies.

Sir Vernon smiled in the darkness, and throwing out his chest he strutted back to the big tent where he drank many cups of wine, happy in the knowledge that he had done his duty.

CHAPTER 4

WHEN DARKNESS FELL, THE air cooled quickly as the hot land, which had baked all day, radiated its heat back into the cloudless sky. The grandeur of the stars and the bright splendour of the moon erased the harshness of the landscape, making the jagged rocks, the deep chasms, and the almost permanently dry wadis appear to be welcoming and magical.

John walked his black horse, Celestial, slowly down the gradual slope of the long valley stretching away before him. He was limping and fatigued, and although he had some water in his flask, he knew it was not enough for himself and his horse to last another scorching day in the high desert. It was essential he find a source of water and some sustenance before the next sunrise.

He was leading Celestial, because the horse was exhausted and uncertain.

The animal had endured both the rigours of the battle, and the frantic charge as John had tried, in vain, to catch up with the Giant. Then the earthquake struck, and Celestial had kicked and bucked like a mad creature, the earth shaking beneath its hooves. When the convulsions ceased, the terrified horse galloped for more than a mile until John had eventually regained control. He had climbed wearily from the saddle, and spent a long time calming the beast. Now, conscious that the night was the best time to travel, he was leading his skittish companion westwards in the hope of finding some habitation.

John had been determined to catch up with the Giant before darkness fell, but the earthquake changed everything. As he galloped from the battle, he had imagined he would be able to confront the huge warrior in a final and victorious contest. He knew from past experience that the power was not something he could control, and that it manifested itself through him without any desire or ability on his part. He was merely the vessel. This time, however, it seemed to be leading him on, and he had been certain the ongoing nightmare of the Giant would soon be ended. However, when the aftershocks finally ceased, and after he had pacified his horse, he realized the pulse in his right hand no longer throbbed and the outline of the runes was no longer guiding him to his enemy.

Now he was lost. Behind him would be the Moslem forces. Either a victorious army, mopping up the remains of the Crusaders, or a defeated and fragmented body of men bent on revenging themselves on any soldiers from Christendom they came across. When he followed the Giant he had believed he had no need of mortal weapons, trusting in the superhuman force he had occasionally experienced. He believed it would turn the Sword of Power against its present owner, as it had done once before in the Flower Meadows of Wessex. He had given his sword, Tegwen's Gift, to Ralph, lost his shield during the earthquake, and had been forced to discard his heavy body armour further up the track. With only a dagger he was unwilling to risk an encounter with the enemy, and for this reason was walking west.

When the first dark figures materialized silently in front of him, John was convinced they were phantoms created by his tired mind. He stopped and Celestial whinnied loudly, frantically trying to turn his head to the right. John glanced about and saw he was surrounded by a large group of men; their robes and turbans were clearly outlined in the silvery moonlight.

He drew his dagger and prepared to die. He had heard stories of how the Arabs and Turks did not spare their captives, but enjoyed making them suffer long and painful deaths. Rather than endure torture he resolved he would fight to his last breath. John experienced a brief moment of regret that Gwen would never know what had happened to him, and then he faced his opponents.

"Stand back!" he yelled. "I'll kill the first man who comes too close!" He did not imagine these people spoke English, but his words fortified his resolve and he hoped his chain mail suit would deflect some of the early blows and enable him to die bravely.

There was an unnerving silence as the men formed a solid circle around him. In the dim light their faces were shadowy, and only their eyes and their weapons gleamed. As he stood with his back to the side of his horse, the reins in his right hand and the dagger in his left, John realized that some of the men were already the other side of his horse and were even then holding its harness.

"Do you speak French?" The speaker displayed a cultivated French accent.

"Yes," John replied, conscious he had not spoken the language for a while.

"Good. You will put down your weapon, and I will guarantee your safety."

"How can I trust you?" John's eyes darted about the group, trying to identify the speaker.

"You must believe me. You have no choice."

"Why would you guarantee my safety?"

"Because you are a knight. One of the iron men. You are worth ransoming." The speaker laughed. "You are worth more alive, than dead. So, throw down your weapon."

John found himself biting his lower lip in desperation. Could he believe this man? He looked about the circle and knew he had no hope of fighting his way out. Either he believed this French-speaking Arab, or he died. He could not believe the unseen leader would go through this charade merely to have the pleasure of torturing him. "All right. I surrender myself to you." He dropped his dagger on the ground, and was immediately rushed by the shadowy warriors. His arms were pinioned and he was forced to his knees, letting go of the reins. Celestial stamped his feet, and tossed his head violently.

The leader spoke sharply in Arabic, and the men holding him loosened their grip.

"Stand up, if you please." John rose to his feet and found he was facing a slim man who was of equal height. The Arab's face was hard to discern in the desert light, but John could see he had a large nose and a full beard. "Does your horse have a name?"

"Celestial. He's a one-man horse."

"Indeed?" Once again, there was a hint of humour in the voice. He took hold of Celestial's bridle, and breathed softly into the horse's nostrils, then ran his left hand gently down the muzzle, and spoke softly to the powerful horse, displaying a complete confidence in his ability. Within a short while the big animal was standing quietly, his eyes fixed on the man. "Celestial." He breathed the name, as though experimenting with the sound, and in a fluid movement vaulted into the saddle. The horse reared up, tossing its head, and prancing in a sideways motion, trying to unseat the serene rider, who remained firmly in control. After a short contest Celestial stopped moving, and fixed his large eyes on John.

"He's still a one-man horse," the leader said, looking down at John. "Mine." Again, there was the slight hint of a laugh.

John remained silent. He knew he had only to whistle and Celestial would unseat this proud man onto the rocky earth beneath, but he also realized it would be a short-lived victory, as his captors would enjoy cutting his throat. Strong arms restrained him, as his wrists were tightly bound in the front and a long rope was attached to his wrists.

"I'm sure you won't mind walking," the leader said as he attached the other end of the rope to his saddle. The irony of having to walk behind his own horse was not lost on John, and it also ensured that he would not try to upset the animal. He just hoped the leader did not lose control of Celestial, as he could imagine few worse deaths than being dragged across rocky ground behind a galloping horse.

After a short march the leader turned into a broad gulley, where two men were guarding a herd of tethered horses. The small army was soon mounted and John noticed their animals were considerably smaller than Celestial. The riders carried short bows, curved swords, light round shields and only limited body armour, and therefore these horses bore only a fraction of the weight carried by the average Crusader war horse. In battle, a knight carried a heavy long sword, thick iron body armour on top of his chain mail, a large shield, a cumbersome helmet and a long and weighty lance. In order to use these weapons and move easily with the heavy armour, knights had to train for years, and were often huge men with bulging muscles. In contrast, the Arabs around him appeared to be lean and agile, and he suspected their horses could easily outrun Celestial.

"If you walk fast we should arrive before the heat of the day," the leader said. Already, the darkness was giving way to an iron light, and dawn was close.

"Can I have a drink?" John indicated his water flask on the side of the horse. He could have managed without, but it seemed useful to see how much the leader would allow. It would help to prepare him for the treatment he could expect in the immediate future.

The leader shrugged his shoulders and reached for the flask. He undid the stopper and passed it down to John, who drank quickly, holding the flask awkwardly, but determined to build up his reserves. While he was drinking, the leader said something in Arabic to his men, and they all laughed. "I was telling them how generous I was to let you drink your own water."

During the next three hours they gradually descended from the high ground and eventually reached a valley with a shallow, slow moving river running through. There were trees and bushes and irregular, cultivated fields. Small boys tended herds of goats, and there were a number of camels in the distance. After another mile, when John was finding the heat almost unbearable, they reached a village of low mud buildings and loud, excited children. Veiled women stared from doorways, and dogs and chickens scattered noisily away before the feet of the horses.

Many of the warriors stopped and dismounted, while the leader continued on down the one street towards a group of larger buildings constructed around a pleasant courtyard. A small band of riders continued on behind, preventing the children from coming too close to the prisoner. As the leader approached the gateway into the courtyard he acknowledged a group of older men with long, wild beards, who were standing outside. They pointed at John and angrily shook their fists at him, calling out and spitting on the ground. John was past caring as he staggered past them;

his feet were blistered and he was drenched in sweat. His mouth was parched and his arms ached from the constant pulling of the rope. The leader laughed and shook his head at the elders, pointed proudly at the horse, and proceeded grandly into the courtyard, where he guided Celestial towards a water trough, dismounted, and allowed the horse to drink.

John came to a halt a few feet behind his horse. He swayed as though drunk, fighting his exhaustion and determined not to collapse. Around him the other men dismounted and led their horses up to the trough. When Celestial had drunk as much as the leader allowed, he undid the rope on the saddle, handed the reins of the horse to another man, and approached John. "I think your one-man horse will suit me well."

He contemplated the knight in front of him, noting the swollen lips and the red eyes in a face that was otherwise well formed. Like all the knights he had encountered this one was without a beard, had long hair, and stank. He signalled to one of the soldiers and spoke rapidly with little emotion. He turned towards a fountain in the middle of the yard, filled a pottery cup with water, and drank leisurely with much enjoyment.

The soldier approached John and slowly withdrew a sharp knife from the folds of his robe. John watched him cautiously through half-closed eyes as the soldier gradually raised the knife in front of John's face and passed it threateningly backwards and forwards. The man was stocky, muscular, and had bad teeth, which he revealed as a cruel smile formed slowly on his vicious face. He spoke softly in Arabic, repeating some words with increasing vehemence and bringing the knife closer to John's skin.

John tried to swallow and forced his dry lips apart. "I don't speak your language, you devil, so don't threaten me!" he yelled in French.

The leader spun round and bellowed an order. It was the first time John had heard him raise his voice. The soldier paused, curled his lip at John, and quickly cut the thongs that bound his wrists. John let out a gasp as he tried to use his hands. The circulation was slow to return and when it did, it caused exquisite pain making him clench his teeth in agony.

"Remove your chain mail."

John raised his aching eyes to glare at the leader. "No."

"Do it, or I'll order my men to do so. They will enjoy humiliating you."

Without a word John removed his sword belt, and then his tunic. He slowly dragged the heavy hauberk over his head and dumped it on the ground. Beneath, he wore a light fabric shirt, soaked in sweat, and long leggings. He carefully picked up his tunic and slipped it back on, but as he picked up his belt, the leader snapped his fingers and the soldier snatched it from him.

"You will have no need of a belt with an empty scabbard." The leader gave another order and the soldier filled a wide pottery bowl from the fountain, and poured it over John's head. The other soldiers jeered, enjoying the humiliation of their prisoner. But for John it was a sensation of sheer ecstasy as the cool water trickled down his face; he forgot for that moment he was a prisoner.

"I need to drink," he muttered already moving towards the fountain. The soldier barred his way, his knife drawn.

"He will give you some water," the leader warned. "You will not go near the fountain. You are unclean. Wash yourself in the horse trough."

John took a deep breath and fought down the desire to hit this man, whose insults were clearly calculated. Then he reflected on his situation. He was dirty and sweaty and he needed to drink. "I understand," he said wearily, and walked towards the trough.

• • •

SOME HOURS LATER HE awoke from an exhausted sleep. He was in a small bare room with a narrow aperture on the back wall that allowed in a slither of light. The cell was clean with a hard mud floor, drab white walls and a solid wooden door. In one corner was the woven blanket on which he was lying and along the other wall was a large pottery container, the use of which was unpleasantly obvious. There was also a jug of water.

John had never been a prisoner or ever been under anybody's complete control before, and he found the situation unnerving and insulting. If it had happened to him three years ago he would have coped better. At that time he had been an untutored country youth. He had possessed some reading and writing skills, but had been ignorant of the world and used to uncomfortable living. Since then he had become familiar with the lifestyle of a young lord, skilled in fighting, physically strong and used to commanding soldiers. To be locked up and forced to obey the orders of others, especially the orders of mere desert farmers, was difficult to accept.

After he had been allowed to wash in the trough, the soldier led him to this small cell on one side of the courtyard. He remembered being pushed savagely from behind as he entered the doorway and had collapsed against the opposite wall. A few moments later his captor had arrived and smiled at him in a self-satisfied way. "Get some sleep, and we will talk later," he said, indicating the worn blanket. He had waved an index finger at him as though to a naughty boy. "Do not think of escaping, there would be no point." The soldier had slammed the door and secured it with a wooden bar.

John stood up, stretched and moved slowly round the small space, examining everything very carefully. He drank from the jug, conscious he had not eaten for more than a day. There was no doubt in his mind that his captors intended to make him more submissive and he wondered what was inferred by the word 'talk'.

It was twilight when two soldiers opened the door. Both were wearing light body armour and one carried a curved sword; in the dim light John could see he was the same man who had threatened him earlier. The other held a torch and having indicated he was to be followed, led the way across the enclosed yard. As they walked swiftly in single file, the swordsman prodded John constantly with the point of his sword, encouraging his prisoner to react.

"You wait, my ugly friend, until I have a sword," he muttered.

It was clear the soldier did not speak English, but understood the general direction of his prisoner's speech. He reversed his sword, and brought the pommel down heavily on John's right shoulder, causing him to gasp with pain. Instantly, the sword was against his throat and he was forced to continue moving. The torchbearer stopped at the entrance to a large room and the soldier replaced the sword in his belt. Watching him, John understood the soldier had deliberately avoided causing any obvious wound and had contented himself with inflicting unseen injuries, as though under orders not to abuse his master's prisoner. He tucked this thought at the back of his mind, as the door curtain was pushed aside. They entered the room and the two soldiers stood silently on either side of their prisoner.

In front of him was spread a rich carpet on the floor with an array of large cushions, on which the leader was sitting cross-legged. He was wearing a fine, multi-coloured robe with a thin belt from which hung a small, decorated dagger. On his head was a blue and white turban and he wore rings on many of his fingers. Two boys, perhaps having recently attained manhood, sat on either side. They also wore expensive robes and had clean, bright turbans in the same blue and white. Both sat cross-legged with their backs straight and identical fixed frowns on their young faces. John felt they expected him to be impressed and maintained an impassive expression, revealing nothing of his thoughts, while he considered the situation. The room was disconcertingly pleasant with a comfortable, cultivated atmosphere. Bead curtains hung across the back wall and oil lamps provided tasteful lighting. Tapestries in deep, muted colours decorated the sidewalls and there was a small table with an assortment of glass objects. After his confinement in the bare cell, John had expected to be taken to a similar room to be interrogated. He had prepared himself for the worst and this display of wealth and elegance was startling. In the background he could smell cooking.

"Come forward," the leader said, breaking into his thoughts. "Sit there, if you please." He indicated a thick, long cushion opposite and about eight feet away from him. The rest of the cushions formed a loose circle. Behind him John could hear the two soldiers move out through the curtain.

He did as he was asked and sat awkwardly, trying to imitate the people in front of him. He had never sat on cushions on a floor and his shoulder ached from the recent blow. The leader was watching him carefully and John stared back at him, ignoring the youths, and wondering why the Arab was treating him in this way. He had been made to walk for miles, when there had obviously been a spare horse; yet, he had been unshackled in his bare cell when they could have had him chained to a wall. It was clear the soldiers had been prevented from abusing him too seriously and now he had been invited to sit at what appeared to be the start of a family meal. Most strange of all he was aware that the leader had used the courtesy, "if you please," on two occasions, whereas John's brief contact with the Crusader officers had shown him that they treated their Moslem prisoners with extreme brutality and contempt.

"What is your name?" the leader asked.

John's first reaction was to admit only to John, but it was clear that this man considered him to be a valuable prisoner, and would expect a more distinctive name. "Gilles de Plantard. What is yours?" It was the reply that Ralph would have given and John decided to model his responses on those of his friend, who feared nothing.

The leader stared thoughtfully at him. "I am Ibrahim al-Din. You may call me Ibrahim, and I will call you Gilles." A ghost of a smile passed across his face. "This is my elder son, Rashid," he indicated the boy on his right. "This is my second son, Saif." He turned slightly towards the boy on his left. "His French is not good, unlike his elder brother's, which is why he will attend our discussion, and I will question him afterwards as to what he has understood." Saif blushed deeply and gave a weak, embarrassed smile.

Ibrahim clapped his hands and two young women, heavily veiled, entered carrying bowls of water, and towels. One bowed in front of Ibrahim and he dipped his hands into the water and dried them on a small towel. She then turned to the two youths starting with Rashid.

"You have been provided with soap to clean your hands." Ibrahim remarked as the young woman bowed in front of John.

It was a clear hint that was not lost on him, and he proceeded to wash his hands thoroughly. Afterwards, the young woman offered him a towel, and he carefully dried each hand. "Thank you, you are most kind."

The girl did not understand the words, but nodded her head as she withdrew backwards from the room.

"We will eat first and after we will talk." Ibrahim said, and nodded at Rashid, who immediately clapped his hands. Three young women, supervised by an older woman, entered with plates of food and served John first. He sat uncomfortably, nodding to the young women as they heaped different aromatic foods onto a wide plate, that they eventually handed to him, together with a cup of water. They were clean, perfumed, and dressed in bright colours and he was painfully aware that although his hands were clean, the rest of his body was not, and his clothes were stained and smelled of days of dried sweat.

He waited until the others were served then looked down while Ibrahim said some words in Arabic. After what John assumed were prayers the women left and Ibrahim and his sons began to eat with their fingers. It had been more than a day since his last meal, and John ate steadily, occasionally taking large gulps of water, experiencing a gradual feeling of wellbeing. He ate with his head down, unaware and uncaring of the curious stares of the two youths. The women entered with more water, took away the empty plates and returned with bowls of grapes, dates and figs. Finally, the women returned again with bowls of water and towels, and the meal was over.

"Now we will talk," Ibrahim announced. He stretched out his legs and leaned back on his elbows, his sons did likewise. John cautiously manoeuvred his body into a more suitable position, and began to realize how comfortable it could be.

"That was a good meal. Thank you," John said. He was keen to promote a continuation of this friendly treatment, but aware that there must be some price he would have to pay.

"You are clearly an intelligent man, Gilles, and I would like to treat you as such." Ibrahim gazed across the circle with dark, thoughtful eyes. "You are obviously a strong knight, and you have displayed some courage." He paused. "As you may have guessed, I had a spare horse. The reason I made you walk, locked you in a cell without food, and let you experience the hostility of Hassan, my bodyguard, was to show you how your life could be. This evening indicates another type of captivity. You must choose."

"How do I choose?"

"By giving me your word, as a knight and a warrior, that you will not try to escape. By keeping strictly to the limits I impose and by providing me with stimulating discussion, and my sons with an education."

"I am no teacher," John protested.

"Ah, but you are." Ibrahim spoke persuasively. "If my sons are to survive in this new age, when Christianity and the Crusaders may become a permanent and increasingly powerful influence in our land, they must learn about the beliefs and the intentions of the invaders. It is a time of new weapons, new fashions and new philosophies. You understand these things, and can explain them."

"I'm a soldier. I have some education, and some training in leadership and how to run an estate, but I am not a philosopher, and I know little about the politics of the Crusader leaders."

"I think you will be surprised how much you do know when you begin to examine your thoughts." He smiled. "Anyway, I am willing to take the risk, especially as you and I will be discussing such matters long before you have to teach such things to these two." He looked proudly at both his sons. "They can read and write in their own language, and speak some French. Rashid is almost fluent. However, they do not know how to write the language. I have some books in French, and you will teach them how to read and write your language."

"French is my second language, and I have never read a book in French," John paused, "at least, I don't think I have." He saw the question on Ibrahim's face. "That is a long story."

"Indeed. Let us first agree on the terms of your..." he paused, "your stay with us."

"How long will you keep me prisoner?" John retorted.

"Until I can get a suitable ransom for you, Gilles," Ibrahim replied smoothly. Again, a gentle smile appeared on his face. "It may take a while, such things do not happen quickly." Then he frowned. "In the meantime you can fester in that little cell, be forced to work in the fields with my servants, have Hassan to be in charge of you, and eat the leavings we feed the animals." His two sons looked very serious. "Or, you can agree to my terms, and live the life of a valued guest in my house, be provided with clean clothes, good food and a large amount of freedom." He smiled again. "Under my protection you could move freely around this valley, but if you tried to escape you would die in the desert, or be killed by the local people. There is none of your kind in this area, and if you ever tried to escape you would never return alive."

There was a long pause while each man stared into the eyes of the other. John had no doubts about Ibrahim's sincerity, and was slowly beginning to realize he was in the presence of a remarkable man. In most other situations he could imagine either he would be dead, or lying manacled in some foul prison. He rose slowly to his feet. "All right, Ibrahim. I agree to your terms. I will not try to escape, and I will teach your sons as much as I am able."

Ibrahim stood up and crossed the circle. He stopped in front of John and gripped his right arm with his right hand. "I believe this is how you seal an agreement," Ibrahim said. John nodded and returned the grip, and repeated the gesture with the two serious youths. John was impressed with their impeccable manners, and wondered how they would perform as students with an unqualified tutor.

"You must be tired. Hassan will show you to your quarters," Ibrahim gave a small bow. "Hassan will behave himself from now on."

CHAPTER 5

THE REMAINS OF THE English army were gathered together in makeshift accommodation in a rocky area south of the main encampment. As a way of raising morale and reintroducing some form of discipline, Ralph had insisted that those who were uninjured and the walking wounded, would reform in their platoons and sections, and had agreed with the officers of the relief army and with the Knights of the Order to have their troops billeted separately. While the officers met to exchange information and discuss the results of the battle, it was felt that those soldiers who could still fight should remain with their original armies to avoid confusion and panic mongering.

"Halt! Give the word!" The challenge of the sentry cut through the quiet air.

"Stonehenge," Ralph replied, keeping his voice as low as possible.

"Pass, m'Lord." The young soldier replaced his sword in his scabbard, as Ralph approached out of the gloom.

"Well done!" He gave the sentry a friendly pat on the shoulder. "Have you had to challenge anyone else recently?"

"No, m'Lord. Except the Sergeant. 'E comes round regular."

"Good. Keep alert. Give a loud challenge whenever you have to. Understand?"

"Yes, m'Lord." The sentry stared after Ralph as he disappeared into the darkness. "Don't ye worry, nobody'll get past me," he murmured, and drew his sword, just in case.

Martin was standing outside one of the tents, a torch flickered behind him, and his powerful frame cast a big shadow. "All's well, m'Lord. Gwen be fast asleep." He sounded like a doting father, and Ralph restrained himself from making a joke.

"Good. When do you change the sentries?"

"I changed 'em a short while ago, m'Lord," Martin frowned. "Did ye catch any of 'em asleep?"

"No. The one who challenged me was well awake." Ralph came closer. "I noticed when I was challenged just now, how sound carries on such a night. Anyone wanting to get through our lines could easily hear the password if they hung around out of sight."

"What do ye want me to do, m'Lord?" Martin sounded alarmed.

"Nothing we can do. We have agreed the password for tonight and some of our officers are still in the officers' tent." He rubbed his unshaven chin. "The perimeter sentries will stop anyone entering from outside. We are the only ones to have our own guards inside the camp. All I can suggest is that you tell all of them to challenge very loudly so we are all aware of people entering this area."

"D'ye think Gwen could be in some danger, m'Lord?"

"I think the Order wants to discover if she's alive, and if so, where she is."

Martin cleared his throat. "Do them knights 'ave any right to protect 'er, m'Lord? I mean they was in charge of 'er safety before the battle. Especially that Lord Longsword, and his friend De Bois, but they be dead now. So do we take over?"

"From what I hear, I don't think Longsword and De Bois were friends," Ralph said. He gave a humourless laugh. "But you're right, Martin, we're going to provide her security from now on. We're going to be her Praetorian Guard." He smiled broadly.

Martin nodded his head. He had no idea what a Praetorian Guard was, but it sounded fine. "I'll go now, an' make sure them guards keep alert." He picked up his circular-rimmed helmet, and walked off quickly tying up the strap as he went, his sword banging against his left leg.

Ralph unfastened his sword belt as he quietly entered the tent, and laid it on a large wooden box that had been rescued from the pillaged wagon train. At the far end of the tent was a dark curtained-off area, behind which Gwen was sleeping. In the middle of the accommodation the red embers of a fire glowed in the dim light created by the outside torch. He settled down on a blanket and covered himself with his cloak. Within moments, he was asleep, utterly exhausted by the events of the past two days.

•   •   •

GWEN WOKE WITH A start and lay still while she tried to control the thumping of her heart. She had been dreaming of the horrors of the battle, once again the enemy soldiers were rushing at her, their mouths open, their eyes blazing. Barbara, her loyal friend and servant, was falling towards her with a spear in her back, and when Gwen turned to flee, she was facing the huge red cross as it toppled over. Shields and armour were catapulted into the sky in slow motion and then began descending like iron hail. She was running, but was getting nowhere, and a heavy shield was coming straight at her.

She sat up in the dark, holding her face in her hands. Slowly her breathing settled and she remembered where she was. Reaching out, she touched the curtain and pulled it aside. Close by was the red glow of the fire, and beyond was the entrance to the tent with the dim flicker of the torch outside. As she stood up Gwen could see the outline of a sleeping body and was sure it was Ralph. She tiptoed towards him, but in the gloom could see little except his blond hair. Kneeling down, she touched his long locks, caressing them with her hand. Ralph slept deeply, unaware of her presence. She bent down and gently kissed his forehead. "Thank you," she whispered. "You are a good friend."

Stepping carefully, she made her way to the entrance and pushed open the flap. Outside it was cold and very still; uncountable numbers of stars glimmered in a cloudless sky. A half moon cast a stark, silvery light, making everything about her look strange and unreal. There was no sign of Martin and she assumed he was on patrol or asleep close by. She smiled to herself when she remembered how she had found Martin guarding her room in the French inn. In this situation Martin would not be sleeping.

Wrapping her arms around herself, she paced quietly back and forth, slowly regaining her faculties after her deep sleep. Her head felt tender under the bandage, but otherwise her body seemed remarkably intact considering the violence she had undergone. She turned her mind to John, and immediately stood still. What would she do if he did not return? In recent weeks, her mind had been focused entirely on him. Since her joyful reunion in Cyprus, after their separation for nearly two years, she could not imagine life without him.

Following her isolated sojourn in the French Nunnery, it had taken some while for her to catch up on the important news. She had discovered that the giant warrior, one of the two brothers who had tried to capture her in Wessex, now possessed the two swords known as The Swords of Power, and how the Knights of the Order considered him a threat to all the Crusader Kingdoms, Principalities and Counties. John had often explained why he felt he was the only person who could oppose this embodiment of evil, and how his apparent control of the swords was triggered by the runes in his right hand and the speaking of the name Giles Plantard, which the Knights pronounced as Gilles de Plantard. Now, he was missing and she feared for his life. Gwen had never seen John use the power that he claimed he possessed, and although she found the idea of such a power difficult to imagine, she never doubted him. There were things they had experienced together for which there were no rational explanations, and although she had never met the strange man called Owl, whom John described as mystical, she had encountered ordinary owls acting in remarkable ways. While she was cautious of the word magic, she believed strongly in the power of goodness, and liked to think that their many recent escapes from death were part of an overall plan in which they played an important part.

She was so absorbed in her thoughts that she failed to notice how she had moved slowly away from her tent and into an area where wagons and horses had been assembled. Inside the wagons she could hear the snoring and occasional groans of injured men, and the tethered horses shuffled and snorted as she approached. Gwen wondered how the wounded would survive the coming day, with the long, hot journey back to Antioch. She was just turning away when she heard a sudden bellow, as a sentry issued a challenge. There was a short pause, and the challenge was repeated, the voice loud and angry.

Gwen's eyes had accommodated to the moonlight and she moved swiftly around a supply wagon, curious to see whom the sentry was challenging. From the shadow of the empty wagon she could see the sentry, about sixty paces away. His sword was drawn and he was facing two figures that appeared uncertain in their movements.

"What's the word? I won't ask again!" There was a nervous aggression in the voice.

"Stone revenge," one of the men answered. He had a French accent.

"That's still not right. Stay where you are!"

"Sorry. It was something like that." The voice sounded embarrassed. "We're looking for a friend, we just want to know she survived the battle."

"Ye looking for a woman?" he sounded amazed. "What's 'er name?"

"Gwen," the man lowered his voice, and moved closer. "She's quite tall, long dark hair. Good looking. You must have seen her?"

"Don't come no closer!" The sentry took up a defensive position, and the two men took a pace back.

"Sorry," the man hissed. "We don't want everyone to know. Just tell us. Is she here?"

"Ye can't come in without the password."

"We don't want to come in," the first man persisted. "We just want to know that she is alive."

"Suppose she be? What then?"

"Just give her a message."

"What message?"

"Tell her that her friends will escort her back to Antioch tomorrow."

"What name shall I tell 'er?"

A large shadow appeared behind the sentry. "What's going on 'ere?" Martin advanced threateningly with his sword drawn.

The two men quickly turned and ran into the darkness.

"Who were they?" Martin's voice was deep and angry. "What'd they want?"

"They didn't 'ave the password right. "Said they be looking for that young woman called Mistress Gwen."

"What'd ye tell' em?"

"Nothin', Sergeant." The sentry sounded guilty. "They said they be friends of 'ers, and that they be going to take 'er back to Antioch tomorrow."

"So they knows she's 'er, then?" There was an awkward silence and Martin strode angrily away. The sentry shook his shoulders and paced dejectedly up and down, while Gwen made her way silently back the way she had come.

Martin was standing outside her tent, and looked surprised when she approached.

"So, the Knights of the Order know where I am?" Gwen said. Martin nodded slowly, he was unsure what to say. "I don't want anything to do with them, ever again! Why can't they leave me alone?" she stormed, pacing swiftly backwards and forwards in front of the tent.

"Don't ye worry, Gwen," Martin said. "Ralph and me, we won't let 'em get near ye." He looked fiercely into the darkness.

"I'm probably the only woman who survived the attack on the wagons; the only woman in the whole camp." She shook her head. "Even in all this chaos I will easily be identified. There are many of them and they want to take me prisoner again. They pretend they are keeping me safe from danger, but really they want to use me in some plans they have to gain power in this country. I don't know what they really want, and I don't care. I will not be used in this way!"

"Nor will you be, Gwen." Ralph had appeared in the entrance to the tent. "Martin and I will guard you on your journey back to Antioch and there we will make plans to get you to a place of safety. Perhaps, back to Cyprus."

"They know I'm here," Gwen said. She spoke as if it was the end of the discussion. Her shoulders drooped and with the bandage across her forehead, she looked vulnerable and defeated.

The two men frowned at each other. Ralph raised his eyebrows in a questioning manner as Martin's face became animated.

"I saw ye once, at Christchurch, dressed up as a soldier." Martin smiled at her, and then turned to Ralph. "Gwen looked the part an' all. I reckons her can do it again."

"That's it!" Ralph exclaimed. "Well done, Martin! We'll dress you as a soldier, Gwen, and add a few bloodstained bandages, and you can travel among the injured in one of the wagons. Martin and a few of our men can mount guard, and I will keep an eye on the Knights." He seemed, suddenly, wildly optimistic. "I might even let it be known that Gwen has left camp at first light with a small detachment of the Governor's men, who departed early to report to the Governor and prepare the city for the injured." Ralph grinned at Gwen. "You must let me have your dress when you have changed. I think I have a use for it."

. . .

AT FIRST LIGHT A small group of mounted knights and their retinues escorted an injured woman across the camp. The woman, in a torn blue dress, and with her head covered in bandages, rode her horse in the manner of a man, with her legs on both sides of her saddle and her dress tucked under her thighs. The group stopped at two of the sentries, gave the password, and galloped off into the brightening dawn in the direction of Antioch.

"The woman looked in bad shape," a sentry reported to his sergeant, "but she could ride a horse as well as any man."

Further down the trail, well out of sight of the camp, the woman vaulted off her horse, unwrapped the bandages around her head, and removed her dress. The other riders whooped and cheered as Vernon de Kari took a bow.

"I know I'm good looking," Vernon said, sweeping back his hair and parading about, "but I don't fancy any of you fellows so you keep your distance." Vernon's antics convulsed the riders and he took a final bow. "On a more serious note, remember you know nothing about any woman and you've never heard of a Mistress Gwen. Lord Ralph d'Escosse will pay you for your silence."

He handed the blue dress to Philip, his squire. "Hide this, and destroy it once we are back in the city." He turned to his armourer. "I'll put on that armour now, Giles. I don't want to get a reputation for being inappropriately dressed."

As the horses moved off, the riders were unaware they were being watched. More experienced men would have known that in the desert, regardless of the cruel terrain, there are always eyes that miss nothing.

• • •

IT WAS DARK WHEN the armies arrived back at Antioch. It had been a long, hot journey through a parched landscape and although the majority of the journey had been downhill, the speed of the march had been limited by the progress of the slowest wagons, the majority of which were pulled by fractious mules. But, in spite of their discomfort, most soldiers were grateful that there had been no sign of the enemy, and they could look forward to fresh food and unlimited water. The expectant city gave a silent gasp of relief as their depleted garrison was reinforced, and the injured in the wagons gave thanks that their suffering was soon to be eased. For many hours after their arrival the officers and their sergeants were kept busy organizing the billeting of their soldiers, ensuring food and water distribution was a priority. Eventually, when they had dealt with the most urgent problems, the huge army of men settled down for the night. Hundreds of small fires were lit around the outside walls of the city, while inside, the severely injured were accommodated in large halls and covered places. In spite of the numerous braziers and torches the city was essentially a dark and shadowy place, and amid the noise and bustle of the masses of soldiers, servants and local people, there were some cool, quiet places occupied by the influential and the resourceful.

In the great hall of the Knights of the Order, the High Lord was in close conversation with his most senior knight. The other members had retired early, having consumed a fine meal and generous amounts of wine. Some had survived the battle, while others had merely taken part in the relief column, but the return journey had wearied all of them. The meal had been lavish, but the conversation had remained muted, as the knights reviewed the outcome of the engagement with their enemy. It had not been a success in any sense, although some reflected with mixed feelings on the loss of some of the most senior Knights in their Order.

The High Lord was angry and his voice was loud and petulant. "I tell you again, the woman was not with those few knights who returned early! They were all men who reported to Maurice de Maron." Sir Raoul de Warron's thin face was a mask of anger. "The Governor was grateful to get their reports in order to prepare the city for the wounded. I have seen those reports, and there is no mention of Mistress Gwen or of any other woman!"

"The reports of the camp guards were quite clear. She left with the vanguard at first light," Sir Raymond de Wulfric growled. He was not used to being contradicted. "My servants were certain she was alive, and was recovering in the camp last night. They traced her to the well-guarded English section and she was not there this morning. I repeat: she left with the Governor's men."

"But why? She was safer with the army." Sir Raoul was convinced there was something he had not been told. "Why would she travel through enemy country with only a few cavalry to defend her?"

"The reports indicate severe wounding to her head and face. Perhaps she wanted to avoid the worst of the heat, or maybe she wanted to get immediate treatment for the injury to her face." He gave a dismissive snort. "Women are concerned about their looks."

"Perhaps." The High Lord was unconvinced and moved over to the window, where he stared up at the moonlit sky. "You're certain she was not with the evacuation force today?"

"I have said." Sir Raymond fought to contain his anger. "She was not with the English forces. I had men watching d'Escosse throughout the day. I, myself, inspected the whole army during the course of today's journey. If she had been with the column, I would have known. She must have escaped with the Governor's men."

"But why is there no mention of her arrival in the city?" Sir Raoul was visibly unsettled. "Are we to assume she went somewhere else?" He rubbed his hands together as though washing them. "Where would she have gone? There is nowhere she could have gone in this arid land. There is nowhere between the plateau where they were ambushed and this city. It does not make sense."

There was a silence as both men stared at each other. It was Sir Raymond who broke the tension. "Do you have the names of de Maron's men who returned early?"

Sir Raoul walked over to his writing table, and produced a scroll with a list of names. He handed it to Sir Raymond without comment.

Raymond cast his eyes down the list. "I know this one!" He narrowed his eyes. "Is Sir Vernon de Kari known to you?" The High Lord shook his head. "I met him briefly two days ago. He's newly arrived and is part of the Governor's retinue. He is young, stupid and annoying, but he does know how to fight and his family are rich, which is why de Maron has given him a post." He stood quite still, slowly rubbing his mouth with a thick forefinger. "If anyone can tell us what happened to Mistress Gwen, I am sure he can."

He walked towards the door. "I will find him tonight and I think he will tell me what I want to know." Without a backwards glance, Sir Raymond strode out of the room, slamming the door behind him.

For a while the High Lord stood still, carefully reading the list of names. Finally, he moved to his writing table, replaced the scroll with a number of others, sat down and began to write. After a few minutes he called his servant. "Pierre, make sure you deliver this to Lord d'Escosse. He is with the English section, near the river. Give it to no one else. You understand?"

The servant nodded, and quietly withdrew. He had been the personal servant to Sir Raoul since he was appointed the High Lord. Pierre was well treated and valued his job; he knew when to give advice and when to keep silent. He had listened outside the door to the exchange between his master and Sir Raymond and was concerned by what he heard. Although Sir Raoul could be vicious in his verbal attacks he rarely used physical violence. In contrast, Sir Raymond was known for his violent temper and his brutality towards his servants. None of Pierre's acquaintances had a good word to say about the powerful knight. The consensus in the kitchen was that everyone hoped the Moslems would get him before too long.

However, Sir Vernon de Kari was another matter. He was a young Lord who, although ridiculed by other knights, was liked by the servants who encountered him, and as of a few hours ago, Pierre had a special reason for liking him.

. . .

IT WAS IN THE late afternoon, some while before the main body of the armies returned from their unresolved battle on the plateau, when Pierre, dressed in the distinctive grey and brown uniform of his Lord's household, was shopping in the city's main market. He had already bought most of the provisions he needed for a dinner his master was arranging for the senior Knights of the Order, and his final stop was at a stall that sold live chickens, water fowl and song birds in small cages. He did not speak Arabic, using a mixture of his native French and some Latin to barter, after turning for help to a young French-speaking Arab boy, who was carrying most of the purchases. Pierre had reached the final stage of the bartering.

"Tell him it's too much," he said, pointing to three live chickens in a wicker cage. The trader continued to hold up both hands and gabbled at the top of his voice.

"He says you are a foreign devil who would not know his mother and that you are trying to rob him." The boy grinned broadly. He appeared to be enjoying the exchange.

"Tell him it's my final offer. If he doesn't agree I'm off to spend my money where the merchant knows who his father is." The boy spluttered gleefully and rapidly translated. The trader stopped waving his hands, became very sullen and handed over the chickens. Pierre blinked in surprise, counted out the money from a large purse he kept inside his belted tunic, and gave it to the boy, who put down the previous purchases and slowly handed the money to the trader. As they moved off the man spat angrily on the ground.

"What did you say to him?" Pierre demanded as he picked

up the cage. He could not believe the Arab had agreed so easily because of the return of an insult.

"I told him that unless he agreed, you would return with soldiers and take all his fowls for nothing." The boy said, as he staggered along with the supplies.

"Very diplomatic," Pierre muttered. "Next time you translate what I tell you."

"Yes, ferenghi," the boy nodded seriously. It was an insulting term used by the Arabs, which in its broad sense meant foreigner. Pierre believed it meant master and both sides were happy in the exchange.

The return journey to the Great Hall took them through a narrow, busy part of the market, where traders and customers squashed together, and where the noise of voices and animals was a constant assault on the ears. Pierre was in front pushing his way through the throng when he heard the boy yell out behind him. He turned quickly and was just in time to see, amid the press of the crowd, two tall, bearded men knock his servant to the ground. They were dressed in black and one man was holding a short wooden club and lashing out at the boy who, abandoning his bags, was seeking refuge among the legs of people unable to escape the fight. The other, who was only an arm's length away, was glaring at Pierre and holding a long knife at waist height.

The boy was yelling and others took up the cry of alarm. Pierre swung the cage of hens forward as the attacker lunged with his knife. The sharp blade cut through the thin structure, killing one of the birds and causing the knife to become entangled with the woven material. The man tried to shake off the cage and Pierre lost his balance and fell backwards, as all around him people backed away. Using his other hand, the assassin withdrew his knife and cast the broken cage and its hysterical occupants to one side. He raised the weapon above his head and rushed at the horrified Pierre, who lay prostrate on the ground and could only raise an open hand in defence.

• • •

VERNON DE KARI WAS in a good mood. He had enjoyed Ralph

d'Escosse's prank, which is how he saw it. He did not think to question why a powerful young lord wished to smuggle a young woman out of the camp, or even how it was accomplished. His role had been simply to dress up as a woman, bandage his head and give the impression to the guards that he was a she. It had been great fun and he was aware that the other knights in the group had thought him to be "a good fellow". He could not ask for anything more. On arriving back at Antioch, he had reported the numbers and condition of the wounded to the Governor, Sir Maurice de Maron, who had entrusted him with contacting other officers to arrange hospital accommodation. The lovely Lady Elizabeth, the Governor's wife, had exchanged some kind words with him, and on a burst of youthful energy, he had decided to explore the market, having ordered his squire, Philip de Gortz, to do the hospital arrangements, and Giles, his armourer, to clean his horse.

He was dressed in his chain mail with a grubby tunic, which he felt gave the satisfying impression that he had just returned from a dangerous mission. His sword, in its tooled leather scabbard, hung on his left side, a precaution after his experience with the would-be assassins in the alley, and he also carried his dagger on his right hip. He had left his helmet and other armour with his servants and was savouring the smells and sounds of the crowded market. It was everything he had imagined: romantic, exciting, and above all wildly different from the tedious repetitive life he had lived in England. It was doubtful if he would ever appreciate the fact that he had lived, and still lived, a pampered, elitist existence, and the only reason he had been bored in England was, as the youngest son, nobody had ever expected anything of him.

As he looked around the sea of faces he was aware of a few other Europeans, mostly soldiers, forcing their way through the dense crowd. On his right hand side he noticed a pale skinned man in a smart uniform, who was followed by a young Arab servant. The man, who boasted a large stomach, carried a wicker cage with birds peering anxiously through the bars, while behind him the young servant was bravely struggling with a load of provisions.

They were unaware of two tall, bearded men who were rapidly advancing from behind and clearly intending to reach them.

Vernon turned away as a heavily veiled woman bumped into him. He apologized to her, and when he looked back he saw that one of the bearded men had knocked the boy to the ground, and the other, an older man, was attempting to stab the European. Instantly, Vernon pushed his way through the ring of retreating spectators. The bearded, older man was struggling to rid himself of the cage of birds, which encased his knife hand. Amid the screaming and yelling and the chaotic movement of panicking people, Vernon had no room to draw his long sword. He saw the attacker raise his blade as he moved towards his defenceless victim, who lay squirming on the ground. In a blur of spontaneous activity, Vernon drew his dagger and launched himself at the bearded attacker, crying, "Stop! Murderer!"

The attacker spun round. He had not expected any interruption. People in crowds never responded quickly to assassinations that were over before the onlookers could determine what to do. The crowd parted and a small figure, dressed like a soldier, rushed forward, yelling some foreign language. The bearded man lashed out with his knife and, as he did so, he registered with apprehension both the chain mail and the bright dagger. He sprang back and took up a defensive position, no longer confident in the outcome.

Vernon's responses were quick, yet he understood that the assassin was equally skilled. There was a split second as both men faced each other; the Arab feigned to Vernon's left, trying to force him towards the second attacker, who having turned away from the boy, was intending to attack from the right. Trusting in the power of surprise Vernon did a half movement to the right, as the assassin had intended him to do and then reversed the movement, meeting the Arab as he lunged forward.

It was over in a moment. Vernon's dagger whipped up under the assassin's defence and before the man could bring down his knife, the dagger entered under his rib cage. With a look of incomprehension in his eyes the attacker staggered back and collapsed on top of Pierre, who was screaming like a banshee.

Vernon did not pause to consider his actions, but pivoted on his right foot and dodged as the club, aimed at his head by the second assassin, passed safely over him. The Arab was momentarily off-balance and Vernon lunged with his dagger. As he did so one of the surviving chickens, having escaped its broken cage, fluttered up in a flurry of feathers in front of him and completely confused his counter attack. The assassin, fearing for his life, threw the club at Vernon and rushed into the crowd, pushing and punching at anyone in his path. As Vernon was recovering from the shock of the unexpected frenzy of the chicken, the club hit him on the forehead and he fell to the ground.

He recovered quickly, but not before the blood-drenched Pierre had cradled him in his arms. "Thank you. Thank you," Pierre intoned as he inspected Vernon's bruised forehead. The servant boy had recovered from the assault and was busily trying to collect his master's purchases, before other boys stole them. People stood around in animated groups and discussed the incident. But apart from Pierre, none of them offered any assistance to the young knight.

A patrol of soldiers pushed their way through the crowd and the sergeant acknowledged Vernon, who was standing unsteadily, holding his head with one hand and holding on to Pierre with the other.

"You all right, Sir?" He was a thickset man, with broad shoulders and powerful arms, and as he saluted, he surveyed the dead Arab with an experienced eye. Vernon nodded and took some deep breaths. "'Glad to see ye got the best of 'im, Sir." The sergeant was surprised how young the knight looked.

"The murdering fiends attacked me," Pierre interjected. "Two of them. They attacked my servant, and tried to kill me." He sounded indignant. "This man saved my life."

The sergeant glanced at Pierre, and recognizing he was of no importance, ignored him and continued to speak to Vernon. "We'll take the body back to headquarters, Sir. We got a prisoner who might know him." He noted the knife the dead man had been carrying and the blood on Vernon's dagger, which lay on the floor. The young knight had proved himself in a knife fight.

As a hardened soldier, the sergeant knew that Europeans rarely survived such attacks.

"Your prisoner? Was he brought in two nights ago by Sir Raymond de Wulfric?" Vernon tried to stand up straight, aware the sergeant was at least six inches taller and twice his weight.

"Yes, Sir. It were an attempted murder near the Main Square. Three dead, one captured, some got away. That'll teach 'em to mess with Sir Raymond." The sergeant let out a bellowing laugh. "No one in their right mind gets in 'is way." The soldier noted Vernon's scowl, and wondered if he had said too much. "If ye pardon me saying so, Sir."

"I was the one they attacked, not Sir Raymond," Vernon was outraged that his involvement had gone unnoticed. "He came in at the end of the fight." He clamped his lips together. A knight did not have to explain such things to a sergeant, however experienced. Vernon turned away, feeling his face colour up.

The sergeant returned to supervise the removal of the body. "Wet behind the ears," he joked to one of his men. "Good with a knife, but just a boy." A ripple of laughter flowed among the soldiers.

Pierre knew the sergeant had snubbed him and disliked all such men. However, Sir Vernon was a different matter. Without the bravery of this young man Pierre knew he would have been dead by now, just another body in the gutter. "I am in your debt, Sir," he said. He looked around at the curious faces of the crowd, any of whom could be holding a knife. Pierre did not feel as confident as he had been. "Perhaps we could walk together?" He smiled encouragingly.

"Good idea," Vernon mumbled. His head ached and he felt uncertain of his balance. "I need to get back to the Governor's House." He placed an arm around Pierre's shoulders. The Grand Master's steward puffed out his chest and having given the servant boy a warning frown, he swaggered towards the Main Square, happily supporting the hero who had saved his life.

CHAPTER 6

T HE IMPOSING VILLA WAS set in its own grounds near the river, and was protected by a high wall on three sides. It was situated outside the walled city, but in a wealthy area along the eastern part of the river, where wealthy merchants had built fortified homes. Two soldiers guarded an impressive iron gate, that was kept closed, and other soldiers patrolled the grounds and the area near the river. Inside the building a late meal was coming to its close. Sir Ralph d'Escosse and Gwen sat opposite each other and sipped wine as the servants cleared the table, refurbished the candles, and bowed their way out of the door. Ralph and Gwen had said little during the meal, the first well-cooked food they had enjoyed for many days. Both were conscious of an unspoken awkwardness in their situation, and the presence of the servants had been a further inhibition.

Gwen yawned into her hand. "I'm sorry. It's been a long day."

"It's been three long days." Ralph smiled sympathetically. "How's your head?"

"Getting better. The motherly woman in the kitchen washed and dressed it for me. She said it was healing well. Just a graze really." She tentatively explored the bandage with her left hand. "I'm sure I can take this off tomorrow."

"I imagine you're ready for a decent night's sleep?" His blue eyes shone in the candlelight, as he savoured the delight of Gwen's company.

"I can't go to sleep, not yet. I'm still overwhelmed by the recent events." She took a deep breath. "There has been so much horror and killing. So many men died. My loyal Barbara killed for no reason. Then, the earthquake, and that enormous red cross crashing down. I had dreams of the whole event when I was in England." She was speaking fast and her eyes were wide with fear. "When I recovered after the battle I was so relieved to find you and Martin were still alive," she dropped her eyes, "but not knowing about John, I can't think…" her voice trailed off. "Then the escape from the Order and the journey back…."

"Not much fun spending a whole day in a wagon with injured and dying people." Ralph reached across the table and took her hand. "You were very brave."

"Not as brave as those soldiers. The heat was unbearable. It was like being in a furnace, and the awful smell and the persistent flies. I'll never forget it." She shook her head. "It was a nightmare. We remember battles in terms of glorious victories and well-deserved defeats, never in terms of human suffering. So many people died, so many wounded, and what for? What was achieved?"

"Women are not usually as involved in the aftermath of battles as you were," Ralph said, trying to lighten her mood.

"Oh, but they are. It's mainly women who take care of the wounded." She took a sip of her wine. "It's the men who bury the dead." Her face was a picture of misery. "Some soldiers go missing and their bodies are never found. Their families and friends never get to know what really happened and continue to hope that one day they will reappear. They might spend their whole lives hoping."

A small tear ran down her cheek as she thought of John. She withdrew her hand and wiped her cheek as she looked up at the concerned face of the handsome man in front of her. "I'm sorry. I'm bad company."

"Not at all," Ralph said. He sipped his wine and nodded thoughtfully. "Anyway, I think your ordeal will be worth it. Thanks to that young knight, Sir Vernon de Kari, I believe we have confused the Knights of the Order into thinking you either died in the battle, or that you have somehow managed to slip away on the return journey to Antioch."

"Do you really think so?" Gwen stared fiercely at him. "This terrible day's suffering would be worth it to be rid of them. I never knew what they wanted of me, but I always felt my life was not my own. Originally, they placed me with Tom Roper, and knowing nothing else, I was quite content. I don't think Elizabeth, my stepmother, ever really liked me, but she was never unkind to me. As far as I knew Tom was my real father. When the Knights returned they educated me, guarded me, and even provided me with fine clothes and good food. But they never allowed me to be myself. They tricked me with warnings that my life and Tom's were in danger and they told me lies about John. Always they tried to keep us apart." Her large dark eyes were deep pools of tragedy. "I wish they would leave me alone!"

"I won't allow them to come near you again." Ralph said, confidently. "After a few days, when the city has returned to its usual chaotic life, we will leave for Tripoli. I will dress you as one of my soldiers and we will go on a prolonged reconnaissance. Never to return."

"Where will we go?" Gwen asked, holding her palms upwards.

"We could stay in Tripoli for a while, it's a large trading port, or we could go back to Cyprus and stay at Stephen de Bois' estate until a suitable ship can take us back to England. It will be months before the Order begins to worry about the property of its dead knights."

There was a knock on the door. Ralph stood up, his hand on his sword. "Enter!"

A servant opened the door, and handed Ralph a sealed parchment. "M'Lord, this be from the Grand Master of the Knights of the Order." He bowed, and was about to leave when Ralph called him back.

"Who delivered this?"

"Sir Raoul de Warron's steward, m'Lord. Pierre's his name."

"What did he say?"

The servant shrugged his shoulders. "Just to give this to ye, m'Lord." The servant bowed, and was about to leave, when he added, "Oh, I forgot. Pierre asked me if I knows where Sir Vernon de Kari can be found."

Ralph made an exasperated noise. "What did you say to him?"

"That I didn't know, m'Lord. Pierre said Sir Vernon could be in danger. Something about how the knight saved his life in the market place today." With a red face, the servant bowed out of the room.

"I'm beset with idiots!" Ralph exclaimed.

Gwen smiled encouragingly. "He must have thought it was just servant chatter and that you would not be interested. Don't be hard on him." Gwen approached Ralph. "Do you think it's important?"

"It could be," Ralph murmured as he quickly scanned the letter. "He would like to see me tomorrow at noon to discuss an issue of mutual importance."

"About me?"

"Almost certainly. He knows we were together with Stephen de Bois, when we arrived in the city. However, I am certain he does not know where you are now, or he would have paid us a sudden visit, with a strong escort." He rubbed his forefinger on the bridge of his nose. "I think Sir Vernon could be in danger as Pierre indicated."

"In danger? The Order can't do anything against a knight, can they?"

"Certainly they can." He frowned. "If the Knights want to find him, it must be because they think Vernon knows where you are and young, rather silly knights have a habit of disappearing." Ralph walked back to the table and finished his wine. "I don't understand how they have identified him so quickly." He strode to the door. "I want you to stay here, Gwen. I am going to see if I can get to Vernon before Sir Raoul and his merry band find him. Nobody will be allowed into this house while I'm away and I'll double the guard." He forced a smile. "Keep away from the windows, we don't want beautiful women attracting unwanted guests."

Gwen smiled at his attempt at humour. "Take care. I'll stay up until you return."

"I'll try not to be too late." Ralph smiled broadly and gave a small bow. "I'll probably have to bring Vernon back with me, to prevent him getting into trouble."

He closed the heavy, inlaid door and paused at the top of a broad, curving marble staircase. Since his arrival back in the city he had not had time to appreciate the building allotted to him as his own billet, and he stood for a moment savouring its space and quality. Below him was an airy vestibule with large stone pillars, graceful statues, and a small fountain that splashed into a wide richly glazed bowl. The design echoed the influence of Classical Greek architecture and the effect was both cool and peaceful. Bright tiles covered the floor and an ornate mosaic of flowers decorated the area around the imposing entrance. It was unlike anything he had known in England and the house was a clear testament to the wealth and power of its former owner.

Two soldiers stood guard at the bottom of the staircase and came to attention as he descended. One of the soldiers was a giant of a man with powerful shoulders and a wild black beard, flecked with grey. Formally a blacksmith on Ralph's family estates, and promoted to sergeant before leaving England, Little was deeply proud of his military status.

"Nothing new to report, Sir!" He saluted vigorously.

Ralph grinned and returned a casual salute. "Stand at ease, Sergeant Little." He usually called him Little, having known him first as a peasant and later as a loyal friend. But knowing how much the blacksmith enjoyed his role as a soldier, Ralph always emphasized the military title in the presence of other soldiers. "How many guards are outside, Sergeant?"

"Four, Sir. Two in the front and two in the garden at the back."

"I want the guard doubled, Sergeant, and make sure they are checked every two hours."

"Yes, Sir." Little looked worried. "You be expecting trouble, Sir?"

"Yes," Ralph said reflectively. "It's possible. I want you to stay on duty until I return, no matter how late that may be."

The sergeant took a deep breath. "I will, Sir." A knowing look came into his eyes. "Am I to stop anyone coming into the house?"

The emphasis was not lost on Ralph. "Yes, Sergeant, prevent anyone from gaining access, even Knights of the Order." He frowned. "Especially Knights of the Order."

"I will, Sir." Little glared at the soldier next to him. "Ye keep guard while I sorts out the others." He thrust a spear into the soldier's hands. "Remember, nobody passes," he growled, as he followed Ralph out of the door.

. . .

INSIDE A LARGE BUILDING near the centre of the city, in an area where most of the citizens abstained from alcohol, the officers of the occupying armies met to socialize and drink copious amounts of wine. They discussed the recent battle, the numerous attacks on their soldiers within the city, and the best places to get a decent meal. Among the more rowdy members of the group was Sir Vernon de Kari, who, having told his story of the attack in the market place innumerable times, was becoming increasingly ponderous as the wine took effect. "I don't know how many there were," he paused to take a deep breath, "but I wasn't worried. At times like this," he paused, having lost his thread, "there are times, when... when all that matters is being noble." He felt so good about being noble.

"Well done, Vernon. Good man." A young knight patted him on the back. "I couldn't have done better." He staggered away, leaving Vernon to contemplate his recent victories by himself.

"Damn good, indeed," he muttered. He finished his wine and looked about vacantly for a servant to refill his mug. When a soldier approached with a civilian, who could have been either a merchant or a servant, Vernon peered at the man as though he was an unusual specimen. "More wine," he waved his empty mug, but remembering he was noble, he added, "if you please."

"This man wanted to speak to you, Sir." The soldier put an emphasis on the last word, conveying his contempt for a young knight who couldn't hold his drink. He pushed the civilian forward and stepped back a pace.

"It's me, Sir. Pierre. You saved my life a few hours ago."

"Pierre!" Vernon almost embraced him. "You mush have some wine with me." He tried to turn his head, but found it difficult to focus his eyes. "In a moment." He winked at the embarrassed steward.

"M'Lord, I've come to warn you. You could be in danger." Pierre looked around, trying to identify any Knights of the Order, among the dozens of men who filled the large candle-lit room.

"Danger? I'm used to danger." He smiled benevolently and slowly shook his head. "We knights, you know, we're noble. Bravery to us is second…" he paused, and nodded with profound dignity, his eyes trying to focus on the rotund man in front of him, "…schecond nature."

Pierre was alarmed. He recognized that Vernon was very drunk and might not understand what he was told. He looked anxiously around and tried another approach. "You are needed outside, my Lord. This soldier," he turned to the waiting guard, "will help you." He took a coin out of his purse and handed it to the soldier. "Help him outside onto the balcony." He pointed across the room.

The soldier smirked, helped the drunken knight to his feet, and frog marched him out to the balcony that overlooked a wide square. Pierre followed and picked up a flask of water on the way. He waited until the soldier had departed, and pushed the flask into Vernon's hands. "You must drink this, quickly."

Vernon tried to focus on this man who was giving him orders. "I'm a knight. I'm noble." He took a deep breath and the oxygen seemed to clear his brain for a moment. He took a long drink of the water, and banged the flask down on a table. "You're Pierre. You're the Grand Master's Steward. I saved your life." He smiled contentedly, sat down on a bench, and promptly collapsed over the back and onto the floor, where he lay unmoving.

"Sir Vernon!" Pierre whispered, he patted the knight's face in an ineffectual way; his fear was fast giving way to panic. There was no valid reason for him to be here and there was a high chance he might be recognized. Sir Raoul de Warron's orders had been unambiguous, and having delivered the message to Sir Ralph d'Escosse, Pierre would be expected to report that he had completed the task. If his master heard he had been talking to Sir Vernon there would be awkward questions to answer. "Sir Vernon!" He shook the young man urgently. "Wake up!"

Vernon opened his eyes and tried to focus on Pierre. He closed one eye, and nodded gravely. "I'm noble," he stated, and passed out.

Although Pierre was the larger of the two men, he was also overweight and physically unfit. He stared down at the unconscious knight and knew he could not lift him. The balcony was in shadow and when he looked into the lighted room where the rest of the officers mingled, he realized that nobody had noticed Vernon's exit. Pierre knew he had to react quickly and he dragged the unconscious Vernon to the side of the balcony, behind the door, and pulled him up into a sitting position. It was possible that if people should walk on the balcony, they might briefly admire the flickering lights of the city, and yet be unaware of the recumbent body.

He picked up the flask in the darkness and studied the lighted room. When he was certain there was nobody he knew in the mêlée of soldiers, he pushed back his shoulders and marched purposefully across the crowded room and out of the main door.

Once outside he nodded meaningfully to the smirking guard and decided to return to Lord Ralph d'Escosse's villa. He would tell the young lord where to find his friend and then he would have repaid the debt. There was only so much one could do. "A life for a life," he murmured and walked quickly in the direction of Ralph's villa, trying to ignore the dark shadows on each side of the road and the numerous side alleys that resembled black open mouths filled with potential horror.

·   ·   ·

RALPH MARCHED SWIFTLY TOWARDS Sir Vernon's billet in a house close to the Governor's Mansion. Two of his soldiers accompanied him, one carried a flaming torch and both were fully armed. With recent reports of yet more attacks on the Crusaders and their servants, Ralph was unwilling to risk his life unnecessarily. "Keep your eyes open for anyone who takes an interest in us," he ordered, "and tell me if you see any of the Knights of the Order."

The soldiers were well aware of the increased danger in the city and had little love for the members of the Order or their servants. "The trouble with 'em, m'Lord, is that they reckons they got God on their side, which makes it difficult for the rest of us."

Ralph nodded at the soldier. "Very true, Dan. However, I'm not sure God agrees." He gave a short laugh. "Stay close. This is the area where there's been a number of attacks."

They were taking a short cut through a run-down district of the old city. Buildings of different sizes were crammed together on both sides of the main street. Some had torches burning outside their open doors, where groups of bearded men stood or sat on their haunches in small circles and stared with undisguised hostility at the three Europeans as they hurried past. There were also stretches of shadowy, crumbling buildings where closed doors and shuttered windows gave the impression of emptiness and decay, yet behind which could be an army of cutthroats. Frequent narrow alleys on both sides disappeared around sharp corners and provided perfect cover for ambushes. At times they could see fleeting figures on the flat roofs of the buildings, some of which were lit with torches, while others were dark and threatening.

"Draw swords!" Ralph ordered, as they approached a large group of men who blocked the street. He drew his long sword, and holding it in front of him with both hands, he marched forward with a soldier on each side. The Arabs looked alarmed and moved aside, unwilling to test the resolve of the three English soldiers as they continued quickly down the street.

"I thought we be in for a fight there," Dan remarked, as he checked behind to ensure they were not being followed.

"They might have had some such thoughts, Dan, but your ferocious expression changed their minds." Ralph winked at the other soldier.

"That's good then," Dan stuck out his chest. "They better had watch themselves an' all."

They were a few minutes from their destination when they heard a frightened cry in the night. It was the sound of a man who was suffering pain and whose life might be in danger and, most importantly, he was crying out in French.

"Follow me!" Ralph yelled as he ran towards the sound, which had changed to a high-pitched scream.

• • •

SIR RAYMOND DE WULFRIC feared nobody. He was aware of his

reputation of being a dangerous and unpredictable opponent and it pleased him that other people, even knights, were cautious and even fearful in his presence. As he made his way along the ill-lit streets he displayed an overt contempt for the local citizens, even when they were gathered in groups of ten or more. He was a powerful, skilful fighter, and in a pitched battle could swing his long sword with one hand for longer than most knights could continue using both. He was ruthlessly ambitious with fixed beliefs and had no compunction in taking human lives to achieve his aims.

Sir Vernon de Kari had not been in his billet, but a servant had thought he might have gone to the Officers' Mess. Raymond did not mind the exercise and disdained the use of a horse in the city unless it was necessary. He did not think it would take long to persuade the young knight to tell him how Gwen was spirited away from the battlefield, and where she was being kept.

He strode into a main thoroughfare. Flickering braziers illuminated parts of the almost empty street, silent now after the noise and activity of the day. Arabs, singly or in small groups, scuttled past on the other side, deliberately ignoring him. His alert eyes noted them; his mind assessed them and dismissed any danger. Since becoming a knight his quick reactions and his immense self-confidence had proved invaluable in preserving him from serious injury. Other battle-hardened knights spoke of his bravery, but he dismissed the word. As he feared nobody, how could he be brave? Those who feared him and yet still opposed him showed bravery; they were brave, but dead.

In the midst of this satisfying contemplation, he rounded a corner and entered a wide square surrounded by gloomy, hulking buildings with narrow passageways on either side. He turned to his right and saw at the other end of the square the familiar figure of Pierre, the High Lord's servant, walking quickly towards him. In the same instant the figure darted into a dark alley. Raymond knew the servant had seen him and he wondered why he was attempting to avoid recognition, and what he was doing in this part of the city.

Sir Raymond passed the alley without turning his head, giving the impression he was unaware of the person hugging the shadows. Once past the alley he flattened himself against a wall and inched his way back along to the recessed doorway of a mud-clad building. He silently drew his dagger and waited, convinced the servant would reappear.

After a brief wait, Pierre crept out of the shadow of the alley, glanced quickly to his right, and turned left, unaware that Sir Raymond was immediately behind him. Pierre yelled loudly as a huge hand grabbed him, forced him into the gloom of the alley, and banged his head against the rough mud wall. Pierre continued to scream until a hand blocked his mouth.

"Where have you been?"

Pierre was terrified. He recognized Sir Raymond's voice and wondered how much he knew. Perhaps the knight had been at the officers' party, or maybe Sir Raymond had simply seen him on his return journey to the Governor's house. Either way Pierre knew he was in mortal danger. "I was looking for someone, Sir." He gasped as the gloved hand moved down to his throat.

"Who?" Sir Raymond tightened his grip on Pierre's fleshy neck.

"Sir Vernon de Kari. My master sent me to find him, Sir."

"Why?" The enormous hand tightened around his throat.

"I don't know, Sir," he squeaked. "My master sent me to find Sir Vernon, and arrange for him to come to a meeting at his house tonight." He could hardly breathe.

"Did you find him?" There was a slight relaxation of the frightening grip on Pierre's windpipe.

Pierre took a deep breath. "No, Sir. He was not at the officers' gathering. I was just going to report to my master."

"So, you didn't find him?"

"No, Sir." Pierre swallowed loudly.

"Why did you try to avoid me?

"Oh, no, Sir! I wasn't trying to avoid you, Sir. I just needed to relieve myself." He gave an uncertain laugh.

Sir Raymond shoved him away and Pierre staggered out of the alley, falling like a stuffed dummy on the hard ground, his water flask rolling away.

At that moment Ralph entered the shadowy square, followed

by his two soldiers, and seeing a European in obvious distress he ran towards the alley just as Sir Raymond emerged from the blackness, his hand on the hilt of his sword.

They stared at each other for a long moment. Ralph had drawn his sword and his two soldiers were equally prepared. Sir Raymond sniffed. "To what do I owe this belated assistance?" He gave a mock bow. "Ah, we meet again, Lord d'Escosse."

"My Lord de Wulfric," Ralph nodded his head in recognition. "We heard someone cry out for help." Ralph tried to keep the loathing out of his voice as he met the confident eyes of Sir Raymond. Pierre staggered to his feet, groaned, and rubbed his neck, a frightened expression on his face.

"You must have heard this lying mound of fat screaming his pretended innocence," the knight said contemptuously. He lashed out with his foot and Pierre collapsed, once again, in a heap in the dust. "I intend to return him to his master where I will extract the truth." He bent down and grabbing Pierre by his left arm dragged the terrified servant to his feet.

"The truth?" Ralph queried.

"I believe you know a young knight called Sir Vernon?"

"Should I?" Ralph raised his eyebrows.

"I need to speak with him."

Ralph shrugged. There was a silence as both men glowered at each other. Dan picked up the flask that Pierre had dropped and held it out to him. The angry knight smashed it to the ground. "This creature will tell me what I want to know." His eyes bored into Ralph's. "We need to find Mistress Gwen and I think you know of her whereabouts."

Sir Raymond searched Ralph's face for a reaction and seeing none clutched Pierre's arm in an iron grip and turned away. Pierre mouthed two words at Dan as he was dragged off.

The three men watched in silence as Pierre was hustled out of the square.

"He whispered two words at me, m'Lord." Dan said.

"What two words?"

"He said, 'Officers' party'."

"Did he now?" Ralph nodded thoughtfully. "Then that's where we'll go. Keep close."

Ralph's thoughts centred on de Wulfric as they marched quickly towards the centre of the city where the Officers' Mess was located. The knight was a relatively new arrival in the Holy Land and had quickly moved up in importance in the Order. According to information he had elicited from the Governor's officers, de Wulfric was wealthy, well connected and a powerful fighter. He was merciless towards his enemies and unforgiving towards any friend who failed to support him. Servants feared him and lesser knights either kept their silence and their distance, or gave him their whole-hearted, sycophantic support. Ralph was unhappy with de Wulfric's treatment of the Governor's servant, but he could not have intervened. However, this behaviour had confirmed that the Order was looking for Vernon, and it was imperative to find him before he was forced to disclose his knowledge of Gwen.

Ralph arrived at the Officers' Mess, and identified himself to the soldiers guarding the door. "Is Sir Vernon de Kari inside?"

"I don't know, Sir. There be a load of officers in there." The guard was formal but unhelpful.

"He's young, not very tall, and newly arrived in Antioch." Ralph stared intently at the faces of the guardsmen and noticed a slight flicker in one man's eyes. He smiled encouragingly at him.

"There's a young knight, Sir, what I helped out on to one of the balconies."

Ralph noticed the slight grin on the soldier's face and drew the obvious conclusion. "Was he drunk?"

"He'd had a bit, Sir."

"Where will I find him?" There was steely note in Ralph's voice and the soldier composed his face instantly.

"At the top of the stairs, Sir, there be a door into the main room. The balcony be directly in front." He was aware of the intensity of the knight's stare. "At the other side of the room, Sir."

"Thank you. If others come looking for Sir Vernon you will tell them he has left. You have no idea where he has gone or whom he was with." Ralph frowned at the soldiers. "Is that clear?"

The soldiers nodded in unison.

"Good. I knew I could count on you all." Ralph gave them a dazzling smile. "I want you all to have a good time after your guard duty." He passed a few coins to the soldier who had helped Sir Vernon and raced up the stairs.

The two soldiers who had escorted him acted as though this was common practice. "He always does that," Dan said. "But he'll cut your gizzards out if you disobey him." The soldier was suitably impressed and grinned at his friends. "Seems like the drinks will be on me, lads!"

Sir Vernon was lying unconscious behind the door as Pierre had left him. Ralph ordered the two soldiers to carry the young knight down stairs, where they loaded him onto a horse, and shortly afterwards deposited him at the Governor's house.

"I hopes he has a rotten headache in the morning," Dan muttered as he and his friend staggered up the steps with the semi-conscious Vernon. Under Ralph's guidance they sat him on a couch in the Governor's hallway while Ralph instructed the servants how to care for Vernon. As they left they heard him mutter, "I'm noble."

Dan scowled. "Ain't no different to me when 'e be drunk. A pig's as noble as he be."

. . .

IT WAS APPROACHING MIDNIGHT and Gwen was pacing around the main room of the villa, anxiously awaiting Ralph's return. She had tried to engage the servants in conversation, but all of them had been tongue-tied in her presence. The two local women who worked in the kitchen were unused to leaving their area of work and had blushed and giggled when she tried to speak to them of anything other than the next meal or her head injury. The soldiers were all men from Ralph's estates in England and none had met Gwen before. Their answers to her questions were brief, formal and awkward, and she was quite unaware of the hormonal effect her femininity had on them. As one of the soldiers remarked, "She be like an angel, too beautiful to be true, even with the bandage."

Little had let it be known that the lady of the house, as he called her, was Ralph's woman and any soldier who made unsuitable comments or stared would have him to answer to. The result was that everyone treated Gwen as though she was royalty and bowed or saluted whenever she appeared and stared fixedly at some spot over her head.

She stood at the top of the stairs leading down to the well-lit vestibule, where four soldiers were talking quietly among themselves, their voices sounding anxious and uncertain. As she began to descend they formed up quickly on both sides of the bottom step, standing rigidly to attention. Gwen smiled at them but was unable to make eye contact.

"Thank you. Please stand at ease," she said awkwardly. She had no experience of having a bodyguard. The soldiers relaxed but still remained staring ahead, their faces impassive. "Is your Sergeant Little about?" she asked tentatively.

There was a brief pause, and then one of the soldiers turned towards her, his face red with embarrassment. "The sergeant be outside, M'am. Um... Mistress Gwen. He um..."

Gwen smiled invitingly at him. "Yes?"

The soldier licked his lips. "Sergeant says ye were not to come down them stairs, 'cos there be trouble at the gate."

"What sort of trouble?" Her voice hardened.

The soldier turned to the other soldiers, but none of them would make eye contact. "We understands," he looked desperately at the other men, "we understands that a knight called de Wulfric wanted to enter but Sergeant Little would not let him."

"What happened?"

The soldier took a deep breath. "He went off. He weren't happy though."

Gwen felt the tension wash out of her. "Thank you. Thank you all. Just don't allow him to enter. Don't allow any of them to enter while Lord d'Escosse is away."

She turned to walk back up the stairs and heard the soldiers murmur their agreement. It was late and she felt so tired. She reached the top landing, opened the door to the large room in which they had had their meal, and sank down onto a padded couch. She tried to focus on the problems of the present situation, but was unable to resist the need for sleep. The extremes of the past few days had exhausted her and in a short time her eyes closed and soon she was in a deep slumber, unaware of the noisy confrontation that suddenly erupted below her room.

• • •

IT TOOK ONLY MOMENTS for Raymond de Wulfric to get a complete confession from the frightened Pierre. When faced with the prospect of being painfully injured, the servant decided his debt to Sir Vernon was paid.

"So he was unconscious when you left him?" The knight held the point of the dagger against Pierre's neck.

"Yes, m'Lord. Out cold." His tongue moistened his dry lips.

"And you're sure d'Escosse is at the officer's party?"

"Yes, m'Lord. I was just trying to help… he saved my life today, and I…."

"Enough!" The knight replaced his dagger in his belt. "Think yourself lucky you work for an important man, or I would have your ears removed for listening at doors." He sniffed contemptuously at the snivelling servant. "Report to your master, immediately. Tell him the person we are looking for is almost certainly at the house of Lord d'Escosse, in the English section, outside the city. You understand?"

"Yes, Sir. Thank you, m'Lord."

"You will hurry with this report." Pierre nodded furiously. "Tell Sir Raoul I will meet him there and to bring a strong guard. Go!"

Pierre rushed away, moving surprisingly quickly for such a large corpulent man. He kept to the middle of the road as he raced past groups of Arabs and was delighted to see a small patrol in front of him. "I'm the Steward for the Grand Master of the Order," he announced to the unimpressed Corporal. "You will accompany me to his house."

The Corporal was about to indulge himself in some venomous expletives, when Pierre produced some coins. "You will be well rewarded, Corporal. My master is always generous to those who deserve it." He breathed a sigh of relief as the Corporal accepted the money and directed his men towards the house of the Grand Master. As he scurried along beside the soldiers Pierre wondered if he could avoid a beating by appearing to be the bearer of important news.

. . .

MEANWHILE SIR RAYMOND HAD reached the torch-lit gates of Ralph's villa, and was outraged that a mere sergeant should disobey him. "I said, open up, Sergeant." He glared at the equally large man who faced him at the other side of the wrought iron gates, which were fastened with a simple latch. Behind the sergeant were four well-armed soldiers who carried spears, shields and short swords.

"I'm sorry, m'Lord. I have strict orders not to open these gates until Lord d'Escosse returns. Nobody be allowed to enter until he says so." Little enjoyed the frustration of this arrogant knight in front of him.

"Tell me, Sergeant, what is so special about Lord d'Escosse's headquarters that normal courtesy is refused to another knight?" He smiled, but the tone of his voice revealed his anger.

"I just follow me orders, Sir."

"Do you have a young woman in this villa?" The question was so casual as to have the initial effect of being of no consequence.

"We has a number of young women in the kitchen, Sir." Little smiled back.

The knight drew in a loud breath. "Tell your Lord, I will return." He paused. "When I do I will expect the gates to open for me." He turned and marched off in the direction he had come.

"Well done, lads," Little acknowledged each of the soldiers. "I reckon we've seen the last of him for tonight. I'm going inside to check on the house. Keep awake now, just in case." He strode off towards the house.

"It could be a long night," one of the soldiers said, "and it be about time we got our reward." The soldier reached behind a rock and produced a goatskin of wine. He took a long swig and passed it to the next man. The empty road in front of the gate was dark and silent. The candle-lit villa, with its broad steps up to the front door, was fifty paces away. "We're safe enough. We'll see the sergeant as soon as he comes out," he reached for the wine as it passed back from mouth to mouth. The other two were very ready to agree, and it was only a few minutes before the majority of the wine was consumed.

All three were facing the house, a warm glow had spread through their tired bodies, and they were intent on finishing the dregs of the wine while still watching for the return of their sergeant. When the gates behind them suddenly burst open they were completely overwhelmed as a platoon of soldiers stormed into the grounds. In moments the guards were subdued and the platoon, spearheaded by a number of Knights of the Order, raced on towards the villa.

Inside the building the three guards were discussing the merits of Gwen. They had never seen her before their brief meeting a few minutes before and each had his own particular views of her accomplishments. These ranged from the agreement that she was "special" to individual assertions that she was "beautiful, a goddess, and very desirable." The last comment met with a hard stare by the other two guards, who felt that it was an unsuitable observation, no matter how accurate it was.

They were all taken by surprise when the doors burst open and a platoon of soldiers raced into the house. Within moments the three guards were overwhelmed, and either ended up kneeling with hands on their heads, or lay unconscious on the floor. The invaders, led by Sir Raymond, raced up the stairs and paused in front of an ornately carved door. "Stay back. I will enter and you will follow if I call," he ordered as he inched open the door.

Looking inside Sir Raymond saw an almost unbelievable sight: the young woman whom he had been so determined to find, was asleep on a couch in front of him and there were no guards in the room. He signalled to his soldiers to patrol the landing and quietly closed the door. When all was silent he walked quietly across to the sleeping Gwen and stared at her for a long time. She possessed a beauty that surpassed any woman he had previously encountered and it unnerved him. Perhaps Longsword, in spite of all his ranting, had been right. Gwen, even with a bandage across her forehead, was strikingly unusual.

Eventually he knelt down beside her and very gently shook her left hand. "My Lady." He raised his voice. "My Lady!"

Gwen awoke with a start, panic etched across her face. "Who are you?" she gasped.

"A friend. I am here to provide your safety. You are in grave danger and I will defend you against any threat."

Gwen sat up and rubbed her eyes. She looked quickly around and realized that there was no other person in the room. "Where is Lord d'Escosse?"

Raymond smiled. "He's not here and if I had been an enemy, you would be dead." He sat back on his haunches. "He has just demonstrated that he is unable to guard you against attack. However, you will be safe with me." He stood up and offered her his hand. "It is time to leave this place."

Gwen took a deep breath and tried to understand the situation. In front of her was a very large knight with an emblem on his shoulder indicating he was one of the Knights of the Order. She did not recognize him. He wore fine chain mail and his tunic was immaculate and he seemed immensely strong. He was confident and arrogant, yet strangely gentle in the way he spoke, as though he was making an effort to be friendly. She shuddered. He was her worst nightmare: a powerful man who felt he had the right to control her life.

"Come, Mistress Gwen. It is time we left for a safer place." Raymond placed a hand on her arm and pulled her to her feet.

"Let go of me!" Gwen screamed. "How dare you break into this house and try to abduct me." Her eyes flashed and she brushed off his hand on her arm. "I don't know you. I don't trust you. I want you to leave this house. Now!" She backed behind the sofa and her eyes searched for anything she could use as a weapon.

Raymond grinned. He liked women with courage and found himself marvelling again at her beauty. She was exceptional: graceful, determined and intelligent and he had no doubt that she was the one whom the Order had identified as the survivor of a powerful bloodline. "Mistress Gwen, believe me, I am here to protect you and ensure that you return safely to Jerusalem."

"Return to Jerusalem? She glared at him. "I have never been to Jerusalem. I do not want to go there. I want to return to England." She picked up a small vase. "Now get out!" She threw the vase across the sofa and forced Raymond to duck out of its path. It smashed against the wall behind him.

"My Lady," Raymond straightened up, "you must do as I ask. I insist." As he moved quickly round the sofa, Gwen fled for the door.

"Guards!" Raymond bellowed.

She reached the door as it burst open and two large soldiers blocked the door space. They had their swords drawn, and seeing the situation quickly replaced them. After their dramatic entry they stood very still, staring just above her head.

By the time Gwen had recovered from the shock of the soldiers, Raymond had come up behind her. "Lead the way," he ordered, and with a firm grip on Gwen's left shoulder he shepherded her out onto the landing and towards the stairs.

Below she could see two bodies on the ground, and Sergeant Little and others of Ralph's company standing in a sad little group against the far wall. Some of them were injured and all had been disarmed and had their hands secured behind their backs. Around them was a strong guard with spears and drawn swords; many of the weapons were wet with blood, as were others lying on the floor near the stairs. It was clear to Gwen that Ralph's men had fought bravely in spite of overwhelming odds. Little towered above the rest, he was swaying slightly, with closed eyes. Blood trickled down his face and his huge shoulders were slumped forward. He looked defeated.

As she was hustled down the stairs she called out to Little. In spite of his posture she knew he would hear her. "Tell Ralph the Knights have taken me!" It was all she had time to say before she was forced out into the dark night. She had thought to scream, but it would have been of little use and would have merely confirmed her helplessness. She thought to collapse on the stairs, but she knew the knight would easily lift her and carry her. In the end, to maintain her composure, she walked down the stairs supported by Sir Raymond and followed the soldiers out of the main entrance and towards the gates.

CHAPTER 7

I N THE WEEKS FOLLOWING his capture John settled into a routine.
He would rise at first light and wash and exercise himself. He
grew a beard and learned how to wear Arab clothing, even taking
to wearing a turban, which he found cool and serviceable and was
aware that it also helped him to blend in with the local people.
After the equivalent of breakfast by himself he would tutor his two
enthusiastic students for the rest of the morning. During the heat
of the day he was allowed to do as he wished and after a light meal
would often sit in the shade of the main courtyard reading from
Ibrahim's valuable collection of French books, which had been
acquired through a relative who traded around the Mediterranean.
John could not remember meeting anyone who possessed books,
let alone a library. From late afternoon until the evening meal he
would discuss various topics with Rashid and Saif, ranging from
details of the English countryside to the training of knights.

Sometimes Rashid would explain their way of life: how
Moslems worshipped and why they prayed at certain times of
the day, and the meaning of readings from the Koran. At other
times Saif would introduce John to local people and translate
their questions and observations with a rapidly increasing French
vocabulary. John began to master some words in Arabic and his
struggling pronunciation provided huge amusement, especially for
Saif. After a short while he found the language made sense to him
and soon he was speaking in sentences, developing his vocabulary
at a rate that amazed the boys.

"How is it you can speak our language so quickly?" Saif
demanded. "I think you knew it before you came here."

"You might be right. I was probably around all the time and you never saw me," John joked. But he began to suspect it was just one more example of his slowly revealing past.

During the evening meal Ibrahim and John would discuss a wide range of ideas and throughout, the sons would listen quietly, their grave faces revealing nothing and speaking only when asked to. It was a pleasant time in many ways and John felt he was learning as much as he was teaching; yet always his mind would return to the important questions of who had won the battle and were Gwen and Ralph alive? He had discussed the battle with Ibrahim, but the Arab leader claimed to know nothing of the result. As the weeks passed by he pressed Ibrahim with more insistence for details of his ransom. How much was demanded and to whom had this request been sent?

Ibrahim was evasive and said there was a process.

"But who pays the money?" John asked. "Is it paid in gold? Did you apply to the Governor of Antioch? To King Henry I of England? To the Lord d'Escosse?"

Ibrahim shook his head. "Your name is given to intermediaries, who contact the leaders of your army."

"But which army? There are a number of different lords and kings, each with their own army. How do you know they will find the right people? I could be here for years." John was appalled at the prospect. "I want to go home."

"But would you?" Ibrahim wondered aloud. "Would you go back to the green forests of your England or would you rejoin your friends, the other knights, and continue waging war on this, my poor country?" He bowed slightly to John. "We are friends now. I know much about you, and you of me. Is it not better to continue together in this peaceful life rather than return to war and killing? My sons admire you and consider you their friend, but what would happen if you returned to your army? Suppose the lord or king whom you served decided to conquer this area. Would you burn our houses and kill my children?"

"No! Of course not." John was appalled by the suggestion.

"Yet, that is what might happen."

John shook his head. "I would not take part in such a crime."

"But the other knights would, especially that fanatical group called Knights of the Order. They hate Moslems, any Moslems. They slaughter mothers and small children and yet they claim they are doing it for God. Their God."

This was the first time the Order had been mentioned and John was surprised that Ibrahim knew of them. In his short time in the Holy Land John had heard reports of knights, not only from the Order, who considered the ruthless destruction of Arab and Turkish villages to be God's work. They believed the greater the slaughter, the greater the reward in Heaven. John felt the need to disassociate himself from such people. "The reason I am in this country is to observe that particular group of knights and report back to my liege lord, King Henry I of England. I am no supporter of the Order."

"Your King is concerned by the behaviour of these Knights of the Order?" Ibrahim was agitated.

"I don't think the King worries about their behaviour on the battlefield," John said bitterly. "His concern is with their fanaticism. It is what they believe in that worries him."

"Why?"

"I am still learning." John's eyes glazed over. "I think the King sees them as outside his control and perhaps he thinks they might eventually be a threat to his rule." He ran his fingers down his beard. "What I do know is that they possess great wealth and are very secretive in their affairs and in their beliefs. They seem to think that Gwen, a young woman I know, has some religious or mystical power. It's absurd. She's an intelligent, but very normal young woman. Yet they claim to want to protect her and when we were attacked by the Giant and his army, there were some of the leaders of the Order who thought she would win the battle for them."

In the past weeks Ibrahim and John had discussed the battle at great length and Ibrahim had revealed that the Giant was known and hated throughout the surrounding area. "From here to Aleppo that creature is feared by our leaders and yet many simple folk follow him. He is said to have the Swords of Power, whatever that means, and his aim is to unite the whole of the Moslem world and conquer the Christian countries. The monster is truly mad and evil and has nothing to do with the teachings of the Prophet."

At the time John had remained silent, unwilling to reveal that for a brief time he had once owned one of the Swords of Power.

"What is the aim of the Knights of the Order?" Ibrahim moved closer to John as though expecting some deep secret.

"I have no definite idea," John said. "It has something to do with Jerusalem and they believe that when they get Gwen to the city, something will happen. That's all I have been able to discover. I think that many of the Order are unsure what they hope to achieve." He took in a deep breath. "They talk in terms of returning the Holy Land to Christian rule, but my understanding is that this land was never owned by Christians, but by Jews and Moslems. It is almost as though they and the Giant are at opposite ends of a violent world of fanaticism."

Ibrahim rubbed his eyes. "You and I should eat. We have talked too long on such a subject." The earnest expectation had died in him and he seemed suddenly weary.

"I'll wash, and then I'll join you," John said, and turned away. Once again, he seemed to be running on the same spot: lots of energy but no progress. He wondered if Ibrahim had really contacted any intermediaries, or whether this was just a ploy to keep him happily teaching the two sons. He could not believe that Ibrahim wanted to keep him forever as an extension of his household and John decided to set a date in his own mind by which time he would expect his exchange to be agreed.

In many ways his life with Ibrahim was ideal, but he missed his friends and the excitement of his previous life. There were unresolved issues constantly nagging at him throughout his waking hours and occasionally in his dreams. He had to know whom he was and what was meant by the title Keeper of the Grail; he felt certain it was his destiny to confront the Giant, which would certainly involve the Swords of Power. Finally, he was convinced that although he had been moving forward in a definite direction, his life had stopped. Now he was merely languishing in some backwater, unable to continue along the bright road that he and Ralph had travelled. Time was passing him by.

John stared unseeing at the bare hills that surrounded the village and finally acknowledged his real concern: Gwen. Although he recognized the importance of his fleeting passion for Tegwen, and his more developed and intense relationship with Aelfreda, it was always Gwen who had remained like a brilliant star in the darkness: permanent and untouchable. There was a strong chemistry between them and it had existed from the first moment he had seen her in the Flower Meadows, causing him to risk his life for her safety and changing him from a callow, lost boy into the person he had become. Always, no matter what had occurred in the subsequent years, he had felt her presence and an unexplainable attraction. Until the old priest had asked the question it had never occurred to him that they might be brother and sister, and since then, unable to discuss it with her, he had avoided the physical relationship, which Gwen had clearly intended.

John dipped his hands in the fountain and splashed the cool water on his face. He made his decision. He would give Ibrahim four more weeks to produce evidence of the negotiations of his ransom, or he would initiate his own release.

• • •

"So, you have nothing to report?" Lord Ralph d'Escosse's voice betrayed his frustration.

"No, Sir. I've heard back from all the platoons we sent to the towns and villages in this area." Sergeant Little stood to attention, trying to convey the seriousness of his report. "There be no sightings of any knights, with or without a woman in their company passing through on their ways down south." He took a deep breath. "I've conducted a thorough search of this city. Every Arab what could be bribed 'as been enlisted. I've checked the port and there be no unusual departures in the past weeks. I've paid spies to report on any unusual movements of people. There be nothin'."

Ralph glared at the anxious face in front of him and his own face gradually relaxed into a forced smile. "Stand down, Sergeant Little. I know you've done everything possible." He grunted. "And even the impossible. Well done. I can't expect anything more."

"Thank ye, Sir." Little relaxed, and gently explored the thick scab on his head, a reminder of the night Gwen disappeared. "Must be nearly four weeks since she were took?"

"Yes."

"We'll find Mistress Gwen, m'Lord. Them Knights can't have made 'er disappear." Little blew out his cheeks. "Should I continue to search the city?"

"Yes. Keep up the pressure, just in case they have her hidden in a safe place and are waiting for us to relax our search." Ralph rubbed his eyes. "That will be all, Sergeant Little."

Little recognized his Lord's exhaustion and without another word withdrew from the room.

Ralph walked slowly over to the open window and stared out at the grounds. It was late afternoon and the city was coming back to life as cool breezes, blowing in from the coast, replaced the heat of the day. Below, the iron gates with their new locks were closed and many soldiers on both sides of the barrier were on constant guard. "Locking the stable after the horse has escaped," he muttered to himself.

It was hard to believe more than four weeks had passed since Gwen's abduction. He remembered his anxiety as he had approached the villa with his two soldiers to find the gates open and no guards on duty....

He ran towards the house with Dan and the other soldier behind him, their swords drawn. The door was ajar and he rushed in prepared for the worst and found his soldiers dead, wounded, or trussed-up like chickens. The loyal Sergeant Little lay unconscious on the floor. Ralph ran up the shadowy stairs, bellowing orders to the two men to check the kitchens and with his heart thumping burst into the main room to find it empty but with obvious signs of a struggle.

"Gwen!" he yelled as he raced from room to room. A cold fear settled on him, and with a wild look on his face he careered down the stairs calling her name, yet knowing she was gone. At the bottom Dan was pulling an unwilling girl from the kitchen. She was crying hysterically and was clearly terrified.

"She be the only one here, Sir. I found 'er hiding in the cool room." Dan pushed her forward and the young woman collapsed on the floor in a kneeling position, her arms crossed in front of her. Dan was a good soldier but not very bright and his experience with women had been limited to coarse suggestions and physical horseplay with the young girls of his village. In Dan's mind the servant was foreign, and worse still, she didn't speak his language.

Ralph took a deep breath. "Thank you, Dan." He tried to regain his composure. "Check outside. See if they have escaped by water. Check everywhere!"

Dan saluted, pleased to be released of his prisoner and vanished through the main door. At that moment the other soldier appeared in the hall. Ralph ordered him to untie the soldiers and check the wounded, especially the unconscious sergeant.

He turned his attention to the sobbing girl in front of him and very gently raised her to her feet. She continued to shake with emotion, refused to look at him, and fixed her eyes on her feet. He desperately needed immediate answers, but tried to control his impatience. He had exchanged some brief words with her in the days following his adoption of the house and knew she spoke some limited French and probably understood more than she spoke.

"You are safe now," his voice was encouraging. He repeated the words and waited as she gradually stopped shaking and snivelling. When she was more composed, he placed an index finger under her chin and gently raised her head. After a moment she looked into his eyes; his calm smile was reassuring. He was much taller than she was and she looked up, nervously chewing her lower lip. "Tell me," he said, "where is Mistress Gwen?"

It did not take long to establish what had happened. The servant had escaped into the grounds when she heard the soldiers fighting in the hallway. Soon after she had witnessed a tall knight, whose description fitted that of Sir Raymond de Wulfric, hustling Gwen towards a covered wagon in the driveway. When they had gone the servant crept back towards the house, entering by the backdoor. Moments later Ralph and the two soldiers had appeared and she had hidden in the cool room, afraid for her life.

Once he was certain the Knights of the Order were responsible for the attack on the house and the kidnapping of Gwen, Ralph had mustered a large force of his soldiers and, with the agreement of the Governor, had marched into the centre of the city intending to surround the headquarters of the Order. But in the courtyard and in the streets around his mansion the High Lord had massed his knights and soldiers, as if for battle. There was a fragile standoff while the Lords on both sides negotiated. Eventually, after more than a day the High Lord agreed to a search of his headquarters by the Governor's knights and allowed Sir William de Bracey and Sir Vernon de Kari to enter all of the rooms, but they found no evidence of Gwen or of Sir Raymond de Wulfric.

. . .

LATER, THERE WAS A heated debate, chaired by the Governor, Maurice de Maron, and attended by knights of all factions. The High Lord, Sir Raoul de Warron, denied any knowledge of Gwen's abduction and suggested that she may have run off with the strangely absent Gilles de Plantard.

"We have no idea where Giles Plantard is," Ralph said, using the other name that John had favoured. "We have not seen him since he forced the Giant off the field of battle."

"Forced the Giant off the field!" Sir Raoul exploded in a mirthless laugh. "Others have suggested that the Moslems withdrew because of the earthquake, and that your multi-titled, would-be knight, also known as John, fled the battle, having lost his sword."

"That is a lie! He gave me his sword and chased after the Giant, who had ceased fighting and was fleeing for his life."

"He gave you his sword, so he could chase the most powerful warrior in the Moslem army! What did he want to do? Fight him with his bare hands?" The knights that surrounded the High Lord roared with laughter and banged their mailed fists on the tables.

Ralph struggled to control his anger. There was no way he could reveal that it was John's unusual power that had forced the Giant to flee. It was something he did not comprehend and he knew John himself did not fully understand this power. There was nothing to be gained by trying to convince this gathering of knights. John's unique power smacked of magic and the knights would see it as either childish nonsense, or as an example of sorcery. It was dangerous to be associated with curious and unexplainable things.

"I understand," Sir Raoul smirked and nodded meaningfully to his knights, "that another title this coward calls himself is the Keeper of the Grail!" His eyes flashed. "Is that the Holy Grail he refers to? Does he claim to be the keeper of the holy chalice that is reputed to have held the blood of Christ?"

Ralph's blue eyes stared back at him contemptuously. "My Lord, I had no idea you were such an authority on religious and mythical matters." He paused to increase the dramatic effect. "But I had forgotten the Order is involved with many strange customs and beliefs. I have heard some reports that your secret rituals involve human sacrifice and satanic worship!"

Instantly, the High Lord was on his feet, his hand reaching for his sword. "You perfidious Saxon oaf, how dare you spread these calumnies!" Roars of agreement and disapproval filled the hall as knights from both factions drew their swords.

"Enough! I order you all to sit down!" Sir Maurice bellowed, struggling out of his chair. "You are here under my authority. Sheath your swords!" After a short interval, while the opposing knights snarled and muttered at each other, Sir Maurice regained control of the meeting, but not before his second-in-command, Sir William de Bracey, had marched in a platoon of men-at-arms. "I will not tolerate any outbreak of violence. Anyone, no matter his position or status, will be arrested if he draws a sword." He banged his chubby fist on the table and, with his overweight body heaving with the exertion, he stared fiercely around at the angry faces. "You are the cream of Crusader chivalry in this part of the Holy Land. Outside, our enemies outnumber us ten fold; we must not weaken our forces by these petty and disruptive disputes." The volatile mixture of belief, arrogance and ambition, when combined with anger and hatred was a dangerous and unpredictable composition, but the Governor knew that no knight would risk being arrested by common soldiers.

When the hall was silent, the Governor sank back gratefully into his chair and indicated that Sir Ralph could speak.

"My Lord de Maron," Ralph said, his voice sounding resonant, yet humble. "I, and my fellow knights, seek only to determine the whereabouts of Mistress Gwen. May I proceed with questions to Sir Raoul de Warron, High Lord of the Knights of the Order?"

"Proceed."

Ralph turned to the High Lord, who sat opposite to him across a polished table. Sir Raoul sat with his hands in front of him, as if in prayer. His long nose rested on the tips of his manicured fingers, his blue eyes stared unblinking at Ralph. There was a pause while each regarded the other.

"Where is Sir Raymond de Wulfric?"

"How should I know? I'm not his mother." There was a ripple of laughter from the Knights of the Order.

"I believe he is the new second-in-command in your Order?" There was an icy silence. Ralph continued. "It was only a short while ago that every man in your Order was outside your headquarters facing my men, and those of the Governors. It was a serious confrontation that could have led to a huge loss of life by the knights in this room. Is it not strange that the second most important knight in your Order was not present at such a time and is still missing?"

All eyes turned to the High Lord, who gave a derisory snort. "The confrontation was not of my making. You and your English soldiers are to blame."

"I spoke to Sir Raymond de Wulfric on the night that my headquarters was invaded and Mistress Gwen abducted. You say your men were not involved. But I have witnesses who clearly identified de Wulfric as the man who abducted Mistress Gwen. She is still missing and so is he. You must know where he is!"

"It is you who should be charged with abduction!" The High Lord spat out the words. "Mistress Gwen was under our protection. Lord Longsword and Sir Stephen de Bois brought her over from the Argenteuil Convent near Paris, and she was on her way to Jerusalem. Her welfare is important to us. Yet after the battle and the deaths of her two protectors, you abducted her! If she has gone off with Sir Raymond it is no concern of yours. If you continue to disrupt the peace of this city and make wild accusations I will take out charges against you."

"She did not want to be under your so-called protection." Ralph felt that his argument had suddenly lost strength, like a rock that had turned to sand. "My Lord de Maron, my headquarters were attacked, my soldiers killed and injured, and Mistress Gwen abducted. I seek compensation and the safe return of this young woman."

"My Lord Governor," Sir Raoul sounded like an embarrassed father whose son has misbehaved in church. He pushed out his thin lips judiciously. "I can prove, without a doubt, that Mistress Gwen was voluntarily in our safekeeping for the weeks leading up to the battle. After the battle, she disappeared. By his own admission Lord d'Escosse has confirmed he was hiding her in his headquarters. If Sir Raymond rescued her and had to kill some of the English guards in the process, then it would seem he had every right to do so. I have no knowledge of where Sir Raymond is but it would appear to me that neither he, nor I, nor any member of this illustrious Order has committed any crime or has anything to answer for. I leave it to your good judgment, my Lord Governor, to decide if Lord d'Escosse need stand trial for abduction." He stood up, bowed to the Governor, and walked out amid loud clapping and cheering by his supporters.

The Governor sat back in his chair, stared stony-faced at Ralph, and declared the meeting over.

· · ·

RALPH CONTINUED TO GAZE unseeing at the main gate and was unaware that the soldiers guarding the entrance were unusually attentive to their duties.

"He still be staring at us," Dan murmured. "Best keep alert, lads."

"He ain't been the same since that young woman disappeared," a soldier commented.

"I remembers when 'e would 'ave a joke with ye. Now he'll bite ye 'ead off if ye speaks out of place," another agreed.

"That be the problem with women," Dan sniffed. "They always causes trouble."

"Hark at 'im," the first soldier jeered. "The voice of experience!" A roar of derisive laughter went up from the group.

The hilarity cut through his thoughts and Ralph frowned and opened his mouth to yell a rebuke, but stopped himself. He was aware how agitated he had become and how his soldiers no longer greeted him in a relaxed way. Shaking his head, he turned slowly away from the window and flopped down on a couch. The room was warm and he was aware of the odour of his own sweat. Ralph stared dejectedly at his hands and began to notice how grubby they were, the nails broken and dirty. He sat up and considered the stained, creased condition of his white tunic and felt the two-day growth on his chin. He had neglected himself since Gwen's abduction. Until the past four weeks he had always prided himself on his appearance and washed at regular intervals. Although the Moslems grew long beards, he knew that the men were scrupulous in their body hygiene and considered the Crusaders, especially the French soldiers, to be sweaty, unwashed barbarians. He smiled; he had no knowledge of French women.

"This won't do!" he said, conscious that since the disappearance of John and then Gwen he had begun to talk to himself. He strode to the door, yelled for a servant to bring a towel and ran down the stairs. An anxious Sergeant Little greeted him: "Is everything all right, m'Lord?"

"I'm going swimming, Little. Do you want to come?" After a brief pause, he added, "Sergeant?"

"I don't swim, m'Lord, but I be 'appy to come and keep ye company."

"Good," he gave the sergeant a broad smile, the first for weeks. "You can mount guard and keep all the young women from staring at my youthful body. Advance to the river!" He rushed out of the main door, followed by the attentive Little. All the men at the gate came quickly to attention.

• • •

IT WAS ANOTHER WINDLESS day and the lateen sails hung immobile from the two masts of the sturdy freighter. The triangular sails were popular in this area of the Mediterranean because, unlike the traditional square sails, they enabled the boat to sail almost into the wind. But on such a day and like the previous days, even these sails could not find a breeze. The sky was a deep blue and the merciless sun blazed down relentlessly, forcing the crew to seek what little shade there was on the burning deck. The passengers had the doubtful choice of roasting in the small cabins or sitting motionless under improvised covers.

"I should have used a slave ship with oars!" Lord de Wulfric bellowed at the silent Captain. "I should have transferred to another vessel when you were unable or unwilling to leave port. Because of your tardiness we missed the wind!"

"It was your choice, my Lord."

De Wulfric smouldered with rage. He was well aware he could have changed to another vessel, but had refused to do so, in case others became aware of Gwen's presence. "I could be in Ibelin by now! We should be in Jerusalem, not rotting away on this God-forsaken cesspit of a boat."

He glared at the two sailors standing dejectedly by the solid tiller that was too hot to handle, as though they were guilty of some plot to annoy him. They did not speak French, but understood the drift of his angry protestations and did not dare to look him in the eye.

"He's a monster," one of the sailors muttered in Arabic. "May the sea god take him." He joined his fingers behind his back in the sign of a wish.

The elderly captain stared straight ahead. He knew from recent experience that the knight could not be pacified. In all his many years as a trader on this coast, he had never experienced such weather conditions. The sea was unnaturally calm: barely a ripple stirred the surface and the distant coast remained blanketed in a dark mauve haze. There had been no wind for days and the heat was oppressive. The voyage from St. Symeon was supposed to have taken seven to ten days, but was already in its third week and he believed he was only off Tripoli. To make matters worse he was running out of water and wine and the food supply was nearly exhausted.

"How much longer to you think this infernal weather will

continue?" The knight stationed himself next to the captain and
stared sullenly at the featureless coast.

The captain was fluent in French and had suffered a barrage
of similar questions throughout the day. "Only God knows the
answer, my Lord."

"But, in Hell's name you're a sailor. You must have had this
happen at other times? What do you usually do? What have you
done before?" He beat a powerful fist into his other hand. The
weather had forced him to discard his chain mail, his gauntlets
and his heavy boots, but dressed only in his tunic and sandals, he
still stood head and shoulders above the captain.

"I have experienced times when the winds have dropped for
hours on end, but always a breeze would arise by the end of the
day. I have never sailed in conditions like this, my Lord." He had
explained this before.

"Perhaps you should point the boat out to sea? There is bound
to be wind out there."

"There is no wind to point the boat in any other direction, my
Lord. We are here in this spot until God decides to give us a wind.
Then we will sail immediately to the shore and to the nearest town
or village."

"You will do no such thing! Are you mad? Did I not make it
clear to you that we have to sail directly for Ibelin?" The knight
was shouting and his eyes were wide with anger.

"My Lord, we must reach the first port as soon as we can. We
are out of water and wine and we will soon have nothing to eat."
The captain spoke firmly, keeping his voice at conversational level.
He was used to giving orders and was not afraid of the knight.

"We must go straight to Ibelin! It is too dangerous to go anywhere
else. I cannot endanger the lady I am escorting."

"My Lord de Wulfric, we may have more than two hundred
miles still to go. Your lady may be dead of thirst by then. I will not
endanger her life or the lives of my crew and your men." He raised
his head to stare into the wild eyes of the knight. "If, and when,
the wind rises we will sail directly for the coast."

Gwen was sitting on the captain's only chair, at the other end
of the boat, and beneath a small canopy suspended from ropes

attached to the front mast. Like everyone else on deck she had heard the argument, but unlike the crew she knew what the knight was saying. Two of Sir Raymond's soldiers were on guard on either side of her, facing away, and preventing the crew from coming too close. If she walked about they followed, glaring at the sailors and preventing any of them from approaching her. Most sailors believed it was unlucky to have a woman on board ship and they blamed her for the unusual weather. When the captain had mentioned this the knight had remarked, sardonically, that it had more to do with sailors' sexual urges and the arousal a woman caused in such a confined male world, than with the matter of bad luck. Having overheard the conversation Gwen was relieved that the knight was aware of her predicament. She found the constant frowning and leering of the crew disturbing. Once before she had been on a long voyage surrounded by staring men, but at least her loyal servant, Barbara, had been with her. Thankfully, de Wulfric could control his men and the crew; it was the only point on which she felt grateful to him.

The boat groaned as it rocked gently. A small swell passed mysteriously by, and the sails flapped momentarily. The boredom and discomfort was intense and to avoid dropping off to sleep she tried to recall the details of her capture.

• • •

SHE REMEMBERED WAKING UP to find the huge knight kneeling beside her and recalled how quickly he abducted her from Ralph's mansion. Her struggles were in vain and she remembered the horror of seeing the dead and the injured as she was hustled down the stairs and out into the grounds. By the gate two more bodies lay on the earth and nearby the rest of Ralph's soldiers were kneeling with their hands on their heads, surrounded by heavily armed guards. "Why did you have to kill them?" she protested, as the knight propelled her through the open gates. "You should not have killed anyone on my behalf."

"I would kill half the world for you, my Lady." He gave an exultant laugh. "You are safe now. No one will harm you."

"I don't want you to kill anyone," she wailed. "Don't you understand? I don't want your protection."

"It is God's will," he answered, and with a broad smile on his face that reminded her of a wolf, he lifted her effortlessly into a large, horse-drawn wagon. There was no way for her to escape. She sat dejectedly on a side seat as he climbed in and secured the flaps of the canvas door. Around her she could feel an assortment of boxes and bags and on the other side of the canvas she could hear the sounds of a troop of horsemen as they escorted the wagon on its bumpy journey along what she assumed was a little-used track. It was impossible to see anything in the wagon, apart from some small pinpoints of light around the door flaps. Outside, the night sky was clear and bright and the small convoy travelled without any lamps or torches. But it was hot and stuffy in the wagon and Gwen sat rigid and alert, wondering what the knight might do. To her relief he remained silent and immobile by the door. After about an hour the wagon stopped and he opened the flaps.

"This is where we change our mode of transportation." He seemed very pleased with himself and Gwen's sullen silence did not appear to affect him.

Sir Raymond climbed out of the wagon and talked quietly to a knight who had dismounted. Gwen stood by the opening and looked about. It was a deserted area close to the silent river and there were no lights or signs of habitation. To scream for help seemed pointless and she felt vulnerable and frustrated: once again the Knights of the Order had interfered with her life, denying her the freedom she desired and insisting she travelled with them to Jerusalem. She had no idea what awaited her in the Holy City, but she knew it was not a choice she would have made no matter what wealth and influence she might be given. She wanted only to find John, be reunited with Ralph, and travel back with them to England. Most of all she wanted to regain her liberty and distance herself from these fanatical men who constantly pursued her.

She pondered the shadowy figures of the mounted soldiers as they waited for their orders. The horses were restless and skittish and the soldiers cursed them in whispers, tugging fiercely at the reins. Gwen wondered if she could slip off the wagon and lose herself in the darkness, but the horsemen were watching her and she abandoned the thought. The knights had walked towards the river on her right, deep in discussion, and were silhouetted against the night sky as they stopped on a raised bank. There was a slight cough close to her left and she glanced down to see a large soldier staring up at her, his horse against the wagon. He wore an iron helmet with a faceguard that obscured his features and for a moment she thought he was going to attack her. The whites of his eyes seemed unnaturally large and there was a desperate appeal on his dark face.

"Don't say nothing," he hissed. "Just know I be with ye." He turned his horse away and moved sideways into the restless circle of riders.

Gwen gripped onto the canvas flaps, fearing she might lose her balance. At once her fear and resignation lifted: she was not alone. It seemed impossible, but she recognized the voice: Martin was with her.

"Sergeant!" Sir Raymond's voice cut through the silence. Gwen watched, as the big figure walked his horse towards the knights. There was a brief exchange and Martin returned to the soldiers. He selected six of them and they all dismounted, handing the reins of their horses to others.

"Allow me, my Lady." Sir Raymond reached up and before Gwen could object, lifted her off the wagon and placed her carefully on the ground. "We have a short trip down the river in a small boat, and then a slightly longer journey in a more comfortable and much larger ship." He was smiling broadly. "I think you will enjoy the experience." He gave a slight bow and with a strong grip on her arm he escorted her to the river, while the six soldiers under Martin's direction unpacked the wagon.

On a raised bank, they watched as the broad boat was quickly loaded with supplies. They climbed aboard and the knight insisted on guiding her, ignoring her attempts to break free of him. Behind them the remaining horsemen and the wagon and spare horses moved off into the night, and the sergeant and the six soldiers clambered in at the bow. Four local river men handled the long oars in the centre of the craft and waited patiently while Gwen

and Sir Raymond arranged themselves on a bench near the stern.
Behind them the owner of the boat manned the tiller and on
his command the stable craft moved cautiously away from the
rocky bank and into the main current. The river flowed slowly:
there were few insects and a cooling breeze stirred the reeds.
In other circumstances Gwen might have found the experience
enchanting, but instead she sat staring into the blackness, silently
pondering her fate. She knew it might be impossible for Ralph
to follow her and if John returned there would be no one to tell
him what had happened. She fought to control her breathing and
her racing pulse, but knowing that Martin was in charge of the
soldiers was reassuring and something to believe in. After a few
minutes she overcame the panic attack. The key was Martin. As
long as he was near there was someone she trusted.

Eventually, she started to think positively and wondered if
Martin could help her to escape before she was forced to board
a bigger ship that would take her south. It was a small hope, but
she held on to it like a thin candle in a dark room: no matter how
weakly it flickered, it still provided a possible way forward.

In the early hours of the morning they reached a sprawling
port at the mouth of the river, where Gwen's hopes of escaping
were quickly dashed. A large vessel with two masts was anchored
far out in the harbour and, in the iron light that preceded the
sunrise, the riverboat rowed up alongside and quietly shipped its
oars. Gwen was quickly and firmly guided up a rope ladder onto
the gently rocking deck and without a chance to look around, was
shown into a small cabin lit by a single lamp.

"You will be safe here, my Lady, this cabin is for your use only."
De Wulfric ducked his head as he entered the gloomy, cramped
space. He gave one of his rare smiles. "Within a week we will
arrive at the port of Ibelin and then it is only a few days journey
by horse to Jerusalem." He bowed and appraised her with an
approving eye.

Gwen turned away. "And what happens in Jerusalem, my Lord
de Wulfric?"

There was a loud intake of breath. "There you will learn of your
greatness and your exalted position within the Order. You will meet

with the King of Jerusalem; you will become the inspiration that will enable us to regain all of the Holy Land for Christianity."

She kept her back to him and he could not see the defiance in her face. Although he had revealed more than any other Knight of the Order, it still made no sense to her. It was part of the on-going manipulation of her life and she wanted none of it. "My Lord, I do not wish to be part of this."

"Mistress Gwen," he spoke softly, "it's God's will." With a brief bow, he left the cabin and she could hear a key turn in the lock.

De Wulfric's plan appeared to have unfolded without a problem, and she wondered gloomily if Martin would ever find a chance to release her. It was then she heard the knight bellowing on deck. There was a long and angry exchange between de Wulfric and another person, but although she listened carefully she was unable to understand what was going on.

After many hours, when the heat in the small dark cabin was increasing and the ship had still not left its mooring, de Wulfric appeared. Gwen noticed his face was grim as he came through the door, but as he turned towards her he forced a smile. "Mistress Gwen, our short journey to Ibelin, the port near to Jerusalem, has been delayed. It would appear our Captain and his crew have social and religious reasons for remaining in port a few more days." He breathed in noisily through his wide nostrils. "However, I will escort you around the deck whenever you wish to take the air and I will ensure you have everything you need."

He clapped his hands and a soldier entered with a tray of fruit and a flagon of wine with two cups. "Perhaps you will join me?" He poured the wine.

"I would like to go ashore."

"Mistress Gwen, much as I would like to grant your request, it is not possible." He forced open the shutters of a small porthole and a light breeze entered the cabin. "Our delay is unfortunate as there is a suitable wind at the moment, but it will only be a short delay." He handed her a cup. "Let us drink to a calm sea, steady winds and a safe journey to Jerusalem."

It was eight days before they left the port and after only a few hours at sea, the wind dropped completely.

. . .

"M'Lady, would ye like some water?"

She awoke with a start. Martin was standing in front of her holding an earthen cup. He showed no signs of recognition and she was quickly aware that others were staring at them. "Thank you, Sergeant." She drank thirstily, needing the water. It was warm and unpleasant tasting, but she was grateful for it. She handed back the empty cup. "Are we short of water?"

"Yes, m'Lady." Martin ran his thick tongue over his cracked lips. "Not much left."

She looked about. Something was different. There was a cool feeling on her hot cheek. At that moment the sails billowed out with a loud crack and the boat came alive with movement. The wooden masts creaked and groaned and sailors ran barefooted across the scorching deck, pulling in ropes and calling to each other in excited voices. The Captain yelled his orders and, in spite of the muttered protests of the Knight, the ship turned towards the land.

"Have we reached the port for Jerusalem?"

"No," Martin shook his head. "We be a long way away from Ibelin. I reckons we ain't reached Tripoli yet."

"Is that good?"

"I reckons so." Martin pretended to be interested in the vigorous activity around him as the sailors tried to coax life into the reluctant sails and the heavy ship gradually increased its motion towards the shore. No one was looking at them. He dropped his head. "Be prepared when we makes land. It might be our only chance to get away." He straightened up and began yelling at the guards.

Gwen stood up and moved carefully across the deck. If she were to escape there were things they needed. She realized the sudden change of weather had excited everyone and all heads were faced to the shore as the blurred mauve line gradually gave way to recognizable cliffs and rocks. Very quietly, she retired to her cabin.

CHAPTER 8

THE LATE AFTERNOON WAS the perfect time to swim. Throughout the hot day people did their work and sweated. In the late afternoon, as the heat was abating, swimming became a sensual pleasure for some, children in particular. When released from their chores, they gathered by the riverbank to swim, splash each other and boast of their imagined achievements.

Ralph swam slowly down river towards a large gang of boys who, having exhausted themselves in the water, were lying on rocks along the left bank, telling tall tales about their families, their supposed riches, and their epic adventures. As he swam past, about fifteen paces from the group, the boys stood up to watch him. One boy, taller and older than the others, shouted at him, waving his fist in the air. Ralph did not know much Arabic, but he understood from the sound of the words and the anger on the boy's face that he was being sworn at. The other boys clapped their hands, pointed and waved fists, some giggled. Egged on by the group, the tall boy picked up a large stone and threw it at Ralph. It missed, but it could have caused injury and Ralph frowned, deciding to swim for the bank and deal with the problem. Another stone hit the water in front of him and he dived, swimming strongly down towards the river bottom. At first it was dark, but as he swam towards the shallows the water lightened and he was surprised how clear it was. As soon as he could see rocks, he swam to the surface.

He had expected a final stone and was preparing to rush out of the water as soon as he emerged, in the hope of charging down the stone thrower. Instead, as he stormed naked out of the river, he saw Little, standing like a statue on the rocks with one arm around the tall boy's neck and the other in a relaxed pose, holding Ralph's clothes and towel. The boy was struggling furiously, but achieving nothing. He was unaware that his supposed audience had run away, terrified by the huge soldier who had burst into their group,

"What shall I do with 'im?" Little asked. He released the chokehold and set the boy down in front of him, gripping his shoulder. The boy stopped writhing, glanced round to see his friends had vanished and stood silently staring at the ground. His legs started to tremble.

"Not so brave now, eh?" Little winked at Ralph and handed him his towel and clothing.

Ralph slipped on his tunic and ran his fingers through his wet hair. "Do you speak English?" There was no response. "Do you speak French?" There was a slight reaction and Ralph raised the boy's head and stared into his dark eyes. The boy stared back and although he knew his captors could inflict serious injury, he remained composed and defiant and Ralph admired his bravery. He smiled, "You do speak French, don't you?"

He nodded. "A little."

"What is your name?"

There was a pause and Ralph motioned for Little to release him. The boy rubbed his shoulder. "I am Kalil."

"Why did you throw stones, Kalil?"

"You are the enemy."

It was as simple as that. Ralph wondered what he would have done if the situation had been reversed and England had been overrun with Moslems. If he was a boy of eleven who saw a single enemy swimming in his river, he knew he would throw stones or something worse.

"You're very brave."

Kalil frowned.

"You understand the word brave?"

The boy nodded. He seemed confused.

Ralph took out a silver coin and held it between his forefinger and his thumb. "Would you like to have this coin?"

"Yes." Kalil glanced at Little, as though suspecting a trick.

Ralph indicated a smooth rock. "Sit down."

After a quick look around, Kalil did as he was asked and Ralph sat opposite him. Little moved away, ensuring that the other boys did not return.

"Raise you hand when you do not understand what I say," Ralph said, miming the action. The boy dipped his head in agreement and chewed his lower lip.

"You are not my enemy." Ralph smiled. "Have you heard of the Knights of the Order?"

"Yes." Kalil knew of them. They were the iron men who killed Moslems for sport. They were the worst of devils.

"They are my enemy too."

"Why? They are like you."

"They are not like me. I do not kill innocent people." He paused and stared thoughtfully at the boy. "I am looking for a young woman. The Knights have captured her. You understand?"

Kalil nodded and glanced hopefully at the silver coin.

"I think they took her away on a boat. Do you know people who have boats that travel down to the sea?"

He glanced around to make sure none of his friends were near. "Yes. I know everyone around here."

"Have you heard of a boat that left here at night? It would have carried some Knights of the Order and this one young woman. It would have travelled down to the sea. This number of days ago." He held up both his hands and opened and closed them twice.

"I heard of this." Kalil nodded solemnly. "I cannot tell you the name of the owner."

"I don't want his name. I just want to know if they went this way. Are you sure they went down river?"

"I am sure."

"You are a brave young man." Ralph stood up and handed the boy the coin.

Kalil looked carefully at the coin and then put it in a small pocket inside his short robe. "Can I go now?"

"Yes." Ralph grinned. "Would you like me to yell at you as you go? To impress your friends?"

For the first time, the boy smiled. "Yes. That would be good." He turned and ran off, avoiding Little, as Ralph bellowed a string of rude insults at him.

As the Sergeant approached, Ralph completed dressing. "We need to travel to St. Symeon immediately. They took Gwen down river."

"No one told me that, m'Lord." Little sounded indignant. "Not even when I offered money."

"That's because they see us as the enemy."

"Well, what about the boy?"

"He hates the Knights more than he hates me." He put an arm around Little's powerful shoulders and was reminded of the fact that he had known this man all his life. "Find me a boat. Choose two reliable soldiers. Get some supplies for a week or so. You decide who is to take over your position while you're away." He put the towel around his neck. "I think I know who can stand in for me." He chuckled, as they hastened back to the house. "And it's bound to upset the Governor!"

.   .   .

Sir Vernon could not believe his luck. One moment he was an obscure young officer doing menial tasks for the Governor, and the next he was in a position of authority. He had no idea how or why the Governor had transferred him to be Sir Ralph d'Escosse's aide or why this powerful young Lord had accepted him. Considerations of that sort never bothered Vernon. Life was for the living and he lived in the moment, never worrying about the future and rarely regretting the past.

"While I am away, you will make all the decisions regarding the day-to-day management of the troops. The officers and the sergeants are experienced and you should have little to do other than sign the requisitions and make sure the men get paid." Ralph looked away to prevent himself from grinning. Sir Vernon reminded him of one of his English hunting dogs in training: bright eyed, bursting with enthusiasm and likely to make a mess on the floor at any moment.

"Your most important task will be to hide the fact that I am no longer here. Let no one in this house. Check on the guards regularly."

Sir Vernon nodded furiously. "How long will you be gone, my Lord?"

"I don't know. I'm taking Sergeant Little, and two of the men. I hope to catch up with Sir Raymond de Wulfric before he reaches Jerusalem. We leave within the hour." He looked around trying to remember all the things he wanted to take with him. "It should be a quiet time. After the recent bloodletting I doubt there will be any military action for a few months."

"Mistress Gwen is with Sir Raymond?"

"I am certain of it."

"Suppose she went of her own free will?" Sir Vernon was pleased with his suggestion; it was something this young Lord should consider.

"Sir Vernon," there was an icy note in Ralph's voice, "there are some things you do not understand and I have no time to explain them."

"Ah!" Vernon's eyes opened wide. "I quite understand."

"No, you don't." Ralph picked up his sword and paused in the doorway. "Remember, stay put, don't get drunk and speak to no one about Mistress Gwen."

Sir Vernon stood to attention, and saluted as Ralph went out of the room. "You can rely on me, my Lord."

At the bottom of the stairs, Little was waiting. "Everything's arranged, Sir."

"Well done, Sergeant." Ralph looked back up the stairs. "What will be, will be." He found himself grinning as he left the house.

. . .

"WHAT IS THIS PLACE?" Sir Raymond thundered. He glared around, unhappy with what he saw.

They were approaching a bay with high broken cliffs dominated by an extinct volcano. On the seaward side of the black mountain was an imposing castle, not large by Norman standards, but cleverly positioned to control the bay and provide adequate defence for its inhabitants. Two hundred feet beneath the tall towers of the castle a picturesque village nestled around a small harbour with a wide, stone breakwater that curved round in a half circle. Fishing boats anchored behind the breakwater and a variety of small craft was pulled up on the rocky beach. The houses, built one behind the other, were haphazardly arranged around a stream that flowed from a rapidly ascending valley that eventually reached the height of the castle. The buildings were a ramshackle collection of single storey, flat roofed hovels, but against a backdrop of blue sky and rolling surf, the village was inviting to everyone that is except the knight.

"This is Marqab, and that," the Captain pointed at the sombre stone bastion, "is Al Marqab castle. My grandfather helped to build it, about fifty or more years ago." The pride in his voice was evident, even to the knight. "Then the Byzantines captured it and now it's part of the Principality of Antioch."

"So, we have not even reached Tripoli?"

"No, my Lord. Tripoli is at least forty miles away. With this variable wind we could die of hunger and thirst before we reached it."

Sir Raymond gritted his teeth and drew in a deep breath. "Is it safe here?"

The Captain raised an eyebrow. "Safe? As safe as any Arab or Turkish village will be to an invader. A young knight from Christendom is holding the castle at this time. His name is Payen de Montdidier. He comes from Flanders."

"How do you know all this?"

The Captain shrugged his shoulders. "I have relatives who live here."

"So that's why you've brought us to this God-forsaken place!"

"It was the nearest port, my Lord." The Captain steered the boat behind the breakwater. "Also the safest."

Gwen moved up behind the Knight and watched as the crew dropped the sails and anchored among the smaller craft in the harbour. A crowd had formed on the quay and the Captain waved. Some men waved back and yelled across the water in Arabic.

"What are they saying?" Sir Raymond stared suspiciously at the villagers.

"They are welcoming me, and asking who you are."

"You and I will go ashore with some of my soldiers. I want you to get the necessary supplies and prepare to leave immediately."

"My Lord de Wulfric, I want to go with you," Gwen said. She moved up beside him.

"Impossible," he snapped. "I cannot allow you to leave the safety of this ship."

"Is the ship safe without you?" Gwen's eyes flashed, "Are you and the Captain going to leave me to the mercy of these men of yours? Do you trust them?"

The knight hesitated. "You're right. I will stay aboard with you, and the Sergeant and two men can go with the Captain."

At that moment the crowd on the quay parted as a small group of horsemen approached. The men were well armed and wore smart uniforms.

"That's Montdidier's men," the Captain explained, as though it was obvious to anyone.

One of the soldiers dismounted and yelled to the ship in French. "My Lord, Sir Payen de Montdidier requests the pleasure of your company, and invites you to dine with him. I am here to escort you up to the castle."

This was not the reception that Sir Raymond had anticipated and he looked about in a paroxysm of uncertainty. "Tell them we will be over shortly," he ordered the Captain. He turned to Gwen, "This was not anticipated, my Lady. Would you prefer to stay?"

"My Lord, I am desperate to get off this ship and have some civilized entertainment. Nothing will prevent me." Gwen was interested in the effect her speech had on the knight. It was as though he was in awe of her.

"I agree. I think it best that we attend. We will leave this port tomorrow. Another day's delay will be of no account." He clenched his fists as he watched Gwen return to her cabin. It was strange that each encounter with this beautiful young woman left him ever more unsettled. It was as though, for the first time in his life, he did not have complete control over his emotions and was unwilling to admit such a thing, even to himself. He turned away from the port and gazed out to sea. Mistress Gwen was his responsibility. His pledge was to escort her to Jerusalem, where certain Knights who supported him would induct her into the Order as the surviving member of a most important bloodline. It was his mission, his sacred duty to get her safely to Jerusalem and achieve great power for himself.

The sergeant approached and saluted. "Do ye reckon I should come with ye, m'Lord? I be worth twice the rest of 'em."

Sir Raymond scowled. His first reaction was to dismiss the advice of a mere soldier. Then he reconsidered. The man was built like an ox and he would be useful if there was any trouble. "Yes. I want you and four others to provide an escort. Make sure the remainder know that they have to defend this ship and prevent it from being occupied by those locals." He turned away from the Captain. "They must also stop this Captain, should he wish to leave without us," he muttered.

Martin almost smiled with happiness. "I'll deal with the men, Sir. 'Ow soon do ye want to leave?"

"We leave this ship as soon as Mistress Gwen appears on deck. Get prepared."

The Captain had been watching and listening intently. "There will only be your men on board, my Lord. All of my sailors are going ashore until tomorrow. So your men will be responsible for making sure this ship will still be here when the sun rises." With an ironic smile and a brief bow, he marched over to the stern of his vessel. "Two of my men will wait until you are ready to be rowed ashore," he said, as he disappeared over the side and climbed into a large rowboat.

· · ·

GWEN WAS STANDING IN the main tower of Al Marqab castle, gazing out over the small port and marvelling at the panorama. Below, she could clearly see the soldiers on the deck of the two-masted ship on which they had arrived and the local fisherman moving slowly around their boats on the beach. Dark, majestic cliffs stretched out on both sides of the castle and in the cloudless blue sky a large hawk floated on the currents of rising air.

"You must be delighted to own a castle with such a view, my Lord de Montdidier."

The young knight smiled self-consciously. "I don't own this castle, my Lady. I am merely holding it for King Baldwin until he appoints a new Lord. The previous knight died of a fever shortly after taking control. I was on my way to Jerusalem with a reduced retinue when I was requested to guard this stronghold for a brief time. Translated, it is called the Castle of the Watchtower." He indicated the space they were in. "I imagine I will continue my journey when the King is ready."

Although in his early twenties, Sir Payen de Montdidier was a serious-minded man, and unlike most knights could read and write. He was fluent in French and English, and had quickly assimilated a basic knowledge of Arabic that had helped to create a working relationship with the local people. In spite of having only a few soldiers, he had quickly established his control of the area. He was of medium height with the thick neck and powerful shoulders of a knight. Yet unlike the fashion his black hair was cropped short and his face was clean-shaven. In some ways he resembled an athletic monk and even his tunic was plain and unadorned.

"Why were you travelling to Jerusalem, my Lord?" Gwen was anxious to know more about this aesthetic knight. Would he support her against de Wulfric? Could he be persuaded that she travelled to Jerusalem against her will?

Sir Payen ran his tongue over his lips in a nervous gesture. He felt uncomfortable in the presence of such a beautiful woman and her unexpected arrival at the castle gates had stirred up feelings that he had spent several years trying to overcome. It was his aim to reach Jerusalem and offer his services as a fighting monk: a role that combined his religious beliefs with those of knighthood. He wanted to offer himself to King Baldwin and, with other knights of his persuasion, protect the many pilgrims who travelled to the Outremer. In return they hoped the King would allow them to act independently within the City. Only then could they begin the search for an ancient truth that only he, and a few other members of a powerful and secret group, believed was hidden under the great temple of Jerusalem. He tried to look at her without blushing.

"I hope to be part of a small force of knights who will keep the roads to Jerusalem free of thieves and murderers, my Lady."

"That is a very noble intention." Gwen smiled encouragingly. He seemed unlike any of the Knights of the Order and apart from Lord Ralph d'Escosse, he was the first young knight she found even remotely likeable. She was conscious of her travel-worn clothes and had been disappointed that there was no lady in residence. The ship's captain had given her a comb, and she had been able to wash, but her dress was sadly worn.

"Has King Baldwin given you permission to take on this 'noble' role?" Sir Raymond's voice cut through their conversation like cold water on fire. He had been sitting alone at the other side of the room, drinking steadily and was unhappy with this upstart knight who seemed to encapsulate all that he had imagined he would become when he was a young knight. Now, in older age, he felt such intentions were naïve and unworldly. "I thought the Hospitallers were undertaking that role."

"The Knights of the Hospital are overstretched, my Lord. They are unable to deal with the unimaginable numbers of sick pilgrims and soldiers who seek their help, let alone try to patrol the roads." There was a sharp edge to Sir Payen's voice. "I believe it is God's will that I undertake this mission."

The older knight sniffed loudly, but did not respond.

"You will meet other knights in Jerusalem?" Gwen felt a sudden burst of optimism. "Knights like yourself?"

"Yes, my Lady. There are some others and we are all Soldiers of God."

A group of servants appeared at the doorway with an assortment of food, and began to set a table near Lord Wulfric.

"Supper is served, m'Lord," an older servant announced.

Sir Payen nodded to the servants and bowed to Gwen. "Let us break bread. The meal is prepared." He ignored Sir Raymond and offered Gwen his arm. As they moved across the room Gwen saw Martin standing guard at the top of the winding stairs. He winked at her as they passed by. No one else noticed.

The three of them sat down at a heavy rectangular table of great age, which could have accommodated a dozen people. They all sat at one end with Payen at the head, Gwen on his right and Raymond on the left. The food was plain but ample and consisted of bread, olives, goat cheese and dates. There was also a flagon of local red wine and a jug of water. To Raymond's surprise the servants brought bowls of water and towels for them to wash their hands. "A local habit," Payen explained. He said a brief prayer and nodded to the servants to serve the guests.

"No meat?" Raymond exclaimed.

"I do not eat meat," Payen said. "If I had received prior notice, I would, of course, have arranged for the servants to kill a goat for you."

Gwen was aware that the young knight was enjoying the challenge. She indicated for a servant to fill her goblet with red wine and slowly savoured the quality while she silently observed the developing tension between the two men.

"We leave tomorrow," Raymond announced abruptly, as though the previous exchange had never occurred. "I will require water, wine and enough supplies to reach Jerusalem. I will pay in gold."

"My Lord, you are a fellow Soldier of God. I am happy to give you all the supplies you may require. Keep your gold for a more needful occasion." He raised his goblet and observed Gwen over the edge as he drank. Raymond grunted an acknowledgement and there was a silence as everyone concentrated on the food. Gwen chewed meditatively, pretending to be unaware of the young knight's attention, yet secretly pleased. As they ate, Payen described the history of the area and how the castle was part of the Principality of Antioch. "As you will have observed the castle's situation makes it difficult to attack and needs few soldiers to defend it. In times of unrest we could quickly accommodate a large force and use this as a base for quelling any insurrection."

"But, you do not expect to be here for much longer?" Gwen gave him her full attention.

"No more than a month or two, my Lady." He accepted some dates from a servant and watched Raymond as he demolished a pile of bread and cheese. "Perhaps you would like to stay here until that time and we could travel together?"

"We leave at first light." Raymond sat up straight and placed both hands on the table. "We must reach Jerusalem as soon as possible."

"Why are you in such haste to reach Jerusalem?" Payen asked.

"This lady is under my protection," Raymond glared at Payen as if he might disagree. "In Jerusalem she will come to know her destiny."

"My Lord, I have already made it quite clear that I do not want to go to Jerusalem."

"My Lady, I have explained that you are in constant danger and the Knights of the Order have dedicated themselves to your defence and security." He raised his goblet to her and emptied it in a single draft. Fortified, he adopted a less aggressive manner and turned to Payen. "Throughout her life, The Order has protected her from her enemies. We have arranged her education and her welfare, and soon Mistress Gwen will know the reason for our dedication to her well-being. She does not yet understand what her role in life will be, but you can be assured, Sir Payen, that I and the others of my Order have nothing but her safety in mind."

Gwen felt insulted by his arrogant discussion of her as though she was some chattel. She turned to the young knight. "Have you heard of these Knights of the Order?"

"Of course, my Lady. The Order has provided the Crusade with some excellent fighters." He selected a piece of cheese and balanced it between his fingers. "However, I am not aware of the reason for their independent approach to the defence of the Holy Land or what their interest in Jerusalem may be," he paused, "other than to serve the King."

"The Order is a secret society and as such we will not discuss it." Raymond brushed off the servant behind his chair and refilled his own goblet.

"If your society is so secret, why do you and your knights make such a show of being different?" Gwen asked, innocently.

Raymond gave an exasperated snort. "Because we are different! We are the Knights of the Order. Not just any group of would-be knights," he looked pointedly at Payen. "We are men who are of good birth and experienced in warfare, who fight the heathen not just for our liege lord, but for our God and for the preservation of a powerful bloodline that one day will enable us to regain the entire Holy Land, or Outremer as the settlers like to refer to it."

"It is my understanding, Sir Raymond, that we have never owned the Holy Land, so how can we regain it?" Gwen smiled at Payen.

"Jerusalem is the holy city of God. It has always been so." He finished his wine. "Solomon built the great Temple to God's glory."

"He was a Jewish King, not a Christian King," Gwen exclaimed. She remembered how her broad reading in the library at the French convent had frequently brought her into conflict with the simple beliefs of the nuns. "So, therefore, Christians cannot regain the Holy Land, they can only invade it. We would all have to be Jews to regain it."

"This is not a subject for women," Raymond said with an air of finality and poured himself more wine.

"If it is a subject only for men then why is the Order so keen to take me, a mere woman, to Jerusalem?" Her cheeks were aflame and her large eyes flashed with indignation. "I understand that I am in some way important to you in a religious sense, whatever that may be, yet you tell me I cannot discuss religious matters. If that is so then why did you have me educated at the convent?"

"Mistress Gwen," he sounded tired. "You are a very intelligent woman. I know you have some questions regarding your future. Just believe me when I say that I have your best interests at heart. When we reach Jerusalem, all will be revealed." He took a loud gulp of wine. "Then you will understand why I am unable to discuss such matters."

"Perhaps because you do not understand them yourself?"

There was a brief panic in Raymond's eyes, which he quickly masked by refilling his goblet. "My Lady, I have sworn an oath of secrecy. You are part of that oath." He turned to Payen who had been watching the argument with interest. "Have you had any problems in this area with a giant who leads part of the Moslem forces?"

Payen narrowed his eyes. "I have heard of him." He drank some water and refilled his goblet. "I have heard strange things about this man, or as some say, this creature. I have heard he carries a magic sword and is invincible in battle. He was supposed to be the reason why Bohemund and Tancred were defeated at the Battle of Harran in 1104. It was our first important defeat; we lost many good knights that day." He glanced at Gwen. "I do not believe anything about magic, but I do believe he is a powerful enemy." He looked at Raymond. "I understand he has red hair?" There was a note of incredulity in his voice.

"He does, my Lord, I have met him!" Gwen's face was a mask of fear. "And he does have a sword, two swords now, which are," she paused, "most dangerous in his hands."

Both knights stared at her, neither knowing how to respond.

"Have you heard of the recent battle?" Raymond said, appearing to ignore Gwen's outburst.

"I have not. I hear very little in this remote castle."

"There was a sizeable battle some miles outside Antioch, but an earthquake ended the conflict, and both sides withdrew." Raymond glanced across at Gwen. "It was thought that the Giant was leading the enemy forces."

"I understand the monster would have beaten our armies if it was not for a knight called Gilles de Plantard." Gwen was speaking quickly. "He calls himself Giles Plantard, I know him as John. He is the only person who can defeat this evil creature. He is—."

"We will not discuss him!" Raymond stood up and drained his wine. "It is time for us to return to the boat."

"My Lord, that is not possible," Payen announced emphatically. "You will notice that darkness has fallen. I would not attempt to leave this castle to descend to the village, let alone force a woman of quality to risk the dangers of that path."

Raymond looked confounded. He strode to the open window and looked out at the dark night. Far below, a few tiny lights indicated the village and the harbour, but besides these faint gleams nothing was visible. "Very well, we will stay. But I suggest Mistress Gwen is shown to her room. We will need an early start."

Gwen was about to contest Raymond's patronizing decision, when she realized that the sooner she withdrew, the sooner the knights would retire, and the greater her chance of escaping with Martin's help.

"As you will, my Lord," she said.

"I will show you to your accommodation, my Lady." Payen bowed to Gwen. "You and I, my Lord, will share my room."

With a grunt and a hand wave to indicate it was of no importance, Raymond refilled his goblet and moved over to the window. "Where is Mistress Gwen's room situated?"

"Beneath this room." Payen turned to Gwen. "My room, which I will share with Sir Raymond, is on the other side of the tower. We will not disturb you."

Gwen paused. "Are there any women servants in this castle?"

"No, my Lady. It is easier for men to be celibate when there are no women around." Payen felt the colour rising from his neck to his cheeks.

"You don't miss women?" Gwen smiled sadly, noting his clear blue eyes and his generous mouth.

"I try not to think about them. I have taken an oath to live simply, avoid women and fight for the greater glory of God." He dropped his eyes and turned the movement into a small bow. "I believe it is my duty to serve God." He breathed out and forced himself to look at her again.

In spite of his powerful physique he seemed unbelievably young. Gwen found his awkwardness attractive; he spoke with such sincerity she wanted to hug him.

They stared into each other's eyes for a long moment. He coughed self-consciously, and moved towards the doorway. "I will show you to your room, Mistress Gwen."

In the hallway, Gwen could see Martin walking slowly backwards and forwards like a caged bear. She hesitated and turned back to Sir Raymond who was lost in thought as he gazed down at the flickering points of light below. "My Lord de Wulfric?"

"Yes?" he growled.

"Your sergeant seems to be a trustworthy man."

"He does his job well enough. Why?"

"My Lord, I would feel safer in this castle of men, if he was to guard my door."

It had not occurred to him that Gwen might feel unsafe in a castle occupied by himself and a celibate knight. He could not believe any soldier would dare approach this part of the castle unless on duty, but he was never certain about foreign servants. He shrugged his huge shoulders. "I will arrange it."

She followed Payen out of the room, aware that Raymond was watching her, and forced herself to ignore Martin, who stood to attention as they passed. As she descended the circular stone stairs to the lower floor she heard Raymond's voice: "Sergeant! Get yourself something to eat. You'll be on duty tonight."

CHAPTER 9

H ER ROOM WAS SPARTAN. It was a large space, capable of accommodating a platoon of men. Its walls were rough stone, with no ornamentation and the ceiling was perhaps three times her height. Two large, open windows looked down on the bay and the inset stone blocks were several feet thick. The heavy, dark wood door, the only artistic feature, was carefully carved with a variety of birds and had a solid iron bolt on the inside. The bed was a basic straw palliasse and, apart from a bench, a small table with a flagon of water and a mug, there was nothing else in the room.

"Not the most comfortable bedroom for a lady," Payen acknowledged, as he placed a metal candleholder on the table. The candelabra had seven arms emanating from a single stem forming a half circle and giving out a comforting light.

Gwen stared at it for a moment. "Is that locally made?"

"Yes. It's a menorah." When Gwen did not respond, he added, "It's a Jewish candlestick used for religious ceremonies."

"Why do you use it?" It seemed strange that this young man who had taken Christian vows should have a religious symbol of another faith.

"Why not?" He smiled broadly revealing unusually strong and even teeth. "It is very attractive and is not being used for a religious purpose at this moment. It was in a storeroom when I arrived."

They stood on either side of the table; the flickering light illuminated their faces, softening their features, yet emphasizing the gleam of their eyes. Gwen had a sudden desire to continue the conversation. After her days of boredom on the ship, this young knight was a refreshing change from the stilted conversation of de Wulfric and the unsettling stares of the Arab sailors.

"Do you think Jews use Christian religious objects around their houses?"

Payen laughed. "What an interesting thought. I've never considered it." He placed an index finger on his nose. "I doubt whether they ever have a cross in their houses. It would serve no purpose." He paused. "However, some Jews might keep one around the place to avoid persecution by pretending to be Christian."

"Does that happen in some countries?" Gwen often felt that her learning exceeded her experience.

"The persecution, you mean?"

She nodded, and he made an effort not to stare at her. "Sadly, that is the case. There are always people in every society who have to hate someone."

"Do you hate the Moslems?"

A frown appeared on his unlined face. "I don't hate anyone." He took in a deep breath. "I fight against the Moslem armies because they wish to control the Holy Land. I don't hate them as individual men, but I will oppose them as long as they wage war against me, and as long as they strive to dominate those places that are important to Christian beliefs. If we could all live in peace together, I would like that."

Gwen felt elated. Here was a man who was prepared to answer her questions and who treated her as an equal. He was direct, honest and without any of the pompous, paternalistic attitudes that she associated with the Knights of the Order, all of who spoke down to her while still pretending to acknowledge her importance to their secret society.

She moved around the table and stood close to him; she felt she was at an important point in her understanding. There were things she needed to know. It seemed elements had conspired to create this moment: the lack of wind, the unlikely fishing harbour, the castle and its unusual and attractive knight. John had told her how Old Mary always said that everything would be revealed when the hour was right.

"There are some things I need to know." She was breathing

quickly and he was aware of her sweet breath so close to his face.

"What do you want to know?" He felt unsteady as he looked at her, as though his legs might collapse. His pulse was racing and his vows seemed strangely unimportant.

"What do you understand by the Grail?" There had been no reference to it in the Convent's library, and John himself had never understood the title 'Keeper of the Grail'. Now, she must know. Yet as she asked the question her body wanted another answer. She placed her left hand tentatively on his right arm.

He turned to face her, finding it difficult to answer. "The Grail?" He swallowed loudly. He had never been this close to a woman other than his mother and he felt overwhelmed. "The Grail is thought by some...." He lost his way, unable to remember what the question was. He could not draw his eyes from her's.

"Yes? What is the Grail?" Her voice was a horse whisper.

"Some say it's a golden chalice that contains the blood of Christ. Others say...." He placed his hand on top of hers and moved closer. He was on fire.

"Yes?" She murmured. "Yes?"

"De Montdidier! Where are you?" They sprang apart at the sound of de Wulfric's voice on the stairs, as though they had been hit by a thunderbolt.

They had barely assumed decorous positions when de Wulfric appeared in the doorway. "Ah! There you are, my Lord." He bowed to Gwen. "We must not keep you from your sleep, my Lady. We have an early start tomorrow." He placed a fleshy hand on the young knight's broad shoulder and propelled him towards the door. "I wanted to talk to you about this area, perhaps you could advise me?"

As he began to close the door behind him, he paused. "I have arranged for the Sergeant to be on guard outside this door throughout the night. He will be here shortly." He gave a small bow and then noticed the bolt, which he tested with his fingers. "Secure the door immediately. You will be quite safe, my Lady. Be ready for an early rise."

Gwen was convinced he was laughing at her as he closed the

door and she drew the bolt across with a bang. She remained standing for a long time with her back against the carved wood, staring unseeing at the candles. Her breathing eventually slowed down and she moved to a window, enjoying the cool breeze on her flushed face. What was happening to her? She had spent nearly two years in the convent, many weeks travelling with the annoying Stephen de Bois, a brief but frustrating stay in Cyprus with John and Ralph and an equally frustrating time in Antioch. This had been followed by the disastrous march to Tripoli, the horrific battle, her injury and the loathsome journey back to the city of Antioch. She had become aware of Ralph's suppressed passion and knew they both missed John for different reasons. Before regaining her equilibrium she had been forcibly abducted and made to suffer the heat and squalor of a botched voyage, with only Martin to give her any hope. Was it any wonder that she was attracted to this ardent young man with his fine looks? He possessed the strong body of a warrior and the innocence and sincerity of a boy. Did she want to mother him, or did she feel a bond in their enforced chastity? His by personal commitment, and hers by a series of events that threatened to overwhelm her.

She banged her fist on the smooth stone of the casement. "Stupid!" she muttered. "Quite stupid!" What could have happened? A kiss to remember him by? The warmth of a fleeting embrace? Hot tears rolled down her cheeks. "I will not be used like this," she muttered, as she vigorously wiped her face with both hands. "I will escape the control of these misguided men who are denying me my freedom. I have a right to live my life as I choose!" She began to walk about the shadowy room, slowly regaining control of her emotions, beginning a rational review of her circumstances.

The Knights of the Order offered nothing that she wanted. She had experienced poverty and knew she could be happy without the trappings of wealth that were so important to the powerful people she had met. Their ambition and power led to ruthlessness and cruelty, and often they were unaware and uncaring of the people they controlled, as though power enabled them to see the world differently from those whose lives they dominated. The Knights had promised her power, wealth and influence, but she wanted none of it. She had learned that nothing came of nothing and she was certain their promises came with an awful cost: her complete lack of freedom. It was as though she was a mere puppet that the knights manipulated as, somehow, they sought to achieve control of the Holy Land.

After an hour of pacing backwards and forwards on the stone flags, there was a soft, insistent tap at the door. She quietly slid back the bolt, relieved to see Martin standing in the shadowy hallway. He was without doubt the biggest man in the castle and she felt reassured when she saw him.

"Come in, quickly."

Martin looked awkward, but after glancing behind, slipped silently into the Gwen's room. He felt uncomfortable in the large, shadowy room. "I reckons we have a few hours before they wakes up." He looked closely at her, enjoying the moment of togetherness. He did not seek much, just the chance to be with her and protect her. His dreams had long since avoided the impossibility of a physical relationship; he was content just to be with her and know that she trusted him and counted him as a friend.

"Can we escape this castle?"

"I reckons we can. I've arranged for my soldiers to have the night off. I found them some wine an' all." He winked at her, like a large naughty boy. "Sir Payen's men think our men be sharing the guard. I've already dealt with their sergeant."

Gwen thought it best not to ask for too many details. "So, we can leave the castle?"

Martin nodded. "There be two of their guards on duty at the gate. I've already made myself known to 'em, so they won't be expecting no trouble when I approach 'em." He unrolled a bundle he had kept under his arm. "I got you this big cloak with a hood. Ye put it on now, just in case we meets someone unexpected."

She donned the dark cloak, and smiled. Martin was enjoying himself.

· · ·

THE BOAT RIDE TO St. Symeon was uneventful, apart from the

stifling heat and they reached the port before sunrise. By the time
the copper sun had risen over the distant mountains, Ralph had
located the harbourmaster and established an uneasy relationship
with him over a breakfast of goats' milk and newly baked bread.
He was a Syrian called Unur, a portly man, with dark, shifty eyes
and a prominent hooked nose. Ralph had quickly discovered Unur
had a working knowledge of French and was particularly fond of
silver.

"About four weeks ago a large craft with two masts was in port."
Unur licked his cruel lips. "It is called the Banyas, after a town
between Acre and Damascus." He smiled with his mouth, but his
eyes were hard as they assessed the small pile of silver coins in
front of Ralph. "It often comes to this port," he said meditatively.

"Why?" Ralph could tell the Syrian was hinting at something.

"He trades," he waved his left hand. "In many things."

"Yes?" There was an edge in Ralph's voice.

Unur paused and slowly lifted his gaze from the money. "He
comes from Marqab." He stared, unblinking into Ralph's eyes.

"Marqab?"

"It is a port on the way to Tripoli. About fifty miles away."

"So?"

"He carries passengers," he paused and looked at the coins, "if
they pay enough."

"When did the Banyas leave?"

"Sometime in the early morning."

"Did this captain from Marqab take any passengers?" Ralph felt
it was like drawing teeth.

The harbourmaster slowly scratched his belly, shrugged his
shoulders and held his calloused hands palms up. "Maybe."

With a quick movement Ralph snatched up the silver coins
in his left hand and leaned over, his face close to the Syrian's.
"This silver has to be earned. There is no more and you will get
nothing unless you tell me something that is worth paying for!" He
slammed his right fist on the table.

Unur flinched. He was not used to having his power challenged.
"Look over there," he said, unable to contain a nervous twitch at
the side of his mouth.

Ralph glanced out over the port. Nothing was moving. Some fishermen were mending nets, but none of the handful of large boats was preparing to leave. There was not a sail in sight. "Why is it so quiet?"

"Because there has been no wind for many days."

"What are you telling me?" Ralph was standing and his right hand rested on his dagger. The time for playing games was over.

The movement was not lost on Unur. "The Banyas was hired by some Knights of the Order. They boarded before dawn with a woman."

"You could have told me this before now." Ralph glared at the Syrian, who was feeling uncomfortable in the presence of this dominant young knight.

"They remained far out at anchor for about eight days and eventually left at dawn on the ninth." He could read the question in Ralph's face. "I don't know why they waited so long." He shrugged his shoulder. "Soon after, the winds dropped. It has been most unusual. I do not recall weather like it." He was speaking quickly with a fawning smile on his lascivious face. "If the Banyas was becalmed the captain would almost certainly aim for Marqab to get supplies." Unur held out his hand. "That is all I know."

Ralph released the coins into the outstretched hand. "Is there a galley in the harbour?" For a moment Unur hesitated, as if to ask for more money, but Ralph's hand on the dagger deterred him. He nodded.

"Is there a captain and men to crew it?"

Unur nodded again. He hated giving free information.

"Could we reach it in a day if the ship was well manned?"

Again Unur nodded. Seeing the annoyance on Ralph's face he grunted his agreement.

"Good. You will make the arrangements to have us transported to Marqab. There are four of us."

He was about to protest, but Ralph produced a gold coin and slowly waved it in front of him. "I will pay well if you act quickly. I want to leave within the hour. You can do that, can't you?

"Yes, my Lord!" Unur jumped to his feet and bowed deeply.

"I will arrange it myself." He bustled along the quay, moving surprisingly fast for such an overweight man.

"Sergeant Little!" Ralph yelled. The tall soldier quickly appeared. "Follow that creature and make sure he hires strong rowers, not the dregs of this God-forsaken hole."

"Right, m'Lord." Little beckoned to his two soldiers. He was going to enjoy this. As far as he was concerned all foreigners were Arabs, and all Arabs would either steal, bribe or murder you. "I'll keep an eye on 'im. Ye can leave it to me." He set off in fast pursuit, followed by the two soldiers who were glad to be doing something physical.

Ralph finished his breakfast and called for the owner of the inn. He was a young man who had recently taken over the business on the death of his father. He approached the knight with a worried face.

"It was not good?" He spoke in broken French and indicated the empty plates.

"Very good," Ralph reassured him. He produced some silver coins. "I need to talk to you. I will pay well for information." He indicated the seat opposite him. "Now, what can you tell me about the Banyas?"

. . .

THE TWO HORSES WALKED quietly, their hooves covered in sacking and their riders sitting upright and watchful. There was a slither of a moon in a star-bright sky, but it was dark as they manoeuvred carefully along a little used track away from the silent castle. After a few minutes they joined the wider path from the port and turned to their left, heading towards the hinterland.

"It won't be long before someone realizes the guards aren't on duty," Martin whispered. He was starting to worry as the implications of their escape began to sink in. It had been easy to overcome the two unsuspecting guards at the gate, and the Arab servants in the stable had gratefully gone back to sleep when Martin had indicated his wish to saddle-up the two horses by himself. With Gwen's help he had covered their hooves with sackcloth taken from the tack room; they had walked the cooperative beasts out of the gates and beyond arrow range before they mounted.

"Should we take these covers off their feet?" Gwen asked. She was excited and almost light-headed now that she was free from de Wulfric.

"I reckons we should keep them on a while longer. They won't leave no hoof prints," Martin explained.

The roadway was wide enough for wagons, but the surface was potholed and strewn with rocks. On either side low, bare hills faded into the gloom. There were jagged patches of lava rock; huge boulders stood like giant sentinels, their silhouettes outlined against the heavens. Gradually the road opened up and they began a slow descent into a wide plain or valley whose size could only be guessed in the darkness.

"Where are we going?" Gwen whispered. There was no longer any need to travel silently, yet she felt overawed by the emptiness and the strangeness of the place.

"As I sees it, we needs to get as far away from the castle as possible," Martin said, also speaking in a low voice. "Then, in a few hours, we 'ave to find a place out of the sun."

"Do we have water?" It seemed a strange question to be asking at this point in their escape.

"I got enough for a few days," Martin said confidently. "We should 'ave found a place with water by then."

They continued for the next few miles without talking and watched in awe as dawn gradually erased the darkness: the sky erupted in a violent composition of greens, blues, pinks, yellows and blood red. The copper orb of the sun emerged from behind the distant hills and they were bathed in a warm light, raising their hopes for the day.

"I've never seen a dawn like this," Gwen murmured. She turned in her saddle and surveyed the desolate landscape. Dry valleys and low, rocky hills surrounded them and in front the stony path wound its way through clumps of thorn bushes and boulders, some as big as a two storey house.

"Enjoy it now," Martin said. "It'll be mighty hot in a few hours." He stopped his horse and looked carefully around. "We started by movin' east and then, a while back, we turned south. I reckons this should keep us close to the coast, an' it might help us hide from them knights." He was not used to giving long speeches and he felt encouraged by his performance.

"I agree," Gwen said. "You decide, Martin. I'll do whatever you suggest. Just keep me away from de Wulfric and any other of the Knights of the Order." She smiled at him. "It's good to have you with me, Martin. You have no idea how much I value your friendship."

Martin flushed with happiness. This was like one of his unbelievable daydreams: he was alone with Gwen and only he could save her. She was smiling at him; he was in charge of their future and would not fail her. Whatever the sacrifice he would protect her to the bitter end. In his dream he saw himself fighting off hordes of Moslems and defying the Knights of the Order; John was no longer in the picture and even Lord d'Escosse was unable to help. It was up to him, Martin, to oppose the enemies and keep Gwen safe. His dour face broke into a huge, beaming smile.

"Martin? Are you all right?" Gwen's anxious voice broke through his reverie.

"Oh! Yes, I was just thinkin' about somethin'." Martin averted his adoring gaze and his eyes swept briefly over the landscape behind her. "Oh, dear. There's trouble."

Gwen turned in her saddle and saw, way in the distance, a small cloud of dust at the farthest point of the road. "Is that de Wulfric?" she asked, her voice taut with fear.

"I reckons so," Martin said. "We best get off this road now. Don't go too fast. We don't want to raise no dust, like they be doing."

"You lead, Martin. I'll follow you."

With a gasp of pleasure Martin turned his horse west and trotted off into a shallow valley. Within a few minutes they were out of sight of the road and before long they reached a complex system of dry valleys and huge boulders. He turned right and, after a brief canter up hill, they found a natural depression that enabled them to look down on the way they had come, without their horses being visible.

"We'll watch from 'ere. See if they be following us." He looked proudly at Gwen. "Good thing I kept them hooves covered. Even a good tracker won't be able to follow us." He handed Gwen a water flask and she drank gratefully. She handed it to back to him, but pretended not to need it.

"Martin," she spoke firmly to him, "you must drink as much as I do. I can't cope if you fall sick."

He nodded and drank deeply, wiping his mouth with the back of his hand. He felt this was the happiest day of his life.

. . .

AN HOUR BEFORE FIRST light de Wulfric awoke and quickly donned his chain mail. He was used to waking at this hour and felt a disdain for those who slept in. He would never have admitted it, but he felt more alive at dawn than at any other part of the day. Guttering candles were still flickering in a corner of the room and he could just make out the figure of Sir Payen kneeling in prayer by the window. The young knight appeared to be unaware of the movements of Sir Raymond. He continued to pray in a passionate whisper, alone with his God.

Raymond watched him for a moment and, with a contemptuous snort, left the large room they had shared. With a solitary candle he descended the stairs to Gwen's room and was disturbed to find there was no guard outside her door. Swearing he would demote the sergeant, he advanced to the door to find it ajar. He paused, then banged loudly on the frame. "My Lady! It is time to rise. Mistress Gwen?"

Receiving no response, he pushed open the heavy door. It was dark inside and it took him a few moments to realize that the room was empty. A cold touch of panic seized him. Had something unspeakable happened in the night?

He rushed out onto the landing and called out for Sir Payen, who emerged from their room above as Raymond raced down the stairs to the courtyard. The castle was asleep. It was not until he reached the main gates that his worst fears were confirmed. Two soldiers lay trussed and semi-conscious on the ground, and no other guards were to be seen.

Moments later Payen appeared in the courtyard, equally confused by the lack of guards. "Where are they all?" he yelled.

"How should I know!" Raymond yelled back. "This is your castle. You're in charge. Something has happened to Mistress Gwen! We must find her."

In a short while Gwen's absence was confirmed. Raymond's sergeant was also missing and reports showed he was responsible for the lack of guards and for disarming and imprisoning Payen's sergeant.

"Has your sergeant abducted Gwen?" Payen asked. He remembered the man as being a fine soldier, who seemed to have the confidence of Sir Raymond and Gwen. It did not make sense to him. Subconsciously he had been looking forward to seeing her again and perhaps persuading the knight to stay a few more days.

"She has suborned him." Raymond muttered. "She does not understand." He walked in a broad circle, punching his mailed left fist into his right hand. "We must find her. She is in grave danger. She has enemies she does not know of and an importance she cannot visualize." He faced a bemused Payen. "She must have persuaded the sergeant to help her escape, yet she is confused. She does not know who her real friends are."

"I thought she was with you voluntarily? Why would she run away into the desert?" Payen stared in disbelief as Raymond paced about like a caged lion.

"Because she does not understand!" He bellowed. "We must find her before it's too late."

Payen did not respond. He could not comprehend why such a beautiful woman would leave the safety of his castle to risk her life in the desert, no matter how strong and able the sergeant was. There was no logic to it, unless this Knight of the Order was hiding the truth.

He cast his mind back to the moment she had arrived at his castle. He had not expected a woman of such refinement to be travelling without female servants, and although his experience of women was extremely limited, he had noticed that she arrived with no change of clothes. The dress she wore was of good quality, but showed hard use and there had been an odd and distant relationship between her and Sir Raymond. Payen remembered standing with her in the flickering candlelight and being overwhelmed by her beauty and by a deep desire to hold her in his arms. The image was so vivid; he let out a deep groan.

"What?" Sir Raymond had stopped in front of him.

"My Lord?"

"I said I would need horses. How many do you have?"

Payen took a deep breath and cleared his mind. "I have only nine horses. Two have been," he paused, "borrowed", and one is my warhorse. We are undermanned at the moment and do not travel far by horse. In other words, I have six local horses."

"I must insist on the use of them." He gave a perfunctory bow. "She cannot have travelled far and I should be able to return them to you before nightfall."

"I will come with you, Sir Raymond. I will leave my sergeant in charge." He gave a sideways glance at the man who was standing to attention at the foot of the stairs. His blackened right eye was nearly closed and his lower lip was swollen and bloody. "It will give him time to lick his wounds."

Raymond grunted his agreement. He returned to his sleeping quarters to get his sword and armour while Payen gave orders for the security of the castle and the preparation of the horses.

In the torch-lit courtyard there was a bustle of activity as the soldiers donned their armour and prepared for the expedition. Some were barely able to function, having drunk themselves insensible only a few hours ago; others were privately threatening severe punishment on Martin. They had previously respected him as a tough sergeant and a fine soldier, but one who had seemed to be their friend. Now, he was their enemy and they looked forward to the hunt.

"He's got that woman with 'im as well."

"Perhaps she's put a spell on 'im?"

"Her would put a spell on any man." There was crude laughter that ended abruptly as Raymond strode into the yard. The soldiers formed up as servants dragged the unwilling horses out of the stables. One of Raymond's soldiers staggered as he tried to stand to attention.

"Wake up, you drunken oaf!" Raymond shook the man so violently his helmet fell off. There was stifled laughter. "You're no use to me!" He dragged the hapless soldier over to a horse trough and pushed his head under the water. The drowsy man seemed to come alive, spluttering and coughing. "Do I have to do that again?"

"No, m'Lord. Sorry, m'Lord." The soldier seemed diminutive beside the towering knight.

"Get down to the ship and tell the others not to allow the Captain back on board, or any of his crew. You understand?" The soldier nodded furiously. "If that ship is not there when I return I'll cut you into pieces and feed you to the dogs." Nobody laughed.

"My Lord de Wulfric," Payen spoke formally for the benefit of the soldiers, "do your men ride?"

"They're soldiers, for God's sake!" Raymond turned his back on the men. "They'll ride if they have to."

"Some of my men have been trained to fight on horseback and I have one local guide who is also a translator. He would be invaluable."

"Do you trust him?"

"Yes." Payen beckoned to a young man with a thick black beard and a pale headdress. He stepped forward and Raymond could see he was dressed for riding. "This is Ishmael." The guide bowed slowly.

"Agreed," Raymond grumbled. "But the other three will be my men."

• • •

DAWN WAS BREAKING AS the six riders left the imposing confines of the castle. The air was cool but the spectacular colours on the distant mountains presaged another hot day. Sir Raymond knew he had to push the horses while they were fresh; he would worry about their return journey after Gwen had been recaptured. He was riding one of the small Arab horses and, like Payen, was wearing only a chain mail shirt and hood, a light tunic and loose trousers. He had left his heavy armour at the castle, including his helmet, and carried only his long sword, a small round Saracen shield on the side of his saddle and his metal gauntlets. As he urged his mount forward he reflected sorely on his conversation in the courtyard.

"These horses are not used to your weight and certainly would be unable to carry you very far if you wore your armour," Payen had explained.

"I'll ride your horse then," Raymond had responded, pointing to Payen's warhorse, which stood several hands taller then the smaller local horses.

"My Lord, you must be aware that such a horse is suited for battle, but useless as a fast pursuit animal." Reluctantly, Sir Raymond had conceded the sense of the argument and although he had chosen the largest of the other horses, his long legs almost touched the ground when he sat in the saddle. This had produced some malicious grins from his soldiers, the majority of whom had little love for this arrogant Lord.

Payen rode hard; his experience and local knowledge enabled him to keep ahead of Raymond, who soon found the going difficult and frustrating. Ahead, the young Arab named Ishmael was leading the group. He was a proven tracker and could follow the trails of deer and lions. Payen had befriended Ishmael soon after taking charge of Al Marqab castle and was pleased to use the youth's skills for this mission. Payen reviewed the situation as he rode skilfully along the rocky path; he had been faintly amused at the knight's lack of experience in the desert, but was still confused as to what had led Gwen to flee his castle and seek refuge in this savage and unforgiving land. His agreement to accompany Raymond was motivated by his concern for her welfare and ultimate survival, rather than any wish to see her returned to the apparently unwanted protection of the Knights of the Order.

Ishmael slowed his horse to a walk as soon as they descended into a broad valley. After a while he stopped and dismounted. The two knights drew rein and watched as Ishmael squatted down and examined the rocky ground. The three soldiers drew up behind them, grateful for a brief rest now that their earlier enthusiasm had abated.

"Make up your mind, you damn heathen!" Raymond bellowed.

"It's obvious where they've gone." He edged his horse around Payen's mount. "Let's keep going. We're losing time."

The Arab appeared not to hear and walked slowly up to Payen. "They have left this path and gone up there," he said in broken French, pointing to a shallow valley that joined from their right.

"Are you certain?" Payen asked. Raymond was guiding his horse away from them, determined to continue in their original direction. The tracker nodded, and cast a sneer in Raymond's direction as the knight urged his horse into a trot.

"Good. Well done, Ishmael." Payen pointed to the soldiers. "This way," he said as he indicated the side valley. The tracker mounted quickly and led the group in the new direction. Raymond's soldiers glanced anxiously at each other, but obeyed the order.

Raymond was outraged when he glanced round to see the others moving quickly away from him. He yanked on the reins, and cursing volubly, galloped after them. "You'd better be right," he muttered, "or I'll flay you alive." He hated all foreigners, particularly those who pretended to know more than he did.

It was a while before he caught up with them. The group was moving at a modest trot, with Ishmael eventually slowing to a walk and finally stopping. On both sides of the trail, cliffs rose up to a hundred feet or so, punctuated by shallow ravines, indicating the fast passage of water during the infrequent rains.

Raymond was pretending to be unaware his horse was limping; during his angry gallop he had ignored the difficult terrain and the animal had stumbled, damaging its right front fetlock. It had reduced its speed to a hobble, regardless of the savage beating he gave it. When the others stopped the injured horse raised a front hoof off the ground. Its eyes were wild with fear and it trembled uncontrollably.

"Ye horse's limping, m'Lord," one of the soldiers remarked helpfully.

"I know it's limping, you idiot! Swap horses!" Raymond dismounted and stalked towards the alarmed soldier.

"M'Lord?" the man seemed unable to grasp the logic or the fairness of the order.

"I said swap horses!" he roared, reaching up and dragging the hapless soldier from his horse. The man's cry of surprise gave way to a grunt of pain as he fell heavily onto the ground. This time the other soldiers did not smile. Without a backwards glance Raymond climbed awkwardly into the saddle. He urged his new mount towards the place where Payen and Ishmael were in earnest conversation. "Well?" he demanded.

"It would appear their trail has gone dead," Payen shrugged his shoulders. "Ishmael thinks they have gone off into one of the side wadis somewhere in the last half mile."

"How convenient," Raymond snarled. "How do we know he's not in league with that sergeant? Taking us off the track in a wild goose chase! Does he think I don't know what he's up to?"

"I trust this man in the desert," Payen spoke sharply and he locked eyes with Raymond. "His first duty is to me. I would always trust his advice over someone who knows nothing about this country."

Raymond clenched his gauntlets, gave Ishmael a withering scowl and abruptly rode his horse up the track. He stopped thirty feet away. In spite of his conviction that she was miles ahead of them on the main trail his eyes scoured the cliff tops and the dry ravines as though he expected to find Gwen looking at him. Behind him the soldiers discussed the health of the injured horse, concerned as to how they would travel with only two able horses between the three of them. The third soldier was massaging his shoulder and muttering foul curses on Sir Raymond, who had not given the incident a second thought.

Payen noticed the injured horse and the mutinous attitude of the soldiers towards Sir Raymond; he wondered why the knight had insisted on bringing his own men, in spite of their lack of knowledge of local conditions. He shook his head; such arrogance and intolerance were unfamiliar to him and he wondered how the situation would resolve itself. "Do you think you can find the place where they left this track?" he asked Ishmael.

"Perhaps." The Arab pursed his lips. "I can try." He glared at Sir Raymond. "I will not help him, only you."

Payen wiped his brow, aware of the increasing heat. "We only have water for a short journey. If you are uncertain, we will return to the castle."

"These flat surfaces tell me nothing," he said, pointing to the wide stretches of rock that lined the track. "If I can find a soft area, perhaps there will be a sign." He looked into the knight's eyes. "Do you want me to find them?"

Payen smiled uncertainly. "I want to save them from dying in this desert."

Ishmael bowed his head. "If I think they are safe, perhaps I will not find them?"

He had a fleeting memory of standing close to Gwen in the dark room, moments before Raymond had burst in. He could understand her dislike for this Knight of the Order and suspected the sergeant was her ally. Perhaps she was safer in the desert with her powerful soldier than she would be if she were reunited with her apparent jailer. Part of Payen wanted to see her again, but another part, his religious, moral and unworldly self, wanted to keep away from her and not experience again the pointless and upsetting yearnings she had awakened in him.

He looked up at the bare cliffs. "I think you should do what is best for the lady." He glanced at Raymond who was fifty paces away, grimacing at the rocky landscape. "You should find her only if she appears to be in danger." There was a brief moment when they exchanged looks as Raymond approached them.

"We should split up and check each of these gulleys," he said.

Payen shook his head. "I think we should allow Ishmael to do his job."

There was a long pause as Raymond fought with the desire to lash out at this presumptuous young knight whose sickening virtue and naïve open-handedness was an insult to his concept of soldierly behaviour. Raymond knew he could not search the area by himself, even with the doubtful help of his unwilling soldiers. The situation had become intolerable and he blamed himself for allowing Gwen off the ship. He also regretted his decision to travel without the assistance of another knight, but he had been unable to resist the opportunity of being the sole consort of the young woman who would change the political and spiritual balance in the Holy Land. He had imagined his triumphal entry into Jerusalem....

"My Lord?"

He glared at Payen. "Yes? All right. He can lead. But God help him if he fails to find them."

· · ·

IT WAS MIDDAY. THE heat was intense and the horses stood like statues in the deep shade, their eyes closed. Every now and again they would shake their heads or flick their tails to dislodge the troublesome flies, but they were local horses: they were used to flies. Martin had removed their saddles and he and Gwen were using them as headrests, as they dozed under the protective shadow of a wide ledge.

Three hours before, from a hidden vantage point, they had glimpsed the riders moving slowly back along the shallow valley. The heat was increasing and they could see the soldiers were suffering, and one was leading a lame horse.

"That one in front looks like he be their guide," Martin observed. After a long pause he shook his head. "That be mighty queer."

"What is?" Gwen asked. She had been watching the horsemen moving slowly down the valley and had noticed nothing strange in the way they progressed.

"That one in front," Martin said. He waved for Gwen to keep her head down. "I been watchin' that one. I reckons he knows where we left the trail, but for some reason he ain't telling them knights."

"You think he's on our side?" Gwen found this impossible to believe. Why would a local man employed by a knight support them?

"Perhaps." Martin stroked his beard. "Or perhaps he's been told by that young knight not to find us. I don't think 'e likes Sir Raymond."

"But why did he follow us down this valley if he didn't mean to find us?"

"Ye got me there," Martin agreed.

They watched as the small party disappeared back towards the main trail.

"I reckons we find somewhere out of the sun, and we decides what we do when it gets cooler."

Slowly the heat of the day began to lessen as the sun dipped behind them, framing the hills and increasing the shadow in which they slept. Martin awoke with a start, sat up and rubbed his eyes. He looked quickly around and got carefully to his feet, trying to avoid waking Gwen, who slept peacefully. For a moment he stood gazing down at her, marvelling at her loveliness, savouring the moment. He reluctantly averted his eyes, not wanting her to suddenly wake and find him staring. Cautiously he moved towards the ridge and crawled up to some rocks at a place where he could look down on the valley below. He blew out his lips in relief when he saw it was deserted. It had not been sensible for them to doze off at the same time, and he had worried that he might see their pursuers advancing swiftly towards their makeshift camp.

As he lay there on his stomach he relaxed and carefully studied the landscape, noting the numerous small valleys and the way the hills stretched out towards the south and west. The sun was fading to his right and he knew he should get the horses down to the valley bottom while it was still light. He was about to get up, when he noticed a movement to his left. Wide-eyed, he froze as he saw a column of horsemen moving like shadows along the trail. They were dressed in black robes with black head coverings and he watched with increasing anxiety as scores of the riders passed below. The men were attentive and watchful, scanning the cliffs on both sides as they moved silently towards the west. They appeared to be experienced warriors: each man carried a small round shield, a curved sword and either a short bow or a lance. From his vantage point Martin could judge the horses were in good shape and showed no signs of exhaustion, or anything to indicate they had been ridden hard.

Eventually the main column passed by, followed by a rear guard of about twenty. Martin assumed they must be on patrol as they carried no supplies, which indicated that their camp could not be too far away. They had taken the path he had intended to follow, which led in the direction of the sea. He realized his simple plan was no longer possible; he stared fiercely around as he considered the alternatives. The light was fading and if he was to get Gwen safely off the high ground, he had to move fast.

Gwen was saddling up the horses when Martin returned. While they prepared for their journey he described what he had seen.

"So, which way shall we travel?" Gwen asked, her dark eyes wide with concern. Their escape from the castle had suddenly become a more serious issue. No longer was this an enjoyable flight to freedom, but rather an unplanned venture into a dangerous and unforgiving land, where their enemies were everywhere and where the influence of the Crusaders stopped outside the safety of their castles. Somehow, she had ignored the huge risks of her escape. Her mind had focused solely on regaining her freedom, regardless of the consequences, but now her first concern was for Martin, whose friendship she knew she had exploited. Since his unexpected reappearance as a soldier outside the door of her vile room in a French inn, she had always felt secure in the knowledge that someone she trusted knew where she was. Even now, after somehow getting himself included in the guard taking her to Jerusalem, he was, once again, risking his life for her.

"I reckons we can't go the way them soldiers went. They could have a camp in the area. So, it might be best if we goes the other way, towards the east, and then turn north back towards Antioch. Once we gets past Al Marqab, we could travel near the coast. There be plenty of Crusaders up that way. We got enough water and a bit of food to last us a few days. We could make it if we goes careful." He was speaking with the intense concentration of a man who rarely gave long speeches.

"How far do you think it is?"

"About sixty or seventy miles." He looked pleased with himself. "In the castle last night, I asked them soldiers."

"Well done, Martin, you've thought of everything." She gave him a hug. "I don't know what I'd do without you."

"Right, then," he said, clearing his throat. He turned towards the horses and took a deep breath, expelling the air through his thick lips. He could not remember when he had been so content.

"We'd better get down to the valley floor before we lose the light. You best follow me."

They picked their way carefully down the slope and Gwen reflected on her change of mood. Moments before she had felt fearful and guilty, but now, in spite of the danger, she was optimistic and looking forward to the journey ahead. It was the first time for more than two years that she had completely escaped the constant supervision of members of the Order. With luck she and Martin would meet up with some Crusader patrol, or reach a safe castle. At the worst they would travel all the way back to Aleppo, which might take three days. She was certain that Ralph would be organizing search parties for her in the area. He might find her long before she and Martin reached the city.

Her thoughts were interrupted when her horse disturbed some loose stones that rattled down the side of the gulley, sounding loud in the silent, windless evening. Martin turned to check on her; she waved her hand to reassure him. They were soon on level ground and, turning left, they walked the animals carefully until they reached the wide valley. The last vestiges of sunlight disappeared and they stopped their horses to stare up at the clear sky. In the desert the immensity of the heavens and the wonder of the uncountable stars were awe-inspiring, and neither said anything for some minutes. Their eyes adjusted to the starlight and with nods of agreement, Martin led the way towards the east, following a clear path. There was an unspoken understanding that speech was unnecessary, perhaps even out of place, in the quiet wastes of the stony desert.

As they trotted carefully along the track, Martin loosened his sword in its scabbard, checking the shadows on either side. Although unfamiliar with the desert, he knew that humans were not the only enemy they were likely to encounter, and he was keenly aware of his responsibility for Gwen's safety.

After a while, as the journey began to unfold, she pondered the different possible results of their journey: the enemies they might encounter, the places they might reach and even the wild beasts that might attack them. Eventually her thoughts returned to Antioch: she thought of Ralph and his original plans to convey her secretly to Cyprus, then on by boat to England. Her thoughts turned to John and she screwed up her eyes as though in pain. He might be dead. In spite of Ralph's optimism she was beginning to accept the fact that John had not survived the battle. Ralph had assured her that no one had found John's corpse, so there was every hope he might be alive. But if he had followed the Giant, as many reports agreed he had, it seemed logical that either he, or their evil adversary, was dead. If John had killed the fiend he would have reported the fact. But, if John had died in the resulting conflict, then who would know? She took a deep breath. Perhaps he had been injured and had died later in some lonely place. If, on the other hand, he had been captured, surely there would have been a demand for a ransom? Someone would have reported it.

She wondered what would happen to her without John. In spite of the refined qualities and friendship of Ralph and the dependable strength and devotion of Martin, she did not feel any real emotional attraction to either of them. Both in their own ways were remarkable men, and she loved them as friends. But it was John she wanted and she could not imagine how her life would unfold without him.

CHAPTER 10

"**Y**OU ARE VERY POPULAR with my sons, and I have come to know you well. I believe you are a good man even though you are an infidel." Ibrahim chuckled as he spoke. It was early evening and there was unusual activity around the buildings.

"You are a good man too, Ibrahim. Even though you beat your wife and terrorize your daughters." John tried to look serious, but failed. It was an open secret that Ibrahim worshipped his wife and doted on his daughters. It was as though he wished to shield them from the unpleasant aspects of life; he was forever complimenting them and arranging little treats. In contrast, he was severe with his two sons, constantly urging them to work harder at their lessons, rarely allowing them freedom of action. His favourite homily to John was: "They are not yet men. Boys will always get into trouble if they are not given enough to do." Ibrahim took his sons' obedience for granted, seemingly unaware of the enormous respect and admiration they had for him.

As the two men stood together in the courtyard, a casual observer might have thought they were related. John was the taller and younger of the two and lacked Ibrahim's prominent hooked nose. But with their thick beards and similar clothing and the easy, relaxed way in which they jostled with each other, they seemed like brothers. Both had intelligent dark eyes and tanned skin; both stood their ground with confidence and authority. A stranger would have been astonished to discover that one was the voluntary prisoner of the other.

Ibrahim looked thoughtfully at his two sons standing anxiously some distance away. "They are very keen to take you to see the ruins of a Greek temple. It is not far from here." He spoke as though it was the first time the subject had arisen, although he and his sons had talked about little else for days. "I have decided that such an adventure would be good for them. You might find it interesting. I took them there last year, but now they are older they might benefit more from the experience." He put both hands together, as if in prayer, placing the finger tips beneath his cavernous nose. "You will take Hassan with you; he will be fully armed in case of trouble."

"Do you think I will run off with your sons?" John raised his eyebrows in jest.

"No, my friend, you are a man of honour. You have given me your word. But there are villains outside this valley who will kill you, just for your clothes. They have little compunction in abducting children." He looked up at the hills. "Also, there are wild animals to consider." He sighed deeply. "But boys will be boys and need to prove themselves, which is why I am only sending Hassan." He looked into John's eyes. "I think it best that you are armed also. I will return your sword to you," he smiled, "and the temporary use of your horse, Celestial." He turned towards the boys and clapped his hands. They immediately ran over and stood in front of their father, rocking from one foot to the other in anticipation.

"I have decided that you can take your teacher on this expedition." There were howls of delight and Ibrahim shook his head and waved his hands, pretending to be annoyed by the outburst. "Listen quietly. You will leave early tomorrow and Hassan will lead you. He has been there many times. It will take you about three hours. You will be back before it is dark. You will do exactly as Hassan says and you will be respectful to your teacher." Both boys nodded happily. "Now go and groom your horses, and prepare my new horse, Celestial, for your teacher." As the boys ran off he called out: "Groom Hassan's horse as well." He turned to John, "Wait here, I'll get your sword for you."

John watched him walk quickly away. He was a confident man who was proud of his sons, even if he did not demonstrate this to them. As John waited, he reflected on Ibrahim's firm yet loving relationship with his sons and felt an intense sadness as he wondered about his own father.

He had very few clear memories of his early life, until the year he spent near Woodford with the old woman called Mary. Occasionally, he experienced faint recollections of a religious establishment, which might have been a nunnery or a monastery; at other times he recalled a castle and a great hall with banners. But his most vivid memory was as a young child on a large, rolling ship in a terrible storm, with howling wind and driving rain. Dangerous waves crashed over the deck and the water was swirling around his feet. With him, holding him safe, was a tall thin man dressed like a soldier. He was gaunt and seemed unwell, but no matter how hard John tried, he could neither recall the soldier's face, nor even the sound of his voice. Was the man his father? He had no way of knowing. But, as a lonely child will invent an invisible friend, John had clung stubbornly to the belief that this man might have been his father. As for his mother, he had not the faintest memory of her, or of any woman, before he met Old Mary.

The two boys led the horses out of the stables, chattering excitedly. John wondered what he would have become if he had been loved and instructed by a mother and a father. He realized he had learned so much in the past few years: Old Mary, like a mother, had instructed him in many things, and had provided him with a powerful symbol on his hand that had protected him from his enemies; he glanced down at the clear, intricate design on his right palm. Then, there was Owl: the strange, unbelievable man with his warm, fatherly advice who had appeared only twice in John's life, but each time as though to guide him along a new path. He would not forget Tegwen, who had taught him physical love, or Aelfreda who had awakened his spiritual love. The brother in his make-believe family was Ralph, who was more than just a friend. His sister would be....

He chewed his lower lip. Was Gwen his sister, or the true passion of his life?

"Are you not happy?" Saif was standing in front of him, his dark face creased with worry.

John forced a smile. "Very happy. I was just worrying myself over a big problem."

"Oh?"

"I wondered how I might keep up with you fine horseman tomorrow, as I have such a small horse."

Saif giggled delightedly and clapped his hands. "Come and see how we've groomed your small horse," he said, happy to join in the joke. "We're all ready for tomorrow."

. . .

THE FIRST PART OF the journey to the Greek ruins was uneventful. They left at first light and followed narrow dirt tracks away from the familiar fields, gradually climbing up into the surrounding high lands. The relative lushness of their damp valley gradually gave way to dry, stony ground as they gained height. Gone were the palms and small trees, the olive grooves and the herds of goats, while ahead of them, and on their left, the bare hills stretched away into a bluish obscurity as the sun began to dominate the sky.

For two hours they rode slowly, only occasionally breaking into a trot. Hassan led the way, making no attempt to speak to John, who continued an animated conversation with Rashid and Saif. The boys were keen to explain everything they thought John should know, and Saif was anxious to show that he knew as much as his elder brother.

"The place we are going to is very old," Rashid said.

"It was here before the Romans came," Saif added.

"The Greeks built it to worship one of their gods, but...."

"We don't know which one," Saif interrupted.

It was clear to John they had been given a lesson by Ibrahim, so they could demonstrate their knowledge and be the perfect guides in their local terrain. As they continued their joint lecture, he kept a watchful eye on their surroundings, occasionally glancing back to check the empty trail behind them. He had no doubt that Hassan was doing the same. This was confirmed when the bodyguard abruptly stopped his horse and pointed ahead of them. They all halted and shaded their eyes as they searched the landscape. After a moment, John was finally able to identify some movement almost out of sight.

Hassan spoke briefly to the boys, his deep voice quickly gliding over the guttural sounds. He did not address John, knowing his Arabic was limited and indicating, once again, his contempt for foreigners. John picked up the word: *goats*.

"Hassan says there is a flock of goats and three herders," Rashid said.

"And he does not think we need to worry," Saif added.

John smiled. "Good. He has amazing eyesight."

Rashid translated this to Hassan, who gave a disdainful grunt and urged his horse into a trot. He rode well. With his tooled leather body armour and his domed helmet, he looked more like a leader than a bodyguard. On his left side hung a curved sword, and a round embossed shield was attached to the saddle. Across his back he carried a short bow, with a quiver of arrows below his right arm.

As they passed the herdsmen, John noticed their dark, thin faces, their ragged beards and the pitiful rags they wore. It was impossible to tell their ages. The men stood still, watching resentfully as Hassan rode straight through their flock, causing the goats to scatter in all directions. John and the two boys did their best to prevent their horses causing further disturbance, but their attempts were in vain. Wide-eyed with fear and bleating like banshees, the goats broke into a terrified rush, some springing in the air and landing on each other, while others avoiding one horse, ran into the path of another. Saif's horse reared up and almost threw the boy, but he held on grimly as the powerful hooves of the animal flattened a goat in its path.

When he saw the herdsmen were yelling and waving sticks, Hassan turned his mount and raced back to ensure the safety of his two wards. One man rushed at Saif as he was trying to control his anxious horse, and hit the boy a violent blow on his left shoulder. He screamed with pain and fear, barely able to remain in the saddle, but before the incensed herdsman had time to swing his club for a second time, Hassan attacked him from behind. It was over in seconds. Hassan's sword sliced into the unsuspecting herdsman and he fell in a welter of blood, his sad excuse for a weapon falling unnoticed at the side of the track. His two friends, outraged by the death of their goat, attacked Rashid, seemingly unaware that Hassan was charging down at them. John was at the rear of the group, and realizing the danger of the situation, rode his horse in front of Rashid's, forcing the herdsmen to retreat. The two men backed off, and at that moment saw their fallen friend, and the murderous Hassan. They howled, their voices indicating a complex mixture of fear, outrage, and loss as they became aware of their mortally wounded companion. There was a look of incomprehension on their faces, and John felt deeply for their loss. At that moment, he looked up to see Hassan urging his horse into a gallop as he charged back at the two bewildered herdsmen; his sword was raised in the air, and he had the blind bloodlust of battle in his eyes. Without hesitation, John drew his long sword and urged his mount forward, intercepting Hassan's charge.

"Stop!" John yelled. But the bodyguard was intent on killing the men who had dared to assault his master's children. He galloped forward as though John was not in his way. "Hassan!" he yelled, but it did not have any effect on the blood-crazed warrior.

John turned Celestial to the side. Hassan, his eyes fixed on the two herdsmen, charged by, an arm's width from John's horse. As he passed, John brought down the flat of his sword on the back of Hassan's neck. There was a jarring in his arm, and then John watched relieved as the powerful warrior collapsed in his saddle. He did not fall from his horse, but dropped to one side, his sword falling to the ground. John cantered over to the frightened creature and led it back to where the two boys were waiting. Saif was crying and clutching his arm; Rashid was trying to comfort him. The two herdsmen were gathered around their dead friend, screaming and beating their chests. All the anger had gone out of them and they appeared lost and frightened.

John dismounted and eased the unconscious Hassan from his horse. He removed his helmet, his bow and quiver, and laid him on the ground. Having checked he was still breathing, he walked over to the two boys. The unnecessary killing sickened him. He glanced back to see the two herdsmen unceremoniously drape the corpse over a large goat and hasten back the way they had come. The scattered goats followed slowly behind, seeking safety in numbers.

"It wasn't my fault," Saif wailed. "I didn't mean to kill the goat." His breath came in hiccups, and he trembled violently, gripping his shoulder with his right hand as Rashid tried to support him.

"Let me see," John said. He kneeled down and placed his hands on the boy's shoulder, instantly aware of the uncontrolled power surging through them.. Saif stopped crying and dropped his right hand, a look of awe on his face. John was aware he was using the voice that came with the tingling in his fingers, speaking soothingly and precisely. Knowing he had the power to heal, he removed the boy's robe from his shoulders and gently massaged the damaged joint, all the while reassuring him. He had not experienced this feeling since chasing the Giant off the battlefield; it was both wonderful and terrifying, for he knew he could do amazing things while he had this power, but it worried him that he had no control over it.

"My shoulder doesn't hurt anymore," Saif said. There was a tone of wonderment in his voice.

"You should be able to move it now." John was conscious that the tingling in his fingers had stopped. He stood up, feeling strangely weary and helped the small boy to his feet.

"How did you do that?" Rashid was staring in disbelief. "Was that magic?"

"No, it was not magic," John said quickly. "It was just something I learned in England." He wanted to downplay the event. It would not help if they began to see him as a magician, or some weird infidel with superhuman powers. It had taken a while to gain their acceptance and their trust, and he felt a deep sense of responsibility for them.

Saif flexed his arm gingerly and smiled. "It doesn't hurt anymore," he repeated. He stood up and gazed adoringly at John.

"What will we tell father?" Rashid said. His worried eyes moved from John to the prone Hassan and back again.

"You must always tell your father the truth," John said reassuringly. "Tell him how Hassan rode through the herd, and how Saif's horse was frightened by the goats. You will tell your father how Hassan killed the herdsman and how I had to stop him killing the others."

"What about the way you healed my shoulder?"

"Does it hurt at all, Saif?"

"No." Saif swung his arm about. "It's like the man never hit me."

"Well," John said, "you could pretend it never happened." He shrugged his shoulders.

The two boys regarded him gravely. After a moment, Rashid walked over to the unconscious Hassan. "Will he be all right?"

"I hope so." John stood by Rashid. "He's a very strong man. He should recover."

"Can you make him better?" Rashid was scowling at the warrior.

"Do you want me to?" John asked.

Rashid nodded, and Saif said nothing. They both stared at the huge body, as though they had never imagined him in this state. John bent down and placed his hand on Hassan's neck, waiting for the tingling to happen in his fingers. But he felt nothing. He prodded the thick neck, trying to sense if it was broken or out of place, but was unable to feel any broken bones. He was unsure whether he was achieving anything and, feeling unsuited to the task, he rose slowly to his feet.

"Did you fix his neck?" Saif screwed up his nose, as though he might sneeze.

"I think he'll recover. Pass me the water from his saddle."

Rashid fetched a water bladder from Hassan's horse and handed it to John. "Are you a healer?" he asked cautiously.

John took the water bladder and released the top. "Yes, I'm a healer." It seemed better to answer his question. "But I can only help with certain things," he added. "I don't know if I can help Hassan recover."

"We don't like Hassan," Saif said. His brother scowled at him.

John paused, about to pour water on Hassan's head. "Why?"

"He's very loyal to our father," Rashid said bitterly, "but he bullies us. He tells our father that he will make men out of us and yells and threatens us if we do not do exactly what he wants. Sometimes, he gets so angry that his eyes go funny." He took a deep breath. "I think he might murder us one day."

"Are you afraid of him?" John turned to Saif.

"Yes. He can be very scary."

"Why don't you tell your father?" John stared down at the thick neck, and the large ears and nose. Everything about Hassan was big and strong. Even in his unconscious state he had a contemptuous twist to his mouth.

"My father has known Hassan since childhood. They are friends. Our father would not understand." Rashid stared unseeing at the retreating flock of goats.

"Would he believe you?" John persisted.

"He would not disbelieve us," Rashid said, and Saif nodded earnestly, "but he would not understand. He would be disappointed in us, as though we are not worthy, as though we are failing to become sons able to rule our tribe." He stared down at Hassan. "My father expects me to become a warrior, like Hassan, so I can protect the valley and provide leadership when he is dead."

"If Hassan is loyal to your father, why is he so hard on you?"

"He says we are weak-willed. Hassan enjoys killing and hurting people." Rashid spoke with an intense distaste in his voice. "We would not have galloped through that goat herd. I would not have killed that herdsman. That was murder."

Saif punched the air with his fist, enjoying the movement of his arm. "Hassan hates all foreigners, especially you. He will kill you if you ever break your promise to our father. He would enjoy it."

This was the first time the boys had talked about their bodyguard, and although their information came as no surprise, John marvelled that he had been so unaware. In the first hours of his capture by Ibrahim, he had endured the rough treatment meted out by Hassan, accepting it as the natural behaviour of an enemy. But since his agreement to teach the two boys, the bodyguard had remained in the background, rarely acknowledging him, but always lurking in the shadows, constantly on watch. John had slowly become used to him. Over the weeks he had stopped noticing; Hassan was like the flies, always in evidence, but merely an irritation of no importance.

"What will you do with him?" Rashid asked.

"Perhaps, I should try to wake him." John drank and then

poured water over Hassan's head, but there was no response. He handed the water back to Rashid, who drank deeply and handed it on to his brother.

"I'm going to throw him over the saddle and take him back to your father."

"But we'll miss the ruins," Saif muttered.

"Another reason for hating him," Rashid added.

"He may need medical help," John said. "Your father would not be pleased if he died because of my neglect."

The two boys glared at Hassan's limp body, before turning away and remounting. As John struggled to get Hassan secured on his horse, he was aware of a muted conversation between the two boys.

"We'll be travelling at the hottest time."

"I know," Rashid hissed. "But John's worried about Hassan."

"We're almost there," Saif persisted. "There will be water for the horses."

"We have to do as we're told. Father said we must obey our elders."

"But he's a prisoner. He doesn't know this area."

"He is not a prisoner, he's our teacher. If Hassan dies, father will blame him." John looked up to see Rashid shove Saif's shoulder. "Just shut up, and do as you're told."

. . .

SLOWLY, THEY BEGAN TO retrace the path back to Ibrahim's valley, with the boys leading the way. John rode beside Hassan's horse keeping a close watch on the unconscious man, who showed no sign of recovery. The sun was high in the sky and the dry heat became intense. Everything around them was so bright that the deep shadows of rocks and thorn bushes appeared unnaturally dark, as though beckoning them to take cover from the merciless radiation. Nothing moved. The desert stretched out before them, a seemingly unending pattern of small rocky hills, dry valleys and desiccated bushes. The boys did not speak. With their heads drooped down and their hoods covering their faces, they clearly expressed their disappointment. John wondered if he had made the best decision. As if aware of his doubts, Saif turned towards him and pouted.

"If we had continued to the Greek temple, it would have been cooler there, and we would have been able to bathe in the cool water."

"Hassan would have been better there than frying in this desert at this time of the day," Rashid added. "We could have stayed there until it was cooler."

Cooler, that was the word. John had rarely experienced heat of this intensity. He knew his experience was limited, and that these young boys knew more about survival in this barren land than he did. He stopped his horse. "All right! We'll go back to the Greek temple."

The two boys cheered, and turned their lethargic horses.

"How much further is it?" John asked.

"We should be there in less than half the time it would take us to return home." Rashid sat up eagerly on his horse, his earlier tiredness forgotten.

"Good. You can lead the way." John smiled to himself as the two boys set off at a brisk trot. He glanced at Hassan, who remained unconscious, and imagined the satisfaction of dumping him in cold spring water. The boys were right; it was madness to travel any further than necessary in this searing heat. Yet, as he acknowledged the sense of the decision, a small voice in his head was warning of danger.

· · ·

AFTER NEARLY AN HOUR, they began a slow descent into different country. The barren rocky desert gave way to stunted bushes, thin grass, and small olive trees. As the path curved around a jagged hill, John saw the tops of large trees on the horizon.

"We're nearly there!" Said exclaimed excitedly. "The temple is in a hidden valley over that way." He pointed towards the green blur in the distance.

Their horses, sensing the promise of water, began to trot. John kept close to the unconscious Hassan to prevent him from slipping off the saddle.

"This place is full of giant cedars," Rashid explained, as they entered a small forest and followed a well-marked track. "They're sacred trees, not like this stone pine which is more common." He looked very proud, as though he was showing John around his country estate.

"There are apple trees here as well, and big olive bushes," Saif added.

As they moved into the shade of the forest, they slowed down to a walk, enjoying the cool, damp air, giving John time to admire the size of the trees. Some of the cedars were as tall as any he had seen in England; their thick rugged branches reached out in all directions, like guardians of the forest.

"There it is!" Saif yelled.

They rode out of the tree cover on high ground. Below them, a large open space was revealed, dominated by a long rectangular lake with the remains of the ruined temple at the far end. The track sloped down to a narrow path that followed close to the water, with thick forest on the right and dense clumps of reeds and bushes on the left. From above they could see the undisturbed barrier of water plants prevented access to the lake, except in front of the temple where rows of grey stone steps stretched from the water up to what had once been a majestic portal. Four marble columns, topped by a decorated lintel formed an imposing façade, behind which only parts of the walls and broken pillars remained. From a distance, the impressive ruin with the quiet lake appeared almost magical, like something conjured up in a dream. Yet in spite of its beauty, John felt there was a strange brooding quality about it.

Saif manoeuvred his horse down the track onto the narrow path, and galloped off towards the temple. He was cheering wildly, his voice echoing around the lake, causing an explosion of sound as a multitude of waterfowl burst into the air.

"Is it safe here?" John asked, his eyes searching the area for any sign of movement. He urged Celestial forward to keep Saif in sight, while still trying to keep the unconscious Hassan in his saddle.

"We have never met anyone here before," Rashid said. His

smile changed to a frown as he registered John's concern. "Saif!" he yelled. "Wait for us."

When they reached the ruin, Saif had already dismounted and was standing on the top step surveying the lake; his horse was standing in shallow water drinking gratefully. "I am King of the Greeks!" he yelled. "I am king of all I can see!" His voice reverberated like a trumpet.

"Saif, come down. Shut up!" Rashid called. Again the echo announced their presence.

"I was only having fun? What's wrong with that?" He came down the steps and made a rude face at his brother.

Rashid scowled at him, before helping John lower Hassan's heavy body to the ground. "There could have been Assassins for all you know," he said. "Father said you were to do as you're told."

"There are no Assassins here. You show me an Assassin!"

While the two boys argued, John dragged Hassan to the side of the steps, where there was a flat, sandy area in the shade of a large cedar, whose strong branches pressed against the wall of the temple. He doused the grim face with water, once again checking his neck, but there was no tingling in John's fingers. After a few minutes he stopped.

"Is he going to live?" Rashid asked.

"I think so. He's very strong." John was not as sure as he sounded, but there was no point in scaring the boys. "At least he's out of the hot sun, and he's more comfortable."

The boys stared at their dangerous servant, wondering what he would do to them if he recovered and what their father would do to them if Hassan died.

John stood up and carefully surveyed the lake: the waterfowl had returned and there was no sign of any danger. He realized he had put a damper on the expedition and decided to make the best of the situation.

"I think Hassan is as safe as he can be. We can stay for a few hours." He smiled encouragingly, concealing his nagging worry about their safety.

The boys cheered up immediately. "We can swim in the lake. It's wonderfully cool," Saif said. Rashid looked hopefully at John.

"Good idea. But first, show me the temple."

They quickly watered the horses and tethered them in the shade. Birds were singing in the trees and around the lake the air was thick with insects. It was cool in the shade, but in the open the sun was merciless. They climbed the worn steps, shielding their eyes from the brightness and walked slowly into the imposing ruin, examining the stone carvings and commenting on the craftsmanship. Saif raced ahead and disappeared behind a pile of stones.

"He will jump out on us and see if he can scare us," Rashid said disapprovingly. "He is still a child."

John ruffled the boy's hair. "Whereas you're a warrior."

"I can use weapons and I am good with a bow. Hassan has taught me." Rashid smiled broadly. "Are you very good with a sword?"

"I can manage. I had a good teacher."

"Did he bully you?" He glanced back at Hassan who lay silently in the deep shade below them. Close by, the horses grazed contentedly.

John laughed. He remembered his long tuition with Ralph as one of the most enjoyable phases of his life. "No, he was my friend; there was no bullying." He wondered where Ralph was now. Had he survived the battle? If so, would he have remained in Antioch, waiting for John's return, or would he have moved on to Jerusalem? There was Gwen. Would she still be under the control of the Order, or would Ralph have taken her back to Cyprus? He imagined the two of them… He glanced quickly at Rashid, aware that he had spoken. "What did you say?"

"Is he dead? Your friend. Is he dead?"

"I hope not." He moved into the body of the temple. "He was always very lucky and very brave. I think he would have survived." He glanced down at his feet; stretched out across the floor was an intricate marble mosaic in a large square. It depicted a woman with a bow and arrow, hunting a stag with a large rack of antlers. She was dressed in a white robe tucked up above her knees, a quiver of arrows on her back, with a dog following her. Above them was a half moon. Around the edges of the mosaic were images of babies, dogs, and strange runes.

"Do you know who this is?" John pointed to the woman. She had flowing hair with a small crown on her head.

Rashid shrugged. "Some Greek queen?"

"No. This is Diana, the goddess of hunting. The Greeks called her Artemis, and she was thought to be the goddess of the forest, the moon and of mothers." He indicated the babies.

"What are these?" Rashid pointed to the runes.

"She was also the goddess of magic. Those are mystic signs."

"They are like the tattoo you have on the palm of your hand. Can I see?"

John turned up the palm of his right hand, and they both looked at the vivid inscription on his skin. The detail was bright and clear. It had not faded in the four years since he had received it, following his horrendous experience with the man with the twisted jaw. It all came back to him: the early magical events with Old Mary, the remarkable Owl, the mystical swords, and the inexplicable power that he occasionally felt. How could he ever explain these moments?

"Does that sign on your hand have something to do with the way you healed Saif?"

John was not sure how far he wanted this conversation to go. He looked fondly at Rashid. In the relatively short time John had been Ibrahim's prisoner, this young boy, the elder son, had become a man. "I think it does. Can you keep a secret?"

Rashid nodded his head. "I promise," he said seriously.

"I have no idea how I cure people. But I think this sign has something to do with it." He slowly shook his head. "I have discovered, Rashid, there are things that cannot be rationally explained: the chance meeting of people, the unexpected event, the power to cure and to survive almost certain death. I have experienced all of these things, but I am no wiser. I think I am a channel for a power I cannot control. I think it is a power for good."

The youth was staring; his face was a mask of concentration. "Should I tell this to Saif?"

"Perhaps not. I don't think he is old enough to understand."

Rashid smiled. He felt proud to be trusted with John's confession. "I will tell no one. You can rely on me."

"Good." He looked around. "I think this temple was dedicated to the goddess Diana. I prefer the name Diana to Artemis, it sounds more feminine," John said. He was keen to change the subject. "Look at that statue." He pointed to a partly destroyed figure at the far end of the temple. The life-sized figure of a woman had lost an arm, and someone had removed the head, which lay damaged on the floor. Even in decay, the face had a serene quality. "Nothing lasts forever, Rashid, remember that," John said, feeling at once unbelievably old.

It was a moment that would remain in Rashid's memory for all time. It was the first occasion that an adult, whom he revered, had treated him like a man. It was also the instant when his ordered existence changed forever. He looked back, admiring the light on the pillars, and noticed movement at the far end of the lake. He ran to the doorway, ducking behind a pillar and calling to John in a hushed voice.

"What is it?" John asked as he came up behind Rashid. Then he saw what the boy's acute vision had seen: a party of horsemen was coming out of the forest and slowly descending to the lake. They wore black robes.

"Assassins!" Rashid whispered, his voice shaking with fear.

"Quick!" John ordered. "Find Saif, and meet me at the back of the temple."

Without a word, Rashid ran off towards the back, as John scurried half-bent to the side of the building. In one area, near the front, the sidewall had collapsed leaving a pile of broken stone. He climbed through the gap and found himself high above the place where the horses were tethered; the same trees providing the shade had grown up against the massive blocks of stone that supported the floor of the temple. The thick cedar branches provided a possible way down as well as cover for his descent. He knew he had little time to debate the issue.

After checking his sword, he lowered himself onto a broad branch and holding on to those above, edged his way towards the trunk of the tree. It was a difficult climb down, made more precarious by the awkwardness of the sword, which entangled itself with small branches. By the time he was able to jump the last few feet to the soft ground, his clothes were torn and his legs and arms were grazed and bleeding.

During his descent he had considered the possibilities, and knew he had very little time. His first concern was for the boys: if he could get the horses to the back of the temple before the riders appeared, there was a good chance Saif and Rashid could flee the valley without the Assassins seeing them. He realized there was no way he could save Hassan: there was not enough time to heave his heavy body across a saddle. But if John left him under a tree with his horse by his side, the warriors might leave his unconscious body alone. It would certainly give them something to discuss, and would provide extra time for the boys to escape.

The horses were about ten paces away. John raced towards them, his mind focused on the problems of how to untie each animal quickly. He reached Celestial and was releasing the animal when a large figure, sword in hand, staggered out from behind the other horses.

John jumped back and instinctively drew his sword. He quickly realized it was Hassan, but the recognition did not encourage him. The bodyguard was still groggy, but his huge strength and hatred was enabling him to function in a way that would have been impossible for a weaker man. His eyes were red-rimmed with a manic gleam in them.

"Where are the boys?" he growled, edging closer.

"Assassins! There are Assassins coming." John's urgency had no effect on Hassan's deliberate advance.

He was like a nameless creature out of a nightmare: large, violent, and seemingly indestructible. His lips were drawn back, revealing clenched teeth and his breath came in loud gasps. Both hands gripped his sword, which he held in front of him; he limped forward in a rolling motion. "I will kill you, infidel," he hissed.

"The boys are safe," John insisted, slowly retreating. He knew if he could not persuade Hassan, he would have to fight him, providing a fascinating spectacle for the Assassins. "They're hiding behind the temple!"

Hassan raised his sword above his head and swung at John with a violent, but misjudged, movement. John dodged to the left. The bodyguard, unable to keep his balance, dropped heavily on one knee. He used his sword to force himself painfully up on his feet, his anger driving him like an enraged bull. It took a moment before he could locate John, who was standing behind him, pointing down the track. A look of amazement passed across Hassan's face as his coordination let him down. His mind was telling him he could attack this hateful foreigner, but his body was slow to respond.

"Hassan!" John yelled. He could hear the sound of the horsemen behind him, and there was no longer any point in hiding his presence from them. "Assassins!" he screamed, pointing frantically down the narrow path.

The warrior paused, and his face slowly cleared. The mad gleam faded in his eyes as he suddenly realized what John was screaming. He looked down the path as the first of the black robed riders galloped into view. Rubbing his face with his free hand, he shook his head slowly from side to side. "No!" he roared, grabbing his shield from the side of his horse and lumbering onto the narrow path. "Assassins!" He took no further notice of John, but concentrated on the advancing horsemen. These were his lifetime enemies. He would enjoy killing them.

Other riders appeared behind the first horseman, urging him on from behind. He drew his sword and raced towards Hassan. The big man blocked the path, wielding his sword in his right hand and thrusting his shield forwards with his left; he lurched forward, screaming like a maniac. The first horse skidded to a near stop, reared up on its back legs, lost its balance, and crashed down, crushing its rider. There was immediate chaos as riders and horses entangled each other. One rider leapt from his mount, pushing his way round the first horse, which was frantically kicking out as it tried to regain its feet. The Assassin lunged at Hassan, who deflected the blow with his shield, following through with a mighty swipe that knocked the fighter to the ground. Another rider forced his mount into the reeds in order to squeeze past the mêlée, but the left side of the horse sank into the mud, causing the warrior to be momentarily off balance, allowing Hassan to dispatch him with a single slashing stroke. Most of the riders were unable to see clearly what was happening, obstructing each other in their eagerness to fight. Hassan took full advantage of their confusion.

John mounted Celestial, released the other horses, and led them towards the side of the temple. He glanced back, relieved to see Hassan wreaking havoc on his enemies. He was advancing relentlessly along the narrow path, his sword cutting a swath through the seething mass of men and beasts. Further back, beyond the immediate fray, John saw an Assassin draw his bow. "Good luck, Hassan!" he yelled, as he broke into a trot, steering the boys' horses through the trees and up the steep slope. He left Hassan's horse behind, although he knew he was unlikely to need it.

The ground rose abruptly. Leaning forward in the saddle he urged Celestial up the steep incline by the side of the temple. Despite his predicament, he noticed how the ancient builders had made good use of the contours of the land, building a high platform at the front to allow the majestic wide steps to stretch down to the lake, and lessening the height of the platform as it moved back into the hill. At the rear of the temple, it was possible to gain access to the building through what had once been a back entrance, but was now a level pile of rubble. John rapidly assessed this as he rounded the corner, where the boys were waiting anxiously for him. Without hesitation, they both ran forward and scrambled onto their horses.

"Rashid. You lead the way. Saif, follow your brother. Travel as fast as you can, and do not stop for anything." He was speaking quickly, but trying to smile encouragingly at the same time.

"What about you?" Rashid asked anxiously.

"I'll be following, after I have delayed them a bit."

"By yourself?" Saif asked.

"Hassan has recovered. He's holding them off for the moment." The boys exchanged worried glances. "There won't be many left by the time he's finished with them," he joked. "Remember,

KEEPER OF THE GRAIL

don't stop. Rashid, you are responsible for your brother, and I am responsible for both of you."

Saif regarded him with big eyes. "Will I see you again?"

"Of course you will, Saif." John patted them both on their shoulders. "Now go! God speed, and warn your father!"

They both nodded their heads, unable to answer. Rashid led the way up a steep track, closely followed by Saif. After a few paces he turned, giving a short wave, his dark eyes full of fear. John waved back. The two horses quickly disappeared into the forest which stretched up to the end of the valley. As he turned his horse, John felt a deep sense of loss welling up inside of him, uncomfortably certain he would never see the boys again.

He urged Celestial over the rubble, onto the floor of the temple. In moments he was looking down at the lake. On his left he could see the last stages of what had been a furious battle: Hassan was still standing, but his head was bowed; he was covered in blood. In his right hand he still held his dangerous sword and those facing him were keeping a safe distance. Around him lay many horsemen; a few were motionless, others were slowly crawling away, nursing their wounds. Some horses lay on their sides, or stood trembling, their saddles empty. Hassan had two arrows in his left shoulder. He had dropped his shield, but in spite of these wounds and the overwhelming numbers, he had successfully prevented the Assassins from reaching the temple, proving to be more than a match for these feared desert warriors. Eventually, they outflanked him. As John watched, a group of soldiers attacked from behind, rushing out of the trees, throwing their spears at his undefended body. One penetrated the leather armour in the centre of his back and a second lodged in his thigh. Hassan's sword dropped out of his lifeless hand. He fell to his knees, gradually toppling over to one side, where he lay motionless.

The warriors nearest to the dead bodyguard went silent, breathing heavily and resting on their weapons. Others approached cautiously, standing around the body, staring at their fallen enemy with a mixture of curiosity and awe. After a long pause, a warrior bent down and picked up Hassan's sword. He held it high in the air, letting out a raucous cheer taken up by the whole group.

Their voices echoed around the valley, as the last of the Assassins arrived.

John felt a lump in his throat. He had never liked Hassan, but the bodyguard had fought bravely, sacrificing himself to save the sons of his lifelong friend. Celestial snorted impatiently, reminding John of the need for action. He knew many of the Assassins would have seen him departing with two horses in tow, and if any of those had survived the battle, it would not be long before they were in pursuit. His first reaction was to attack them while they were unprepared, to create a temporary distraction, but with no armour, no shield, and only a sword and a dagger, he knew it would be a futile gesture; his main purpose must be to draw them away while the boys raced for home. From his vantage point, he could see a path running along the other side of the lake. It looked more overgrown than the one they had used when they entered the valley, but almost certainly joined up with it at the far end.

He took a deep breath and rode the horse carefully down the wide stone steps of the temple in a diagonal direction, towards the other side of the water. Almost immediately, he was noticed. A shout went up, followed by a roar of anger, as the Assassins saw another enemy trying to escape. Those on foot raced towards the steps, many carrying bows, while the horsemen forced their way past the carnage in front of them.

John reached the path as an arrow dropped into the reeds nearby. In spite of the danger, he raised himself up on his stirrups waving his sword above his head, yelling some of the Arabic words used by Ibrahim's goat herders when their flocks caused problems. He was not entirely certain of their literal translation, but guessed they were highly insulting. The effect on the warriors was instantaneous. As he galloped off, he glanced back to see outraged Assassins riding their horses into the lake in front of the steps, only to discover the water was too deep, forcing them to swim. Others were urging their mounts to cross along the stone steps, getting in the way of the archers, preventing them from seeing their target.

He was soon out of range of the arrows and half way down the lake, before the first horseman reached the path behind him. If he could maintain his lead, he intended to continue round the lake and join the track that led out of the valley. It would provide a perfect place to fight a rearguard action if the warriors came too close. John's confidence sagged however, when he became aware of a large band of horsemen galloping along the path on the other side, only a few lengths behind him. Although he was in front on his side, they would certainly reach the track that led out of the valley before he could gallop around the top of the lake. He would be trapped between the two groups.

Celestial rounded a bend in the path, and skidded to a halt. A large pine had fallen across the path, its trunk hidden in the forest, its ragged branches splayed out, forming an impenetrable barrier. With no time to consider the limited alternatives, John returned his sword to its scabbard, and wheeling round, headed up into the dense trees. The horse forced its way through the tangled undergrowth, while John kept low in the saddle, trying, in vain, to avoid the low hanging, spiky branches. With a sixth sense, Celestial found a way up the increasingly steep hill, using animal tracks, taking advantage of gaps caused by fallen trees.

John felt a sense of unreality as the bright sunlight of the path gave way to the gloomy darkness of the forest. It was cool and damp, and there was an absence of bird song. Large trees grew close together, their high branches forming a dense canopy, allowing only the occasional shaft of light to penetrate the obscurity. Behind, he could hear the distant yelling and crashing of men and horses as they attempted to follow him. Somewhere to his left, some large creature fled away, the sound of its departure loud in the surrounding silence. In the half-light he lost his sense of time and direction, relying on Celestial to find its own way out of the valley.

Without warning, the hill levelled off, the trees thinned, and soon he was back in the dazzling sunlight, on a broad plateau, with the moist, hidden valley behind. In front and on both sides the dry land spread out before him, with bushes and palms growing only in shallow depressions, the heat rising up from the baked rocks. The change was dramatic. He paused to remove twigs and pine needles from his hair while he looked about.

He was aware of the faint sounds of his pursuers, as they fought their way up the hillside, and was glad they had not given up. If he could occupy them for another hour or two, then the boys should get home safely. The sun was on his left, and assuming it was mid to late afternoon, he was able to work out the direction he wanted to travel. John turned to the right, setting off at a canter towards a small rise about half a mile away. He decided to lead the Assassins towards the north and west. Only later would he try to ride east and cut across the path the boys would have taken. When he reached the rise he stopped, and although Celestial pawed the ground impatiently, John sat easily in the saddle, facing the spot on the rim of the valley where he had emerged.

After a short while, riders began to appear out of the distant trees, like a plague of black spiders. Some were weaving about as they waited for orders, while others sat staring at him, assessing the distance, appraising the large black horse on which he sat. When John was convinced he had their attention, he drew his sword, holding it up, deliberately allowing the sinking sun to reflect off the blade, sending a challenge to the assembling warriors.

He sheathed the sword as the Assassins broke into a ragged charge. Their small, sturdy horses leaped forward like hounds, each rider determined to have the glory of making the kill. John turned and galloped away, keeping low in the saddle, allowing the reins to go slack. It was up to Celestial now, and he wondered how long the big animal could outrun the desert horses, whose reputation for endurance was second to none. When he reached another mound, he glanced behind; the pursuers were no nearer, and focusing on a distant hill, he relaxed into the saddle.

CHAPTER 11

NIGHT WAS FALLING AS Sir Payen de Montdidier returned to his castle at Al Marqab. The search party had failed to find Gwen and the English sergeant, yet Payen was not dissatisfied with the result. The expedition had given him the chance to observe the behaviour of Sir Raymond de Wulfric, and the young knight had disliked what he had seen. From the moment Gwen's disappearance had been discovered this senior knight of the Order had bullied, ranted, and demonstrated such an uncontrolled anger that Payen was convinced Gwen was safer in the desert with her soldier, than to be returned to the doubtful security of a fanatic.

As they reached the main gate, Raymond turned to stare balefully back at the darkening desert. "We leave at first light tomorrow!" he bellowed. "And this time we will take enough supplies to enable us to complete a proper search to find the Maid."

"My Lord, we could have taken enough supplies today, if you had not been in such a hurry to leave," Payen replied sardonically.

"We should have found her today! Your so-called tracker couldn't find a jakes in a castle." He glared at Ishmael who stared back, his dark eyes unblinking, his olive face revealing nothing.

"I think it best if we continue our discussion inside," Payen said quietly, leading the way into the castle. Payen dismounted, handed his horse to a servant, and bowed slightly towards Ishmael, who returned the gesture. Ignoring Raymond, he bounded up the stairs to the refectory.

There was a mutinous silence in the courtyard as Raymond laboriously dismounted. His three soldiers, who had been forced to share two horses, were exhausted, each having taken turns to lead the injured horse. They handed their mounts to the servants and exchanged knowing looks with their friends. The young guide quickly merged with the Arab servants, who kept a safe distance from this tall and fearsome knight. Raymond cast a contemptuous glance at them, concentrating, with difficulty, on not staggering while leaving the courtyard. He had been suffering throughout the day in the saddle of a horse unsuited for his large physique, and was painfully aware that it had been many weeks since he had ridden so far. Gritting his teeth and staring straight ahead, he strode heavily towards the steps, where he paused, gripped his sword, and climbed slowly up the stone stairs.

"The bastard can hardly walk," observed one of the soldiers.

"I hope 'e rots in Hell."

"With luck, 'e won't be fit to ride tomorrow."

"Don't ye believe it. That devil's indestructible."

The soldiers continued to bicker and complain. Shoving the servants out of the way, they trudged off to find a much-needed drink.

In the refectory, the servants had laid out a simple meal and a jug of wine. Payen poured himself a cup, pausing before reluctantly filling a second for Raymond. He took a deep breath, blew out through his mouth, and gradually relaxed as he appreciated the wine's bouquet. After swirling the deep red liquid around the cup, he drained it, his eyes closing as he enjoyed the sensation. He refilled his cup as Raymond appeared in the doorway. Payen silently indicated the wine, before turning to stare out of the window.

"You'll have to find another guide." Raymond emptied the cup and helped himself to the wine jug. "That idiot you insisted on believing, led us astray. We'd have found them if we'd gone in the direction I wanted to go." He was conscious that he was sounding like a whiner, but his indignation, coupled with his aching joints, made him less circumspect than was his usual behaviour.

Payen did not reply but continued to stare down at the harbour.

"We need more horses," Raymond muttered. He limped up to the table and noticed the meatless meal. "Get someone to kill a goat or catch a bird, even a fish would be better than dates, figs and cheese." He helped himself to more wine. "I've had nothing but swill on the ship, and a man needs meat if he is going to survive in this God-forsaken place!"

Payen smiled. "You're talking about the Holy Land, my Lord. Hardly God-forsaken."

Raymond scowled and cut himself a hunk of bread. "We must find Mistress Gwen. I am responsible to my Order for her safekeeping. She is more important than you can imagine." He glowered at Payen who did not appear to be listening.

"There is another large ship entering the harbour. A galley. It looks like we have company."

"Do you recognize the ship?" Raymond demanded. He limped over and gazed malevolently down at the port, which was only just visible in the fading light. His curiosity changed to anger as he watched the galley store its oars and anchor close to his ship. "What are they up to?"

"I imagine it must contain soldiers from Christendom. You needn't worry. I'm convinced they are not pirates."

"What makes you so sure?"

"Pirates would not enter in that way." Payen spoke confidently. He had made it his business to learn the ways of the local people. He knew there would have been an obvious reaction if an unknown craft had entered the harbour. "Very few traders use galleys, they are too difficult to man, and they don't carry enough cargo. They are most useful for quickly transporting soldiers, especially as they don't rely on the weather."

"Where do you think it comes from?" Raymond's voice betrayed his anxiety.

Darkness soon blotted out the harbour and only a few flickering lights could be seen. Payen left the window, and picking up a lighted candle from the table, moved carefully around the room lighting the others. "I know there is one galley for hire in St. Symeon."

"St. Symeon?" Raymond almost choked on his wine. "I was not told there was a galley. I could have been in Jerusalem by now!"

The young knight relaxed in a chair and regarded Raymond over the rim of his cup. "I imagine whoever arranged your transportation was more concerned with the lady's comfort." He was keen to move the discussion around to Gwen, as he was certain she would not have fled the security of the castle unless she wanted to escape from Raymond, or from the secret organization he represented.

"You think this galley has come from St. Symeon?

"Almost certainly."

"You must send down a servant to discover who is aboard. Immediately!"

"It's almost impossible. The path is difficult by day, and dangerous at night. I will not impose on my servants or my men to undertake such a life-threatening mission that can wait until first light. Nothing is going to change during the hours of darkness."

"Then I will send one of my men!"

Payen gave an affected yawn. "Your three men are either unconscious with exhaustion, or drunk."

Raymond could not escape the awful logic of the situation. He fought down his desire to thrash this self-righteous prig who seemed to be enjoying his frustration. He drank another cup, his back to Payen. "Tomorrow, at first light, you will send a servant to discover who is on that galley."

"Perhaps you will want to travel down and assess the situation for yourself. After all, you are in need of more soldiers to search for the maid, and it might be possible to hire donkeys from the villagers." Raymond turned and glared at him. "Better than walking," Payen smiled.

After pacing the room in an agitated silence, Raymond sank onto a stool, focusing on the problems. He had to find Gwen; to accomplish the task he needed more men and more horses. It was important to restart the search as soon as possible and the galley could be a blessing or bane. In his worst nightmare, he imagined the galley might contain the accursed Lord Ralph d'Escosse, or other knights who sided with him. Raymond knew of d'Escosse's reputation as a talented leader; he knew he had been sent by King Henry to report on the intentions of the Order, and he was worried about d'Escosse's questionable association with Gwen. What had seemed an innocent visit to this castle had turned into a disaster. His status in the Order and his ardent wish to have the glory of entering Jerusalem with Gwen by his side, were both threatened.

"Why do you think Mistress Gwen fled the safety of your

protection?" Payen asked. His voice was uncritical, as though he were discussing the weather.

Interrupted in his reverie, Raymond sprang to his feet. "How the Hell should I know!" he thundered. He reminded Payen of an enraged bull as he rushed awkwardly across the room, his limp betraying the agony of his stiff joints. He stopped by the door. "Be ready at first light!" he roared.

Payen watched him go, before sauntering over to the doorway. He beckoned to a servant in the staircase. "Find Ishmael. Tell him I need him, now." The servant nodded and raced down to the courtyard. After undoing his sword belt and removing his chain-mail vest, he slumped down on a seat by the table, quickly devouring a makeshift supper. A few minutes later, Ishmael appeared in the doorway. He was a slim young man, of medium height, with the graceful movements of a cat.

"My Lord?"

"Ishmael. Come in and sit down." Payen spoke to him as to a friend, not as a servant. He gestured to a seat at the table, and indicated the food. There was an amicable silence as Ishmael sat and selected some dates. "Tell me what you think."

"They were in that valley, my Lord. I caught a glimpse of them watching us."

"Where do you think they'll go?"

"I am sure they would have followed along the same valley, and aimed south once they were close to the sea. But it is possible they were prevented.

"How so?"

"After we had left the narrow valley, we turned south for a long distance until you were able to convince that barbarian there was no trail to follow. On the return, as we came to the opening of the narrow valley on our left, I saw evidence of many horsemen who had recently crossed our previous path and headed along that same valley."

"Who do you think they were?"

"Almost certainly Assassins, my Lord." He chewed meditatively on an olive.

Payen passed his hand over his head, gently rubbing the

cropped hair. "Assassins?" He pursed his lips. He knew about these fanatical warriors who occupied a large area between the Principality of Antioch and the County of Tripoli. They were ruthless fighters, who would kill Arabs and Turks as easily as they would attack the infidels from other lands. Powerful tribal leaders paid the Assassins' demands, rather than risk being stabbed in their own beds. Only rarely did these men in black robes fight pitched battles, preferring to murder those who opposed them, creating a fearsome reputation for themselves. They were known to have a well-tuned spy network, which further enhanced the general belief in their invincibility. Local people spoke of them in hushed whispers; leaders doubled their guards if they wished to oppose the Assassins.

"There have been reports of a large camp near where we were searching."

"What would have happened to Gwen and this sergeant if they were caught?"

Ishmael wiped his hands on his smock. "The Assassins would take them prisoner and see if they were worth a ransom. If no money was offered, my Lord, their lives would be short."

"I think we must hope Gwen and her soldier avoided the Assassins." He pushed a jug of water towards Ishmael, who never drank wine. "Assuming they avoided capture, what would you have done if, like them, you saw the Assassins passing by? Where would you go?"

"If I was them, I would travel back towards Antioch and hope to meet some friendly forces on the way." He drank some of the water. "Perhaps, my Lord, you would wish me to search for signs of them by myself?"

"Good. You are more likely to find their trail without Sir Raymond harassing you." He paused. "However, I want you to take someone with you. I have few horses, so whether you take one or two will make no difference. Make sure you leave before first light."

Ishmael nodded his agreement, and stood up. "My Lord, if I find them, should I do anything?"

Payen gripped Ishmael's arm. "Give them any help you can. May God go with you."

They bowed to each other and Ishmael vanished silently into the dim corridor.

. . .

"I KNEW IT WAS too good to be true," Sir Vernon muttered as he looked at the parchment in front of him. He had only been in charge for four and a half days, and already there was a summons to appear before the Governor. He wondered which of his small escapades had reached de Maron's ears. There had been a minor upset with Ralph's quartermaster, whom Vernon had suspected of stealing from the stores. This had resulted in some heated words, and the previously trusted soldier had departed in high dudgeon. Later, Vernon had tried to energize the guards, despite warnings by his squire and his armourer, by insisting on a full inspection in the heat of the day. This had not gone well, revealing his gross inexperience. Finally, there was the business with the pretty girl in the kitchen. He blanched. Surely, that couldn't have got back to the Governor?

He tightened his sword belt, checked his appearance, and with his helmet under his arm, marched out on to the airy landing. "Watch my back while I'm away," he said to Philip, who never knew what duties he might be called upon to perform. "Oh, and tell Giles to keep his hands off the cook." He winked at his squire, remembered the reason for his departure, choked on his humour, and with a worried face clattered down the wide staircase.

As he crossed to the main door, the pretty girl from the kitchen appeared and gave him a broad smile. He stopped, unable to decide if she was happy to see him, or triumphant that he was going to pay for his little indiscretion. He nodded awkwardly in her direction, coughed self-consciously, and walked into the closed door with a resounding crash.

A moment later, the door was tentatively opened as the guard outside came to investigate the noise. He was one of the soldiers who had suffered the inspection. "All right are ye, Sir?" he asked, a big grin forming on his grimy face.

"Thank you, soldier. That will be all," Vernon snapped. He went out of the door and marched towards the front gate. A number of guards formed up to attention as he approached. He had the distinct impression that they were being amused by something going on behind him. Turning quickly, he saw the guard at the front door suddenly snap to attention, his right hand furiously rubbing his nose.

"Corporal!" he yelled as he marched past the gate "The guard at the front door... put him on duties. I want a report when I return." Red faced, and trying to prevent his sword tripping him up, he marched down the road, kicking up dust as he went.

"What a pillock," one of the soldiers remarked.

"I hear he be mighty good with a sword and a knife," another replied.

"All officers are pillocks."

There was a general murmur of agreement.

· · ·

"WHERE IS LORD D'ESCOSSE?" Sir Maurice de Maron demanded. He was poring over a large rudimentary map on a table, surrounded by a crowd of knights, many of whom Vernon had never met. He stood to attention, overawed by the number of important people whom he believed were gathered to witness his trial and condemnation.

"I believe you sent for me, Sir?" He resisted the desire to blow out his cheeks.

"No, Sir Vernon, I sent for the leader of the English forces." The governor was at a loss with this young man. He was never sure whether he was just a brave but inexperienced knight, or a total nincompoop. "Why has d'Escosse sent you?"

Vernon felt a wave of relief pass over him. The Governor did not intend to demote him or review his recent problems. He must have misread the message. Vernon's face relaxed and took on the appearance of a lovesick idiot.

"Well?"

"Ah!" Vernon quickly refocused his mind. "I'm in temporary charge, Sir." As he completed his sentence he remembered Ralph's absence was supposed to be a secret.

"I mean, he asked me to attend this meeting on his behalf, Sir."

"Why?" It was clear the Governor was not pleased.

"Why?" Vernon regained his wide-eyed village-idiot look. "Well, um, because he, um, he…."

The Governor had serious matters to attend to, and he was conscious of a ripple of sniggers and grunts from the assembled knights. He advanced threateningly towards Vernon, determined to wring an answer from him. At that moment, the door burst open and Sir Raoul de Warren, High Lord of the Knights of the Order, strode in followed by a dozen others.

"Sir Maurice." He bowed in a perfunctory manner. "I understand there is an emergency?" He glanced around the room, recognizing many of the other knights. "Sir William." He nodded to Sir William de Bracy, the Governor's most senior knight.

"Indeed, Sir Raoul, we do have a problem. Let me explain with the help of this map," Maurice indicated the table. Both men were being scrupulously polite to each other, but there was a tension between the junior knights, who did not understand the way high politics was played. Raoul advanced with an affected swagger, and stood next to the Governor. The rest of the knights, of both sides, formed an outer circle around the two men, their eyes fixed on the Governor's hand as he began to point to the main features on the map. Vernon was forgotten. His relief was so great that for a moment he wondered if he could slip away unnoticed. Quickly, he regained his courage and silently positioned himself where he could best view the table.

"We have had reports that there has been a large gathering of Assassins around the area of Marqab." There was a loud intake of air; the knights had heard of the Assassins. The Governor pointed to the area on the map. "This could be in preparation for an attack on the County of Tripoli, or even on Tripoli itself."

"The Assassins rarely, if ever, attack in strength," Sir Raoul declared, and looked around for support. "They are famed, or should it be feared, as creatures who murder in the night." He smiled with his mouth as he returned his gaze to the Governor.

"Normally, they never gather in the numbers our reports suggest, but I cannot believe they would assemble in hundreds to kill a single person in the middle of the night, my Lord." The Governor smiled humourlessly at Raoul. "So, I can only assume they are not after a man, but a city or a County." It was a fine verbal retort, and the High Lord scowled and focused his eyes on the map.

"The second set of reports refers to the monster who attacked our forces some weeks ago as they attempted to march to Tripoli. Many of you were there." Sir Maurice had everyone's attention. "It is believed that this giant with the red hair leads a large force from the area of Damascus, and that they intend to attack Tripoli. In other words it looks like a concerted attack."

Sir Vernon craned his head forward to look at the map. His geography was minimal; having reached Antioch he had done little to improve his knowledge of the area. Looking at the map, he could see that Tripoli was on the coast and approximately one third of the way, as the bird flies, from Antioch to Jerusalem. He listened intently as Sir Maurice indicated that Marqab was an important coastal castle, situated over a small village and harbour, over half way between Antioch and Tripoli. He had heard of Damascus, but was not aware that it was a large inland city and just over half way from Antioch to Jerusalem. Although he had often heard people talk about the Holy City, he had never understood that Jerusalem, the city of David, famous in the Bible, was more than fifty miles inland and situated just west of the northern end of the Dead Sea. It was just over two hundred and fifty miles from Antioch to Jerusalem, but only if you were a bird.

"We've had a message from King Baldwin," Maurice continued. "He asks us to assemble our largest army and march down to Tripoli to prevent the enemy from taking that strategically important city." He looked round at the assembled knights, trying to ignore Vernon's eager face. "If the enemy succeeds in taking Tripoli, they would effectively have cut the Crusader Empire in half. It must not happen!"

The knights cheered, stamped their boots, and hammered on the table. Vernon was so excited that he pushed forward until he was at the table facing the Governor on the other side. "We'll smack 'em one!" he yelled. Then, realizing it was not the language

of a knight, he added, in a subdued voice, "You can count on me…
Sir."

"Ah, Sir Vernon," Maurice said, in a distinctly patronizing tone.
"I'm sure you've met Sir Raoul de Warren, the High Lord of the
Knights of the Order."

Sir Raoul nodded his head, mystified at the introduction.

"Sir Vernon is the acting head of the English forces!" There
was almost a tone of jubilation in the Governor's voice, and a look
of blank disbelief on Raoul's. "I understand, Sir Vernon, you can
make the necessary decisions regarding our march to Tripoli?"

The excitement of the situation had suddenly evaporated.
Vernon felt as though an iron hand was gripping his throat. He
was quite convinced that Lord d'Escosse had not intended him to
do anything more than be a presence in the mansion and pretend
his Lord was otherwise engaged. Suddenly, in the time it had
taken him to say, "You can count on me," the world had changed.
He stared at the Governor, like a rabbit facing a stoat and was at a
loss for words. "Sir," was all he was able to say.

"I'll take that as a yes," the Governor turned to Sir Raoul. "Can
I rely on your forces?"

"Certainly." The Grand Master's dour expression belied the
excitement he felt. Very recently, he had received confirmation
that Sir Raymond, after reclaiming Mistress Gwen, had decided
to take her to Jerusalem without the agreement of the Order.
Raoul had received news of the unnatural calm on the sea, and of
its effect on shipping. He was convinced it would have delayed Sir
Raymond. The entry into Jerusalem was a sensitive issue, and he
was amazed that Sir Raymond, the second most important knight
in the Holy Land, would have acted in this way. He could only
assume the wondrous Maid, who was soon to raise the Order to
unparalleled heights, had affected Raymond's judgment. If anyone
was to benefit from the reintroduction of this glorious member of
the most powerful family in the Holy Land, it was going to be
the Grand Master. Now, thanks to this news, he had a legitimate
reason for moving his forces down south. Once he had settled
what he considered a minor problem with the Assassins, he would
continue on to Jerusalem. He did not believe the reports that the

Giant was back in the picture. His intelligence had confirmed the Giant had fled back to the Damascus area, but had also indicated that his battered army had evaporated as a fighting force. "We could be ready to march at first light, tomorrow, Sir Maurice." He had spent the previous hours arranging for a strong force of his Knights of the Order to travel down to Jerusalem, but had yet to give the order. Now, all would fall into place. Once in Jerusalem, he would relieve Sir Raymond of his duties.

"Can the English forces be ready by tomorrow?" De Maron frowned at Sir Vernon, unable to believe that a commander of such ability as Lord d'Escosse had put his faith in such a ridiculous knight. But it did appear to mean less division at this emergency meeting between the English commander and the Order. It was an open secret that the English King had sent d'Escosse to keep watch on the activities of the Order, and d'Escosse and De Warren disliked each other intensely, especially since the disappearance of the young woman, known as Mistress Gwen.

The Governor's frown increased as he watched Vernon appear to ponder the question. The young knight was rubbing his forehead and staring fixedly at the map. Sir Maurice could only assume that Vernon had talents that he had not been revealed during his brief service in the Holy Land; certainly, Lady Elizabeth had found him likeable. It occurred to the Governor that his wife liked all the young knights who worked for him. He put aside these unwelcome thoughts as he waited for Vernon's delayed response. "Well?"

De Kari looked up. He felt like a condemned prisoner. There was no way out. He had briefly considered feigning illness or losing his voice, but he knew he had to answer. "Yes, Sir Maurice. I have reviewed the situation carefully, and in spite of the short notice, I believe our forces can be ready to leave at first light." There was a murmur of surprise and encouragement from the surrounding knights, most of who towered above him; even the Governor had stopped frowning, and had raised his eyebrows in near amazement. Vernon was delighted with the way he had handled the situation. Suddenly, he had exchanged the role of the buffoon for the position of the experienced commander.

If he could have rested on his laurels, all would have been well, at least at the meeting. But, with a flash of knightly bravado, he added: "Sir Maurice, as this could be a risky campaign, I'd better pop round and say goodbye to Lady Elizabeth."

He bowed, and marched defiantly towards the door, sublimely unaware that the red-faced, fleshy Governor was grinding his teeth.

CHAPTER 12

THEY STOPPED TO REST their horses as the sun erupted on their right. During the dark hours, the path had turned north and Martin was confident that they were heading in the right direction for Antioch. In spite of his optimism, he knew they were in a dilemma: either they used this well-worn path and hoped to avoid meeting unfriendly forces, or they left the path and risked getting lost or falling prey to wild animals.

"I reckons we'll stop 'ere for a while, an' then press on until it gets too hot," Martin said. He carefully checked the trail in both directions, slowly running his eyes along the rocky hills surrounding them. "Can't see no one about."

"Good." Gwen slowly dismounted and stretched her arms in a languid manner. With her eyes closed and her black hair gleaming in the bright rays of the rising sun, she was the most attractive woman Martin had ever seen. He paused in the act of dismounting, unable to draw his eyes away. Gwen yawned and began to run on the spot, massaging her thighs as she did so. "Oh, I needed to get out of that saddle," she said.

"Ye be all right then?" Martin murmured. He dismounted and absent-mindedly rubbed the muzzle of his horse.

"I've never felt better." She gave him a dazzling smile. "Tired, but happy." She took a drink from her water flask. "I think this is the first time for more than three years that I have felt truly free of the Order. Not one of them knows where I am!" Her smile faded. "They seem to think they have the right to control my life. They educated me, guarded me, and always with the intention of taking me to Jerusalem."

"Why's that then?"

"They have never fully explained. They say I'm important. They hint that I come from an influential family and that I will soon have a life of power and wealth. But, I don't want those things. I want to be free to lead my own life." She offered her flask to Martin. "You have no idea how grateful I am to you, Martin. You have always been my friend, and without you, nobody would have known where the Order had taken me. The Knights see me as some sort of commodity to be used as they see fit."

Martin glowed and took a small sip of the water. He did not know what a commodity was, but if Gwen was grateful to him, it was all that mattered. "Ye been my friend too, an' friends need to look after each other." He felt his cheeks burning, and taking the reins of his horse he led the way towards an opening between some large rocks. "We best get off this trail, just in case." He did not want to worry her unnecessarily. "I don't reckon them horsemen in black be looking for us, but best not take any chances."

She patted her horse, and smiled at his retreating back. "I realize we could be in a lot of danger. But you mustn't worry about me, Martin. I can look after myself, and together we will get back to Antioch safely. Mark my words." She followed behind, leading her tired horse and aware she was being wildly optimistic.

"That's good then," Martin said contentedly. He stopped in the shadow of a large jagged boulder that dominated a wide blind gully. The sun was slowly illuminating one side, leaving the other in deep shade "We should be cool enough 'ere for a couple of hours. Then, we can push on a bit."

They unsaddled the horses, and allowed them a long tether so they could browse the desert bushes that lined their makeshift camp. "Ye can tell them be local beasts," Martin observed. "The ones I used to ride at Linford Mill were bigger and good for pullin' carts, but they wouldn't last long out 'ere." He unpacked a saddlebag and sitting on a broad, flat rock, distributed some hard bread and some soft cheese. Gwen joined him with a water bag and watched with friendly amusement, as Martin tucked into the basic meal with a ravenous intensity.

"What'll ye do when we gets to Antioch?" he asked, as he chewed vigorously.

Gwen took a long drink of water. "I hope we'll join up with Ralph and go back to England. I know he would find you a job." She noticed the uncertain look in Martin's eyes. "That is, unless you want to get back to your father's mill?"

Martin chewed thoughtfully on the bread. After a short pause he glanced across at her. "What do ye think ye'll do?" he asked tentatively.

"I don't know." She did not want to mention John. She remembered how negatively Martin had reacted in Cyprus when she had told him of John's unexpected reappearance. If he were dead, there was nothing to be gained by discussing him with Martin. "I know Ralph would offer me a home, but I..." she shrugged, "I don't know what I'll do. What I do know is that I will never again allow the Knights of the Order to offer their so-called protection." She was about to expand on that theme, when one of their horses whinnied loudly and almost immediately the other joined in; both began pulling at their tethers, their eyes wide with terror.

Martin was on his feet in a bound. He pulled on his gauntlets and drew his sword, and after putting a finger to his mouth, rushed over to calm the anxious horses.

Gwen darted over to join him. "What is it?" she whispered; she felt for the dagger at her waist.

"Don't know," Martin whispered back. "Might be a lion? I heard they 'ave some around 'ere."

They stood together, unmoving, their eyes searching the edges of the gully for any sign of movement. Suddenly, from among rocks at the other side of the frantic horses, they heard the deep, menacing growl of a large predatory animal.

"Get behin' me," Martin ordered. He moved back very slowly, holding his sword in both hands, his eyes searching the dark recesses of the rocks. The horses smelt the creature and reared up in panic, pulling free of their tethers. Gwen's horse turned sharply and bolted towards her. She lunged for its reins as it careered past, but was knocked aside, and fell heavily to the ground, narrowly missing the pounding hooves. She was badly winded and for a moment could not take a breath, but rolled on the hard ground, holding her arms around her stomach with her knees bent up towards her chin.

Martin's horse reared up once more before racing for the opening in the gully, and as its front hooves began to descend, there was a dark blur as a huge lion bounded over the rocks and landed on top of the horse, forcing it to the ground and biting deeply into its vulnerable neck. Amid the screaming of the horse and the triumphant blood-roar of the lion, Gwen could hear Martin's angry bellow. He rushed forward, his sword level with his shoulder, intending to drive the creature away before the horse was mortally wounded. But his horse was between him and the lion, and as he tried to position himself, the dying creature forced itself to its feet in a last attempt to shake off its attacker, causing Martin to leap back. The horse staggered and collapsed, its legs convulsing in a final spasm, with the powerful cat still sucking the lifeblood from its throat.

By jumping to his left, Martin found himself behind the lion as it fought to control its prey. He raised his sword in a two-handed grip and swung the weapon down with great force, intending to behead the creature. At the last moment, the lion became aware of its danger and with unbelievable speed whirled round as the blade approached, and succeeded in avoiding the deathblow. The sword cut deeply into its shoulder and, although maimed, the lion launched itself at Martin, almost without a pause. It was four hundred pounds of muscle, bone and uncontrolled ferocity, and its pain and anger blinded it to anything beyond its immediate compulsion to kill its enemy.

Martin barely had time to bring his sword into a defensive position before the injured creature attacked. The blood was pumping out of its left shoulder, and it sprang forward on its mighty back legs, as though propelled from a catapult. He was a big man, immensely strong, and had never been bested in a fight, but Martin knew fear for the first time. He had a vision of a cavernous mouth, large bloodstained teeth and murderous eyes and one large clawed paw. He jumped to his left, slashing out wildly, knowing there would be no second chance. His sword dug deep into the chest of the lion, and it fell heavily onto its injured side, but not before the sharp talons on its right paw had raked across Martin's face.

He could barely see, his face was a mass of blood, but he hacked furiously at the fallen animal, carried on by an unrelenting need to protect Gwen at all costs. Eventually, his strength failed him, and reason returned. He dropped his sword, and slowly removed his gauntlets. There was blood in his eyes, and he gently tried to clear them. In a dim, watery haze he could just discern the lifeless bodies of the lion and his horse, and beyond, at the far edge of his limited vision, he glimpsed Gwen: she was rolling slowly on the ground, her arms clasped around herself.

It was at that moment, the second lion attacked. Martin was trying to focus, his fingers gently rubbing his scarred eyes, when he was knocked down violently from behind. His chain mail vest prevented the sharp claws from penetrating his shoulders, but his large, hairy head was unprotected from the assault of the lion's powerful jaws. Martin fought bravely, twisting his body in a frantic attempt to break free of the awful teeth. A smaller man would have died instantly, but Martin's wide head and strong, muscular neck enabled him to survive the first assault. With his left hand, he tried to grip the lion's throat, while his right hit out in a vain attempt to force it away. The power of the beast was immense, and it was driven by hate and revenge. As Martin blinked at the ferocious eyes, he knew he was going to die.

Gwen gradually began to breathe. Fighting for air, she forced herself into a sitting position. She raised her head and for a moment was relieved to see Martin was standing, holding his face, his great body swaying from side to side. At least he had survived. Her relief turned to horror as the second lion attacked, and in the blink of an eye, Martin was on the ground and the furious beast was savaging him.

She staggered to her feet, screaming at the top of her voice. It was the worst of nightmares. For a moment, she was unable to decide what she should do. Her dagger was a mere toothpick against such a creature, but she had no other weapon. Martin was going to die unless she helped him. Anger overcame her fear. She picked up some sharp stones and ran forwards, throwing her missiles at the lion. It crouched over Martin's still body, and although it snarled when a stone hit, the lion continued to attack its prey.

"No," she yelled. "No!" and hurled more stones. One hit the lion between its eyes, and drew blood. With a deep, angry roar it sprang from Martin's body and advanced in short bursts towards her, its tail flicking dangerously from side to side. She backed back and drew her dagger. The creature's large unblinking eyes, regarded her without a trace of fear or pity, bright remorseless eyes preparing for the kill. Gwen was breathing fast, her mind racing, unable to accept the inevitability of her death. She held the dagger at arm's length, waving it from side to side as she waited for the huge beast to leap at her. It paused a few paces away from her, and bunched its legs in preparation for its attack.

Suddenly, it jumped to the side, screaming in pain, with an arrow in its throat. As Gwen watched in frozen disbelief, another shaft embedded itself in the creature's chest and it rolled over, collapsing lifeless on the ground, only an arm's length away. She found she was trembling violently, unable to utter a sound. Her eyes locked on the monstrous creature. In a blink of her eyes, beyond her comprehension, her death sentence had been annulled.

"You are safe now, Lady." It was the voice of a young man, with a precise way of speaking. She felt him gently take her dagger, and although she allowed him to lead her to a flat stone where he helped her sit, she was unable to look at him or control her shaking that racked her body.

"Drink this," he said, and placed a flask of water to her lips. She drank some, and moved her head slowly as he splashed water over her face. "Breathe deeply, and slowly. You are in shock, Lady."

She was aware of another man. He walked past her towards where Martin lay, and bent down to examine him, after a short while he returned. "Is he…?" her lips would not form the words. "Is he…?"

"The man is dead, Lady." For the first time, she looked up and saw the two Arabs looking down at her. Their young faces were grim, yet concerned. She wanted to tell them they were wrong. Martin couldn't die. He was strong; the strongest man she'd ever known, a survivor of fires, earthquakes and battles. He could not die here. It was not possible. She shook her head, her mouth opening and shutting mechanically, unable to say anything.

She tried to stand. Before the men could react, her eyes rolled up and she dropped to the ground, unconscious.

. . .

IT WAS THE MOST traumatic night of Vernon's life, as he tried to cope with the myriad of decisions he had to make before hundreds of men could be ready to march. His previous fall-out with the quartermaster had resulted in a great deal of squirming from Vernon to ensure the man's co-operation, made especially difficult as Vernon was still convinced the man was guilty. Never before had he considered the complexities of organization: composing written orders to requisition extra horses for the cavalry and more mules for the wagons; ensuring there were adequate supplies of food, water, spare weapons, boots, armour and wood for siege engines; even allocating wine for the officers, and rougher wine for the soldiers to be distributed before a battle. There were arrangements to be made for cooks and their equipment, for sappers and their tools, for priests, medics and the personal servants and equipment of the officers.

Sergeants and junior officers had reported problems in contacting the large numbers of troopers who had received permission to visit the city's nightlife before the officers had known of the order to assemble.

"We're searching all the bars and brothels, Sir. But many of the men are already drunk, and won't be sober by first light," a senior officer reported.

"If they can stand, they can march it off," he replied. "If they're dead drunk, throw them in a wagon. Put them on fatigues as soon as they come round."

There was a constant stream of officers and messengers throughout the night, all wanting answers, seeking advice, and receiving orders and counter-orders. In the midst of the seemingly unending chaos, Vernon found he was enjoying himself. He liked being in charge. The more he made decisions, the easier they seemed to become. No one in his family had ever expected anything of him, and he had never been in charge of anything important. It was a novel experience, one he embraced with the enthusiasm of youth, and the certainty of wealth.

In the early hours of the morning, when there was a sudden lull in the activity, his squire appeared. "I think you should eat something, Sir," he said, handing him a plate of cooked meat and a hunk of bread. He went over to the table and poured Vernon a mug of wine.

"Ah, thanks, Philip." He gave him a beaming smile, and savoured the wine. "I think it's about time I got ready for the parade. Got to look the part, you know."

'Everything's ready, Sir. Old Giles is waiting outside with your sword and your armour. He's been working at it for hours."

At dawn, he found himself sitting on the magnificent horse his father had provided, wearing his gleaming armour polished by his squire and carrying a sword and buckler, lovingly maintained by his armourer. He looked every bit the commanding officer to the army of men formed up in strict order in front of him. Few would have recognized him as the gauche, high-spirited knight, who was the butt of many jokes within the officer's mess. Many thought it must be Lord d'Escosse. Those who knew it was Sir Vernon de Kari were baffled by the transformation, and impressed with the way he had organized the hasty assembling of the English forces.

After a brief inspection, he gathered his officers together. "Good work. We march as soon as the Governor's forces are," he rolled his eyes, "finally ready." The officers enjoyed the joke: there was still plenty of activity in the area in which the local forces were forming up.

A young squire galloped over, and jumped off his horse, his face ablaze with excitement. "My Lord," he said, bowing his head, "Sir Maurice de Maron requires your presence, immediately."

Vernon regarded him sternly. "Does he indeed? Tell him I am on my way." The messenger bowed again, jumped into his saddle, and galloped back the way he had come. Vernon stared severely at his officers. "Gentlemen, it looks as though we may be ready to move out," he paused, "sometime today." He winked at them.

Inclining his head towards Philip, he walked his horse slowly in the direction of the disorganized forces on his left, followed by his squire, who carried his lance with the de Kari pennant fluttering from the top. Vernon sat bolt upright on his fine horse, conscious that all were watching him.

"A good fellow," one of the officers observed. "Didn't know he had it in him."

"Quite a surprise, d'Escosse choosing him," another murmured.

"Does anyone know where d'Escosse is?"

There was a shaking of heads.

"I understand it's something secret," the first knight volunteered. "He's taken a sergeant with him. That huge fellow with the unlikely name of Little." There were a few chuckles around the group. "I'd wager it has something to do with Sir Raymond de Wulfric, he's a senior officer with the Knight's of the Order, yet nobody's seen him for weeks."

One of the knights yawned. "Let's hope our Sir Vernon can get them moving. I don't fancy sitting here all day."

• • •

"I IMAGINE THERE'S GOING to be a slight delay, Sir?" Vernon said in a heavily condescending way. Behind him could be heard the shrill yells and screams of abuse, of the sergeants, bullying the reluctant soldiers into their formations.

The Governor was not amused. After disagreeing violently with his wife, finding fault with his officers and coming off worst in an acrimonious dispute with Sir Raoul de Warren over the authority of the army, he was in no mood to have a jumped-up young knight try to be clever. He glared at Vernon, and wondered if his wife had been referring to this strutting cockerel, when she had requested he provide a young knight to be her bodyguard. Sir Maurice was no longer a young man, did not take much exercise, and his armour no longer fitted him comfortably. In recent months, his wife had developed a range of minor illnesses whenever he had suggested that he share her bed; yet, she was always so lively whenever there was a party to attend. As a result, he found himself constantly on the watch for possible suitors for Elizabeth's favours, and was convinced that Vernon was a likely candidate.

"I hope d'Escosse's forces are ready to move out." He glared at the smiling Vernon.

"Absolutely, Sir. We've been ready for a while." He could not resist adding, "I understand you're not quite ready yet, Sir?"

Sir Maurice almost choked. It was impossible that this incompetent knight, in his dandified armour, could have managed this single-handed. Which confirmed that Lord d'Escosse had organized the muster and was still in the city, contrary to some of the rumours he had heard. "Where is Lord d'Escosse?"

"He sends his regrets, Sir. He is unable to attend this meeting, and has appointed me to take his place."

"This is most unsatisfactory." The Governor was barely able to contain his rage. "Go back and tell him I demand his presence, now!"

"I'm afraid he's already left the city, Sir. He took some of his men and went on ahead to reconnoitre the area."

"What! Do you take me for a fool?" He was red faced with indignation.

Vernon paused for a moment, as though unable to understand the question. "No, of course not, Sir." He shook his head indulgently.

"Then, where in Hell's name is he?" de Maron bellowed.

Vernon was very tempted to assure the Governor that Ralph was not in Hell, but restrained himself. "Lord d'Escosse was not impressed with the intelligence provided a few weeks ago, when his army," he gave a nod of his head towards Sir Raoul de Warren, "and yours, my Lord, were ambushed by superior forces. He believes if it had not been for the earthquake, it would have resulted in a huge defeat, Sir."

"You do not have to lecture me, Sir Vernon." The governor was pacing about, chewing at his lower lip. "That still does not explain why he is not here."

"As I was saying, Sir. Lord d'Escosse has gone on ahead to ensure the safety of our forces. He has always been a man of action, and after the last," he paused, "debacle, he decided to…"

"He could have sent scouts ahead! It is unthinkable he would have gone himself."

"That is the way he is, Sir." Vernon had adopted the voice he might have used to deny sweetmeats to a child. He shrugged his shoulders. "Lord d'Escosse is a very brave man."

"When did he leave?" Sir Raoul's voice cut in. He was convinced there was more to Ralph's disappearance than this upstart knight was revealing.

Vernon had pondered this question during the brief intermissions in his long night of organization. "As I explained to you yesterday, my Lord de Warren, Lord Ralph d'Escosse had put me in charge of the English forces," he gripped the pommel of his sword, unable to resist putting one finger over another, "and left the city as soon as he heard the Giant was on the move again." The High Lord did not respond, but glanced knowingly at some of his knights.

The Governor stared in disbelief. "So, you are claiming you are responsible for having the English forces ready to march?"

"Yes, Sir." He adopted a pose, and smiled ingratiatingly at the portly Governor. "It's not too difficult once you get the hang of it, Sir."

There was a long silence as the Governor fought to control his emotions. "My Lord de Warren, I am entrusting you with the local forces. You will have overall command of the whole expedition to Tripoli. Once you have scattered the Assassins, assess the real situation regarding the Giant, and any other threat to Tripoli. Then, you will return immediately to help protect this city." The High Lord silently bowed his head.

Feeling more assured the Governor switched his attention to Vernon. "You, de Kari, will assume the temporary command of the English forces until Lord d'Escosse rejoins his army. At all times you will be under the command of Lord de Warren, High Lord of the Knights of the Order. Understand?" Although he had no time for these fanatical knights and their secrets, it gave him considerable pleasure to clip Vernon's wings. Perhaps, with luck, neither of them would return.

"Absolutely, Sir. You can count on me."

"Yes. I'm sure I can," he said, sarcastically. "My Lord de Warren,

I'm not sure if I made it quite clear: I will remain here to ensure that the city's security. I look forward to your safe return, as soon as possible." He exchanged bows with the High Lord, ignored Vernon, climbed into his saddle, with the invaluable help of his servant, and headed back towards the city.

Vernon drew himself up and bowed formally to Lord de Warren. He sensed it would be dangerous to annoy this man. "What are your orders, my Lord?" Although only slightly taller, the knight radiated authority. His long, boney face was dominated by a large beak-like nose; he had a wide, cruel mouth and piercing pale blue eyes, set wide apart in deep sockets. His thin, blond hair, worn long to his shoulders, made him appear effeminate from behind, but facing him, Vernon was conscious of steely strength and pitiless ambition.

"Your forces will act as the vanguard, and will march immediately. Send out scouts and report back to me throughout the day. Part of my cavalry will join yours, and your wagons will travel with ours. The local forces will guard the supply train. The rest of my army will provide the security at the rear." He stared coldly into Vernon's eyes. "When Lord d'Escosse returns, let me know, immediately."

Vernon felt his confidence evaporate. He realized the High Lord did not believe him, and had effectively taken control of the English forces. Although Vernon had annoyed the Governor with his unlikely efficiency, he had merely played into the hands of this powerful and humourless knight, who now possessed the authority to control him like a puppet. At the back of his mind, a small voice wondered how Lord d'Escosse would react, when he discovered what had happened. Vernon bowed automatically. As he walked back to his horse, he wondered despondently what he could have done differently.

· · ·

AT DAYBREAK, RALPH D'ESCOSSE and his sergeant approached the main gate of Qalaat Al Marqab, the Castle of the Watchtower. They looked an incongruous pair in the steel grey light, sitting uncomfortably on small, long-suffering donkeys. The steep journey up from the harbour had been momentous. Little was so terrified he had kept his eyes tightly closed for much of the journey, unable to look down at the steep drop on his left, his long legs almost touching the uneven path. Ralph, in contrast, enjoyed the experience. He spent the time considering the remarkable view, and the almost impregnable position of the castle.

At the top of the climb the narrow path turned to the right and cut through a short ravine with steep sides, before opening up onto a broad sloping area on top of which was the imposing castle. Scattered about were large black pieces of volcanic rock and the path meandered through these, before joining a wide road leading up to Al Marqab's main gate.

Ralph looked back at Little. His white face was covered in sweat and his teeth were clenched together. "You can relax, Sergeant, the fun's over."

Little let out his breath in a long gasp. "I never wants to do that again."

"Until we go back to the ship," Ralph reminded him. "It'll be much more exciting going down."

A look of horror crossed the tall man's face, as he followed Ralph up to the castle.

The guardsmen were alert and feeling resentful after the mishaps of the previous night, and challenged the two riders in loud, aggressive tones. Ralph identified himself, and waited patiently while Sir Payen de Montdidier was informed.

Eventually, the solid oak doors opened. They passed slowly into the courtyard, where the young knight was waiting to greet them. He was still strapping on his sword belt, but did not appear disconcerted by their early arrival, or their comic appearance on the donkeys. "Welcome to Al Marqab." he said, bowing courteously.

Ralph dismounted awkwardly and handed the reins to a servant. "Fine little beast," he murmured, ruffling the donkey's mane and narrowly avoiding being bitten. "I'm Lord Ralph d'Escosse," he bowed. "This is my sergeant, who answers to the name of Little."

Payen smiled. "I saw your galley come in last night. You must be in need of refreshment?"

"That would be most welcome," Ralph grinned encouragingly at Little, who had finally separated himself from his bad-tempered mount. "But first, I need to know if a knight, by the name of Lord Raymond de Wulfric, and a young woman have arrived in port in the last few days?"

"Indeed. They arrived the day before yesterday. Lord Raymond is still here."

Ralph's face clouded over. "And the woman?"

"Mistress Gwen?" Ralph nodded. "She decided to flee the castle during the first night, accompanied by a sergeant who had been under Lord Raymond's command. A very large man, known as Martin." Payen was interested to see the emotions on Ralph's face. "Lord Raymond was not pleased. I have rarely seen a man in such a temper."

"How long has she been gone?"

"We discovered her missing at this time yesterday. Sir Raymond insisted on a search, but he failed to catch up with her."

There was a certain reserve in Payen's explanation, and Ralph realized he needed to explain the true situation if he was to get the young man's help. "I imagine Sir Raymond is likely to appear at any moment? Can we go somewhere less public?"

Payen nodded and led the way towards the stables. Ralph looked back and catching Little's eye, indicated the kitchens, before following his host through the stables, noting the lack of horses. They climbed up a long flight of steps onto a battlement overlooking the northern coastline. Payen dismissed a soldier on guard duty. As they walked slowly backwards and forwards along the stone walkway, Ralph explained Gwen's association with the Knights of the Order, and how he had become involved.

"So, Raymond abducted her?" Payen mused. "It accounts for the strange relationship between them, and for her lack of clothes and female company. But why Jerusalem? And why, if she is so important to the Order, were there no other Knights to ensure her safety?"

"I think he's acted in defiance of the orders of the High Lord of the Order. I imagine there is much scheming among the ambitious members of that strange and secret society," Ralph replied. "As for Jerusalem, I believe the city holds some great secret for them, which they hope to exploit, with Gwen's help." He shrugged. "Or lack of it." As he turned to enjoy the view, he failed to see the strange look on Payen's face as he reacted to Ralph's mention of a great secret in Jerusalem. The young knight quickly regained his composure.

They had passed the stage of formality, and Payen felt he could trust this vibrant Lord, who was much the same age as himself, but radiated confidence and authority. "Before you arrived, Ralph, I sent out a local guide who is a gifted tracker. He hoped to find Gwen and her sergeant, and give them any assistance they might need to get back to Antioch."

"So, she is returning to Antioch?" Ralph raised his eyebrows.

"It is a logical guess. South of here there's a lot of unexplained activity by the Assassins, who normally are less visible."

"I've heard of them." He stared at Payen. "It's a pity you didn't have your guide with you yesterday, my friend. If he'd found Gwen I could have her safely back in my galley by now."

"He did find the place where Gwen and her sergeant were hiding." Ralph looked startled. "But, as neither of us trusted Raymond, we decided not to reveal their presence to him. It was later we heard about the Assassins. If I had known you would arrive, I might have made a different decision."

Ralph pondered this news. "Is there any point in my trying to find her?"

"None. The desert is huge and unforgiving. Also, I am down to my last four horses. With luck, my guide will return with good news. But not, perhaps, for a few days."

The two men stood side by side looking down at the black volcanic cliffs and the deep blue of the sea. After a while, Ralph clapped Payen on the shoulder. "I could do with some breakfast, Payen. An odd camel or two would do." His infectious laugh resonated around the battlements.

"Of course, my Lord." He gave a mock bow. "But unfortunately, camels are only served on Holy Days. You will have to make do with a donkey." They continued their jesting as they moved towards the stairs. It was a long time since Payen had enjoyed the company of someone of similar intelligence and ability.

They reached the foot of the stairs and as they crossed through

the stables, they could hear the sound of Sir Raymond yelling:
"Well, find him then!"

The knight was standing in the courtyard, his face red and
choleric, glaring at all around him. When he saw Payen emerge
from the shadows of the stable, he advanced in high dudgeon.
"What the Hell do you think you're playing at? We should have
left...." The words failed him as he saw Ralph.

"You have some explaining to do, Lord de Wulfric," Ralph
snapped. He strode determinedly towards the huge knight,
undeterred by their difference in size. His eyes flashed and his
right hand went to his sword.

"I have nothing to say to you, d'Escosse!" Raymond thundered.
He grasped the handle of his sword, and took up an aggressive
stance.

Payen positioned himself between them. "My Lords, nothing
will be achieved by drawing your swords. It is bad for morale. I
urge you both to retire to my refectory."

Both knights glared at each other, while the soldiers and
servants watched with interest. Slowly, both knights released the
grip on their swords. Shaking with anger, they followed Payen into
the tower.

"Pity," one of the soldiers remarked, "I'd 'oped de Wulfric was
going t'get skewered."

"I reckon that knight wiv' the blond 'air could do it an' all,"
another commented.

"'E will, when the time's right," Little added, towering above
them. "Ye mark my words."

CHAPTER 13

FROM THE HIGH GROUND, the view was breathtaking. In the far distance, the blue haze of the Mediterranean merged with the darker colours of the coastal hills, interspersed with green valleys slowly giving way to the yellows and grays of the desert areas. It was late afternoon, and Vernon was enjoying himself. From the promontory on which he sat, he could just make out a small dark blur, which his scouts had told him was the coastal town of Lattakieh, at least four leagues away as the crow flies. His attention returned to the army far below, a long snake of men marching in well-ordered formations, with groups of cavalry riding ahead and on both sides, and with the supply wagons lumbering along in the centre. Behind them, marched the elite forces of the Order with more formations of cavalry forming a rearguard. Soon, much to the relief of the foot soldiers, they would be pitching camp. The army had marched many leagues across desert country and the men had endured the uneven ground and the blistering sun.

He could see the small groups of scouts constantly leaving and returning with their latest reports: the High Lord was not going to risk a second ambush. It was the fourth day since leaving Antioch, and the army was making good progress. Earlier in the day, Vernon had decided to join a party of his scouts, part English and part Arab, in order to assure himself of their effectiveness. At least, that was the reason he had given to Sir Raoul de Warren, who, as Vernon's superior, was entitled to know why his second-in-command was leaving the safety of the corps. In truth, Vernon merely wanted to explore the strange and exciting land through which they were travelling, and the scouts noticed he appeared unaffected by the heat, the difficult terrain or the physical demands on his body.

"What a grand sight, Michael. Could you wish for anything better!"

"Yes, Sir. I mean no, Sir," the scout replied. He had been in the saddle for many hours and was looking forward to returning to camp; he did not share the enthusiasm of his young commander.

Sir Raoul de Warren's decision to march his army down the coastal route to Tripoli was seen by most officers to be a logical alternative to the mountain route favoured by the late Lord Longsword. Those who had survived the previous battle, blamed Longsword for their near defeat and a rumour had circulated accusing him of revealing their position to the enemy in order to precipitate a conflict with the mysterious Arab leader known as the Giant.

"Four days of marching. No sign of enemy forces," Vernon observed.

"No, Sir."

"Tell me, Michael, if you were the enemy commander, and you knew a strong army was approaching, what would you do?" He tilted his head to one side, and adopted a thoughtful expression as he prepared for a man-to-man talk.

"Me, Sir?" The scout looked appalled. He hardly knew this officer and did not want to have a closer relationship. As far as he was concerned, officers gave orders and soldiers carried them out. He always felt uneasy when officers were around. He could not fathom why this knight, who was the newly appointed leader of the English forces, should have joined a scouting party, when he should have remained with the other officers.

"Yes, Michael, I'm interested in your thoughts on the matter." Vernon smiled encouragingly. In his new role as a senior officer, he thought it best to get to know the men and build up a reputation for being 'a good fellow', or whatever it was that soldiers called their favourite officers.

"I can't say, Sir. Never given it much thought."

"Ah," Vernon tried to cover his disappointment. "I just wondered, with you being a scout and all that, whether you'd built up any special knowledge of these things."

"No, Sir." Michael glanced back at his three friends, and raised his eyes. They sat stoically on their horses and, like Michael, waited impatiently for this officer to dismiss them, or lead the way back. Below, they could see the huge camp taking shape as tents were erected and fires lit. If they did not return soon, they would be late for the camp meal, which meant minimum rations. "I should be getting my report back, Sir, before someone reckons we've been ambushed." He saluted smartly.

"Well done, Michael. Dismiss." He looked around regretfully: he was not ready to return to camp. "I'll follow you shortly."

"Thank you, Sir." Michael wheeled his horse, winked at the other three scouts, and trotted off along the plateau in the direction of the winding path leading down the mountainside. They soon disappeared, leaving Vernon to contemplate his good fortune.

He wondered what his father would say if he knew his youngest son was now the acting head of the English forces in Antioch, and soon to liberate the city of Tripoli. He smiled to himself. There was also the attractive Lady Elizabeth. No doubt about it, she had a soft spot for him. Admittedly, she was much older than he was, but.... He sat up straight in his saddle, and stretched his shoulders. Life was full of possibilities.

It was quiet on the top of the mountain, and he was content to watch the four scouts as they came back into view, carefully following a zigzag path down to the camp. They were a couple of hundred feet beneath him, still way to his left, and he estimated it would take them almost an hour to reach the new base camp. The bare mountainside was littered with large, rocky outcrops and loose boulders on their inevitable journey downwards. The scouts appeared immensely vulnerable on this stark landscape, occasionally vanishing from sight, only to reappear in a lower place, becoming smaller each time.

"Well, old horse," he said, patting the animal's damp neck, "time for home." He felt immensely satisfied with his life. Giving the vista a final lordly sweep of his eyes, he gently shook the reins and headed left.

His horse had just begun to move, when he yanked frantically on the reins, dismounted and ran back to the promontory. Vernon stared down, wondering if his eyes had deceived him: he could have sworn he had seen movement behind some angular rocks far below. He could see the scouts gradually approaching these rocks, but in spite of a close examination of the mountainside, he could observe nothing to cause alarm. He was about to relax, when he saw something move. What he had thought were dark shadows in the rocks came to life, and he realized he was looking down at a large band of men in black uniform, with black domed helmets. They were hidden from the approaching scouts, who appeared unaware of any threat, although they were only a few yards away.

It all happened in the blink of an eye: the soldiers stood up and some began to swing something over their heads. As Vernon watched, unable to grasp what was happening, a volley of slingshot was discharged at the unsuspecting scouts. The first horse was killed instantly, and collapsed over the edge of the narrow path, crushing its rider as it fell. The second scout was hit, and sagged forward in his saddle, his frightened mount rearing up and preventing the other two scouts from advancing. It was almost impossible for them to turn their panic-stricken horses. They drew their swords in a vain attempt to fight off their attackers, who surged forward waving curved swords and releasing more sling shot. Within moments the four scouts were massacred, and the victorious fighters turned their attention to the lone infidel who was screaming abuse from above.

Once they realized the raging figure on the top of the mountain was unable to attack them immediately, having no bow, they began a fast, methodical pillaging of their victims, removing the clothes and weapons before pushing the corpses off the path. Others had captured the scouts' horses, and with obvious ability were calming the terrified animals.

Vernon was beside himself with frustration: the attack was over in moments, and he was forced to watch his men being killed and their bodies plundered, while all he could do was make impotent threats. Three warriors deftly mounted the subdued horses, and began an assent of the steep path, with the rest of the band following closely behind.

He ran to his horse, swearing loudly, and climbed quickly into the saddle. He unbuckled the leather shield with its finely crafted metal boss, and fastened it onto his left forearm; he lowered the visor on his gleaming helmet, and drew his long sword with the De Kari device inscribed on the top of the blade. His chain mail was the best money could buy, and he was fleetingly aware of his formidable appearance as he prepared to seek revenge.

The plateau was relatively even, and Vernon reached the top of the steep path well in advance of the ascending warriors, and prepared his plans. The path was narrow, allowing only the width of one horseman to travel safely, but he could envisage the foot soldiers bunching up, even squeezing past the animals, in their haste to reach the top. Once the fighting began, he had no doubt that many of those on foot could leave the path and crawl up the steep side of the mountain to attack him from behind. Apart from his two brief and violent encounters with murderers in Antioch, Vernon had no experience of actual fighting. He had been well trained by Giles, his father's armourer, and was superbly armed, strong and fearless; however, having witnessed the slaughter of his scouts, he was beginning to realize he could easily die. It was not something he had ever considered.

It would not be long before his enemy came into sight, and he struggled with opposing plans. Ideally, he would charge down on them. With the steepness of the ground and his armour and weapons, he would certainly be able to defeat those on horseback and cause chaos in the ranks of the advancing soldiers. It would be a noble and romantic effort: one against many. But, once committed, there would be no possibility of retreat on that steep narrow path, and his horse would quickly lose its enormous advantage once the foot soldiers surrounded him. He took in a deep breath. His other plan was to hold back and attack the horsemen as soon as they appeared over the brow of the cliff. Once he had dealt with them, he would engage the rest of the enemy for as long as possible, while still using the horse to his full potential. There was really no choice. He breathed out, and shook his head. This was not the way the knights had behaved in the many stories he had read, where virtue, bravery and audacity had won through, and where heroism was always triumphant with a beautiful woman as the prize. Slowly, almost reluctantly, he backed his horse away from the edge, and prepared for his first real battle.

The warriors were silent as they rushed up the path. There was no yelling or screaming, merely the grunting and panting of many men, forcing themselves to keep up with their friends and share the honour of killing the infidel. Standing back about thirty paces from the edge, Vernon watched the first horseman appear. There was the flash of a sword, the dome of a helmet, and the head of a horse, its eyes large and its mouth dripping saliva. Finally, the warrior was staring at him. The horse staggered at the top, its legs unable to cope with the sudden change in elevation, its huge lungs almost bursting with the effort.

"Lady Elizabeth!" Vernon yelled as he urged his horse into a charge; it seemed to him to be a chivalrous thing to be dedicating his life to a pretty woman, no matter how brief their association.

The warrior was trying in vain to control the horse, when Vernon cut him down with a powerful blow. The man fell to the side, his foot trapped in a stirrup, and the animal bolted off along the plateau dragging its injured rider over the broken rocks. As Vernon pulled his horse to a stop, the next rider was forcing his mount on to the level. He was a large man with a full beard and staring eyes. In his right hand he gripped a curved sword, and in the other he held a black, round shield. He lashed out at Vernon, who deflected the blow with his long sword, and twisting in the saddle, punched the boss of his shield under the warrior's raised arm, knocking him to the ground. A useful trick he had learned from his training with Giles.

The third rider was attempting to push past the fallen fighter, whose horse was momentarily trapped at the top of the path, and behind him a mass of heads burst into sight. Vernon turned his horse to the left as the third rider lunged forward, his sword coming at an angle. There was a clash of iron as Vernon lent back blocking the warrior's sword thrust and forcing it downwards to his left. He continued with an upward movement to the right, cutting deeply into the man's side, and the sword dropped from his lifeless hand. Vernon kicked hard with his boots and his horse galloped off as the first group the foot soldiers rushed at him.

When he was out beyond the reach of arrow or slingshot, he brought the horse to a stop and turned round to face the warriors. They were bunched together, beginning a slow advance, while at the back two of them climbed onto the captured horses. He raised his visor and estimated there were more than thirty of the black clad soldiers. Without further thought about his own mortality, he flicked down his visor and charged at them, his sword held out to the right side and his body bent slightly forward in the saddle. In his left hand, he controlled the reins and gripped his shield, while his head moved from side to side as he peered through the eye-slit in his helmet. He urged his horse into a full gallop, and the ground beneath him appeared to race by. Vernon was certain of his ability to scatter these lightly armoured soldiers, for he was a knight, and they were mere irregulars. With this simplistic view of warfare, he felt invincible.

There was a sudden and dramatic change in his optimism when he came within slingshot, and his helmet received a direct hit. He felt his head snap back, and his ears resonated with a loud ringing sound. Immediately, a flurry of missiles bounced off his chain mail, and he was surprised at the strength of the impacts. An arrow deflected off the shield, and he realized he was disorientated. He was bouncing up and down on the saddle, as the horse galloped on, and the gap between himself and the enemy shortened unbelievably quickly. Everything was a blur. Unable to raise his sword arm after receiving a direct hit on the shoulder, and blinking away the tears that streamed down his face, he gritted his teeth in agony as he received more direct hits on his helmet. His last moment decision to avoid combat was not entirely his own: a stone glanced off the broad neck of his horse, causing her to veer sharply away to the right, at the same second that his wish to live overcame his foolhardy desire for glory. Urging the horse around in a tight circle, he galloped off, narrowly avoiding certain disaster.

A roar of derision arose from the soldiers. The two on horseback made a half-hearted charge, following the retreating knight until they were certain he was not going to renew the fight. By the time they returned, the main body of soldiers had trotted off to where their horses were hidden, leaving two men to watch the activities in the camp below and pass on the new orders. After a brief exchange, the two guards climbed up behind the riders and cantered off after the others. From their point of view it had been a good day.

After nearly two miles of uncontrolled panic the horse finally tired, and Vernon was able to bring her to a stop. He did a cursory check of the empty landscape, before removing his helmet and slowly climbing down from the horse. The animal was shivering, and blood trickled down her wet neck. She stood with her head bent and her ears back, a picture of fatigue and resignation.

Vernon gently patted her muzzle. "Don't worry, old thing," he croaked. "We gave them something to think about." He staggered round to stare vacantly back along the way he had travelled. He was bathed in sweat, his head was thumping, and his chest and arms ached under the protective chain mail. "Perhaps we'll just have a short rest," he muttered, taking a long drink from his flask.

The sun was low in the sky, and Vernon knew he must soon retrace his steps while he could still see where he was going. But, as he stood staring at the saddle, he could not imagine how he could climb back on it until he had rested. "We both need a short nap," he groaned. He looped the reins on a thorn bush, and unable to find the energy to remove the saddle from the long-suffering animal, he collapsed on the ground beside her, his helmet, sword and shield littered around him. Nothing he had ever read about battles had mentioned the word exhaustion. He closed his eyes.

. . .

IT WAS NOT UNUSUAL for scouts to be delayed when they were operating in enemy country, and it was prudent for the army to think of it as such, for Crusader control was mainly limited to the fortified towns and castles along the coast. Inland from the main cities and fortifications, the land was much as it had ever been: a harsh land where invaders throughout the centuries had eventually succumbed. Although an important crossroad for both trade and invasions, the country had defied ambitious generals and reduced their armies by illness, drought and hunger. Only those born to this cruel environment could survive the unrelenting attacks of the elements.

The camp was about ten miles inland from the coastal town of Lattakieh, and although there had been no reports of enemy scouts or bands of insurgents in the area, the officers were on a high state of alert. When darkness fell, Michael's scouts were reported missing; a sergeant reported the fact to the officer in charge.

"Michael's a good scout, Sir." The sergeant stood to attention in front of the officer. "He 'ad three others with 'im. All good scouts."

"We lose scouts occasionally, sergeant." The officer, a member of the Order, concealed a yawn. It had been a long day, and he had not received reports of enemy encounters from any of the other groups of scouts. The sergeant appeared to be worrying unnecessarily.

"Yes, Sir. But they 'ad that knight with 'em."

"What knight?" The officer glared at him. Knights did not go out on reconnaissance trips with scouts.

"That young Lord de Kari. The one who's in charge of…."

"I know who he is!" The officer jumped to his feet. "Are you sure he went out with these scouts?"

"Yes, Sir. I thought you knew. The men was all talking about it. They…." He shrugged his shoulders as the officer stalked out of the tent, calling for his aide to join him.

Sir Raoul de Warren was enjoying a light supper with some of the more senior members of the Order. It had been a tiring day. Although nothing untoward had occurred, there were ongoing preparations for the inevitable encounter with the enemy, once they approached Tripoli. The wine had flowed, and there was a sense of wellbeing in the group that came with the gradual easing of aching limbs.

"Has the young English Lord caused you much problem, my Lord?" a knight asked. He smiled indulgently. Vernon had gained an early reputation as a rich buffoon and, since his unexpected rise to power, had become a constant subject of discussion among the Order.

"Not at all," Raoul answered, swirling the wine around his cup, "I haven't allowed him to." There was a ripple of laughter.

"I heard he'd gone off with one of his scouting parties?" the knight observed, there was a hint of incredulity in his voice.

"Anything to keep him out of my way." The High Lord drained his mug. "I understand he wanted to check on the scouts, to make sure they were doing their job properly." He raised an eyebrow. "He's obviously very experienced in these matters. Let's hope he doesn't give these hardened soldiers an inferiority complex."

The knights beat their fists on the table to show their appreciation of Raoul's wit, and he grinned wolfishly as his cruel eyes swept the table. He liked power, and since his appointment as High Lord he had established a reputation as a dangerous opponent, who would stop at nothing to get his own way. Since the unexpected, but welcome, demise of the fanatical William Longsword, together with the upstart Stephen de Bois, opposition to his rule had faded. It had come as a shock when his second-in-command, the powerful Raymond de Wulfric, had absconded with the Maid. Again, he was compelled to reassess his own position and plan accordingly.

"My Lord?"

He was jolted from his reverie. The intelligence officer and his aide were standing to attention just inside the tent. Raoul poured himself some wine; it was never wise to respond too quickly to underlings, it indicated weakness. "Yes?"

"My Lord, I have to report Sir Vernon de Kari and a troop of four scouts have failed to return." Everyone in the tent turned to stare at him.

The High Lord listened carefully to the report, and questioned the officer closely.

If de Kari was missing, presumed dead, it was a mixed blessing. With the sudden disappearance of the commander of the English forces, and now the possible death of the second-in-command, it meant that the Order would have full control over the English forces. This was ironic, bearing in mind that the treacherous King

Henry I had sent d'Escosse and Gilles de Plantard, the so-called
Keeper of the Grail, to spy on the Order and try to prevent its
inevitable rise to power in the Holy Land. But, on the other hand,
it was not good policy to lose important officers, no matter how
suspect their appointment. It was bad for morale, and he knew he
had to act decisively.

"I want all scout troops to be away from the camp before first
light. Cover every direction, including Antioch, and double the
number in the area where de Kari might have been." After the
intelligence officer had left the tent, Raoul addressed the rest of
the knights.

"Whatever we might think about de Kari, he is popular with
some of the junior officers in the English forces. It is important for
morale that we are seen to be taking his absence seriously." The
knights nodded their agreement. "I want a strong cavalry unit to
support the scouts in the area in which he disappeared. I want the
army to keep in close formation on the march tomorrow. Spread
the word among the soldiers that we might engage the enemy.
That should keep them alert."

He moved towards the map table, and the knights gathered
round. "We are here," he pointed with his finger at a point to the
east of the coastal town of Lattakieh. "We will turn towards the
coast, and reach Jabala tomorrow. It will mean a fast march, but
the men can cope. In the following two to three days we should
reach Marqab. I intend to leave some of the English soldiers there
to reinforce their small detachment. It will be useful to have a
strong support force to guard our rear." He looked up. "Who knows
anything about Marqab?"

"I stayed there for a few nights earlier this year, my Lord." All
heads turned towards the speaker, an older knight, Sir Godfrey
de Montbard, known for his brevity. He had served with King
Baldwin in 1101, and had been part of the small army of Christians
that had defeated a powerful Egyptian army intent on capturing
Jerusalem. It was rumoured the Egyptian army had outnumbered
the Christians by twenty-five to one. Those knights who were new
to the Outremer regarded him with awe.

"What's it like?"

"A strong castle, my Lord. It can be held by a handful of soldiers. It's called the Castle of the Watchtower, and is situated high on an old volcano. There's a very steep path down to the village, which has a small but useable harbour."

"Good," the High Lord acknowledged the concise information. "How many men can it hold?"

"I would think about a hundred, my Lord," he frowned, "however, the stables are small. No more than thirty horses.

"Who's holding it at this moment?"

"Sir Payen de Montdidier. A young knight seeking holy orders." There was a murmur of interest. "He was appointed by King Baldwin on a temporary basis."

Raoul brought his long fingers together as though in prayer, and rested his lips on the index fingers. It was a mannerism he displayed whenever he was in deep thought; his officers moved away quietly. Any mention of Baldwin reminded Raoul of his biggest hurdle in his path to glory. Once the area around Tripoli was secured, he intended to proceed to Acre with its deep harbour and its powerful connections with the trading fleets of Genoa. There they would replenish their supplies and reinforce their army with the promised forces from Christendom. Finally, he would march to Jerusalem and clear the surrounding area of the Sunni forces that were supposed to be infiltrating from Damascus. In spite of their differences, he was sure to get a blessing from King Baldwin, who was dangerously short of fighting men. Once established, he would reveal his true power, and the Maid would be his crowning glory, in more ways than one. His face clouded over.

The rest of the knights had returned to their seats and were drinking and talking in low voices. The High Lord stared unseeing at the map. Where was de Wulfric, and what was he planning with Mistress Gwen? Raoul was reasonably confident in Raymond's ability to protect Gwen, but his foolhardy attempt to get her to Jerusalem by himself was unexpected and disloyal. Also, nothing could be achieved without the backing of the Order. There was a process to be followed and a ritual to be witnessed, according to the writings of their holy book. De Wulfric was aware of this, which made his actions inexplicable.

Raoul placed his fingers on either side of his nose. In the past few days he had thought carefully about Raymond's reasons for disobeying orders. He knew the man was ambitious, but so what? Everyone who joined the Order was ambitious. Slowly, Raoul was coming to a different conclusion. Supposing de Wulfric had been given no choice but to escort Mistress Gwen to Jerusalem? Perhaps, she had been in extreme danger, and he had acted in her best interests, rushing to the Holy City, intending to await the arrival of the Order? But, if it was so, why had no message been sent?

He looked up and gave a cold smile to the group. "Gentlemen, I won't keep you. I know you have much to arrange before tomorrow." The knights reluctantly left their wine and staggered off to their tents.

The High Lord returned to his musing: de Wulfric could achieve nothing by himself. The Maid was a vital element in their plans, but without the ritual and the power of the Order, she was simply an historical curiosity. He focused on her. She was a remarkable young woman, whose welfare they had tried to ensure for all these years. But there had been constant reports of her unwillingness to embrace her destiny in spite of the education and wealth they had provided. Certainly, she displayed a fine mind, and her training at the convent had prepared her for greatness. But, where was she now?

The High Lord began to pace anxiously around the tent. He was finding sleep difficult in recent days. Even when his tired body ached for sleep, his mind refused to cease its activity, gripped with two opposing thoughts: the attraction and excitement of the possibility of immense power, and the nagging, crippling fear of failure. He poured himself a mug of wine and relaxed in the nearest chair.

Finally, there was Giles Plantard, who answered to the name of John. According to some, he claimed to be Gilles de Plantard, the Keeper of the Grail. Was it possible? Some important members of the Order thought so. Sir Richard de Godfroi, who died at Christchurch, was convinced John might be the Keeper of the Grail. Raoul finished his wine and placed the mug on a table. Both

Longsword and de Bois had been uncertain if he was genuine, but they had not seen fit to challenge him, and now he might be dead. Raoul's eyes began to feel heavy. If John was an imposter, there was nothing to worry about, but if he was the Keeper, then his death could be either a disaster or a triumph for the Order. As he tried to assess the different possibilities, his eyes closed and he sank into a deep sleep.

CHAPTER 14

CELESTIAL WAS BEGINNING TO tire. The last golden rays of the setting sun illuminated the path ahead, and John realized, with a sinking feeling, he was going due west. As the chase had extended, his earlier plan of going north before cutting across to the east and reconnecting with the two boys had given way to necessity. It had soon become obvious that the big horse did better on a well-used path than on the rough desert, where the smaller local horses of the pursuing Assassins held the advantage. In the previous hour, the gap had slowly closed. John knew his survival depended on whether he could maintain his lead until nightfall. Coming upon a path quite unexpectedly, he had made a sudden decision to follow it, regardless of where it led. Since that time, Celestial had succeeded in maintaining the gap between them, but was finally beginning to slow down

On a small hill he glanced back to see the horseman were still some minutes behind. The original tightly knit band had become separated into small groups, the nearest numbering about five, and displaying an unflagging determination. As John galloped down a slight elevation, the sun disappeared behind the distant high ground, leaving a bright, meandering glow along the skyline. It would soon be dark, and if he could find some cover, it might provide a possible chance of escape.

He was bathed in sweat, and was conscious of the gradual change in the temperature as a cool breeze arose and the light faded. The winding path remained reasonably clear and he urged the labouring horse for a final effort, hoping against hope that with the darkness would come deliverance.

As he rounded a bend, he saw some fires in the distance. In

the half-light it was impossible to identify where they came from, but he judged they were about half a mile away. For all he knew they could be coming from an Assassins' camp, or they could be the fires of simple herdsmen cooking their evening meals, but he had nothing to lose. He whispered encouragement to Celestial and, drawing his sword, followed the path down to the flickering lights.

Apart from his unusual horse and long sword, John looked like any other Arab. His thick black beard and his tanned skin combined with his travel-stained robes and his turban, was a description that matched most men in this part of the world. He was tall, lean and had the manner of a man used to authority. So, as he galloped into the centre of a small village, he was not thought to be other than a stranger who had captured a fine horse and an impressive weapon.

"Assassins!" he yelled at the shadowy figures around him, and was fleetingly grateful to Saif and Rashid for their language tuition. "A band of Assassins is coming! Arm yourselves!" It was a good speech in the circumstances, and he had decided to yell it, no matter whom he found around the fires. The villagers heard his call. Although his accent confirmed he was not a local man, they listened intently. It was not a rich village: a few had swords, but the majority had nothing more than knives and wooden staves. However, as in most villages in the region, they all knew how to use slings. Since earliest times, boys had been taught how to use slings to deter wolves and lions, and to catch birds and small animals for the family pot.

John had no concept of how his arrival appeared to the simple people who inhabited this poor village. They had been preparing to celebrate a local feast, when out of the dark arrived a powerful figure on a huge horse, warning them of imminent danger from their eternal enemies, the Assassins. He was tall, with a powerful, commanding voice, and he rode a horse bigger than any creature they could imagine. He was waving a long sword, unlike anything they had ever seen, and he was like a king: something out of the stories that the old folk had told them when they were young. He was a gift from God.

"Prepare to fight!" An old man, bent over with age and arthritis, rushed forward, supporting himself on a strong stick. "Quickly! Everyone grab a weapon! Abdullah, you organize the slings. Bah! Build a barricade quickly. Everyone move now!

As though released from a dream, the people rushed to obey the old man, who, John understood, was the village elder. In moments, two battered flat carts were pulled across the road, stones were placed under the wheels and branches and pieces of wood were piled on top. Further down the village's only road, fires flickered in the light breezes and there was a dark space between their red glow and the front of the makeshift barricade. The women and small children gathered between the mud houses, each holding a small weapon, while the men with slings and swords formed up behind the carts, each transformed almost instantaneously into a potential hero.

After a short pause the thunder of hooves could be heard, and the Assassins appeared at the end of the road. As they galloped past the fires, they seemed like demons, their black robes merging with the darkness. Only their weapons and the eyes of the horses shone in the firelight. The barricade had not been anticipated, and some of the riders continued their headlong charge, realizing too late their mistake. In the flickering lights there was confusion as the first horses pulled up suddenly in front of the carts, their riders crashing their animals into the wooden sides, or falling off onto the makeshift barricade, to be quickly dispatched by the defenders. The majority of the riders stopped in time, their horses moving frantically from side to side, while the warriors tried to understand what had happened.

The old man yelled, "Abdullah, now!" A hail of slingshot decimated the front line of the horsemen. The battle became intense, as other riders galloped up and forced their way past each side of the pitiful barricade, cutting down the nearest villagers who were vainly trying to reload their slings. Other Assassins clambered over the wagons, the blood lust in their eyes, leaving injured horses writhing on the ground behind them. Their black robes billowed as they sprang down from the wagons, and their deep voices rang out with confident war cries. They carried swords and shields, and some had drawn their bows. Furious hand-to-hand fighting ensued, with the villagers rushing forward to defend their barricade. But the Assassins' weapons quickly overwhelmed the lightly armed villagers. John, who sat quietly on Celestial, waiting for the opportunity, charged forward.

He was suddenly the worst enemy the Assassins could have encountered. From his high position, John could clearly see the situation as it unfolded. The warriors tried to gain the upper hand in a particular area, and John charged down on them, his horse and sword overwhelming their attack. With a burst of energy that defied his previous tiredness, he quickly reduced groups of formidable attackers to fragmented and dispirited individuals, unable to believe such opposition. His long sword and his powerful horse were unlike any enemy they had ever encountered. His success reinforced the waning confidence of the villagers, who regrouped and returned to the fight, screaming insults at their hated enemy, and lashing out with clubs and knives.

Small boys climbed onto the flat roofs of their homes. With the encouragement of sisters, they rained down a barrage of slingshot, some of which found their marks on the confined ranks of the riders, injuring both warriors and horses. In the mêlée, the villagers fought bravely, their anger overcoming their fear. Women, unused to the possibility of their men winning, darted out from doorways and the sides of buildings to stab their enemies from behind, or steal the weapons from fallen warriors to pass them on to their men folk. The villagers had suffered for generations from the persecution of the Assassins, whose reputation for murder and pillage had given them an aura of invincibility. These were the men who demanded payments and took goats and donkeys when it suited them; they kidnapped children and took other men's wives. Until this momentous evening, no villager had ever had the courage to oppose them. To do so, was certain death. But with an unimagined warrior to lead them, the villagers erupted with pent-up frustration and the desire for revenge, fighting like men possessed.

The Assassins realized they had seriously underestimated the resistance they might encounter, and finding they were attacked on all sides, forced their way back out of the bottleneck and past the sturdy carts. Suddenly, the assault petered out, and the remaining horsemen wheeled around behind the barricade calling to their friends to join them. The villagers, encouraged by John, rushed forward fearlessly, unusually united in their revenge. The remaining horseman retreated, as more sling shot hailed down on them, leaving their horseless companions without a means of escape. The few survivors tried to form a defensive circle, using their shields to defend themselves, while their swords threatened those who came too close. Their resistance was soon broken as Celestial reared over them, his deadly hooves crashing down on their raised shields, knocking them to the ground as if they were puppets. John's sword cleaved a passage to the barricade, allowing the excited villagers to isolate the last Assassins, who went down in a welter of blows.

When it was over, John climbed from his horse, hardly able to stand. The villagers quickly surrounded him, all wanting to touch the amazing man who had enabled them to defeat their eternal enemies. They sang and chanted "Hero" and "Saviour" and John was uplifted by their enthusiasm. It was hard to believe he had survived, and as he acknowledged the triumphant celebrations, he was aware of something very strange. He had accomplished the victory without feeling the power from his hand. There had been no tingling or heat, and furthermore, he realized he had fought without expecting to be saved by it. He opened his right palm, and in the flickering light of the torches, he could see the outline of the sign, but somehow the runes did not appear to be as bright as he remembered them.

Following the brief celebration, came the realization that some had died and many more were injured. It was like a stormy day when the sun shafts through dark clouds and everything is unusually bright for a brief time, to be followed by intense gloom. So it was when he became aware of the women wailing over their dead relatives, their primitive ululation intensifying the moment. The children who had been screaming their delight went strangely silent. Men quietly embraced each other and, laying down their weapons, began to deal with the sadness and the clearing up.

More unified than they had ever been before, they still had to come to terms with their individual losses.

The old man took John's arm. "Come with me. You have done all you can, and more than you imagine." He looked around the roadway as the villagers attended to their own people, and removed anything of value from the bodies of the Assassins. "They can take care of this." He shook his head in wonder. "They have never had a victory, and in spite of the cost of some good men, this will be seen as the greatest event in the history of this village."

The old man smiled, and despite his weariness and aching joints, John smiled back. "In a short while, after prayers we will feast and celebrate; tomorrow we will bury the dead. In the meantime, you can wash at the well and rest in my house."

· · ·

IN THE REFECTORY, THE spectacular view from the Watchtower held little interest for the three knights. Sir Payen de Montdidier poured wine; Sir Raymond stared unseeing at the deepening blue of the sea, and Ralph strode mechanically around the room taking deep breaths.

"I suggest you join me in some wine," Payen said, taking a cup and relaxing into a chair. His intelligent face suppressed a smile as he watched Raymond; he was deeply interested in how this supercilious knight would deal with what was obviously, for him, an embarrassing situation.

Ralph took a cup. After pausing to consider his action, he sat on a broad stool, his knees slightly up, as though ready to spring into action.

Raymond regarded them both with a dark, resentful stare, marched over to the table and drank a cup down in a defiant flourish, refilling it to the brim. He walked to the far end of the table and sat in a large chair, glowering at them. His face was flushed, and his puffy eyes, with their dark shadows, were clear evidence of a sleepless night.

"Why did you abduct Mistress Gwen?" Ralph's question broke the heavy silence.

"I don't have to explain anything to you," Raymond replied scornfully.

"I won't play games with you, de Wulfric!" There was a furious intensity in Ralph's voice. "You have placed this young woman's life in jeopardy, and you will answer my questions, or we will settle it once and for all." He rose to his feet, his eyes blazing, and his hand on the hilt of his sword.

Instantly, Raymond sprang out of the chair, and drew his sword. "You don't threaten me, you Saxon whoreson!"

Payen had not understood the extreme dislike these knights had for each other, and he jumped between the two men, holding up his arms in protest. "My Lords, you are men of God. There are other more Christian ways to settle your differences." He turned quickly from one to the other, noting the anger in both faces. They had both drawn their swords and were separated by less than ten paces. Payen felt for his weapon, realizing as he did so that his sword belt held an empty scabbard. "I will not allow this, my Lords. I will remind you both, you're in my castle." It was a weak protest, and both men ignored him as they advanced purposefully towards each other.

"You will regret that insult," Ralph hissed, as he studied his opponent.

"I regret nothing." Raymond's face relaxed. He would enjoy killing this young upstart, especially as he was part of the English Saxon detritus that pretended to nobility. Norman aristocracy was the only true nobility, and Raymond's experience in battle was second to none within The Order. He had no doubts about the outcome of the fight. "I should have killed you in Antioch," he sneered.

Ralph did not reply. His instructors had worked him hard since his early youth. He had practiced the use of the sword for many hours a week, for years on end, until his strength and agility had become superior to those who taught him. At this stage, his father had engaged a tutor unlike any the young lord had encountered. Ralph remembered him as a short, wild, bearded man who knew Latin and Greek and talked of strange lands and beliefs. He taught the wonders of the stars, the power of concentration and a belief in ultimate goodness. Ralph had only ever known him as Bracken, remembering him now as he watched Raymond advance towards him. Bracken had improved Ralph's use of weapons, and taken his thinking to a new dimension, showing him how calmness and a cool appraisal of one's enemy would reveal his weaknesses. "Keep your breathing under control, watch his eyes and always let him think he has the advantage." The oft-repeated advice echoed in his mind.

"My Lord de Wulfric!" Payen shouted, placing himself directly in front of the powerful knight, who seemed immensely tall. "I insist you—." His protest came to an abrupt end as Raymond's strong left hand brushed him aside with such force that Payen fell backwards over a bench, cracking his head against the corner of the oak table. He lay on the floor groaning softly.

"Now, you cur, prepare to meet your Saxon God." Raymond's teeth showed in a wolfish grin. He charged forward. Using his immense upper strength, he lashed out at Ralph with a chopping action that would have cleaved him in two if it had connected. Ralph anticipated the move, dodging to the side with the quickness of lightning, repositioning himself, content to let the fleshy knight waste his energy. Raymond swung round, bringing his heavy sword up in a deadly arc. Again, Ralph did a rapid side step, and avoided contact. The fight continued around the room, with Raymond continuing to slice the air, becoming ever more frustrated in his inability to corner the younger, fitter man, who ducked and weaved out of the range of each of his increasingly desperate attacks.

"Not much longer, you Saxon coward!" Raymond's taunt came out in gasps. Ralph was pleased to see the sweat flowing down his opponent's face, the mighty shoulders heaving with the effort of his attack. As the tall knight gathered himself for another onslaught, Ralph retaliated with a two-handed blow at shoulder height, and for the first time Raymond was forced to defend himself. A flicker of uncertainty showed in his eyes. He let out a furious bellow as he parried the stroke and pushing forward, attempted to force Ralph into a corner.

In a trice, Ralph disengaged, and sprung round to his right, jabbing smartly at Raymond's undefended left arm, just below the shoulder. His chain mail, although the best money could buy, was not able to withstand the razor sharp sword. As Ralph withdrew, blood spurted out of the wound. Raymond was unused to injury, and his cry of pain was tinged with blind rage. "Saxon scum!" Holding his sword out in front, he rushed forward, his left arm hanging uselessly behind him.

Ralph held a clear picture of the room in his mind, which enabled him to dart about without having to check the space behind. He retired quickly, allowing the enraged knight to rush forward, encouraging him to use his gradually fading strength. Ralph turned quickly, easily avoiding the deadly sword as Raymond slashed at him from side to side.

On the floor, by the side of the long table, Payen sat up, holding his head and trying to focus his eyes. He was unaware of the action around him. Barely conscious, he crawled forward into the direct line of Ralph's deliberate retreat. With an exclamation of surprise Ralph catapulted backwards over the confused Payen, and fell heavily. His quick mind assessed the situation, even as he fell, and in the instant it took Raymond to realize his advantage, Ralph was able to raise his sword up, in a desperate attempt at defending himself, his pommel on the ground.

Raymond let out a wild, triumphant yell. Swinging his long sword above his head, he rushed forward, determined to end his enemy's life in a single blow. Payen was dimly aware someone had fallen over him. He rolled quickly away, trying to avoid further mishap. Instead, he crashed into Raymond's legs. The heavy man lost his footing and pitched forward, propelled by his own powerful sword stroke. As he dived towards the floor, he was unable to prevent impaling himself on Ralph's long sword. He collapsed, his massive body weight forcing the sharp blade deep into his chest; his own murderous sword imbedding itself harmlessly in the floor next to Ralph's head. There was a moment of disbelief as Ralph realized Raymond's sword had so narrowly missed him. Then, he was crushed to the floor, as the armoured torso crashed down, enveloping his slimmer frame. Raymond's strangled cry gave way to a deep resonant sigh. He shuddered one last time and lay still. An eerie silence descended on the room.

• • •

VERNON AWOKE IN THE dark hours of the early morning and lay very still, uncertain where he was. Lying on his back, uncountable stars gleaming overhead in a sea of blackness, he was overwhelmed with their beauty and grandeur. Somewhere, in the distance, he heard the faint melancholic howl of a solitary wolf, and close by his horse shuffled anxiously, worried by the sound.

"It's all right, old girl. Steady now." He staggered to his feet, quickly aware of the pain in his joints, and the stiffness in his back. It was very dark, but against the star-filled sky he could make out the large, comforting shape of the horse. He stumbled on his sword, returned it to his scabbard, and groped around until he found his shield and his gauntlets. After gathering them, he searched for his helmet, eventually locating it under the horse. The docile animal nuzzled him as he untied the reins and licked his hand; its dry tongue felt like a rasp. He reached for his water flask and poured some into his helmet. The horse drank eagerly, wanting more. "Sorry, old girl, not much left," he said, fitting the helmet on his head, and enjoying the dampness. After a few gulps he replaced the flask in his saddlebag, and conscious of the need to find water before the end of the day, determined to make that his first priority. His stomach rumbled, and he reached into another bag and found some dates. Not much of a meal, he mused, but better than nothing.

Before getting on the horse, Vernon decided he would relieve himself. Being naturally modest, even in front of animals, he walked a few paces away. He was in the midst of this bodily function, when the wolf howled again, this time much closer. Immediately, another answered it. The horse gave a frightened whinny, reared up, and took off at a gallop. Vernon spun round in the dark, tripped on a rock and fell indelicately onto the ground. He lay there cursing loudly, listening to the sounds of the hooves fading away and the wolves howling in a gloating duet.

When he stood up, he realized he had lost his bearings. He turned slowly around in the darkness, trying to recognize any star formation that would point him in the right direction. There was none. He reflected briefly and bitterly on his lack of knowledge, but being uncontrollably optimistic, he soon decided on a route. Vernon had always held the opinion that it was better to act, even if one was wrong, rather than dither and do nothing. The horse had galloped off with his food, his water, his shield and his gauntlets, but he refused to worry about something he could do nothing about. The wolves howled again. He drew his sword, adjusted his helmet and advanced cautiously into the darkness.

. . .

THE OLD MAN WOKE him at dawn. John stood up slowly, careful to avoid waking the others who slept near him. He had been allotted a small mat among the male members of the old man's extended family. Although he had never slept with so many strangers before, he had rarely slept so soundly. As he rubbed his eyes and stretched his aching shoulders, he thought back on the previous night.

Once the bodies had been removed and the injured cared for, the majority of the village celebrated their unexpected victory. Meat was soon roasting on open fires, and women and children rushed around with platters of food for the men, who mostly ate standing up using their fingers and shared knives. While they were eating, older girls moved demurely among them, pouring honeyed drinks and fruit juices, and fluttering their eyes. After the feasting, the men sang and performed their traditional dances, becoming ever more energized as the evening wore on, encouraged by their women, who clapped and sang in support. Throughout the late evening, stories of individual heroisms were exchanged, becoming increasingly exaggerated. Many of the more important men gave glowing speeches in praise of John's miraculous horse, his deadly sword and his unmatched heroism. Eventually, he was called on to speak; he reluctantly agreed.

"I do not speak well," he said, searching for the right words. They cheered and laughed at such a joke: it was impossible this great warrior should be so modest. "You all fought bravely." He raised his cup. "I honour you!" He sat down amid howls of delight, and much encouragement for him to continue. To them, he was a warrior of ancient myth; a man who had appeared as if by magic, enabling them to defeat their hated foe. They all agreed he had a strange accent, but as none of them had ever met a person who was not an Arab, it did not occur to anyone that he might be an infidel.

Eventually, the old man stood up and declared the celebration over. John followed him to his meagre house. After a brief session of acknowledging the village elder's male relatives, he laid down among them and instantly fell into a deep sleep, unaware of the sounds and smells of the many bodies in the cramped space.

In the early flush of the day, the humble village was bathed in a soft golden light that concealed its poverty and made it appear, for a brief while, attractive and even romantic.

"Where will you go?" There was a tinge of regret in the old man's voice, for he was aware of the enormous benefit of a warrior of such stature. With such a man, and with their newly captured weapons, they would soon become the most important tribe in the area.

"Home," John said and pointed towards the northeast. The old man had no concept of distance. He nodded sadly, handing John a bowl of yogurt with dried fruit and a cup of water.

"Perhaps, you will return some day?"

John smiled. "Yes. Perhaps." He finished the satisfying meal, while the old man watched, his dark eyes revealing nothing. John remembered a saying often used by Ibrahim, and placed his hand on the old man's shoulder. "May God go with you. May your children respect you in your old age."

The village elder beamed, and led John to the small enclosure, where two young boys guarded Celestial. They had spent the night in the enclosure, wrapped up together in a blanket, with their wooden clubs by their sides, and they greeted John enthusiastically. Having nothing to give them, he thanked each boy individually, placing his hand on their heads. They blushed deeply, almost overwhelmed by the honour.

As John rode quietly away from the village, the old man stood like a rock, watching him go. The boys waved furiously, their eyes bright with excitement.

. . .

RALPH SAT AT THE long table, chewing meditatively on a hunk of bread, taking occasional sips of water. He was alone, refusing to take any part in Payen's arrangements for the burial of de Wulfric. Sergeant Little, with other soldiers, had attended to Payen's superficial head wound, and carried the heavy corpse to the large room, where Gwen had previously stayed and which served as a chapel.

The young knight, with his religious training, took responsibility for preparing the body for burial, and for conducting the funeral. He made no comment when Ralph refused to attend.

"Well, that's done," Payen said as he walked into the room. He sounded uneasy. Ralph nodded, unwilling to respond. "I buried him in his chain mail and with his sword." He began to pace the room with measured steps. "I have no idea how the Order would have buried him. There's a small graveyard outside. He's not the first Christian to have died here." His thoughts were disjointed, and he felt the need to justify his actions. "I had all the men stand to attention, and afterwards they placed heavy rocks on the grave. I ordered one of the men to carve a stone with de Wulfric's name." He sat on a stool and looked at Ralph. "What do we do now?"

It was the question Ralph had been wrestling with. There was no point in staying on at the castle, or going on to Jerusalem, and without knowing where Gwen was, he felt in a strange limbo. He had no regrets over de Wulfric's death, but neither did he have any satisfaction; he had killed men in battle, but apart from Lord Herlwin, his family's enemy, they had been strangers to him, people without names. De Wulfric had been a bully and a cold-blooded killer, merciless in battle and tyrannical in his everyday dealings with others. As a senior member of the Knights of the Order, his ambition and ruthlessness had been noticed, both within and outside the secretive society, and many would be grateful for his demise. Ralph felt it would be hypocritical to mourn such a man.

He imagined there would be repercussions, for although unpopular, Raymond was an important man and some of the Knights might use his death as an excuse for revenge. It had quickly become known to the Order that he and John were envoys for King Henry, and it was assumed their role was to report on the activities of the Order. The death of yet another senior member might be interpreted as part of an attempt by King Henry to wipe out those who opposed him and his church. Regardless of the truth, there would be consequences. Ralph was not concerned for his own safety, but he found it ironic that everyone, including the King, would misinterpret his actions, when his sole purpose was to rescue Gwen.

"I think your role is to defend this castle from the enemy. Mine is to find Mistress Gwen." He spoke with a sense of dull finality, unable to rise to humour. He regarded the anxious knight who radiated youth and innocence. Ralph felt strangely old: they were about the same age, yet years apart in their respective experiences of life. He made the effort to lighten the occasion. "I'm bad company, so the sooner I leave the better." Ralph tried a half-hearted grin.

"No, my Lord, you must stay," Payen faltered. "At least, stay until Ishmael, my scout returns." The knight stared solemnly at Ralph, noting his long blond hair, his aquiline nose and his bright blue eyes. He was slim, muscular and possessed the hands of an artist, and was unlike any other lord who had come from Christendom. Payen envied his fine looks, his complete self-assurance and his determination to find Gwen. Thinking about her gave Payen a surge of pleasure. In spite of his vows, he hoped his scout, Ishmael, would find her and bring her back to the castle. He felt a deep, irrational longing to see her again.

Ralph stared at the floor. It would make sense to wait, providing the scout found Gwen. But supposing he didn't? The thought of hanging around the castle with nothing to do but worry about Gwen was intolerable. He was a man of action, and knew he could not wait any longer. He glanced at Payen, and imagined him kneeling for hours in the holy places of Jerusalem, taking part in rituals that meant nothing to Ralph. His eyes glazed over as he imagined the huge stones of the Henge, where he had witnessed the ancient ceremonies, whose origins stretched back to the earliest times. It was the place where he and Tegwen... at the thought of her, he felt agitated and confused. He would not think about her, not when Gwen needed help.

"My Lord?" Payen was regarding him strangely, and Ralph realized he was standing and shaking his head. "Are you well?"

"Fine," he picked up his sword belt and fastened it around his waist. "If you'll lend me a horse and a few necessities, I'll be on my way."

"By yourself? That would be most unwise."

"I'll take my sergeant with me," he paused, "so I'll need two horses." He saw the disappointment in Payen's eyes. "If we don't find any trace of her, we'll be back on the second day."

Payen opened his mouth as if to protest, but said nothing.

"I promise to look after the horses." Ralph gave him a friendly pat on the shoulder and marched briskly out of the room. It was time to leave. Fresh energy flooded through him.

CHAPTER 15

THE RUGGED AREA FROM Antioch to Jerusalem, and from Damascus to the Mediterranean had been fought over for centuries. It encompassed ancient trading routes, and had been the natural and most suitable way for the passage of victorious armies, whose empires had blossomed and eventually decayed. Various civilizations, including the Assyrians, the Greeks and the Romans had influenced, changed and finally deserted the people who remained. The ruins of towns, castles, palaces and temples gave silent testament to the power and glory of kings and emperors, whose names perished before their buildings, and whose gods had failed to protect them.

It was with such thoughts John occupied himself on his return journey. He had discussed the Holy Land with Ralph before they left England, surprised at his detailed knowledge. Few people were literate, and of those who were, very few knew anything of the country where the cream of Christian chivalry battled with the forces of Islam.

"I told you," Ralph had replied with his usual indifference to anything he was good at, "I had a very unusual tutor. Bracken is responsible for all the useless information I store in my head," he had grinned, "and for my obvious brilliance."

John paused near the top of a small hill to check the landscape behind him. The path he was following appeared to be heading back the way he had travelled the previous night, and he hoped it would pass near the valley with the Greek temple. Once he reached the valley, he was certain he would be able to find his way back to Ibrahim's lands. He wondered if Saif and Rashid were safely home, and what their father's reaction was to the loss of their teacher and to the death of Hassan, his old friend and bodyguard. As he mulled over these thoughts, he realized he had not questioned his resolve to return to his benign captivity. He had given his word, and Ibrahim had shown his trust by returning both Celestial and his sword. His duty had been to protect the boys, especially after he had incapacitated Hassan, and he had felt bound to ensure their safe return.

As he thought about it, the absurdity of his situation dawned on him. He was a soldier under orders from the King of England; he had been captured and should have been ransomed by now. Ibrahim had treated him well, and in return he had honoured his side of the bargain, but how long should such an agreement last? If the boys had returned home safely, then he would have acquitted himself of his obligation, and if something terrible had happened to them... he shook his head. Then, there was nothing to be gained by returning.

He jerked on the reins, and while the big animal stamped his hooves impatiently, he sat and pondered his options: either he must return to Ibrahim and trust he would eventually be ransomed, or travel north to Antioch and get on with his life. It was important to know if Ralph and Gwen had survived the battle, and John knew there were questions about his own life he had to answer. The time had come for him to seize back his freedom and move on.

With the decision made, he turned off the path and headed north, confident he could find his way. A desolate landscape surrounded him: low hills and shallow valleys spread out as far as the eye could see. It was a desert of parched, bleached rocks with only the occasional desert bush. There were long stretches of sand and gravel, and other areas where wide, flat rocks, smoothed by eons of wind and occasional rain, provided a paved floor fit for giants. Some rocky outcrops were reduced to large blocks with narrow dry channels intersecting them, creating cool shadowy retreats from the merciless sun, and refuges for desert creatures. In the distance, tall mountains reared up on his right, while in front and to his left, a lower range of hills unfolded. There was no sign of human habitation.

At midday, when the heat was almost unbearable, he directed

Celestial into a small gulley with a large boulder almost blocking its entrance. It had steep sides with dark shadows at ground level. As his eyes gradually became accustomed to the dimness, John carefully checked the space for any obvious dangers. He dismounted and stood gazing up at the blue sky framed by the jagged sides. The hours in the intense brightness had made him feel lightheaded, and he drank gratefully from the water bladder the old man had provided. He watered the horse, holding a leather bag to its muzzle, and when Celestial had drunk, he refilled the bag with dry grain and led it to a sandy recess at the end of the gulley, where it could feed unseen by any passing travellers. Although it was unlikely that anyone would pass by, John did not want to take the risk. He ate some goats' cheese and a few dates, settling down in a space close to the horse, from where he had a narrow view of the opening. It was his intention to rest for only a short while, but as soon as he relaxed he was asleep.

Much later, he awoke with a start, unable to believe he had slept so soundly. He left the horse, and walked down to the opening of the gulley to gauge the position of the sun and get some idea of how long he had been asleep. In front of him was the huge boulder. He was moving around it when he glimpsed a movement. He flattened himself against the rock wall, and peered cautiously round the edge of the gulley. To his right, coming from the north, was a large group of horsemen. They were about two hundred paces away, but even at that distance John could see they were not Assassins.

These were soldiers in identical helmets and armour, and all in black. He recognized them as the same soldiers he had fought in the previous battle, and the same ones who had invaded Christchurch. He had no doubts as to their leader. Opening his right hand, he stared intently at the outline of the runes on his palm, wondering if he was to receive some indication of the Giant's presence. Nothing happened, and he dismissed the thought from his mind as he watched the horsemen gradually disappear into the sun. It was late in the afternoon, and he cursed his carelessness in falling asleep. However, he felt refreshed, and grateful he had not encountered the enemy cavalry, which he might have done if he had travelled earlier.

The sight of so many well-equipped soldiers was a worry. Did it mean they had won the battle, and were now attacking the major cities? He took stock of his situation and decided he must continue on his route to Antioch as soon as possible. Only there could he discover the truth. Celestial snickered happily when he returned; he adjusted the saddlebags and galloped away to the north.

After less than a mile he was forced to change direction when he saw a black column of marching men, moving from his right and crossing in a southwesterly direction. He guessed he was looking at many hundreds of soldiers, and logic dictated there would be scouting parties around. Reluctantly, John turned to the east, and galloped off in the hope of avoiding detection. After some miles, he stopped on a small hill to survey the area. The sun was low in the sky and directly behind him, and the bare hills in front were enveloped in bright golden light. He was savouring the moment, when a line of horsemen appeared on a distant hill at the far side of a shallow valley. There was no point in waiting to be seen. He quickly turned Celestial, and moved down the hill at right angles to his original direction.

Twice more he glimpsed large bands of horsemen. Retreating before them, he hoped to avoid a one-sided fight and a pointless death, or worse, the chance of being captured. Whenever he slowed the horse, the fading light and the distant appearance of more cavalry caused him to gallop on. Eventually, as though someone had extinguished a candle in a windowless room, the light vanished and he was forced to reduce the horse's speed to walking pace.

He stared up at the dark sky, and although the star patterns were different to those in England, he was reassured by their presence. Celestial picked his way carefully over the uneven ground. John sat alert in the saddle, the sword in his right hand, listening carefully for any sounds. He knew it was unlikely he was being followed: even if he had been seen from a distance, he would have been mistaken for an Arab; only the size of his horse would have caused interest. It was certain travellers did not journey after dark, and soldiers would, by choice, be in the safety of their camps. Only scouts on special duties, thieves and the feared Assassins would venture the unmapped wilderness of the desert at night.

Once again, he felt he was the victim of unpredictable events, and he reflected philosophically on his situation. His recent years had been a series of phases; some quiet ones, full of learning and discovery, followed by times of great activity and danger. He recognized his enforced stay with Ibrahim as a period of discovery, when he had learned about the local people, their language, their religion and their social values. Through his unusual captivity, he had come to understand them in ways that others from Christendom never did. Now, it was over, and like a piece of driftwood he was back in the maelstrom of life, being driven hither and thither before uncontrollable forces.

He broke off this chain of thought when he realized Celestial was following a clearly defined path. It glowed faintly in the dark, its surface crushed and polished by numerous hooves and feet. He was content to see where it went. Soon, he could distinguish bushes and small trees, and gradually the path began to slope down into a valley. Slowly, the darkness increased as tall trees shut out the starlit sky. The path bent to the right, and almost without warning he found himself in a valley where a large area of water reflected the stars, and where the air was cool and welcoming. At the end of the valley he could see a fire burning on a high platform, and in the flickering light he could discern the outline of tall columns. He sat, mesmerized by the sight: he had returned to the valley of the Greek temple. It was impossible to believe it was a coincidence.

He remained for a long time on the curving path, about ten feet above the level of the lake, carefully watching the fire and listening attentively. It was possible that some of the Assassins had remained behind to bury their dead, and had stayed on to await the return of those who had chased after him. Perhaps, the survivors of last night's defeat in the village had returned to lick their wounds. Either way, he would have an unpleasant welcome. But as he stared, carefully examining the valley, he saw no sign of horses, or of any movement around the ruin. It was unlikely they would light such a large fire and then leave, but at least he was familiar with the valley and with the crumbling remains of the temple. He decided to investigate rather than return to the unknown and featureless desert above.

Cautiously, with his sword resting on his shoulder, he advanced along the side of the lake towards the temple, keeping Celestial at walking pace. The high saddle gave him a clear view over the reeds and bushes that surrounded the tranquil lake, but on his right, the forest was dark and featureless, and small creatures scuttled around. He came to the place where Hassan had single-handedly fought the massed ranks of the Assassins. The ground was chewed up, reeds were flattened and there were dark spaces in the bushes. Further along on the right, where John remembered tethering Celestial, the bodies of two of the Assassins' horses were piled up, and there was a strong stench of rotting flesh. Sensing his horse's unease, John was compelled to move on past the makeshift abattoir, and he advanced towards the ruin quicker than he had intended.

His eyes searched the shadowy structure for any sign of life, but there was none. After peering behind and to both sides, he silently dismounted. He was loath to leave Celestial, and carefully climbed the broad stone steps leading the obedient animal and allowing it to find its own balance before moving cautiously on. At the top of the steps, one side of the imposing pillars was lit with the warm firelight, while deep shadows cloaked the rest. John let go of the reins and sprang forward, sword in hand, darting silently around the stones, quickly establishing that nobody was hiding in the ruins, and no danger appeared to exist.

He led Celestial to the rear of the temple where the altar had once been, and tethered the animal to the remaining hand of the Goddess Diana. It gave him a fleeting sense of satisfaction that, after all these millennia, the Goddess still had a role to play. After carefully searching the back of the ruined building, he found no recent evidence of the Assassins. There were no horses, nor any indication that people had passed through in the past few hours, yet the fire was burning well, and had been recently tended. He walked back to the front platform, and gazed out into the blackness. When he stood in front of the fire, he could clearly see the silent surface of the lake. On each side, the paths stretched into the darkness, like pale arms embracing the water. He listened intently but, apart from the muted calls of the waterfowl, there was no sign of life.

Baffled, he sat down on a long flat stone near the fire, wondering how, during the long hours of avoiding the enemy soldiers, he had returned to this valley. Once again, he felt events were beyond his control, and he waited with a sense of relaxed optimism for what might ensue.

'Well, I'm glad you're here at last. You seem to take a delight in keeping me waiting." It was an English voice, deep and rich and hinting at humour.

John did not jump to his feet in shock, wondering how anyone could have escaped his thorough search, but sat quite still, gazing at the fire, a broad grin on his face. "Owl? How could I have expected anyone else?" He turned towards the voice. Standing a few feet away from the fire was a small, wiry, old man with a large hooked nose, and dark smiling eyes. He was dressed in a brown robe and his large feet were enclosed in rope sandals. In one hand he carried a brace of duck, and in the other a cavernous bag.

"So, do I call you John, Giles or Gilles?" The unmistakable voice had not aged over the past years, and looking at him, John saw he possessed the same energy and liveliness. They had only ever met twice, but each meeting had left an indelible impression, as both events had occurred after John had been in danger, and when he was uncertain of his future. Owl had been a welcome, if unconventional, friend whether at night in a Wessex forest, or by day at the Henge in Salisbury Plain. On each occasion, he had skilfully directed the conversation, drawing from John the answers to questions he had been unwilling to recognize. After each time, he had met people who had guided him along his path; the last had been Ralph, who had become his friend and tutor.

"I think you know I'm still John." He stood up, ready to embrace the old man whom he was genuinely pleased to meet again. Owl did not appear to notice, and dropped to one knee, busily arranging the two birds for roasting on a spit.

"Well then, John, you'd better unpack this bag while I deal with these birds." His enthusiasm was infectious, and soon the birds were plucked and sizzling on a makeshift spit at the edge of the fire, while John unpacked the bag, and laid out platters, knives, two metal goblets, a flask of wine and a variety of food. "It is necessary to eat well, when you have important things to do," Owl said ambiguously.

However, nothing of importance was discussed as they prepared the meal, and John decided he would not ask Owl how he had managed to appear at this moment and in this unlikely place. He knew from past experience that Owl would only answer the questions he considered relevant.

"I'm glad you're here," John said, as he enjoyed the cooked meat.

"Yes, this is a good place to be," Owl agreed, as he poured the wine. "Sometimes, bad things have occurred here, but the essence of its goodness remains in spite of the bloodshed."

John knew it to be true. There was a sense of peacefulness and tranquillity throughout the small valley, and in the firelight the temple was warm and inviting. The violent atmosphere of yesterday had dissipated, as though it had never happened. "Apart from the dead horses, there is little to indicate the bloody battle of yesterday."

"This temple has survived more than a millennium, and will continue to be here after nations have achieved greatness and fallen back into obscurity. In a year, the remains of the horses will be gone, taken back into the earth from which they came. Time is the great healer. Places like this valley, like the stones on Salisbury Plain, will remain sacred, no matter what petty desecrations occur." Owl was staring out at the still waters of the lake, a beneficent smile on his face. He gnawed reflectively on a leg of meat. "So, you are on your way to Jerusalem?"

The question was so unexpected John almost choked on his wine. He was about to ask Owl why he was so sure, but thought better of it. "I was trying to get back to Antioch."

"Why?"

"Because my friends are there. At least, I hope they're in Antioch," he hesitated, "if they survived the battle."

"If they have survived, why would they stay in Antioch?"

It seemed such a straightforward question, yet John found himself struggling with the answer. "The armies were originally marching to Tripoli, and I think, eventually, the Order wants to take Gwen to Jerusalem."

"Ah yes, Gwen. She was the one you were trying to find when we first met, and again you were searching for her when we last met at the Henge." He smiled. "Here we are at our third meeting, and you are still looking for her." He chuckled. "My young friend, searching for Gwen seems to be your life's work."

There was a certain truth to this statement, and John was forced to smile at the absurdity of the situation. Since meeting Gwen, his life had been a series of relatively brief periods of enjoying her company, followed by long separations. There was no doubting the fierce attraction they felt for each other, but since the old priest, Brother Matthew's dying question: 'Is Gwen your... sister?' John's life had changed. From that moment, he had ceased to see her in terms of marriage, and had tried to protect her from a distance; his longing for her was intense, yet his guilt for having such thoughts about someone who might be his sister was greater.

He stared into the fire. "At times I feel my life is not my own. As though I must accommodate to situations which are not of my choosing."

Owl did not reply.

"When we met at the standing stones, I had arrived by accident, yet, you said my arrival was forecast in the stars. Did they tell you we would meet here, tonight?"

"Of course."

"Are they telling you I will be travelling to Jerusalem, whether I want to or not?"

Owl drank deeply, enjoying his wine. "Life is very complex. It is like a profound song passed down through the centuries, and everyone gets the chance to sing it. Some don't bother, that's their choice; we all have choices, even you." John stared at him, his brows furrowed. "The majority learn the song, and sing it quite well, although their lives are unimportant in the big choir of life. But, some come to appreciate the meaning of what they sing, and become teachers, priests and leaders of countries." He shook his head, as though having a discussion within himself. "Sadly, becoming a teacher, a priest or a king does not necessarily mean you have a full understanding of anything, which is why humanity is always moving from one crisis to the next. But, in the great movement of history, there are those who, for a short while, sing the song with passion and knowledge, their influence balancing the evil of those few who come to hate the song, and wish to destroy it. Very occasionally, individuals appear who are considerably in advance of the others, who have come before them in their understanding of the song, and they are able to provide those subtle changes, those advances in wisdom, which enable life to continue."

"Are you one of those people? The ones who alter the song?" John was reminded of the time when, one evening, soon after meeting Old Mary, she had revealed she was a guardian and defender of the old ways. He remembered being afraid of her because, at that moment, she looked different: all-powerful, and ageless. She had reassured him, and her words rang clear in his mind: *One day you will be someone else. Someone you have been before, and will be again.'* He had not understood what she meant; his life was just beginning. Now, he was closer to an understanding, thanks, in part, to Ralph, and also to a gradual reclaiming of skills and knowledge that for years had remained locked away in his subconscious. He looked at the strange symbol in the palm of his right hand. "Am I one of those people?"

There was a pause as Owl cut himself some meat from the plump breast of one of the ducks. He seemed in no hurry to answer. "You will remember Old Mary's caution to you?"

His first reaction was to accuse Owl of reading his mind. But over the years, and in their brief meetings, he had gained an acceptance of the way Owl behaved. He suspected the old man possessed strange powers, but instead of challenging him, he had come to a comforting acceptance. Owl was on his side, and John did not want to know how he appeared or disappeared, or how he seemed to know what others were thinking. John took a deep breath. "Yes, it has annoyed me for years. *'When the hour is right.'* That small statement has been the answer to questions I have wanted answers to for many years, and always there has been the inference that I am not yet old enough to understand."

"Are you beginning now to understand what it means?"

"Yes. I think I do. I am beginning to believe the time is fast approaching when the many questions I need to have answered, and the reasons for the path I have been forced to take will, somehow, be revealed to me."

"Are you prepared for answers you do not wish to receive, and for truths that cut to the heart? Life is not easy, even for those who know and understand the frailty of life and recognize the unfairness of chance. Life can destroy even the most gifted." Owl took a casual sip of his wine, as if his words were unimportant.

Before he responded, John also took a sip of the wine, and inwardly reflected on its quality. He recognized the gravity of Owl's statements, and was certain this meal and their discussion was one of the most crucial periods of his life. "I need to know why I was chosen to have this sign of power on my right hand. I need to know the importance of my name, Giles Plantard, and I want to know why it has the power to protect me on some occasions and not others."

"You appear to be alive. Certainly, you're not a ghost. That would suggest that whenever you thought it necessary to use the power to protect yourself, you were wrong." Owl chortled happily to himself as he drank more wine. "Your name is significant. I am surprised you have not investigated its origin. It is a very old name, and like most old names has changed its spelling and even its meaning. Suffice to say, its symbolism is unique. Whether it is Giles Plantard, Gilles de Plantard, or any other corruption is unimportant. The importance is in the symbolism; it is what the name stands for. In recent centuries, as mankind staggered out of ignorance, there came a need for new gods and new beliefs. Modern man could no longer believe in the Goddess Diana," he waved his hand about, "who represented a narrow, limited belief suited only to hunters and..." he giggled, "those who believe in magic and the moon."

John pondered his answer. "But why me? Why have I been given this..." he breathed in deeply, "this gift? I did not choose it. It was forced upon me."

"Suppose everything that has happened in your recent life occurred without this gift, as you call it. Would you still be alive?"

In his imagination, he saw the other Giant rise up from the flower fields near Woodford; he heard his own voice yell: 'Giles Plantard', and remembered escaping certain death. There was the time in the church belfry when the one- armed man was going to kill him, and the name Giles Plantard had enabled him to escape being murdered. He remembered the beach near Christchurch when the second of the two giant brothers was forced to flee, and the great battle in the mountains south of Antioch, when his hand had glowed and the same Giant had fled before John could use the power of his name. He shuffled his feet. "No. I admit there have been occasions when I was grateful for this 'gift', for want of a better word. But it did not help me when I needed it at other times."

"As I said to you before, you did not need the power, which is why you are still alive today." Although it was a rebuff, it was spoken with a hint of merriment, and John had to acknowledge it as such. Owl continued to attack the carcasses with his knife, and having piled his plate, he smiled at John. "You'd better tuck in before I finish the lot." Again, his laugh resonated with good will and John was forced to laugh with him.

As he chewed on the meat, which tasted better than he had anticipated, bearing in mind that there was no sauce or other condiment, John reflected on his earlier question. "Why should I go to Jerusalem?"

"What do you know about Jerusalem?" Owl responded.

"I know it is the Holy City, and one that the Christians had sworn to liberate on their Crusade."

"Did they liberate it?"

"Well, of course they did. In 1099 they captured the city."

"What about the Christians in the city?"

"What about them?"

"There were many Christians in the city. They were living in harmony with the Moslems, the Jews, and other religions. Did you know the Crusaders, as they were called, slaughtered everyone they could find when they broke into the city, other Christians included?" John shook his head. "When certain knights reached the remains of the Great Temple, what order do you think they belonged to?" Again John shook his head. "The Knights of the Order!" Owl erupted in laughter. "Is it not a sad joke that the men who came to liberate the city destroyed, or almost destroyed, the very reason they had attacked it in the first place?

"What happened?"

"You were in that city and hidden in that temple area. Close to you was concealed one of the Swords of Power. Gwen was also in that temple, and a Knight of the Order, Sir Maurice de Ridefort, recognizing her importance, smuggled her back to England, where she became the assumed daughter of Tom Roper, the blacksmith, as a way of keeping her safe. You, also, were rescued. Your uncle, the last remaining adult of your bloodline, managed to smuggle you back to England, but not before you were seriously hurt in a storm at sea. You were knocked unconscious, and did not fully recover until you came to the cottage of Old Mary."

"The tall, thin knight... he was my uncle?

Owl's dark eyes focused on his, and there was a long pause. "Your father died in the slaughter that followed the breaching of Jerusalem's walls. Your mother also died that night, as did many others of your family."

John took a deep breath. Over these recent years, he had been comforted by the dim memory of a tall knight who had protected him on a large boat in a furious storm. He had a faint memory of a castle with bleached banners, and vague recollections of religious houses, but whether they had belonged to nuns or monks he could never be certain. Now he was faced with the fact that he had no memory of either of his parents. "Are you certain he was my uncle?"

"Your parents died in the slaughter when Jerusalem was captured."

"Is my uncle alive?"

"I am sorry to say he died at sea, which is why you were given to a nunnery. They looked after you."

"I remember a castle with banners."

"Yes." Owl took a long drink of his wine. "The Order took an interest in you for a while, but you were unwell. The injury to your head made you appear stupid. The Order was convinced you would become a lunatic, and they released you back to a monastery. I understand you escaped and were guided to Old Mary's cottage."

"Where my memory begins." John rubbed his face with his hands. The news was both tragic and yet encouraging. At last he knew what the vague memories represented. "What happened to Gwen?"

"I think you know what happened to Gwen. She became an unusual peasant girl, who was carefully tutored by Brother Matthew, himself a member of the Order. You met her when the powers of darkness had tracked her down, and you were responsible for eradicating one of the giant brothers, whom I would identify as a power of evil. He was a person who was intent on destroying the song."

"How did I come to live so close to Gwen's home?"

Owl gave John a piteous look. "It was in the stars."

John almost wanted to scream. It was like pulling teeth. "What is the point of it all? Am I, or am I not related to Gwen?"

"Why should you be?"

"Brother Matthew asked me if Gwen was my sister, just before he died. Until that question, I had not even the faintest thought she might be my sister. Since then, I have been tortured by the idea we might be related." He took a deep breath. "I know there must be some connection. I have heard her referred to as the Holy Grail, and I have been called the Keeper of the Grail. I want to know who we are, and if we are related!"

Owl chewed meditatively on a bone. He did not react to John's outburst. "I can tell you for certain, you are not brother and sister."

"We're not! Why did you not tell me before?"

"You didn't ask."

It was so overwhelming, that John felt he wanted to lash out at this man who claimed to know about his life, and Gwen's, and could have revealed the information years ago. "Why didn't you tell me last time?" he yelled. He was past control.

"Because you had not reached the moment when the hour is right."

"And is this the right hour?" John bellowed.

Owl grinned, sticking out his lean jaw. "Obviously, or I would not be telling you these facts."

John felt like a deflated bladder, and fought to regain his composure. He considered carefully before he spoke. "Am I to understand that Gwen is not my sister?" Owl nodded judiciously. "So what is the connection between us?"

"You are the Keeper of the Grail."

"Yes? What am I to understand by that?"

Owl stood up, and stretched. "Good meal," he muttered. "You, my valued young friend, are exactly what the name implies. You are the Keeper of the Grail, and you and your family, through generations have protected Gwen's bloodline." He chuckled. "Naturally, Gwen is not her name. That is a name Tom Roper, the blacksmith, gave her. But her family is unique. She is the last remaining member of her bloodline that came to importance over a thousand years ago. It was her ancestor who became one of those brilliant people who realized how best to alter the song. The effect of his teaching has lasted over the centuries, but sadly, as time passes, the truth dims." He suddenly stopped, and turned to face John. "You will remember the last time we parted?"

"Yes, we were at the Henge, you told me I would meet someone who would help me become the person I wanted to be." John could clearly picture Ralph approaching the standing stones pursued by a gang of cutthroats. It had been the start of a totally new life.

"You are in for another treat, but this time you will be the leader, not the led. A toast to you, Giles Plantard." John stood up and touched goblets with Owl. The small man smiled warmly up at him, and John felt his goblet was suddenly heavier than it had been. "Who knows when we will meet again, my young friend, but remember, you are surrounded by invisible friends," he began to laugh, and tears flowed down his creased face, "no matter how embarrassing that may be!" He stepped back, and raising his goblet emptied it in a single gulp.

John attempted to do the same, but there was more wine in his goblet than he had anticipated. He closed his eyes, finding himself unable to stop drinking until the goblet was empty. "Wow," he murmured, "that was quite a toast."

He looked up, and Owl was gone, and it was very dark. He turned around, feeling unsteady on his feet, unable to locate where Owl had moved to.

"Owl!" he called, and was aware his speech sounded slurred. "Owl! I wants t'arsh you something." His tongue refused to work properly, and as he attempted to move, he tripped over a stone and fell heavily on the tiled floor. A great sense of loss welled up in him, as he clambered back onto his feet: Owl had not answered all his questions. He sank down on a flat stone, sensing it was the one he had shared with Owl, and tried to focus his eyes. The temple seemed to be moving, and he was suddenly aware that the fire had vanished. Where the bright flames had illuminated the temple's pillars there was a dark space and beyond, in the waving distance, the lake reflected the bright stars on its still surface. He wanted to call for Owl, but his mouth seemed unable to form the word. He tried to stand; immediately his legs folded up beneath him and he sank awkwardly to a kneeling position on the floor. It was then he knew he was not alone.

John felt the skin prickle on the back of his neck. In this ancient place, it was possible to imagine ghosts, and he became aware of things in the air around him. He sensed their presence and was at once reassured of his safety. In a moment he passed from fear to confidence, from unease to contentment. "Thank you," he muttered, as he stretched out on the cool tiles. "Thank you."

In the background Celestial stamped his feet, but John heard nothing.

CHAPTER 16

"I DON'T KNOW HOW FAST they would have travelled, but they have a lead of almost a day and a half. To begin with they went east, cut south and then turned west. The scout was certain they were in a small valley leading to the coast." Ralph was squatting on the ground, pointing with his dagger to a rough map he had scratched in the hard earth. Sergeant Little was kneeling beside him. "The scout, Ishmael, reckons they would have retraced their journey and headed back north if they'd seen the Assassins. He told Payen he would be searching north and east of here."

Sergeant Little scratched his bearded cheek, deep in thought. "Suppose they didn't see no Assassins? They might 'ave continued on to Tripoli."

"Let's hope they didn't go south," Ralph mused. "They would almost certainly have been captured." He stood up and stretched. "I think our only hope is to continue east until we find a well-used track going north. Then we follow it until, hopefully, we find them or we reach Antioch. There's no point in doing anything else."

"Right, m'Lord." Little was also a man of action. He enjoyed serving with Ralph, who never hesitated when a decision was needed. He lumbered over to his horse, and his large face took on a truculent expression. "Ye behave yerself this time, or else." He waved a finger at the horse, which tried to bite it. "Ye're a miserable little runt," he muttered as he climbed into the saddle, "my 'orses at 'ome would make twice o' thee."

Ralph grinned; it was good to be away from the castle, and to sit on a horse again. Even if they failed to find Gwen, it was better to be doing something than waiting around for a report that might never arrive. "Sergeant Little, I've known you all my life, and I've never seen you on such a small horse!" He let out a roar of laughter. "Let's see what it's made of."

They rode off together, each trying to adjust to an uncomfortable saddle, and each determined not to complain.

. . .

THEY EVENTUALLY FOUND A well-used path travelling north and south, and having checked carefully for any sign of other travellers, they turned north. By early evening, when the temperature was beginning to fall, Ralph called a halt. The horses were blown after hours of hard riding, and both men slid thankfully from their saddles, their muscles protesting and their bodies bathed in sweat.

Neither said anything while they drank deeply, and removed the heavy saddles from the suffering horses. Both men sank down on a small ledge of rock, continuing to sip water and sparing small amounts to wash their dust-caked faces.

"I reckons I be ready to stop," Little said. He took off his helmet and gauntlets, and rubbed his rough hands through his thick black hair, which was showing the first streaks of grey.

"Me too. There's no point in travelling at night. We don't know exactly where we are, and I would hate to miss them in the dark." Ralph stood up and slowly stretched, moving his head from side to side. They were in an area of low hills, some of which were mere collections of broken, eroded rock, while others were smoother with large boulders balanced precariously on the tops. The path wound its way through the harsh landscape, following the easiest route. "I think this is as good a resting place as any other," Ralph said, as he surveyed the area. He noticed a high mound close by, with an easy access to its highest point. "Sergeant Little," he said, using the official title, much to the satisfaction of his former blacksmith, "I think we might risk a fire. It could be a cold night. You prepare the meal. I'll check the area." He pointed to the high mound. "If I see an army of Assassins, I promise to let you know!" As he walked away, he could hear Little chortling to himself and was grateful to be in the company of a man who was a life-long friend.

He reached the summit of the small hill as the sun sank below the distant horizon. In the twilight, he stared out in all directions, quietly confident there would be no sign of life. He and Little had travelled for hours without even a glimpse of a wild animal, let alone a human traveller. As he looked casually to the north, his body suddenly tensed. Far up the road he glimpsed riders approaching, their white robes clearly visible in the fading light. Ralph took a deep breath and forced himself to calmly judge the unexpected travellers. He identified three riders, two in white robes and one in a dark colour that was unclear in the dim light.

He ducked below the skyline, and clambering quickly down the slope in the fading light, he assessed the possible alternatives. It was a small group and he was confident he and Little could deal with them if they proved hostile. He arrived back as the campfire burst into bright flame. "Sergeant Little!" he called, unable to see the tall man.

"Any bother, m'Lord?" Little responded, appearing from behind the horses. He had the food bags in his hands.

"There are three horsemen approaching." He stared at the fire, and said nothing for a moment. "We'll keep the fire in; it'll attract them. I want you to move the horses down there." He pointed to the deepening shadows among large stones further away from the path. "Secure them, and return as quickly as you can. I'll keep a lookout until you return." Ralph noticed he was breathing heavily, as excitement coursed through his body.

Little led the horses down a narrow passageway of boulders, and having hobbled the animals, he returned quickly to find Ralph crouching on a ledge about seven feet up. He was staring intently down the path. "What's happening?" Little whispered.

"Nothing. Either they've turned back, they've left the path, or they're moving very slowly." Ralph continued to stare down the empty road.

"Where d'ye want me to be?" Little hissed. He had drawn his sword, and was looking around for his helmet.

"Get back in the shadows. When they arrive we should be able to see them in the firelight. If they are innocent travellers we will not show ourselves. If they want to fight, we should have the advantage."

Little disappeared without comment. He put on his helmet and his gauntlets, and waited in the deep shadows with his sword gripped firmly in his strong hand. He welcomed a fight with any heathens; he believed they were all murderers and had stolen the Holy Land from God-fearing Christians. Like many other soldiers, his understanding of the people of the area was limited. In his mind, all those who did not believe in Christ and the Crusaders were heathen, and deserved to die. It never occurred to him to wonder about the religious beliefs of foreigners. The Church had never explained that Jews, Moslems and Christians all worshipped the same God, but with a different name. To do so might have caused men to question the motives of their leaders.

They waited in silence. The darkness descended and the fire sank down to a vivid red glow, illuminating the surrounding area. Silently, out of the darkness, the three horsemen arrived, their animals moving at walking pace. The riders saw the fire, and stopped, their eyes searching the darkness and their ears listening for any sound. After a tense pause, two of the men dismounted, drew their swords, and advanced cautiously towards the light of the glowing embers. They fanned out, checking the shadows, leaving the third one with the horses. Suddenly, one of Arabs glanced up and yelled a warning when he saw Ralph, crouched on a ledge, his sword drawn. With lightning speed the Arabs moved to the other side of the fire, giving themselves the chance to see their attacker.

Ralph jumped down, landing in a crouched position, and faced them from the other side of the glow. He waited for a brief moment, before springing across the embers, and roaring loudly as he did so, his sword raised high above him. At the same moment, Little burst out of the shadows like a demon from Hell, screaming manically. With his height and his metal helmet he resembled a frightening mythological creature.

The two Arabs immediately retreated back towards their horses, and Ralph and Little charged forward. The white robed figures counter attacked with surprising agility, and caught Ralph and Little wrong-footed. There was a rapid exchange of blows, and the loud clash of steel. It was only the longer reach of the English swords that kept the two smaller Arabs at bay. Little, with his height and long arms, was able to force the shorter Arab to give ground, and Ralph with his skill and experience was more than a match for his agile, but less competent, adversary. As the Arab fighters moved into a more defensive posture, they retreated past the fire, concentrating on blocking the thrusts and slashes of the heavy long swords. Meanwhile, the third rider remained uninvolved, sitting like a dark statue just beyond the light.

Ralph and Little moved to either side of the fire, their faces illuminated in the red glow. "When I give the word, we'll rush them!" Ralph yelled, knowing it was unlikely the Arabs spoke English. He took a deep breath, and glanced across at Little, whose eyes seemed unusually large. "Now!" he bellowed, hurling himself forward. As he did so, he heard his name being screamed. It was a woman's scream. He paused, unable to believe what he was hearing. It was Gwen. In a flash he understood: she was a prisoner.

"Kill them!" he urged Little, and rushed at the two men who defended themselves with a desperate energy. He lunged furiously at the figure in front of him; the man blocked each blow with unexpected strength; yet, when Ralph might have expected a counter move from his opponent, there was none. Little was having more success; his smaller enemy was giving ground rapidly.

"Ralph! They're my friends!" Gwen's urgent cry penetrated Ralph's consciousness, and his determination to revenge himself on Gwen's supposed captors faded instantly. But, not before Little had broken the smaller man's defence, beating him to the ground, and knocking the curved sword out of his hand. The sergeant raised his sword, the blood lust in his eyes, intent on killing his enemy. He heard nothing beyond the loud pulse thudding in his ears.

"No!" Ralph yelled, alert to the disaster unfolding before him. He swung his sword in an upward movement, intercepting Little's weapon as the blade arced down towards its intended victim. The Arab stared up in a paroxysm of fear, as the two swords clashed over his head. Ralph, unable to maintain his balance, collapsed on top of the young man, only just pushing the deadly blade to one side. Little drew back, startled, unable to believe he might have killed his young lord. His relief was overwhelming as Ralph rose awkwardly to his feet.

"That was close," Ralph gasped, wincing as he clutched his sword arm; it was where he had previously received the arrow wound, and his shoulder joint was on fire. He staggered with the pain, dropping his sword on the ground. Gwen ran towards him. He half turned, holding her tightly with his one good arm, as she embraced him and cried uncontrollably.

. . .

LATER, AS THEY SAT around the fire, they assessed the damage caused by their misunderstanding. The young Arab lay on his back, barely conscious, and nursing a cut across his chest. Gwen and Ishmael had cleaned the wound and applied a makeshift bandage to stop the bleeding, but they knew they must get him back to the castle as soon as possible. Ralph was sitting propped up against a rock, his arm in a sling, and bound tightly to his chest. The pain was intense, and he was slowly drinking Sergeant Little's supply of wine, in an attempt to lessen the agony. Ishmael had escaped with a few minor cuts to his sword hand, and Little's only injury was to his pride. He sat away from the others, looking awkward, and frequently glancing towards Ralph, unable to believe he had almost killed him. Little was also having a problem in understanding how Gwen could consider the two Arabs as her friends.

"Once we have recovered, we should start back towards the castle," Ishmael said. His knowledge of the area gave him the right to make decisions, and Ralph was in no state to give orders.

"I reckons we should wait 'ere 'til dawn," Little said, truculently. "We could get lost at night." He did not like taking orders from heathens.

"We will not get lost. I know the way." Ishmael spoke quietly but with great determination. "My friend will get a fever, and we should get him back to the castle before the midday heat." He looked towards Ralph who nodded in agreement.

"Is Lord de Wulfric still there?" Gwen asked. Her voice betrayed her concern.

"Yes. He is likely to be there," Ishmael said.

"He's dead." Ralph muttered thickly. "I killed him."

There was a long silence, as they looked at Ralph, each with individual reactions: Little was proud of Ralph's ability to defeat a man almost twice his size; Ishmael considered it divine justice, and Gwen wrestled with two opposing thoughts: relief and guilt. If de Wulfric were dead, it meant she was free of the Order, but his death was yet another name on a list of people who had died because of her. If she had been left alone in her quiet Wessex village she would have been happy, and none of these senseless killings would have happened. Because of her, at least six Knights of the Order had died; some had been unpleasant men, but others had been well-meaning and even gallant in their way. Her stepfather had been seriously injured while trying to find her, had never fully recovered, and could be dead by now. The peasants, who had followed John when he was searching for her, had died in uncounted numbers. Battles had been fought and soldiers on both sides had died horribly, and all because of her. Even John, the secret love of her life, was presumed dead. "Martin's dead as well," she said. Tears welled up in her eyes. "When will the killings cease, Ralph? When will people stop dying because of me?"

"It's not your fault," Ralph said quietly. His head throbbed and although the wine had dulled the pain in his shoulder, he was having a problem keeping his eyes open. He breathed in deeply. "I met Martin after the battle. A good man." He rubbed his face with his free hand. "He loved you."

"I know," Gwen sobbed. "All the people who love me seem to die."

Ishmael and Little shuffled uncomfortably, and Ralph closed his eyes. "Not all," he said to himself. "Not all."

· · ·

IN THE DEEP OF night, a solitary figure moved cautiously along a path by the side of a lake. The man could see by the stars an occasional flash of water, and had noted from the top of the valley that it was a long lake with some sort of structure at one end. In the starlight, a pale, whitish path stretched along the side of the water, and a quarter moon adorned the sky, but contributed only little to the scene. The helmetted figure advanced nervously along the path, sword in hand, occasionally pausing to listen. Apart from the continuous pulsing sound of multitudinous frogs, and the occasional soft peeping of water fowl, the valley appeared to be unoccupied by humans.

Eventually, the cautious individual reached an impressive ruin of a building, with broad steps leading up to shadowy, tall pillars. Slowly, and with great care, he crept up the stone steps. Behind, the lake was a starlit, peaceful expanse of water in contrast to the ancient building, most of which was in deep shadow. The figure reached the top of the stairs and waited by the tall pillars to adjust to the reduced light. Without warning, there was a long, gurgling groan from the darkness, and the man froze. After a long wait, during which there was no repeat of the sound, he moved tentatively forward, into the outer ring of blackness. There was a sudden, soft encounter as the figure's feet shuffled forward. Two male voices exclaimed loudly; the figure with the sword felt his ankles grasped, and instantly his legs were whipped away from under him. He fell backwards, landing heavily on the stone tiles, his head ringing inside the iron helmet. In the unexpected fall, he dropped his sword and desperately flung himself up into a kneeling position as his assailant, unable in the darkness to find his own sword, made a similar movement. A half-hearted tussle took place, as each person tried to understand what was happening.

"Look, my good man, I didn't mean to wake you." It was an English voice, and one that resonated with the authority of money, rather than experience.

"I'm English as well, we don't need to fight each other." The second voice spoke from a position of strength, as he had begun to force the other man back. He relaxed his grip, and tried, unsuccessfully, to stand up. His head was throbbing and his tongue felt twice its normal size. He had never been drunk before.

In the darkness the intruder stood up. "Good idea. I didn't want to hurt you. I'm Sir Vernon de Kari." He removed his helmet, and gauntlets, and rubbed his ears to stop the ringing.

"I'm..." he stopped himself. "You can call me John." He staggered to his feet, and without a light to focus on managed, by chance, to grasp Vernon's arm. The knight gave a yelp of alarm, and tried to pull away. "Don't panic," John muttered peevishly. "Just help me out to the steps, I can't see a thing."

"Oh, right. Glad to help." As he supported John out, in front of the pillars, Vernon could not resist adding: "I never actually panic, myself."

John groaned inwardly and concentrated on staying upright. Once he was able to focus on the lake, and on the paths on each side, he gradually gained in confidence. Letting go of Vernon's arm, he sat heavily on the top step. "Who are you?" he asked abruptly.

Vernon sat down next to him and could see in the gloom that John was dressed like an Arab. "Pretty poor show," he thought to himself. "He's gone native." He felt it was important to let this fellow know whom he was dealing with. "I'm Lord de Kari. I'm in charge of the English forces in Antioch."

John turned to look at him in the gloom, and tried to remember if he had ever seen him before. "I thought Lord d'Escosse was in charge?" He felt a pit in his stomach, wondering if this knight's appointment to the post meant Ralph had died in the battle?

Vernon cleared his throat. "He was, but I'm in charge at the moment."

"Is he alive?"

"Oh, yes. Fit as a flea, last time I saw him."

This was such good news that John ignored Vernon's supercilious manner. "Where is he now?"

"He should be well on his way to Jerusalem by now."

"Jerusalem?"

"Yes. He went off to track down some young woman who had been abducted by an unpleasant knight called de Wulfric. I must say I..."

"Gwen? Was her name Gwen?"

Vernon was beginning to feel irritated. This Englishmanturned-Arab, seemed to know many people. "Mistress Gwen," he corrected him. "Rather good looking, I quite fancied her myself."

John realized he was clenching his fists. "Does the name Gilles de Plantard mean anything to you?"

"Oh, yes," Vernon affected a small yawn. "The Governor was talking about him. I believe he was a friend of d'Escosse's. He went missing after some recent battle, just before my time. They reckon he's dead." He felt he had put this presumptuous native-lover in his place. Perhaps the man had a horse, in which case Vernon felt it was his duty to borrow it from him. He was just beginning to feel a sense of contentment, when he was thrown to the ground, and a pair of very strong fingers began pressing into his windpipe.

"Listen, you pompous idiot. I am Gilles de Plantard, and if you don't tell me everything you know, I am going to feed you to the vultures," John thundered. The whites of his eyes gleamed in the starlight.

Vernon felt decidedly put down. "I'm sorry about that," he gasped weakly. "I didn't recognize you."

· · ·

By the time the early morning sun beamed into the valley, everything had been discussed and explored to John's satisfaction, and his original anger towards Vernon had evaporated. Although irritating and naïve, Vernon could also be amusing, and once he understood that John was the personal friend of Lord d'Escosse, had ceased pretending to be more than he was.

They sat together on the bottom step of the temple, and as far away from the dead horses as possible. It was pleasant to sit with their feet in the cool water, sharing the food from John's saddlebag. Vernon's head no longer ached, the water from the lake proved drinkable, and as he ate he enjoyed the increasing warmth of the new sun. Close by, Celestial was browsing the undergrowth, and overhead the vultures were circling in an otherwise empty sky.

"The armies are marching to Tripoli," Vernon said. "Perhaps, if we both share your horse, we could make contact with some of their scouts in the next day or so?" He spoke deferentially; the memory of John's fingers around his neck was still a painful one.

"I'm not sure I want to rejoin the army. They all believe I'm dead, and they can obviously do without me." He shot Vernon a wry smile. "My main aim is to catch up with Ralph and help him release Gwen from the clutches of the Order." He withdrew his feet from the cool water. "Which is why I must get to Jerusalem as soon as possible."

Vernon looked dismayed. "What about me?" There was a hint of panic in his voice. "I mean, couldn't we share your horse until we meet up with some of the army? Then I could get back to my command, and you could carry on to Jerusalem."

John shook his head. "I don't want anyone to know I'm alive. Now that I have your confirmation that Ralph and Gwen survived the battle, I know what I must do. As long as people continue to believe I'm dead, I'll avoid being recognized. The Crusade, and what it stands for, no longer interests me. I have stopped believing all Arabs are the enemy." He pretended not to notice the alarm on Vernon's face.

"I know Gwen wants to be free of the Order and get back to England, and Ralph is only out here to protect the family name. With the deaths of Lord Longsword and Sir Stephen de Bois, the English branch of the Order has been severely weakened, and King Henry is unlikely to take further interest in its activities. It would mean Ralph could claim success in his mission and regain the King's confidence, which would allow him to return to his family estates."

"And you?" Vernon asked, blinking in the sunlight.

"I will return to England also, and as the Order will think I am dead, I should have no further problem with them. Then, Gwen and I can get on with our lives."

Vernon looked baffled. "I thought Gwen and Ralph were... well, you know."

"Lovers?"

"Well, I never actually saw them... I mean, I just assumed them to be... um." He stopped, afraid of making another blunder, and dismayed by the frown on John's face. "Ralph seemed concerned," he added weakly.

Suddenly, John was laughing and he leaned over and patted Vernon on his back. "Never, never make a report to the King!" He roared with mirth, shaking Vernon like a rag doll. "You'd lose your head, my friend, in a very short time." Tears were rolling down his face. "Ralph and Gwen are just good friends. He is like a brother to me, and Gwen," he stopped laughing and took a deep breath, "is the woman I'm going to marry."

"Never actually met her myself," he murmured. "Good for you. Hope you'll be very happy." He blew out his cheeks. "What about me then? I'm not sure I'd be very good in the desert by myself."

John wiped his eyes, and gave Vernon a sympathetic appraisal. "What do you think will have happened when you and your patrol failed to return to camp?"

"Well, they'll think I'm dead. That we're all dead."

"You will be the second leader of the English forces to disappear. Who will take over, do you think?"

Vernon licked his lips. "Sir Raoul will combine the armies."

"Exactly. Do you think he will be pleased to see you again?"

"Well, perhaps not." Vernon seemed deflated by the prospect. "But, I mean, I am in charge of the English forces."

"Do you think Ralph imagined you would have to do anything other than cover for his absence?" Vernon sniffed and looked away. "If I understood you correctly, you acted as secretary to the Governor. Somehow, you managed to convince the other officers that you were in charge, and you must have done a reasonable job, or you would have been demoted."

"Thanks," Vernon said, grateful for any compliment.

"So, there is nothing to stop you coming with me, to Jerusalem."

"Jerusalem!" He beamed with pleasure. "I'm most obliged. I've always wanted to see Jerusalem. 'Couldn't go home without a visit to the holy places; my father would never forgive me." He sounded like a young boy, and John struggled to prevent himself from laughing.

"You don't look much like an Arab."

"Why should I?" Vernon gave John's clothes a derogatory glance.

"Because you'll stand out like a sore thumb as we travel. If other Arabs see me, they might comment on the size of my horse, but from a distance I'm just another traveller. But you will be remembered, and word will get out, and we will be soon attacked."

"Well, I'm not going to walk about with nothing on," Vernon said indignantly. "I mean a fellow has to have some modesty, you know. Also, this wasn't cheap," he said pointing to his bright chain mail and helmet." He avoided thinking about the cost of his lost horse and the equipment it carried.

"Quite right," John tried to keep a straight face, "we don't want to shock the natives. However, it just so happens I have an idea." He glanced at the increasing numbers of vultures in the sky. "We need to leave immediately, before those birds attract attention. In the desert, people take note of vultures."

· · ·

"WAIT HERE," JOHN SAID, pointing to an area of scrub bushes. "That's the village I told you about."

They had rounded a bend, and the path they were following sloped down to a shallow valley. In the distance they could see a collection of meagre houses, and a scattering of small fields growing bushes and crops. Vernon slipped down from behind John, and patted Celestial affectionately. "Well done, horse." He looked up at John who was staring intently at the village. "How long will you be?"

"I don't know. Not too long, I hope. You never know what you'll find." He reached down. "Give me your helmet, they're poor people, and I want to leave them something." He looked thoughtfully at Vernon. "In fact you'd better give me the chain mail as well. You won't be able to wear it if you're going to pretend to be a native."

With a show of great reluctance, Vernon removed his outer tunic and his chain mail jerkin. He stood in the road feeling uncomfortable in his thin inner vest and his trousers and long, soft leather boots. Somehow, he looked bigger and stronger without his armour; the years of physical exercise had provided him with a compact and muscular frame, and his thick neck and broad shoulders indicated strength and stamina. "You'd better take the tunic as well, but I'm holding on to the boots until you find me an alternative." He handed the items up to John, who surveyed him approvingly.

"Sir Vernon, you still look like a knight, and I'm sure you can make good use of your sword." He rode off, leaving the surprised Vernon with a satisfied grin on his face.

As he cantered towards the village, people working in the fields recognized his horse, and began running towards him, yelling and waving their arms. The village elder appeared as John dismounted in the middle of the village, embracing him like a long-lost friend.

"You have come back!" the old man raised his hands in celebration, and children jumped up and down with excitement. The older men were looking curiously at the things he was holding.

"I came across an infidel soldier," John said, choosing his words carefully. "I took his armour." He showed them the helmet, the chain mail and the tunic, and they all cheered and patted him on the back, convinced that he had killed a rich and powerful foreigner. None of the men had ever seen pieces of armour like these, and the women were equally interested in the quality of the tunic.

"Did you take his sword?" a man asked.

"No, I let him keep his sword," John said, and laughed as though it was a great joke. The crowd laughed as well, although some looked puzzled. "He is a strong fighter and a brave warrior. I did not wish to take everything from him."

The men nodded their heads; it was the right thing to do. In their minds, John was a great warrior who had helped them beat off their enemy, the Assassins. He even fought foreign soldiers and had defeated a man who had worn amazing armour. With his great horse he was a hero, a man whose word could be believed.

John placed the armour at the feet of the village elder. "I am giving you these, so your strongest and bravest can stand up to the

Assassins, if they should ever return." A gasp went up from the crowd, and the old man seemed speechless. "But you are proud people," he raised his voice so all could hear, "and I know you will not accept these things unless you can give me something in return." There was a strong murmur of agreement, but tinged with apprehension. What could they give in exchange for such wondrous gifts?

The elder looked up from his solemn contemplation of the helmet. "We are a poor village, what could you want that would equal these wonders?"

"Father," he said, adopting the respectful approach used by the villagers, "it is not the value that is important, it is the need. I have no need of these things, but you and your village need them. I, however, need some clothes, and I will barter these things for some simple garments."

Amid much merriment, and their insistence that he accepted a drink and some food, John selected certain of the clothes that were offered, and complimented the owners on their generosity.

"Why do you need these garments?" the old man enquired, asking the question on everyone's lips.

"I have come across a poor man who has suffered. He has no clothes. On my return journey, I promised I would bring him something to wear to cover his nakedness, and to keep the sun off his head and the sharp stones from his feet." He bowed his head.

"May God smile on you, my son." The old man reached up and placed his hand on John's head. There was a brief silence while the village elder performed a blessing; soon everyone began to laugh and joke as those who had contributed garments tried on the helmet. Some of the children were almost hysterical with mirth to see their fathers wearing the metal object, which made them seem like devils.

"So, once again, you are on your way?"

John climbed into the saddle and placed the bundle of clothes in front of him. "I have a long journey to make, and I have kept you from your work for long enough." He respectfully nodded his head at the old man, who, John suspected, understood more than he revealed. Slowly turning the horse, and careful to avoid the small children who were trying to pat Celestial's muzzle, he stood up in the stirrups. The crowd roared its delight.

"Be brave!" he yelled. "Take care of your children!" As he trotted away from the village, the crowd yelled and cheered, and the small children ran after him, falling back as he broke into a gallop. At the beginning of the hill, he slowed down and looked back; the villagers were still waving, and he raised his hand in a last farewell, knowing such moments created legends.

After a few minutes, he came to the patch of thorn bushes where he expected to find the small knight. "Vernon!" he called. There was no answer. He looked about in all directions; at the summit of the small hill, the path turned sharply to the left, stretching away into the distance, with no sign of life. Behind him, in the valley, he could just make out the village and its meagre patchwork of fields, while on either side of him, the dry landscape unfolded in a series of low knolls and broken rock.

"Vernon!" he yelled. There was no answer, and after examining the ground for any clues, he guided Celestial to the left, crossed the path, and began a careful search around the brow of the hill. He had almost completed the circle when he came upon a narrow track moving off to the left. After a short distance it disappeared behind rocks, and appeared to be heading into a steep narrow valley. John checked the barren landscape one more time and, with some misgivings, decided to follow the track. It seemed the only logical direction.

CHAPTER 17

RALPH SAT STARING OUT of the window at the small arbour beneath. It was a hot day and there was no wind, but in the stonewalled refectory of the Castle of the Watchtower, it was cool and pleasant. "The galley is still there, thank God," he said happily. He carefully massaged his sword arm, which was in a sling and securely bound to his chest. "Make sure the Captain waits until I am ready to travel."

"I'll send one of the locals down, m'Lord," Sergeant Little replied, unwilling to attempt the fearful descent to the village until it was necessary. He had no head for heights and avoided looking out of the window; even the panoramic spectacle held no interest for him. "I hear the sailing boat's gone," he added, hoping to change the subject. "I reckons they left as soon as they found out De Wulfric be dead."

"It's a local boat. They need to make a living." Ralph felt strangely philosophical and was content, for the moment, to sit and admire the view. He looked expectantly towards the door. "Have you seen Mistress Gwen?"

Little shook his head. "Not since we got 'ere early this morning, m'Lord. I reckons she's catchin' up on some beauty sleep." He glanced anxiously at Ralph. "Not that her needs any, of course," he added quickly. Ralph appeared not to notice, and Little relaxed. He was still feeling guilty about Ralph's injury, and in his own mind he kept reliving the moment when he almost killed him. Back in England, the Sergeant had become aware of his young lord's affair with a priestess of the Old Religion; now it seemed he was transferring his feelings towards this girl called Gwen. There was no doubt, she was beautiful, but Little and his wife had hoped

Ralph would marry the priestess. "I'll get the message sent down now," he muttered and clattered down the stairs, passing the knight on his way up.

Payen de Montdidier moved quietly into the room and stood by the door, his heart pounding, needing a moment to control his breathing. His ordered, monastic world was, once more, in disarray. Since Gwen's arrival, shortly after dawn, he had barely been able to put two words together. The sight of this exceptional woman arriving back in a shocked and tired state had unnerved him. In her vulnerability she appeared even more beautiful; the feelings of sexual attraction he experienced were painfully at odds with the celibate life he had sworn to embrace.

He stared at Ralph who was in profile by the window, lost in thought. With his good looks, strong physique and worldly experience, he was everything Payen would like to have been, although his views were the antithesis of Payen's beliefs. Payen's parents were deeply religious, and though wealthy, had instilled in their son both humility and a love for austerity that had guided his behaviour and his beliefs. Unlike other young men, he had never had any but the most formal dealings with girls, and being an only child had taken to the rigours of priesthood with a youthful zeal, finding his physical outlet in his training as a knight. He had accepted celibacy as just another spiritual demand. In spite of minor setbacks over the years, he had persevered in his attempts to ignore the sexual side of his nature. Until he had met Gwen, keeping away from women had made celibacy easier. Now, in spite of his determination to remain pure, erotic thoughts wracked him and her reappearance intensified the crisis. To make it worse, he was convinced Ralph was a rival for her affections.

"How's the shoulder?" he enquired casually, as he walked towards the window.

"Mending well, I hope." Ralph gave him a contented nod. "This view is a cure in itself."

"Yes." Payen agreed without looking. He ran his hand distractedly over the back of a chair. "How long will you stay here, do you think?"

"A few days, perhaps a week. I want to get back the use of

this arm before I try a voyage on board the galley." He grinned. "Naturally, if I misbehave you can send me down to the village."

Payen lightened up. "Naturally, I will do that on the first occasion you throw food or spill your wine." He poured the deep plum-coloured liquid into two cups and stood staring at them for a moment, uncertain how to continue. "Is Gwen going with you?"

"That's a certainty. I know she can't wait to get back to England." Ralph accepted a cup. "However, I'll have to wait until she is well enough to travel. She's been through a rough few weeks." He sipped the wine. "I know she's very upset about Martin's death. She'd known him a long time; he was a good friend."

"Yes, Ishmael told me how she tried to defend him. She fought the lion with only stones and a dagger." From an open window he stared out at the wide expanse of blue sea; white crests had formed on the waves, and he noted, subconsciously, a breeze on his face. He tried to imagine what it must be like to attack a full-grown male lion with only a few small rocks. Gwen had risked her life for her friend. Payen marvelled at her courage and her sacrifice. She was without a doubt the most remarkable woman he had ever encountered.

"She's a brave woman," Ralph said meditatively. "Perhaps, one of the bravest people I've ever met. I notice I'm always using superlatives whenever I speak of her." Ralph turned to look at Payen. "What do you think of her?"

"Think? Um…" he felt the blood rushing to his cheeks. "She's beautiful, and very," he struggled for the correct word, "very unusual."

"Yes, isn't she? Unusual. That sums her up. Wonderfully unusual!" Ralph grinned, and raised his eyebrows. "Don't you wish, sometimes, that you hadn't married religion?"

"I've always wanted to serve God." He felt uncomfortable under Ralph's frank stare. "God doesn't tempt you the way a woman does."

"No, he's a bit boring that way, isn't he?" Ralph chortled, delighted with his joke. He noticed Payen wasn't laughing. "I'm sorry, I am not intending to ridicule your beliefs. But, I've always found Christianity lacks a sense of humour. It seems to be a religion that enables priests to feel superior, when in many cases they are not at all special. I also dislike the way the scriptures depict women. Apart from Mary Magdalene, there isn't a woman described in those writings who has any real character."

"You seem to have forgotten the Virgin Mary."

"No, I haven't." His face became serious. "Has it never occurred to you that the gospels are written from an entirely male perspective? Is it not strange that the Church venerates a woman: Christ's mother? Christ comes second. Why, in this male dominated Church, should a woman be the most venerated?"

"You are familiar with the scriptures?" There was a hint of amazement in Payen's voice.

"Priests tend to assume that knowledge of the Bible is the exclusive prerogative of the Church. An unusual man taught me. You would call him a pagan. He was, I'm sure, a priest of the Old Religion, a Druid, yet extremely well informed on other religions." Ralph ran his forefinger down the straight bridge of his nose. "I always wondered why my father, who was a life-long Christian, employed him."

"So, he taught you the scriptures?"

"Yes." Ralph said reflectively. "He also taught me many other things as well. He could recognize the movement of the stars; he understood art and philosophy, and he taught me how to fight with the weapons of a knight. Without his teaching I would be dead." He turned to look at Payen. "But you didn't answer my question. Why do you think your male dominated church is so focused on the Virgin Mary?"

Payen's brow furrowed. This was not the conversation he wished to have. "Because she's the mother of God."

"But isn't this yet another attack on women?"

"What?" Payen looked shocked. "How can that be?"

"Because the Church insists she must be a virgin. In other words, although God invented sex, he did not allow his son to be born in the normal way. Is that not another example of this male dominated Church attacking the concept of sex, and therefore an attack on women in general?"

"It is God's will."

"Is it?" Ralph ran his forefinger down his nose. "Men wrote the gospels; the same men who were afraid of the power of women. That is why the Church insists its priests must be celibate. It's because, as the story explains in Genesis, women tempt men." He laughed. "At least that is what we are supposed to believe. But men also wrote the book of Genesis. Throughout the Bible, women are portrayed as either a problem or as willing and submissive."

Payen gaped, unsure what to say. He felt distinctly uneasy. This young lord whom he admired, was now challenging the very precepts by which he lived. He realized he was struggling for a correct answer; this was an area of religion he had neglected. Women had not been a part of his life, and it had never occurred to him that there was any male bias in the Gospels. "Why did you mention Mary Magdalene?"

"Because, there is obviously something about her that has not been revealed."

"How do you mean?"

"If she is the one, after Christ's crucifixion, who is the first to visit his body, as it says in the Gospels, why was she there? Why was she the only one to report the angels? She must have been fairly important, yet she's not represented in a good light. Is this because she was too important in the story of Christ to fit in with the narrow male views of how the chronicles should be recorded?"

Payen did not reply. He felt he had suddenly walked from a dark room into a very bright room, and needed time to refocus. As he tried to adopt a calm approach to the discussion, a servant appeared at the open door.

"My Lord, there's an army approaching."

"An army?" Payen was confounded. "Are they enemy forces?"

"No, my Lord, they look like us."

Payen waved the man away. "We will continue this discussion at another time," he said, forcing a smile. "I'd better see what this is about."

Ralph leaped to his feet. "I'll come with you." He placed his good arm around Payen's broad shoulders. "It could be interesting."

They climbed a long flight of steps and walked out onto a broad battlement, high above the courtyard, overlooking the main gate. In the distance they could see a small army approaching. The men marching in a tight column, created a dust cloud which rose up like smoke. Ralph could clearly identify them as Crusader forces, from their helmets, uniform and the way they marched. A small group of horsemen, led by a knight in full armour, was cantering towards the main gate. Behind the knight, a young squire proudly carried the lord's heavy lance, with a small banner attached to the point.

"I recognize the banner. It looks as though the Order is arriving in force," Payen said grimly. "I'd better see what this is about." He hurried off, adjusting his tunic as he went.

Ralph watched the riders as they approached, reflecting on the possible reasons for the visit. He felt as though a dark shadow had invaded a day that had begun so well. After a few minutes, he descended the winding staircase and passing the refectory, continued down to the next floor, stopping outside Gwen's room. The guard on duty stepped to the side and Ralph knocked gently on the door. There was no response. He knocked again, hearing nothing he opened the heavy door very quietly and peered in.

The room was large and flooded with sunlight from two tall open windows. On a simple palliasse, at the far side of the room, he could see Gwen sleeping. She was covered in a brown, military blanket with only her head visible; her long, black hair lay in disarray on the makeshift pillow. The cover hardly moved with her regular, shallow breathing and she lay on her right side with only a part of her face visible. On a bench nearby her blue dress was neatly arranged, and although much worn, still retained a quality about it. He smiled as he imagined her naked under the blanket; his pulse throbbed in his neck and he felt a pleasant stirring in his body. Ralph was about to enter the room to wait patiently for her to awake, when he heard the sounds of the arriving horsemen. Before long, Payen would be looking for him. He did not want her disturbed. Regretfully, he closed the door, ignoring the slight twitch on the guard's face, and returned to the refectory.

After nearly an hour, during which time a small army of foot soldiers had entered the castle, Payen returned with two visitors.

Ralph stood up and silently observed their entry into the room. The knight had discarded his armour, wearing only a shirt and a loose tunic. He was of average build, well into mid life, and although shorter than Ralph, radiated quiet authority. His squire was a muscular youth who did not speak unless spoken to. He remained standing by the door, serious and reserved.

Payen appeared nervous, and his face was flushed. He led the way into the room, giving Ralph a warning frown as he turned to introduce the knight. "This is Sir Godfrey de Montbard, Knight of the Order, and his squire..."

"Answers to the name of Rupert," the knight interrupted forcefully. "And you, I gather are...?"

"Lord D'Escosse," Ralph cut in, "Commander of the English forces. At your service, Sir Godfrey." There was a tense pause as each man carefully assessed the other. "But, you may call me Ralph," he said adopting an engaging smile.

Sir Godfrey did not smile back, but contented himself with a slight nod.

"Gentlemen, may I offer you some wine?" Payen said. He was visibly uncomfortable.

"Certainly," Sir Godfrey replied, "but not for him." He gestured with his thumb over his shoulder. Behind him, Rupert remained expressionless, as if he had not heard the sneer in his lord's voice. "Bring me a chair."

Rupert quickly brought a chair from the table, placing it opposite Ralph's. Payen poured wine and the squire handed it to the knights. When Ralph thanked him, the youth looked away as though unused to being noticed. Payen remained standing near the table, staring at Ralph. The atmosphere was distinctly tense.

Sir Godfrey took a sip of his wine, and scowled at Ralph, who gazed back, unblinking. "I understand you disappeared from Antioch," he said, his dark eyes glaring. It was not a question, but a statement of fact. "Why, as Commander of the English forces, did you leave, unannounced?"

"Since when did you assume leadership of the forces of the Order?" Ralph's voice was calm, yet steely.

"I am here as the representative of the High Lord, Sir Raoul

261

de Warron. He is very interested in the reason for your strange disappearance." He smiled with his mouth, but his eyes remained humourless. "I believe you've been in contact with Sir Raymond?"

Ralph glanced up at Payen who locked eyes, and slowly nodded his head.

"I did indeed have that pleasure."

"Where is he now?"

"Don't you know?" Ralph took a sip of his wine.

"If I did, I would not be asking you." The knight had thick brows; they were drawn down in an irritated frown.

"I thought it best that you explain the situation," Payen said, nervously.

"Quite right," Ralph agreed judiciously. He took a sip of wine. "He's dead."

"Dead?"

"Yes. I killed him." Ralph spoke as though he was announcing something unimportant. "Or rather, he killed himself by falling on my sword."

"Sir Raymond is dead?" Sir Godfrey stood up and his hand went automatically to his belt. He was not wearing a sword, and Ralph noted that his squire carried only a dagger. "You killed him?" He seemed unable to accept the fact. Sir Raymond had been one of the best swordsmen in the Order. His strength and determination, coupled with his family connections, had enabled him to rise quickly to the position of second only to the High Lord. With his death came the possibility of Godfrey's promotion within the society. His thoughts returned to Ralph: if this young lord had killed Raymond, then he was a man to be reckoned with. He took a deep breath, and sat down. "I think we've got off to a bad start. Perhaps, you would be good enough to tell me exactly what happened, and why you're here?"

"Yes, we did get off to a bad start, didn't we?" Ralph was enjoying himself. "I think, to begin with, you should tell me why you're here."

Godfrey's mouth tightened. "The armies are moving south to relieve the enemy pressure on Tripoli. I was ordered to bring one hundred men to reinforce this castle, and act as a defensive shield for the rear of our forces." He paused. "Why are you here?"

"To find Sir Raymond, and rescue Mistress Gwen."

"The Maid?" The knight appeared astonished. "Sir Raymond was travelling with the Maid?" He had heard nothing of this. As far as he was concerned the Maid was safe in Antioch; the Order was waiting for the time when she could be safely received in Jerusalem. After the battle, there had been rumours of her death, but before leaving Antioch he had been assured that she was alive and well, under the protection, once again, of the Order. "

"Yes. You didn't know?"

"I'm not privy to everything that the High Lord decides," Sir Raymond replied. His mind was working quickly. "The Maid is still here?"

"I understand Mistress Gwen escaped from this castle shortly after her arrival, and before my galley put into this harbour." Ralph stared blankly at Payen. "She left in the company of a large soldier, who was a friend of hers." Keeping strictly to the facts, he added: "It was the reason for the slight disagreement I had with Sir Raymond."

Sir Godfrey was visibly shaken. All those who were full members of the Order knew about the Maid. In their rituals and beliefs she was their key to power in the Holy Land and eventually throughout Christendom; her value could not be over-estimated. It was unbelievable to think Sir Raymond, second only to the High Lord, could have travelled without his knowledge. Yet, why would Sir Raoul allow her to be taken to Jerusalem without a strong escort? So much did not make sense. "When did she leave?" he demanded loudly.

"About three days ago. I imagine she could have reached Antioch by now, if she was travelling in that direction."

"She might have gone south."

Ralph shook his head. "I think you mentioned there were strong enemy forces around Tripoli? Also, there have been local reports of Assassins, who are mustering just south of here. Is that not right, Sir Payen?"

"That is true," Payen reluctantly agreed.

"So, I think it quite likely that their intention would have been to head back to Antioch." Ralph shrugged. "If it were not for this injury, I, too, would be away from this castle."

"Yes," Sir Godfrey could see the logic of it, and presumed Ralph's injury was from his fight with Sir Raymond. But, one thing still bothered him: "Why did you, the Commander of the English Forces, leave Antioch, without notifying the Governor or the High Lord of your departure? And what is your reason for pursuing Sir Raymond and the Maid?"

"I have my reasons, Sir Godfrey. Suffice to say I did not expect to be away for long, neither did I expect the High Lord to mount an expedition so soon after our last debacle." A thought came to his mind. "I understand the troops you have brought to this castle are part of the English forces? Who gave the High Lord the right to use my men?"

"Your second-in-command, of course."

Ralph's jaw dropped. His mind raced. "Sir Vernon de Kari?"

"Exactly. He organized your army's departure. Then, like yourself, he disappeared." Sir Godfrey was intrigued with Ralph's reaction. "He was leading a scouting party in the area of Lattakieh."

"Sir Vernon organized the army's departure?" The idea was absurd. In Ralph's mind Vernon was the most inept knight he had ever come across. He had left him in charge as a mere figurehead; someone who would not ask awkward questions and would enjoy the semblance of power. "How did he cope?"

"Very efficiently."

Ralph was mystified. "What was he doing leading a party of scouts?"

"A whim, I imagine." The strange behaviour of the English did not interest Sir Godfrey. He stood up and pulled on his gauntlets. "I find it incredible that the Maid should be travelling in this hostile region with only one soldier for protection."

"I agree," Ralph replied, a hint of mockery in his voice. "But, there again, she arrived with only one of your knights for protection, and he died."

Sir Godfrey gave Ralph a withering look, turning sharply towards the door. "Rupert! Prepare the horses. We leave immediately." He approached Sir Payen. "I'm handing over to you the command of the soldiers I have brought. Once I have reported to the High Lord, I will send you further instructions."

Short bows were exchanged, and without a glance at Ralph, the knight strode out of the room. They heard him clatter down the steps, the sound fading into the distance.

"Why didn't you tell him the truth?" Payen asked. "If he'd decided to remain and had sent a messenger instead, he would soon have discovered that Mistress Gwen was safe in the castle."

Ralph grinned, the dark shadow had disappeared; he felt wonderfully animated. "I kept strictly to the truth. I admit, my religious friend, it was not the whole story, but it was enough. Gwen does not want any further dealings with the Order."

"He might have decided to stay," Payen persisted.

"I was certain he wouldn't. I have come to realize how important Gwen is to these Knights of the Order. Godfrey wouldn't have sent a mere servant to the High Lord with the awful news that their beloved Gwen is wandering in the desert, and with only one soldier as protection." He rubbed his arm thoughtfully. "He'll also be keen to be the one to report the death of Lord Raymond. The Order is full of ambitious men. I dare say the humourless Godfrey has his eyes on promotion."

"He's bound to find out. You can't hide the presence of a woman in a castle full of men. It will soon be common knowledge. The first messenger to leave this castle will carry the news." Payen felt bound to defend his point, but was uncertain of his own motives. While he did not want the Order to regain control of this vulnerable woman, he was also unhappy with Ralph's confident assumption that he would direct her future. How did Mistress Gwen feel about this? Payen wondered what role, if any, he might play in her life; once again, he felt amazed he should be considering such a thought. He tried to refocus on the immediate problem. "Also, the Knights of the Order are bound to return to investigate the death of one of their most important members."

"Quite right. Which is why we'll be leaving you as soon as Gwen is well enough to travel."

"What about your arm?" he said, clutching at straws.

"I will be happy to travel as soon as Gwen is able."

"Where will you go?"

"To Cyprus. Although I would prefer you not to mention that to anyone." He smiled warmly. "Promise?" Payen nodded. Ralph drained his wine cup. "Then, back to England."

"But you're the Commander of the English forces," Payen spluttered.

"I have completed my mission as far as King Henry is concerned. The High Lord seems happy to act without me; the soldiers I brought over will not wish to return until they have fought a few battles and grabbed some loot, and of course," he winked broadly, "I have been injured and need to recuperate at home."

Payen took a deep breath, choking back his indignation. He wanted to remind this Saxon lord, who seemed to possess every advantage, of his knightly duties: to fight the Moslems, to uphold the Christian faith, and to serve God. Payen had seen Ralph fight. He knew he was not a coward, yet he was intending to leave his men and retreat back to England. "We'll talk more of this later. I'd better check on the soldiers," he said abruptly. As he left the room, he wondered if this was the usual effect a beautiful woman had on a man. Perhaps this was the reason priests were forbidden to have relationships with women. It was Adam and Eve, the temptation to think of a woman rather than think of God, to give up spiritual duties and manly responsibilities in order to indulge in carnal activities. This was proof.

He felt ennobled and uplifted by these thoughts. As he walked slowly down the stone stairs, he felt smugly virtuous. Ralph must do as he wished, but Payen knew his duty; he was to hold the castle until he could travel to the Holy City of Jerusalem. He would answer God's call.

"M'Lord?" A soldier was standing in front of him. "M'Lord?"

"Yes?" He realized he had been oblivious to everything as he descended the stairs.

"The young woman in there," the guard indicated the door behind him. "Her wants to speak with ye."

"With me?" Payen queried, unable to grapple with the surge of emotions racing through his body. His calm conviction of a moment ago was replaced with a riot of contradictions: hope for something unthinkable, fear of something he longed for and an overwhelming disbelief in his own reactions. Like a man struggling in quicksand, he approached the heavy door. Waving the guard away, he knocked diffidently, while the blood thundered in his ears.

. . .

IT WAS HOT ON the top of the hill and Vernon removed his vest to cover his head from the burning sun. He watched John slowly diminish in size as he rode towards the village, deeply regretting the loss of his own horse. Inactivity was intolerable to him. He removed his sword from its scabbard and tried a few practice strokes, cursing every time the vest slipped off. Eventually, he tied it firmly around his head and continued with his sword practice, but in a very short time he was bathed in sweat and forced to seek the shade of a clump of bushes. But there was only partial shadow, and he soon tired of his own company. When he sat still, he began thinking of the cost of his horse and his expensive armour; these calculations led to feelings of guilt and the prospect of his father's anger and indignation. In order to dispel such gloomy thoughts, he began to walk aimlessly about. He stared at the outline of the distant village, but was unable to see John. Rather than wait around in abject boredom, he decided to explore the other side of the hill.

Vernon's experience of the desert was limited; to him it was just a hot, treeless place where oddly clad natives somehow managed to survive. He did not expect to discover anything of interest as he followed a small track that led down the hillside into a narrow valley, but he hoped he could find some temporary relief from the heat. Below was a deep gulley. The track leading down to the gulley was steep, but not dangerous. He strode down confidently, eagerly anticipating the coolness of the steep-sided channel. The floor of the narrow valley was still in bright sunlight, and he paused for breath. In front of him was the gulley in deep shadow, and to his right the track disappeared around a cliff. He could see the outline of a dried-out stream, indicating water had flowed at some other time of the year, but not a trace of water remained. The valley was like an oven.

The gulley was about twelve paces wide, and stretched away out of sight. It was as if a huge part of the hill had separated, and established itself some distance from the main body, with the two steep sides almost meeting at the top, reducing the incoming light to a mere glimmer. He approached cautiously, and was delighted by the change in temperature. It was cool, and the rocky sides were damp, in glorious contrast to the blistering heat in the valley. There was a sudden change from intense brightness to deep shadow. It was difficult to see clearly. He advanced slowly, allowing his eyes to adjust to the gloom, and was just beginning to feel confident when something hard and boney burst up between his legs. He staggered forward. The shock was so great that Vernon let out a loud cry, and flaying his arms in all directions, crashed into a host of moving bodies. As he fought to regain his balance a cacophonous riot of noise erupted, as dozens of goats fled in all directions, bleating loudly.

Around the dark gulley, shadowy men staggered to their feet, waving long staves and thick wooden cudgels. The air was full of cursing and bleating and Vernon wondered if he had ventured into Hell. He tried to return back to the light, but the goats were all round him, preventing a fast retreat. Before he could reach the opening, he was hit from behind. It was a powerful blow to the head. He sank to his knees, unable to draw his sword before a hailstorm of cudgels knocked him senseless. As he lost consciousness, he remembered he had never liked goats.

. . .

THE STEEP TRACK WAS broad enough for John to ride Celestial with confidence. The sure-footed animal moved slowly down to the narrow valley without showing any concern for the precipitous drop on the right. As they descended, he could see the track passed a deep gulley, which continued along the valley, appearing to follow the dry bed of a seasonal stream. It was intensely hot. He decided to follow the track only until he could see clearly down the valley. If there were no signs of Vernon, he would return to the top of the hill in the hope that the unlikely knight would have returned to their agreed meeting place.

John was passing the gulley when Celestial came to an abrupt stop. Thinking the horse objected to the heat, he gave a gentle kick with his stirrups. Celestial snorted, and stamped his foot, shaking his head from side to side. John patted him gently on the neck, and knowing from past experience the animal's intelligence and sensitivity, took more notice of his surroundings. He looked closely at the ominous cleft in the rock and carefully dismounted, making no noise. There were fresh droppings on the ground coupled with an unmistakable smell of goats. Drawing his sword, he advanced silently, keeping to one side of the entrance, feeling the dampness of the rock wall. He stopped when the darkness increased, allowing his eyes to adjust, and was immediately aware of a strange pale shape on the ground. It was a naked body, but its head seemed curiously large. "What have you been up to?" he murmured.

After he dragged the body out of the gloom, John realized why Vernon had looked so strange in the half-light: his long, brown vest was knotted over his head. In the bright light, he looked like a lunatic. Parts of the vest were soaked in blood and Vernon had gashes on his face and shoulders, with numerous bruises on his back and arms. His boots, trousers, belt and sword had been stolen, but for some reason, they had left him the vest tied incongruously around his head. John wondered if any bones were broken. Kneeling down to check, he was aware of an increasing heat in his hands; even in the bright light they seemed to glow. His fingers began to tingle. Once again, he felt confident in his healing ability, examining Vernon's limbs with a detached, methodical approach, as though he was following a clear plan of how each bone and joint worked. A thorough check found nothing unusual, and he turned his attention to the head.

Carefully removing the blood-soaked vest, he found two deep wounds in the back of Vernon's head, both bleeding profusely. He laid him face down. Taking out his dagger, he cut two small squares from a dry part of the vest and placed them on the two wounds, pressing down very gently. The tingling in his fingers was almost painful, and was not surprised when the bleeding stopped; he knew he was not in control of events. Past experiences had convinced him he was a conduit for a power that healed and preserved; it was beyond his understanding. Sweating, he slowly stood up, flexing his fingers, feeling the tingling fading, his hands cooling. As the power gradually left him, he was conscious of a great weariness, as though he had completed a long and arduous exercise. John stumbled towards Celestial, removed the water flask, and drank deeply. When he returned to the unconscious man, he washed away the blood from his neck and shoulders, and tried to get him to drink; Vernon remained unconscious. John turned him over, propped him up, bandaged his head with strips of the ruined vest and rested him on his side. He sorted the clothes the villagers had provided, selecting a loose smock and gently fitting it over Vernon's bandaged head; it covered his naked body, protecting him from the sun. Finally, he moved Celestial, so his shadow provided some slight shade for the patient. Sitting cross-legged next to him, John pondered their future.

He was certain Vernon would recover. Those he had treated in the past had all returned to full health, but the serious injuries appeared to need a period of unconsciousness to enable the person to mend both physically and mentally. Both Polly Carter and Ralph had needed sleep and rest to recover from their wounds, whereas Saif, with his painful shoulder, had made an instant recovery. But, always, the power came unexpectedly, never when he tried to conjure it up by himself. He still remembered the time when Ralph appeared to be gravely wounded by Lord Herlwin. No matter how hard John had tried, he had been unable to heal his friend. It had been Ralph's sister, Aelfreda, a pagan priestess, who brought her brother back to consciousness.

John drank some water, and turning to Vernon, washed his face. When he tipped a small amount into his mouth, the patient drank, groaned, but continued to sleep. Celestial stood patiently, suffering in the hot sun, his head lowered and his eyes closed, his shadow gradually decreasing as the sun moved round. Soon, John thought, he would have to move the animal to continue the shade it offered; he wondered if he should drag Vernon back into the cool gulley, but was unwilling to disturb him. It was simply a question of waiting.

His thoughts returned to the inexplicable power he had somehow obtained all those years ago in the flower fields. It had come without warning, allowing him to control the two wondrous swords, in spite of their potential for evil. The strange gift had allowed him to heal others and protect himself, but not once was he ever in control of it. He looked at the image on his right palm; it seemed to have lost its clarity. Wondering if it was just the dirt on his hands, he spat on the runes' image, wiping his palm on his tunic. There was no doubt; it was not as clear as he remembered it. Over the years, his attitudes had changed: the original wonder of having the Sign of Power had led to pride, and then embarrassment. He had tried to pretend it was unimportant, a thing associated with magic, unsuited to a young man who sought to be recognized in society. However, more recently he had come to accept the gift, knowing he was on a path that would lead inevitably to a place and a time when he would unravel the secret of his name. Owl was another piece in the puzzle, as was Ralph, and now Vernon. But what did the fading image indicate? Did it mean the power was fading also? Then, there was the Giant and the two wondrous swords; John wondered if he still possessed the power to control them? His eyes closed, his head nodded over and, sitting cross-legged, he dozed off, unaware that next to him Vernon's fingers were starting to move.

CHAPTER 18

GWEN AWOKE IN THE large, stone walled chamber with a feeling of immeasurable loss. She blinked at the bright light that flooded the empty room, and remembered she had stayed here before. Gradually, she was able to recall her arrival when she and the others had reached the castle in the dead of night: the shouted challenges, the replies, the grating sound of the heavy door, the flickering torches and a strong hand helping her up the never-ending stairs. Ralph was here, somewhere. He had been her rock, supporting her when she had nearly panicked, comforting her when she had been hardly able to stand. She recalled the stilted "Goodnight," and her determination to get herself to bed. Suddenly, she remembered Martin; her body shuddered with grief as she wept inconsolably.

Later, when she awoke for the second time, she was more composed. She noticed she had not bolted the door, and hurrying out of bed donned her dress quickly, in case anyone should enter. When she thought about it, she realized her time in the nunnery and her virtual imprisonment with different members of the Order had made her embarrassed by nakedness. She remembered the wonderful freedom in Cyprus, when her swimming had been uninhibited. But even there, men had been prying on her privacy.

Gwen examined her dress, sadly aware of how frayed and dirty it was. She had worn nothing else but this one garment for weeks, and with no other clothes, she felt uncomfortably vulnerable. It was an intolerable situation; she decided she would no longer suffer these indignities. Silently, she opened the large door, and was surprised to see a guard outside. Her warder, Lord Raymond, was obviously not going to be tricked a second time. She paused while she considered her options, and thought of the young knight with aspirations for priesthood, who had so obviously admired her: Payen de Montdidier.

"Guard!" she hissed. The soldier had been drowsing. The unexpected female voice shocked him, and he whirled round to be confronted by the prettiest woman he had ever seen. He blinked in disbelief, suddenly realizing why he had been ordered to stand guard.

"M'Lady?" he mumbled.

"Get me Sir Payen. Now!"

The guard looked confused. "I 'ave to stand guard 'ere, m'Lady." He stared at her, his eyes moving down her body.

"Well, when you can, tell Sir Payen I want to see him," she said, her face burning with embarrassment.

She closed the door and strode over to a window where the warm air soothed her. Once again, she felt like a prisoner: dependent on others and unable to lead her own life. "I will not go with the odious Raymond. I will stay here if I have to." Slowly she calmed down. Ralph was here. He would not allow Lord Raymond, no matter how important he was, to take her away. When Payen arrived she would implore him to get her fresh clothes, and she would assert herself. She was not some chattel to be passed around. She would not cooperate any longer.

With these and similar thoughts she occupied the time until she heard a faint knocking at her door. She opened it cautiously and was relieved to see it was Sir Payen.

"Thank goodness it's you." Her face radiated happiness. She impulsively grabbed his hand, pulling him into the room, closing the door behind her.

Payen was lost for words. She seemed to be showing a preference for him, rather than the experienced Ralph. He flushed with a combination of joy and awkwardness. A warning voice was telling him that he was in grave danger of abusing his religious vows, but it was a dull, old and lifeless voice, and he was young and alive.

Gwen led him over to an open window, releasing his hand. "I thought for a terrible moment it might be de Wulfric. I will not go with him to Jerusalem! You're a good man. I know you'll help Ralph get me to Cyprus." She was speaking quickly, beating one hand against the other, unaware of the expression on Payen's face.

The blood had drained from his cheeks, and he looked utterly crestfallen. "You thought I might be Sir Raymond?"

"Yes." She was puzzled by his reaction.

"He's dead. I thought you knew. Lord d'Escosse killed him."

"Oh?" She raised her hand to her mouth. "Of course." It all flooded back. She had been so exhausted and emotionally drained by the death of Martin, that she had forgotten Ralph's drunken confession. Gwen was confused: she had disliked de Wulfric, feeling uneasy in his company, but he had never physically abused her, or threatened her with violence. She would not have wished him dead. "Ralph killed him?" Her eyes narrowed.

Payen nodded gravely. "De Wulfric started it, he drew on d'Escosse." He was reluctant to portray Ralph in a good light, but was unable to lie. "I tried to intervene, but de Wulfric pushed me to the floor, and Lord d'Escosse tripped over me, and fell backwards with his sword up. De Wulfric impaled himself on the sword as he tried to kill d'Escosse." He took a deep breath. "I'm equally responsible for his death."

"Oh, I'm sure you're not," Gwen said quickly. He looked so young. Although he possessed good looks like Ralph's, he was, in contrast, quite unworldly, exactly like her image of the virtuous priest. She almost grabbed him in her arms to reassure him, but something prevented her. "When did he die?"

"Yesterday morning. I buried him in the afternoon." He was slowly regaining his composure,

"I see." She turned towards the window. After a pause, she said, "Would you do something for me?"

"Of course," he said. He would do anything for her.

"Could you find me some different clothes?" He looked amazed, and she quickly added, "Perhaps, you could get a servant to buy some from the village? I know Ralph will let you have some money."

Payen looked away. It was not the sort of task he had hoped to undertake. "I'll see to it immediately." He marched across the room, disappearing without another word. Gwen knew she had upset him, and gazed thoughtfully at the door.

Later, when she was beginning to become impatient, a servant knocked, staggering in with a variety of local clothes. He laid them on her bed, clearly relieved to be free of his chore. As he stood up, he could not resist staring at her, his dark eyes assessed her body as though she was an object he wished to buy.

"You may go," she said sharply.

He jerked, as though awaking from a dream, and hastily bowed his way out of the room.

Gwen angrily bolted the door, and examined her new wardrobe. There was a number of local dresses, in browns or black; all of them were shapeless, loose fitting and stretched down to her ankles. They had long sleeves, round necks and some had small decorations on the bodices. The woven, hemp-like material was tough and heavy. She understood the dresses had been made to last, rather than to look attractive. Among the pile of clothes were two long, thin scarves, and a pair of flat sandals. There were no underclothes; trying on the dresses, she was aware of the distinctive smells of their previous owners.

Eventually, she chose a black dress, using a reddish scarf as a belt. It was not ideal, but it gave colour and shape to an otherwise drab, loose fitting garment. The sandals were approximately the right size, and to compensate for her wild, unwashed hair, she wound the second scarf of bleached white material around her head and neck, in the manner of the Arab women she had seen in Antioch. There was no mirror. She tried to imagine what she looked like, but she shook her head. It did not matter, there was no one she had to impress, and certainly no other woman to be compared with. She had never been vain; her stay at the nunnery had emphasized her lack of regard for finery. This need for different clothes was simply a reaction to being in a male world, needing something to bolster her self-esteem.

When she opened her door, the guard stared straight ahead, nervously licking his lips. She ignored him and lifting her long skirt, walked slowly up the curving stone steps to the next landing, certain he was staring up at her. At the top, she stood for a moment, feeling strangely weak and tired. The door to the refectory was open. She could see Ralph and Payen framed together near a window, both held cups of wine, and remained unaware of her as she entered. On her right she could see plates of food and a jug of wine on the table, and was reminded of her hunger and thirst, but her attention was drawn to the men's discussion.

"I know it's a bit rough out there," Ralph said, his eyes staring angrily out of the window, "but a galley can cope with most seas."

"I still think it would be wrong to subject Mistress Gwen to the hardship and danger of such a journey. She has suffered enough. This storm is building, but in a few days it will have blown itself out." Payen's voice was firm and direct, and he sounded experienced, in contrast to the gauche young man she had talked to earlier.

"I know all of that," Ralph snapped. "But the longer we stay here, the more likely it is that Sir Godfrey de Montbard, or other Knights of the Order will return. I don't have to remind you that I have killed a leading member of that group. They will want an investigation. They will also insist on removing Gwen into their custody."

A panic seized her, and she rushed into the room. "No! I will not go back to them. I don't care how rough the seas are. I would rather die than become their prisoner, yet again."

The two men spun round, their expressions revealing surprise, awkwardness and concern. Gwen was pleased to note their eyes also showed admiration. Ralph rushed forward, and with his good arm shepherded her to a seat, while Payen fetched a cup of wine. Both men were eager to attend to her, refusing to allow her to discuss her possible departure until she had drunk the wine and eaten some of the bread and goat's cheese.

"You would pass for an Arab woman, any time," Ralph joked. "Although your good looks might give you away."

"This is not the time to be gallant, Ralph," she said severely, although she was amused by the compliment. "Anyway, it should stop the soldiers leering at me."

Payen observed the exchange with regret. He had never been on casual terms with a woman, or even been friends with a girl when he was young, and envied this comfortable banter. "Mistress

Gwen, I think you must wait for calmer seas. I have been here long enough to know the danger of these storms." He winced, not meaning to sound pompous.

"We should leave immediately the Captain of the galley thinks he can get us safely to Famagusta." Ralph stared moodily out at the gathering sea. Waves were crashing against the breakwater; the strengthening wind was beginning to moan around the castle, while overhead dark clouds were blocking out the sun.

Gwen moved to the window and was troubled by the increasing intensity of the storm. It seemed impossible for the weather to have changed so quickly. As she stared out, she was reminded of the terrible storm she had experienced at Christchurch, when she had crossed the raging waters of the estuary rather than stay at the castle with the odious Nicholas de Montford. That also had been a crossing in a galley. She vividly recalled the wet, cold journey, and the awful battering of the huge waves, threatening to overwhelm the small craft. In the darkness, dressed like a soldier, she had been conscious of her own helplessness; because she could do nothing, her nausea and fear had intensified. Could she go through it again? On that occasion, it had been a short, violent trip, but this would be a long journey. Her eyes burned; she remembered Martin had protected her, his great strength and unswerving devotion had supported her throughout the fearful crossing. Now, he was dead.

The two men stood silently on either side of her: Payen hoping fervently for the storm to increase and last for days, Ralph wishing the opposite. Gwen continued to review her situation, aware of the uncanny way her life seemed to repeat itself. At Christchurch she had been fleeing a knight of the Order, and once again she was faced with the same problem. Martin, her loyal friend, had risked his life for her. This time, it would be Ralph, another true friend. Once again, she would be heading into a storm, but unlike before, John would not be waiting for her on the other side.

"I'm going to send a message to the Captain of the galley," Ralph said suddenly, and walked quickly out of the room.

There was a long silence. Gwen and Payen stood side-by-side watching the waves increase in size, feeling the gusts of wind on their faces. She sensed he was preparing to say something, and not wishing to divert him, she waited. He cleared his throat, but said nothing. Glancing down, she noticed his hands were clenched tightly, the knuckles white with tension. She smiled to herself. John and Ralph had always been relaxed in her presence, and the Knights of the Order always self-assured and confident. She was unused to a man of Payen's status being so awkward. "Do you think the storm might last long?" Gwen asked. She could feel the tension evaporate.

"I think it could, Mistress Gwen." He cleared his throat.

"You should call me Gwen, and I will call you Payen."

"Thank you, Gwen," he gulped. The freedom to use her name was like the removal of an emotional dam. Before Gwen could react, he was down on his knees. He seized her hand, and began to kiss it fervently. "Gwen, you must know how I feel. I pledge my life to you. I will forsake the Church. I will...."

"Payen! Please get up." She tried to remove her hand, but he gripped on to it, staring up at her like an adoring pet dog.

"We could be happy," he pleaded. "I will do anything for you."

"Stand up, Payen. Please." Her voice was firm, but kindly. He seemed so young, and although they were about the same age, she felt old enough to be his mother. "You're a fine man," she said, drawing him up from his knees, "and although we are friends, we don't know each other. I admire you as a man and a priest, but I do not love you." She looked into his sad eyes. "Nor do you love me."

"I don't want you to go," he wailed. "I want you to stay. I can look after you."

"Payen," she cut in, "I would be in danger if I stayed here. Ralph would be in danger. We have to leave. If not today, then soon." Her face softened. "You have chosen your life's path. Your destination is Jerusalem. I have not yet chosen mine, but it is definitely not to journey to Jerusalem."

"I would give it up. I would give up anything for you."

"No. You might think so at this moment, but it is not so." She had recovered her composure. "You are a knight who has dedicated his life to God. You have trained for this most of your life. I am simply a temporary distraction. No, don't shake your head; you know it's true. In this male world of soldiers and castles, a woman is a distraction. I have come to realize that." She stepped back, looking closely at him. He was a fine man, but utterly inexperienced with women. In a different place, at a different time, she realized she would have found him attractive. She held out her hand to him. "Let us be friends, and forget these past moments. We each must get on with our life."

Payen hesitated, then took her hand, bowing his head. "So be it." Looking over Gwen's shoulder, he could see Ralph coming up the stairs. "I will always love you, Mistress Gwen," he whispered, and strode across the room, passing Ralph in the doorway. Gwen stared after him, her composure once again in tatters.

Ralph watched him rush down stairs. "Did I enter at a bad moment?" He raised his eyebrows in mock horror.

"No, Ralph. Your timing was, as ever, quite perfect."

. . .

"I say, are you awake?"

John woke with a jump, unable to believe he had fallen asleep. Vernon was standing close by, holding his bandaged head with one hand, and gripping on to the horse with the other. It was still hot, but the sun was lower, and John was no longer in Celestial's shade. "How are you?" he asked, rubbing his eyes.

"Rather unsteady, really. My head hurts like Hell." Vernon swayed on his feet, opening and closing his eyes. "Why am I wearing this dress?"

"It's not a dress." John stood up and handed Vernon the water flask. "Do you remember what happened?" Vernon shook his head; he had difficulty focusing his eyes.

John supported him to a shaded rock at the mouth of the gulley, and explained what he assumed had happened. "I think that outlandish garment you were wearing around your head saved your life. It softened the blows to your skull. The herdsmen left it with you because it was covered in blood."

Vernon nodded moodily, and gently explored the back of his head. "It doesn't seem to be bleeding?"

"No, you must have head like a rock."

"But I was bleeding," Vernon said pointing to the mangled vest. He continued to test the edges of his wounds. "Damn fine job. Thanks."

"Will you be fit to travel?"

"Feeling better every moment." Vernon stood up and gazed with obvious distaste at the garment he was wearing. "I feel like a woman." He looked around. "They took my sword and belt?"

John tossed over a woven belt, a pair of sandals and a wide piece of material. "Sit down and I'll make you a turban," John said, suppressing the urge to smile.

"They're welcome to my britches," he said, brightening up. "I haven't changed them for days."

Eventually, Vernon was ready to travel. After sharing a small meal, John helped him into the saddle. Vernon's colour had returned. Although his arms and shoulders were badly bruised, he appeared not to suffer pain or stiffness. "I don't know what you did while I was having a bit of shut-eye. I look as though I've received a first class beating, yet I've felt worse falling off my horse." He peered down at John. "Are you some sort of a healer?"

Before darkness, they reached lower ground, leaving the desert and moving into a fertile area, rich in trees and plants, with a small river flowing gently between low banks covered in rushes. They had seen nobody, and the contrast to the hot desert was a welcome relief.

"Flowing with milk and honey," Vernon observed. "Old part of the Bible," he explained condescendingly.

"I know," John said. There were times when he felt like pushing Vernon out of the saddle.

Blissfully unaware of his gaucheness, Vernon gave the area a lordly appraisal. "Where do you think we are?"

"We've been travelling south-west. We should reach the coast near Tripoli in a day or so."

They camped by the side of the river, allowing Celestial to drink and splash around in the shallows, while they examined their meagre supplies and set a fire. After a while the horse emerged, shook off the water, and began to browse contentedly.

John stripped off his tunic, and kicking off his sandals, waded in until he reached swimming depth; the cool, slow current embraced him and he felt wonderful. Vernon sat on the bank, wistfully observing. John splashed with his feet. "Come on in. It's glorious."

"Rather not, really. Still feeling a bit battered."

"Take your clothes off, and get in. You need to clean up; you're a disgusting mess." He grinned. "You might even enjoy it."

Vernon felt trapped; he was not used to public exposure, and had rarely dipped in a river. After reflection, he remembered that John had tended his wounds and put the long garment on him. Somehow, it seemed to reassure him. "Right. Good idea." He slowly removed his garments and when John was swimming away, he rushed for the river, tripped on a root and catapulted into the water in a flurry of limbs.

John waited until Vernon surfaced, spluttering and rubbing his eyes. "Most artistic. You must have practised that one."

"Very droll." Vernon made a face. "However, you're right. Most enjoyable."

Later, after a sparse meal, they sat companionably around the fire. It was dark, and a light breeze fanned the blaze, causing bright embers to rise on the hot flames. From the quiet river came the guttural sound of frogs, the occasional twitter of small birds, and the soft hissing from the rushes as the air moved them gently against each other.

"This is a good life," Vernon observed, "and with a bit more to eat, it would be near perfect."

"What would make it completely perfect?"

"Well, I don't know about you, but a pleasant young woman would suit me fine."

John grunted in agreement, but said nothing. He thought of Gwen, and remembered Vernon's comment at the temple. If Gwen and Ralph both thought him dead, would they be attracted to each other, or remain as just good friends? There was no doubt that Ralph was committed to Tegwen, or was he? He had made little comment when John had first arrived with Tegwen's sword. Did Ralph suspect they had been lovers? He gazed into the fire, his dark eyes seeing nothing. As a priestess, Tegwen had told Ralph they could not marry. Did she have other lovers, and if so, did Ralph feel released from any commitment to her?

Vernon began to reminisce about some stable girl he had been keen on back at home. John quickly understood it was a very innocent affair. He thought of his own passion for Gwen, and wondered how they had maintained such a platonic relationship. Tom, her presumed father, had been a big impediment, but also there had been the long separations when the Order had intervened. Without doubt, his biggest inhibition had been the fear that they might be related as brother and sister. They had been so young and inexperienced when they first met, but now they were adults, and with Owl's certain denial of any blood link, John felt free to confess his love for her. Or was he too late?

"I say, were you listening?"

"Of course," he refocused his mind, groping for an echo of Vernon's ramblings. "One can never know how these things will turn out." It was a vague statement, but seemed to satisfy Vernon.

"That's so true, you know. Something to look forward to anyway."

John closed his ears and concentrated on Gwen. They were not related, yet the Order believed she was of huge importance to them, and saw him as some sort of a threat. Owl had enlightened him on some things, important facts, but not all. He spoke out aloud without realizing: "I know, it's because the hour is not right!"

"Yes, I hadn't thought of it that way," Vernon seemed quite animated. "Thanks for the advice, old thing. Good night." He stretched out on the soft grass, and was instantly asleep.

John stared at him in alarm. He had no idea what Vernon had been saying, but was glad to have somehow said the right thing. As he settled down, he felt certain the last stage of his strange journey was coming to a climax. Soon the hour would arrive, and everything would be explained.

· · ·

FOR THREE DAYS THEY made their slow journey towards Tripoli, occasionally stopping near remote villages, where John begged for food. He would leave his horse and sword with Vernon and approach each village, leaning heavily on a stout stick and affecting a slight limp. The villagers were always generous, even when they had little to share. John would often repay them with stories of his travels, or advice on how best to protect themselves from thieves and Assassins. He would listen carefully to their gossip and the closer they came to Tripoli, the more the talk focused on the soldiers in black and their huge leader, who was supposed to have magic powers. According to the local reports, his large army was approaching from Damascus.

"You don't believe this nonsense about giants and magic swords do you?" Vernon guffawed loudly. He was gnawing away at a stale loaf of bread, and was unaware of the effect his statement had on John. "My father used to say that most of the weird things that are supposed to happen in the world are made up by soldiers and sailors who want to scrounge a drink." He washed the bread down with a gulp of water. "How many people have you seen with a heads under their arms? What about a long scaly creature with huge jaws of razor-sharp teeth that lives in rivers and eats people in a single mouthful?" He slapped his knees with delight.

"It's called a crocodile, and it does exist."

"Really? What about the people with heads under their arms then?"

"No." John's attention was drawn to a movement in the far distance. They were sitting on a hillside dotted with cedars, and small bushes. In front of them, a wide plain stretched away towards the coast, while to the south and behind them a towering range of mountains dominated the horizon. It was early in the day, and they were finishing yesterday's charitable donations. "What do you make of this?" He pointed to their left, where the bluish haze of the mountains melted into the browns and greens of the arable plain, above which they were perched.

"Where? Can't see anything, old thing. Better lay off the cheese."

"Look carefully." The edge in John's voice was enough to cause

Vernon to reconsider his frivolity. "The dark line over there. Is it moving?"

"Good Heavens. You're right." He stared at a black smudge on the horizon as it gradually thickened. "Do you think it's a herd of animals?"

"That dark line is increasing. At this distance it must stretch for more than a mile. I'm certain it will be the army from Damascus everyone is talking about. I hope the High Lord has listened to his scouts, or he's going to get an unpleasant surprise."

Vernon frowned. "Is this the army with the fellows in black you were talking about?" John nodded. "You really believe they're led by a giant?"

"Yes. The soldiers you encountered, before you met me, were almost certainly long-range scouts from the army that is rapidly approaching us. The vanguard could be here before the day is out." John glanced at Vernon who was standing with his mouth open, his eyes fixed on the gathering wave that was flowing towards them. "What a pity you allowed two of them to escape."

"Ah." Vernon said, conscious of a certain embarrassment. "It was impossible to kill them all, especially after the horse gave up." He remembered telling John a grossly exaggerated story, claiming to have killed a host of the enemy. The two surviving warriors had galloped away, desperate to save their cowardly lives. He had almost tripped himself up over the loss of his horse, inventing a chance arrow that pierced the creature's eye, killing it instantly.

"Still, I imagine they must have spread the word that English knights were the terror of the Holy Land. You probably did our army a favour, by letting those two live."

Vernon did not reply. He was never quite certain when his new friend was being serious.

"However," John said, changing his tone, "I think we must try to find our army, or at least some of our scouts. Make sure they know what's happening." He picked up the saddle and prepared Celestial for another long day of riding, while Vernon collected their few possessions.

"I just wish I still had my sword," Vernon moaned. "In this dress and without a weapon, a fellow feels very vulnerable, you know."

John vaulted into the saddle and held out a hand. "Would madam like a lift?"

They rode carefully down the hill, following a zigzag path made by animals, finally reaching level ground. Around them were clumps of trees, dense bushes and thick patches of cropped grass, a testament to the herds of grazing animals that were driven across the wide plain. They set off towards the west, keeping Celestial at walking pace, taking turns to stride along beside the tall animal. Occasionally, they crossed small streams cut deep into the landscape with only a trickle of muddy water flowing in them. Most often they were dry.

At midday, when the heat was intense, they decided to take shelter from the pitiless sun in a grove of trees surrounding a medium-sized pond. Part of the area near the pool was boggy, and covered with thick, tall reeds and dense patches of water iris. John removed the saddle and led Celestial to a firm, rocky area at the other side where the animal could safely drink. He washed his face and drank deeply, grateful for this short respite. He looked up to see Vernon paddling about among the reeds, with his long tunic raised above his waist, his white buttocks distinctly at odds with his suntanned face and arms. He realized that if either of them were to reveal his legs or torso while travelling, they would quickly be recognized as foreigners.

Later, he awoke in a panic. High above him was a network of branches, providing a shady canopy. Vernon was snoring gently close by. Behind them, Celestial was standing silently; his head down, almost invisible in the deep shadows of the trees. In front was a screen of tall reeds and yellow iris, and beyond was the pool with the rocky area at the far side. He had not meant to doze. All his senses were instantly alert. His eyes scanned the surrounding area, but nothing moved. Then, he heard the noise his subconscious mind must have registered: the sound of men's voices.

He crept up to the reeds, carefully parting them until he could glimpse the other side of the pool. Two soldiers were watering their horses by the rocky area. John recognized their distinctive black uniforms and the harsh cadence of the voices. They were slim, wiry men, wearing leather breastplates with leather guards on their bare forearms, and black, coned helmets. They carried curved swords and daggers in their belts; the shorter of the two had a quiver of arrows over his shoulder. Both soldiers handled their horses with confidence. Each animal carried a round shield; one had a spear attached to the saddle and the other a bow. There was no doubt these were trained soldiers, and John wished he had more than just his sword. In a regular fight, the odds were heavily stacked against him.

Bent double, he returned to the sleeping knight, and placed a firm hand over his mouth. Vernon's eyes sprang open, and John raised a finger to his own mouth. "Don't say a word. Soldiers are here," he whispered. He buckled on his belt and checked his sword, while Vernon gathered his wits. They crawled down to the reeds and quietly assessed the situation. The soldiers were washing their faces, refilling their water flasks, and looking as though they were preparing to leave. The shorter one mounted his horse, and casually glanced around while the other checked his saddlebags. Suddenly, the shorter man sat up straight and stood up on his stirrups, his eyes narrowing. There was a rapid exchange of words. He began to ride his horse at walking pace, around the pond.

"He's seen Celestial," John hissed. He doubled back to the saddle, which had been left on the ground, and quickly dragged it into the reeds where Vernon was keeping watch. The second man mounted his horse and began to follow, calling out to his friend in a jeering voice. John drew his sword, and handed it to Vernon. "I'm going to use Celestial. When I have their attention, attack from behind."

Before Vernon could respond, John disappeared into the trees. He moved away from the pond in a tight circle, coming up behind Celestial, who was taking a keen interest in the approaching horses. Vernon dragged the saddle out of the way, and gripping the sword with one hand, edged behind a thick cluster of plants, his sandals sinking into the mud. John crawled up to his horse from the back, taking cover in the shade of the trees. He was relieved to see Celestial was standing facing the pond, side on to the oncoming riders, and enabling him to approach his horse unseen.

The first soldier called back to his friend, his voice was surprised and excited; he did not appear to be expecting any danger. His sword hung by his side, and his hands rested on the reins of his small but sturdy mount. The two riders had closed up by the time they reached the bend in the pool, and were only about thirty paces from the horse. Once they could see it was unusually large, they pointed and increased their pace. But, their excited chatter changed to alarm as a lithe body suddenly vaulted onto the horse, which reared up kicking its front legs in the air. Both riders grabbed their curved swords and moved their mounts cautiously forward as Celestial continued to rear up, pawing the air, only fifteen paces in front of them.

Vernon had been crouching in the reeds, like a coiled spring, and had quietly discarded his mud-locked sandals. As the second horse moved past his position, he hurled himself into the air, swinging John's sword in a wide arc, slicing down on the soldier's body at a point where his neck joined his shoulder. The man died instantly.

The other soldier whirled round in his saddle, and saw Vernon, carried by his own momentum, tumble down the back of the second horse, which reared up in terror. As the rider tried to get control of his own mount, his dead friend fell sideways in his direction. At the same time, he was aware of the large horse rearing up in front, its deadly hooves slicing the air, threatening to pulverize him. Overwhelmed by the sudden change of events, the rider urged his horse to the left, forcing his way through the dense reeds. In the panic of the moment, the soldier did not register that John was unarmed, or how many attackers were behind him, his sole aim was to live. With that thought, he galloped away into the trees.

John quickly calmed the dead man's horse, as Vernon emerged from the pond, wiping mud from his eyes, unable to believe the fight was over. John handed the reins of the Arab's horse to Vernon, took back the sword, and galloped after the fleeing soldier. Vernon stood very still, holding the reins. He stared down at the lifeless body, frowning. His arm ached; he slowly became aware of the huge amount of energy and violence he had put into that one stroke. He was conscious of a feeling of relief to be alive and uninjured, but also a sense of sadness, even guilt. The other men he had killed since arriving in this hot, violent country, had all been trying to kill him; he had acted in self-defence. This man, he had killed from behind. Vernon was certain this was not how a knight should behave. Dragging the soldier out of the mud, he laid him on his back; the dead man's head remained at an odd angle, his chest covered in blood. "Sorry about that," he murmured, and was promptly sick into the pond.

After a while John returned. "Well done, Vernon. You saved the day." He smiled broadly, and patted Celestial's neck.

Vernon was on his hands and knees, wiping the mud off Celestial's saddle. "Thanks." He seemed depressed. "What happened to the other fellow?"

"He galloped off. I just wanted to make sure he was not going to return, and ambush us with his bow." John dismounted and stood looking down at the dead soldier. "A fine piece of swordsmanship," he said approvingly. Vernon did not reply, but continued to clean the saddle. "Are you injured?"

"No, not a scratch." He looked up at John. "Was it right to kill him, just like that?"

"If you hadn't killed him, and surprised the other soldier, they would have killed us. They wouldn't have thought twice about it." John patted his shoulder. "In war, soldiers die. As a knight, you've trained for years to kill your enemy. You just did what you were trained for." He wanted to make a joke, lighten the mood, not to dwell on it. In the next few days there was likely to be much killing. The only way they would survive was to see it as something needing to be done. "Remember, it's them or us."

"I know all that." Vernon was unusually sombre. "But as a knight, I was expecting to fight in battles for glory and honour, not murdering people from behind." He stood up. "All my life I've wanted to be a knight. In the stories I read, they did honourable things, fought their enemies face to face, but this was a messy little murder. Although it saved our lives, it doesn't make me feel a hero."

John was abashed. He had not suspected Vernon possessed any deep feelings. "I was grateful for your courage and skill. It's not easy to kill a fully armed soldier. It certainly wasn't murder." He walked over to the newly captured horse, feeling moved to explain something: "I suggest you change into that soldier's armour. You'll have his sword, shield and spear. I'm certain you'll use these weapons to good effect. We're most certainly going to be involved in a battle in the next day or two; it will be your chance to seize all the glory and honour you desire," he patted the horse's muzzle, "but I doubt whether, at the end of the fighting, you will still believe in such things."

CHAPTER 19

"I FAIL TO UNDERSTAND YOU, Sir Payen. Are you telling us that Lord d'Escosse, the Leader of the English Forces, is no longer here?" Sir Godfrey de Montbard's eyes blazed with anger. Behind him stood five Knights of the Order in full armour; a strong detachment of cavalry milled about in the courtyard below.

"He has departed, my Lord." Payen tried to remain detached. It was a confrontation he had known would happen.

Only the day before, as the storm blew itself out, Ralph and Gwen had immediately left Marqab, together with Sergeant Little and his few soldiers. Payen had watched from the castle as the small galley battled its way out of the safety of the harbour, barely coping with the aftermath of the storm's disturbed water, its prow crashing into mountainous waves. For a long time Payen kept watch as the breaking rollers slowly gave way to a huge swell. The craft, though sturdy, seemed immensely vulnerable in the great sea. His teeth clenched tightly as the galley balanced precariously on the top of each advancing mountain of green brine, its slim oars barely touching the surface. Even now, he could feel his heart thumping as he recalled every lurch of the small vessel into the next deep trough. Each time, he had believed it would be its last; each time, when the vessel rose up valiantly, he was grateful for Gwen's safe deliverance. Eventually, the galley disappeared into the brightening distance. He knew he would never again see the lovely woman for whom he would have given up everything. Her departure had left him unsettled and uncertain of his future; all he could do was pray for her continued safety.

"Where has he gone?"

"I was not privy to his actual destination," Payen said, wanting to keep close to the truth. "He arrived in the galley. It was under his control."

"What news of Mistress Gwen?"

Again Payen chose his words carefully. "I have no recent news of her, my Lord. You have heard nothing?"

"Obviously not!" Sir Godfrey turned to one of the knights. "Sir John, send messengers to Antioch. Have Lord d'Escosse arrested if he returns to the city." He whirled round on Payen. "You should have prevented him from leaving. You saw the murder he committed."

"It was not murder, my Lord. Sir Raymond drew first."

"Enough!" Sir Godfrey was barely able to control his anger. "Have you sent out scouts to track Mistress Gwen's progress?"

"I'll send out my scouts immediately," Payen said, bowing his head, so he did not have to look Sir Raymond in the eye.

"You should have sent them out immediately she was reported missing!" Sir Godfrey roared. "She is beyond value to the Order."

"I'm not a member of your Order," Payen replied calmly. "Mistress Gwen seemed quite ordinary to me. I assumed she knew what she was doing."

"If you were not a knight under the protection of King Baldwin, I would have you whipped!" Sir Godfrey stalked from the room, followed by his knights. Payen heard him order a complete search of the buildings, but decided to ignore it. He could have tried to order these fanatics out of his castle, but he doubted if they would have taken any notice of him. It was not important in the general scheme of things. He resented Ralph having the opportunity to protect Gwen, but he was content to accept the situation rather than have her come under the control of these zealots of the Order.

He summoned his chief scout, Ishmael. "I want you, if asked, to lead a search party, but not to find any trace of the woman. Don't ever mention your earlier contact with her. Is that clear?"

Ishmael stared into his eyes. "You are a good man, Payen de Montdidier. I will not let you down."

Sir Godfrey reappeared in the doorway. "Well? What have you arranged?"

"This is Ishmael. He will lead your search party."

There was a tense silence as Godfrey stared at the young Arab. "You will come with me, and you will not return until you have found the Maid." He turned to Payen. "I have just received a message from the High Lord. An enemy host is advancing from Damascus; they appear to be positioning themselves between our army and Tripoli. We need every able-bodied fighter. You will leave this castle to a few trusted men, marshal the rest of the soldiers and march towards Tripoli. You should catch up with our army before tomorrow night, but if you don't, you are ordered to act as a rearguard. Is that clear?"

"Will you be in charge?"

"You have not been listening. I will be in charge of finding the Maid. You will lead these forces against the infidel." Sir Raymond quietly assessed the young knight, and found him wanting. "If you have any difficulties, you will hand over to Sir John." He nodded towards a tall knight beside him.

"Yes, my Lord." Payen gave a perfunctory bow as Sir Godfrey stormed out. He looked down at the sea: balance had been restored; sun-tipped ripples and a welcoming blue had replaced the angry green waves. So it was with his life. It was time for him to leave this accursed castle and fight those who opposed the will of God. Eventually, he knew he would reach Jerusalem where he could pursue the task for which he had been chosen.

• • •

WITH TWO HORSES, THEY were able to travel so much faster, staying well ahead of the main enemy forces. On a number of occasions they had been compelled to hide from large groups of Arab scouts. From a distance their appearance did not arouse suspicion. Vernon rode the captured horse, but was unwilling to wear the dead man's tunic: "It's too short and revealing and I'm definitely not wearing his clout. It's not the sort of thing a knight does, you know." As a result, he wore the long shift with leather body armour, and the conical helmet perched on his head. He carried the captured weapons, but was unhappy with them, finding the curved sword lighter than his English long sword, but less manageable: "It's very sharp, much sharper than the old sword, but it doesn't feel right." He also moaned about the spear, which he found difficult to propel for any distance: "Give me a noble javelin any day." Even the circular shield was a disappointment: "I don't know what the tall fellows do. It would hardly cover their navels."

John ignored most of the complaints, assuring him he would only be required to use the weapons until they met up with the armies from Antioch. "Once we see our men, you can discard them all. I wouldn't want English knights to think you were an enemy soldier, especially one in a dress." It was not a thought that had occurred to Vernon. He began to watch the distant horizon with intense concentration.

In spite of their best intentions, they found themselves delayed in blind valleys while taking what appeared to be short cuts through dry hills. They passed, almost without noticing, from a green landscape of small streams and pools to a patched arid country that languished in a rain shadow. For two days they were lost, finally being forced to retrace their steps having run out of food and water. During this time, they saw neither man nor beast. With the intense heat they began to believe they had ventured into an earthly Hell.

"The horses are close to exhaustion," John said. Both men were walking by the side of their animals, suffering equally from the constant assault of flies. Throughout the heat of each day, the insects attacked aiming to rob them of moisture, buzzing around their eyes and mouths, settling on any parts of their bodies showing the slightest trace of sweat. Shade was impossible to find. They staggered like blind beggars across the stony ground, dragging their suffering horses behind them. Each man, while aware of his friend, travelled in his own mind, ignorant of time, forcing one leg in front of the other, concentrating on the hope of finding a way back to water.

They had not talked for a long time when they staggered out of the desert, down into a small, green valley. It was early morning, still cool. The flies had disappeared as they descended. In front of them, cool water was trickling out of the hillside into a rocky pool.

It was like a miracle. They approached slowly, and feared it was a mirage, until their horses rushed forward.

"It's real!" Vernon gasped, dropping the reins of his horse. He fell face first into the pool, with the horses drinking on either side of him. John knelt down on the edge, taking small sips from his cupped hands, carefully moistening his dry lips and raw eyes. He stood up, and pulled the horses out, preventing them from drinking too much. Vernon clambered to his feet and without speaking they unsaddled the animals, allowing them to graze on long tethers.

Finally, grinning horribly at each other, they shuffled back to the water. Throughout the day, they drank, washed and rested, gradually recovering from the horror. Hunger was their next problem, but that evening they ate well. In spite of his criticism of the weapon, Vernon was able to spear a small deer from a distance of at least thirty paces. "Just a lucky throw," he said modestly.

The sweet smell of cooked meat permeated the air, and once they had satisfied their hunger, John began to worry about their safety. They were camped in a hollow, and though it was unlikely that their fire could be seen from a distance, the mouth-watering aroma of roasting venison might attract unwanted visitors, both animal and human. "Are you fit to travel?" he said, as he wiped his greasy fingers.

"Just about." Vernon yawned. He was surprised how quickly he had recovered. "I could easily sleep for a week, but I wouldn't want to miss the fun." He glanced around, "Also, I don't want some foreign fellow giving me a close shave while I slept. This is a place that could attract visitors."

John yawned in sympathy. "I'll give the horses a final drink. You deal with the water and divide the meat."

Vernon agreed. Killing the deer had restored his good humour, and he was content for John to make the decisions. "When do you think we'll meet up with our fellows?"

"Who knows? It's a big country, and I have very little idea where we are. We can only hope our army is continuing towards Tripoli." He wiped his mouth with the back of his hand. "We have no idea how fast the enemy is moving, but we do know that they are keeping watch on the progress of our forces. The Giant will be able to join battle when it suits him. In which case, he will have a decided advantage." John led the horses to the pool, failing to notice Vernon rolling his eyes.

"You're sure about this big fellow, are you?"

John returned and gazed into the fire. "The soldiers we've met were dressed like those I encountered in England, like the ones I fought on the high plateau. Also, they spoke with the same accent. The local people I've met recently knew about the advancing army. They all claimed a giant, the Giant, was leading it. I'm sure he's in charge."

"Suppose we don't find our men before the battle? What then?"

There was a silence as John looked fixedly at his hand. "Then, I have to find the Giant by myself."

Vernon was dividing the meat into two piles and stuffing it into the saddlebags. "That doesn't make sense. How on earth could you take on an army by yourself?" He sniffed. "Anyway, what about me? I can't speak the lingo; without you I'd be in a fix."

"You won't understand this, Vernon, but the Giant and I must eventually meet." He thought of Owl. "It's written in the stars." This was not the sort of thing knights discussed. Vernon had no answer for it, especially as he realized John was not joking. "I have been thinking about you," he grinned at Vernon. "If we were unable to avoid meeting a large body of enemy scouts, they would wonder why you didn't speak."

"My point exactly," Vernon shook a finger.

"So, we'll pretend you've been injured, and can't speak."

"Ah," Vernon said cautiously, dropping his finger. "How do we do that?"

By the time they were ready to go Vernon had, in spite of his protests, become a soldier known in the army as 'walking wounded'. Around his neck was a thick, dirty scarf, heavily stained with the blood of the deer. Wrapped around his head was another bloody piece of cloth that could, when necessary, cover one eye. "You've been in quite a fight," John said approvingly, adjusting the helmet.

"Wouldn't it be better if you wore the armour?"

John shook his head. "If we were to meet enemy scouts, they would wonder why a soldier was caring for an injured peasant; whereas, they would understand an injured soldier being guided by a local person."

"What about your horse and your sword? They're not local."

"If we're approached, it will almost certainly lead to a fight. But they will not be expecting one of their injured soldiers to suddenly attack them." He began to kick sand onto the fire. "I think we should move on, it's a bright night. If we continue to the end of this valley, we might find ourselves back on the plain."

"I wonder where those Arab fellows are?" Vernon heaved the saddle onto his horse. "For all we know, they could have caught up with us."

"Another reason for moving on."

They travelled slowly and in silence, each carrying his sword across his saddle. As they left the valley, they were relieved to rejoin the wide plain, clearly outlined in the moonlight. They travelled for a while until the ground began to slope upwards on their right towards a range of mountains. In the dark they could discern the black shapes of the summits blotting out the star clustered sky.

"I think we should get some height," John said quietly. "I would hate to meet any patrols on this level ground. If the going gets difficult, we'll stop and wait until morning."

Vernon agreed, content to let John lead the way. After more than an hour of steady climbing, they found themselves on a level area with a precipice on one side, dropping down into the plain and a towering dark cliff face on the other. As they travelled up the gently sloping hill, the easy ground slowly narrowed, gradually leading to a steep rise, forcing them to stop on a wide, flat rock. In the darkness, it was impossible to assess the difficulty of further travel.

"This seems like a useful place to spend the rest of the night," John said. "We should have a good view of the plain when the sun comes up. No one is going to stumble over us accidentally up here."

After dismounting, they hobbled the horses well away from

the edge, took off the saddles and arranged themselves with the horses behind them and the vast empty space of the plain in front and far below. On their left, the ground sloped down the way they had come, and in the bright moonlight they were confident they would not be victims of a surprise attack. Vernon agreed to take the first watch. It was still dark when John took over from him.

"It's cold," John observed. He stamped his feet and rubbed his arms. "'Not the most comfortable night's rest."

"Look over there," Vernon pointed to their left. In the distance, it was just possible to make out a flurry of flickering pinpoints of light.

"Camp fires. They've made good progress," John said. "At least we know where they are."

Vernon had been walking backwards and forwards to keep awake. He quickly removed his body armour, curled up on the warm spot John had occupied, and was instantly asleep.

John stared out at the host of campfires; there seemed so many of them. He felt a faint irritation in his right hand. He looked at his palm; it was as though the runes glowed in the darkness. It only lasted a moment, but it was enough to convince him that his inevitable confrontation with the Giant was close.

"Tomorrow, Vernon, it could be tomorrow." He turned, and realizing his friend was asleep, began to pace about. For the first time he could remember, he felt uncertain. In the past, there was always the feeling that he was protected, and at each deadly engagement the runes miraculously came alive. At the times when they failed to help, it was, as Owl had explained, because there was no need. Was it magic? He remembered the time when he had wanted to be important and not be involved with anything that smacked of magic, believing he could not become a person of influence and still trust in childish things. But, in spite of his opposition, the power continued to appear throughout the past years. In recent times it had enabled him to heal more often than defend. He had grown used to it, like a lord soon gets used to having his own guards to protect him.

Raising his right palm close to his face, he was barely able to make out the design. Tomorrow, if he faced the Giant, would the power return? After his first experience in the flower fields, when he had unknowingly controlled one of the Swords of Power, he had never considered the possibility of the power leaving him. John had approached each conflict with confidence, believing he would eventually defeat the Giant by turning his own swords against him. But now things were changing, he could sense it.

He looked down at Vernon, deep in unworried sleep, a man who saw everything as an adventure, taking each day as it came. "I used to be like him," he whispered aloud, "but I've changed." The darkness seemed to close in. He stared up at the wonder of the stars, looking for an answer. "It's because my knowledge is not complete. Tomorrow, I sense I will face my enemy once more. This time I feel uncertain." Once he had said it, he knew it to be true. He shivered, feeling the cold, but knowing the real reason he shivered was fear. Nothing could save him from the lonely confrontation that was written in the stars. Only at the last moment would he know if he was to die.

. . .

It WAS A PERFECT day, and the view from the Cypriot hill was spectacular. Below them, the blue sea stretched away into the distance where a thin mauve line on the horizon suggested the possibility of the mainland. The storm had blown itself out before they reached the port of Limassol, and the unhurried journey to Stephen de Bois' estate had been a pleasant change after the uncomfortable battering of the storm. When they left the galley, the sailors made signs with their hands. Ralph had cheerfully informed Gwen that they all held her responsible for the violent tempest. "Women and ships never go together," he joked. "It's a combination of sex, confined living and superstition."

The stone mansion was exactly as she remembered it, even down to the neglected gardens and the untidy courtyard that had not been swept for weeks. It was clear that the Greek servants were unaware of Stephen's death. Ralph decided not to tell them, to avoid unnecessary complications, especially as they appeared to have little knowledge of English or French. Some recognized him from the previous visit, and soon the house and grounds were a frenzy of activity, as the ritual cleaning on the arrival of the owners, or their friends, took place.

Ralph went to the stables to supervise the accommodation of the horses he had rented in Limassol, while Gwen inspected the house. The large, cool mansion was inviting. She walked from room to room enjoying the civilized comfort of the place after the rigours of the past weeks. Some rooms flowed into each other with open, curved entrances, continuing the exquisite patterns of the hardwood floors, on which rich woven rugs had been carefully positioned. Each room was sparsely but finely furnished. On one wall was a painting of a majestic-looking man in middle age, whose imperious eyes and prominent nose clearly indicated it was a portrait of Stephen de Bois' father.

Gwen was saddened when she thought of him. Stephen, for all of his arrogant and supercilious ways, had been a decent human being, destroyed by a flaw he could not control. She looked around at all the quality and the artistic comfort that Stephen's father had created for his son to inherit. All for nothing. When she and Ralph left for England, the servants would neglect this lovely building; it would remain unused, slowly decaying, until the Order eventually became aware of it.

She went up the broad, finely carved staircase, wandering from room to room, conjuring up the vivid memories of her last visit. First, she went into the room she had shared with Barbara. Once again, the awful murder of her gifted servant flashed into Gwen's mind. She hurried into Stephen's room, which she had previously only entered when he was recovering from his bout of the falling sickness. She realized when she looked around his room, that Stephen's strange madness when he met John was but a prelude to his death. Finally, she entered into the one which John and the injured Ralph had shared. So many recollections. Always, there had been a sense of moving on towards the conclusion of some grand scheme organized by the Order. Now, for the first time for years, she felt free. But even as she thought it, she realized it came with a price, for without John her freedom was limited. She would be like a nun who, although free to leave the confines of her nunnery, was still denied the physical love which she yearned for.

Standing by the open window, she could see Ralph examining the estate horses with Sergeant Little. She closed her eyes, wishing it were John standing there. Gwen shook her head sadly: without love, she would be like one of those horses, kept in a stable for a rider who never arrived. Her eyes opened wide; the thought was outrageous; she giggled to herself as she went down stairs.

Ralph was in good spirits when he returned to the house. "I've found a man who speaks some English. He's sending his wife up tomorrow. She makes dresses. I thought you might want to get out of your peasant hand-me-downs."

She smiled at him. "You're a very thoughtful man."

"It comes of having a sister. Aelfreda took the business of dresses very seriously."

"What's she like?"

"In what way?" Ralph replied evasively.

Gwen pretended to examine her hands. "Is she beautiful?"

"Well, I suppose so. You can't expect a brother to answer that with any real accuracy."

"What does she do? What is she good at?"

"Let me see," Ralph replied judiciously. "She sings and plays the harp. She rides well and gets involved in all sorts of local stuff."

"Such as?"

"Oh, um, local pageants, and things like that. She likes to encourage the local festivals." He grinned broadly, knowing Aelfreda would be interested to hear her involvement with the Henge and her devotion to Pagan religion described in this way.

"How long did John stay with you?"

The question caught Ralph off guard. He was suddenly aware of the direction of their conversation. "Oh, let me see, a year or so."

"Did John like Aelfreda?"

"Everyone likes Aelfreda. She's that sort of woman. Even my two ghastly young brothers adore her." He found himself playing a part in which he was unsure of his role. If he revealed his sister's relationship with John, it would be the truth. But would it help? He suspected Gwen had loved John. Such a revelation might enable her to move on. But, it might also tarnish his memory, and take away from her something she held precious. He had watched

John when Gwen was around, noting how he seemed to avoid being alone with her, as though he unwilling to risk reviving any previous attraction. John had, almost certainly, loved Aelfreda, and from Ralph's point of view he was content that his sister had not been forsaken. On the other hand, he guessed it would make his courtship of Gwen much easier if he revealed the passion between John and Aelfreda, but his friendship with John, and his respect for Gwen prevented him from doing so. He would progress slowly; there might come a time, after he had won Gwen's heart, when he would reveal the truth of his dead friend. It was not now.

"Did they spend time together?" Gwen smiled bravely, needing to know the answer, but fearing the truth.

Ralph laughed. "I kept his lazy body busy all day long. He was my pupil; I enjoyed teaching him. Once he had mastered the various weapons, we would spend hours practising, or racing our horses. At night, we discussed the management of the estate, the concept of power, religion, even the stars." He adopted a military stance, fighting an imaginary foe. "We defeated my venomous neighbour, Lord Herlwin, and eventually King Henry heard about it. It was his excuse for sending us over to the Holy Land to keep an eye on the Knights of the Order." He grinned at Gwen. "The one subject we never talked about was women." He rolled his eyes, making Gwen chuckle.

"I don't believe a word of it," she said, delighted with his infectious humour. "But there is one thing I would like you to explain."

"As long as it doesn't tax my limited intelligence."

She shook her head. "John carried an unusual sword. It was beautifully made. One time, when he was practising with it, just outside Antioch, I noticed it had a flower design on the blade."

"Really?" Ralph opened his eyes wide.

"Yes, really. I've never seen a man carry a sword with a flowery design. Where did he get it from?"

"He arrived with it. Perhaps your step father made it for him?"

"Tom couldn't have made a sword of that quality." Gwen pursed her lips. "Even if he did, he would never have created such a design. It was almost as if it was a sword for a woman."

Ralph was amazed at Gwen's perceptiveness. He had often wondered why Tegwen had given John her sword, made by her father. Thinking of Tegwen made him conscious of the pulse in his throat. Tegwen, the great love of his life, who had dismissed the possibility of them ever marrying, was still capable of affecting him. He gazed at Gwen; she was not only beautiful but, unlike Tegwen, she would make a perfect wife.

"Ralph?"

He realized he was staring at her. "Sorry. There is no doubt, you are the most wonderful woman I've ever met."

"Oh?" Gwen was at a loss for words.

"But enough of this romantic drivel! This is what comes of too much talk and not enough wine." He reached out his hand for hers. "First, let's go down to the sea, and paddle like children!"

"Yes, let's do that!" she shouted, keen to change the mood. As they raced, whooping, out of the courtyard, Gwen could not help noticing how attractive he was. It seemed as though she had been deliberately looking at him through frosted glass.

•   •   •

"THAT'S SOME ARMY," VERNON murmured as he rubbed his eyes. "I've never seen so many fellows in all my life. 'Makes our army look pretty undermanned."

Below them, the front of the huge horde was slowly passing, with hundreds of cavalry leading the way in well-organized lines; colourful pennants attached to their spears were flapping in a slight breeze. The front sections were mounted on small, tough Arab horses. They were followed by hundreds of camels, their riders rocking backwards and forwards on their ungainly mounts. Behind them, marched dense formations of foot soldiers, spread out across the plain, creating thick clouds of dust, masking their true numbers. There were long columns of carts and wagons drawn by labouring mules, with herds of goats and cattle stretching out behind. Swift moving groups of scouts were constantly arriving and departing. Somewhere in the middle of this ponderous army, were the chief officers and their general.

"I've been watching them for a while." John was lying flat on the ground, staring down at the huge passage of armed soldiers. "There was no point in waking you. We'll be of more use to our men knowing exactly what forces the enemy is putting in the field. I want you to assess their various components. If either of us reaches the Crusader forces, we could be of some value to them."

"Have you seen him yet?" Vernon found it difficult to admit to believing in a giant with magic swords.

"Not yet. When I get close enough, I'll know where the Giant is."

"How will you get close? It's not as if we can just wander up to them."

"That's exactly what we will do. In an hour or so, the main fighting units will have passed. We will approach as though we've been in a fight with enemy scouts. I will explain, if I have to, that you were injured and I captured this horse and the sword. The whole army is on the move. They are looking for massed formations of enemy scouts. We will hardly be noticed, especially with all this dust. Once we are among their supply wagons, we will move forward. We'll be just two more soldiers ready for a fight."

"That's rather dangerous isn't it?" Vernon could not remember reading of any knight who had done such a thing.

"We live in dangerous times, my friend."

"Damned right we do." Vernon was suddenly animated. "I've always wanted to be a hero. My family never believed I was capable of anything." He beamed. "Here we are, two against thousands! This will be something to tell the grandchildren." John tried not to smile. "However, I would have preferred to be armoured like a knight, not dressed like some antic clown."

As the morning wore on, a light wind began to blow across the plain, increasing the dust that billowed high in the air, surrounding the rear elements of the Arab host, and making it difficult to see for any distance. They mounted their horses with John leading, making their way slowly down the hill towards the dense crowds of camp followers, with herds of animals and small groups of guards that moved like a dark wave across the plain. The dust concealed their identity. It was soon apparent that those who travelled in this part of the army were concerned only with surviving the unpleasant conditions, their heads down, their faces masked. As John had forecast, their own arrival, and their subsequent advance through the huge crowd of men and animals, went unnoticed.

By midday, they had passed the flocks of animals, the donkey carts and the masses of people moving along, singly or in small groups. Many wore no armour, carrying only wooden staves, marching to their own rhythm. Others, carried a variety of weapons and odd pieces of armour. Far to the edges of this ragtag body, rode professional soldiers, in tight disciplined formations, guarding the flanks. They appeared and disappeared in the dust clouds like phantoms, but never showed any interest in those they were protecting.

It came as a shock when the vast army suddenly stopped. John had assumed the warriors would settle down to eat and rest, and was surprised when Vernon identified the reason for the delay. "What do you know! They're all praying."

"Get down quickly!" John sprang from his horse. "Hurry! Before we're noticed."

As they huddled together, they could see the Arabs were all facing in the same direction, and John was forcibly reminded of his time with Ibrahim: at certain times of the day, all Moslems prayed. He had forgotten.

"Why are they all facing the same way?" Vernon gasped; he had winded himself falling off his horse, and was unnerved by the display of mass obedience.

"They're facing Mecca. All Moslems pray to Mecca a number of times each day."

"Jolly impressive. You don't get this sort of turnout at our religious gatherings." Vernon glanced around, trying to imitate the postures of the nearest warriors.

After a pause, the army resumed its advance, and John and Vernon climbed carefully onto their horses and continued their journey ahead through the surging mass of people. Slowly, John was aware of larger formations of marching men on each side, with fewer undisciplined men around them. In front were powerful wagons pulled by bullocks, and surrounded by heavily armed guards.

"This is where we might become more obvious," he said, moving close to Vernon. "This dust is going to help, but I think we must move quickly, and avoid getting too close." Vernon nodded, screwing-up his eyes as he tried to peer ahead.

By late afternoon, they had advanced almost into the centre of the huge army. All around them the uniformed troops marched in ordered ranks, some to the beat of drums. Ahead, through the curtains of dust, they could observe grand wagons in which officers travelled, their horses tethered behind. Near them, large formations of camels shambled along, complaining belligerently, while their masked riders struck them with whips. There were very few isolated riders, and their presence, in spite of the dust, had begun to be noticed. Twice, fast moving scouts had approached them, curious as to their mission. On both occasions, John had understood that they were merely trying to help, having noticed the sad state of Vernon's condition. John had laughed it off, explaining that the hero having killed many unbelievers was on his way to medical attention. Once, he had been questioned about his horse; he had demonstrated the long sword he carried and told an heroic tale of disarming an infidel knight. The scouts had been delighted with the news, riding off in high spirits, their minds set on an imminent victory.

"Did you learn anything?" Vernon muttered.

"Yes. They will be making camp shortly, and expect to commence the battle early tomorrow."

"Anything else?"

"Yes. The medical wagons are ahead of us, and we will be able to get you treated once we have set up camp."

"What?" Vernon was confused. He had lost his original enthusiasm, and had found the long journey through enemy forces, with the constant attack of dust and heat, depressing and tiring. He had almost drawn his sword when John appeared to be having problems with the jostling scouts. His relief when they departed had been extreme. It was a situation unlike anything he had ever experienced, and his ideas of heroism and bravery had been severely undermined. "I can't be treated for wounds I don't have."

"Of course not. But we will appear to be going in that direction. I've learned the Giant's headquarters are close by."

"Good." There was a long pause as they trotted on, close to each other. The wind was dropping; the dust was slowly beginning to settle, no longer whirling above their heads, but the movement of so many horses, camels and marching soldiers was still churning up dense clouds. "What will happen to me when you fight with the Giant?" He felt pleased he was able to mention the name, however unimaginable the demonic creature might be. If John believed in an enemy whose description seemed to be dragged up from the depths of mythology, and was willing to risk his life against such seemingly overwhelming odds, then Vernon was willing to support his brave friend. "Remember, I'm your man."

John glanced across at Vernon, and in that moment felt uplifted and strangely guilty: he recognized the moral support of Vernon's friendship, yet found it hard to equate his bravery with his normal buffoonery. "You're a brave man, Vernon. I'm grateful for your support."

"Don't mention it, my good fellow. Glad to help." For the next few minutes, Vernon glowed in John's compliment, while John fought the need to laugh.

Eventually, trumpets sounded, drums rolled, and raucous voices heralded the setting up of camp. Around them there was a flurry of activity as tired soldiers found a place to flop and discard their armour and weapons. Campfires were lit; in a short time a well-organized distribution of food and water was in action. John and Vernon dismounted, and walked their horses through the enormous camp, ignored by the travel-worn soldiers, whose sole aim was food and rest.

"Chew some of this meat," John said, as he handed Vernon a hunk of venison from his saddlebag. 'If we appear to be eating, we'll be less noticeable."

"Good idea. I'm utterly famished." Vernon attacked the meat with gusto.

"Remember, Vernon, you're supposed to be an invalid," John growled, trying to avoid the casual attention of nearby soldiers.

"Ah," Vernon nodded his agreement. "Suck, don't chew."

They moved cautiously through the maze of tents, fires and prostrate soldiers. There were long lines of tethered horses, hobbled camels and compounds of donkeys. Some soldiers were moving around, but the majority lounged around their fires. Guards were posted at the outer edges of the vast camp, and cavalry units were on constant patrol over the otherwise empty plain.

Darkness descended. Vernon and John continued to progress through the camp, beginning to draw the attention of the curious. Soldiers who had eaten and rested were becoming alert to movement around them. They did not suspect enemy infiltrators, but were merely interested in how Vernon had received such wounds and how John had captured such a fine horse.

John adopted the line that they were on their way to find medical help, and he would tell them the whole story when he returned. With shouts of encouragement the soldiers urged them on their way. The silent Vernon slowly passed from extreme anxiety to casual concern, as they led their horses from one section to the next.

They moved into a space where there were no fires around them; only the moonlight and the bright stars lit their way. As they moved across the shadowy landscape, John was aware of a growing heat in his right hand; turning the palm up to his face, he could see the runes glowing in the darkness.

"He's close to me!" John hissed. "I can feel him. The Giant is close by."

"Oh Hell's fire," Vernon gasped. He had been nodding off, and this sudden change of events took him by surprise.

In front of them, some two hundred paces away, large wagons were positioned around a collection of bright, flickering fires. Close to the wagons, a platoon of guards marched past, while others stood to attention at regular intervals, their bright spears reflecting the flickering light of the fires.

"Now what?" Vernon whispered. They stopped, feeling vulnerable. Their horses chewed loudly at their bits, trying to generate saliva in their dry mouths. Around the two men there was the faint hum of the camp, but for the moment, they seemed to be in an oasis of silence, with only the gentle buffeting of the dusty breeze. In front of the wagons, they could dimly see a crowd of men facing towards a massive figure who was waving his arms, and appeared to have the complete attention of his audience.

"That's him," John murmured, "I'm sure it is." The speaker was head and shoulders taller than anyone else. He was waving a large sword in his hand. Even from a distance, it flashed blue in the firelight. The guards had not noticed them; most, caught up in the passion of their leader's speech, were facing towards him. At times, there was loud and sustained cheering, and the beating of swords on shields, but John was not close enough to hear the Giant's words. "I wonder when he'll be aware of me?" he whispered.

"How do you mean?" Vernon squinted as a dust cloud blew towards them.

"The sign on my hand reacts to his presence. His swords turn against him, when I'm near."

Vernon was finding John's statements increasingly difficult to understand. "Turn against him? The swords do?"

"Yes." John's eyes were bright with excitement. "When the runes on my palm begin to throb and burn, I know I have the power to defeat him. When I yell my other name, the swords will come alive, and will destroy him."

A strange expression crossed Vernon's face. His recent friendship with John had not prepared him for this huge leap of logic. If John had suggested they race forwards, into this mass of soldiers, and try to kill the leader before anyone was alerted to their presence, he would have found that acceptable. In spite of certain death, Vernon would have thought himself a hero, dying in a noble exploit. It was worthy of his highest ideals of chivalry. But, when they were so close to success or abject failure, when there could be no retreat, to be faced with the possibility that John was a madman was unsettling in the extreme. "Your other name?" he queried.

"Yes. Giles Plantard," John replied impatiently. He felt under great pressure. During the past years he had known, deep inside, this moment would come. But, in spite of that certainty, he now felt unsure of himself. The runes throbbed painfully in his palm. He was sweating profusely. His eyes stung with the dust and sweat, and his mouth felt dry. "Of course," he muttered, "he won't be aware of me until I shout my name. That will be when the swords come to life."

"Of course," Vernon nodded his head, as though agreeing with a simpleton. "Good idea." This was not the way he had imagined his death, but he was determined he would not be caught alive. "So you're just going to walk up there and yell your name at him, and that's it?"

John breathed out. He turned towards Vernon and in spite of the darkness was aware of his friend's confusion. In a strange way, Vernon's presence, and his simple summing up of the situation made it all seem possible. There was no logic to this, merely a process. It was as though the stars were in alignment; the time was right. John had experienced the phenomenon of his name, the power of the runes and the dramatic danger of the swords. There was no way to explain how it happened, or even why. He felt he was standing on one side of a narrow black abyss, with the Giant on the other. They represented completely opposite values; either he, or the Giant, would be cast down into the darkness. Perhaps they would both die? He placed a hand on Vernon's shoulder. "You're a good man. I know you must find this bizarre, but it will happen. I know it will." He tightened his grip. "With your help, I will defeat this evil creature. We may die. We almost certainly will, but without his evil genius, this army will fall apart. We will achieve greatness, but sadly few will ever know."

Vernon blinked rapidly. He found himself becoming emotional. "I'm your man," he gulped. "What now?"

John felt suddenly alert. The hopelessness dropped away, to be replaced by a confidence and determination he had not experienced before. His right hand throbbed with energy; he knew with a remarkable clarity what he must do.

"We'll walk our horses up to the guards. Leave the talking to me. I'm going to tell them that I wish to present this horse and sword to the leader, and that you are a hero who destroyed a company of unbelievers."

"Then?"

"Then we'll see what happens. When I start yelling, draw your sword and cover me."

"Right." Vernon took in a deep breath. "You might be mad, but you're no coward. I shall be proud to die in your company." He reached out his hand, touching John's arm.

John hesitated, turned and gripped it with his left hand, unable to use his right. After a brief, emotional pause, they moved on silently towards the loud gathering ahead, where the Giant was continuing to harangue the assembled officers of his army.

Soon, they were close enough to hear the Giant's powerful voice urging his men to heroic action. The guards were transfixed by his oratory, and completely unaware of their approach. John stopped behind two guards, touching one gently on the shoulder. The man whipped round, his eyes wide with surprise; it was a moment before his partner reacted. John put a finger to his mouth. "I have something wonderful for our great leader," he whispered, indicating the horse. The guards relaxed, but looked suspiciously at John's apparel. "I want to present the horse, and this sword." He held it in front of him, with his left hand, speaking with such authority, compelling the guards to examine the weapon. "This man is a hero," John hissed pointing to Vernon, whose face was almost hidden by the bandages. "He's killed many of our enemy. We have important news concerning the battle tomorrow. You must give me entry, immediately he has finished speaking."

There was a sudden roar of voices and the crowd around the Giant broke into unrestrained cheering and clapping; many of the guards around the wagons banged their swords on their shields. The Giant stood like a colossus waving both of the mighty swords above his head, their blades glittering blue in the flickering red light. It was a scene from ancient mythology: the huge figure, his bulging eyes gleaming red in the firelight, and his cavernous mouth wide open, roaring like a monster from the depths of Hades. He was all-powerful. Clad in black armour, the solid domed helmet increasing his enormous height, he was a leader like no other these soldiers had ever followed, and the guards were unable to resist turning towards him.

In that moment of inattention, John pushed past them and ran forwards; he surged through the semi-circle of officers, approaching the Giant from the side, where the least number of persons was standing. Immediately, he was in the open space that separated the soldiers from their leader. John's hand was burning; the pain was almost overwhelming, but he thrust it into the air like a shield. The Giant turned to face him; his arms were above his head with a flashing sword in each hand. The reptilian eyes fixed on John's hand, and the fanatical stare vanished to be replaced instantly by shocked terror.

"Giles Plantard! Giles Plantard!" John was screaming the name. The power was flowing from his hand and he felt suspended in time. He was unaware of Vernon bellowing behind him as he fought back the distracted guards; John was only conscious of a strange sucking feeling, as though something was being drawn out of him through his arm and out of the centre of his palm. He felt lightheaded, focusing his full attention on the drama unfolding in front of him, knowing the time was right and understanding it was beyond his control.

A wild, primitive roar was sounding in the Giant's mouth, as both swords, gleaming blue, slowly twisted out of the powerful grip of his hands, and circled menacingly above him. The soldiers had stopped advancing. The officers stood like statues, staring unbelievingly at the strange spectacle. In the darkness, the swords caught the reflection of the firelight, emphasizing the sharp cutting edges of their blue blades, hypnotizing the watchers. The Giant was howling. He seemed unable to move his feet, as his scaly hands tried to beat away the swords that were pointing down at him, their blades only an arm's length out of reach. Suddenly, like bolts of lightning, both swords dropped from the sky, penetrating the thick armour, entering the huge body as if there was no resistance. He stood like a colossus, the swords embedded in his chest up to their hilts, the blades sticking out through his back. There was a strange silence as he stopped roaring, and dark blood poured out of his mouth. He raised his hands to the hilts of the swords, as though intending to pull them out; his fingers fluttered uselessly as he began to sway. His followers stared, unable to respond. The Giant's terrible eyes lost their brightness, and rolled up into his head, revealing blank white orbs. He staggered a half step forward and crashed down, shaking the surrounding ground like a small earthquake.

John felt as though he had been released from chains. His mind was alert, but his body ached all over. He turned to see Vernon staring slack-jawed at the fallen Giant; his sword was bloody, and two soldiers writhed on the ground behind him. With their leader dead, the officers and the guards appeared to be struck dumb, lacking purpose and coordination. They stared fixedly at the huge corpse, unable to comprehend the death of so powerful a creature; many of them had believed him to be invincible; some had thought him immortal. Now, he was just a very large dead body, a vast heap of foul flesh. The two Swords of Power embedded in him had become merely swords, their blue light extinguished, their awful power vanished, as if such evil had never been.

"Vernon!" John hissed, shaking his shoulder. "Quickly! Before they recover."

Transferring his sword to his right hand, which felt sore but cool, he pushed through the thin line of mesmerized soldiers, followed closely by Vernon, who had quickly regained his wits. As they fled for their horses, two guards in full armour challenged them. The men were running towards the silent gathering, drawn by the strange blue lights they had seen in the sky, unaware of what had happened. When they saw Vernon's bloody sword, and the strange weapon John was carrying, they both drew their swords, uncertain what to do. Before they could overcome their confusion, John was yelling at them: "The Giant is dead! They have killed the Leader!" As he approached them, he pointed furiously behind him.

The soldiers stopped, their eyes following the line of John's hand, suddenly aware of the great roar of grief and anger erupting from the gathering. At that moment, Vernon raced past John. He lashed out with his curved sword, slicing into the body of one of the guards, cutting deep into his waist, below the body armour. The man screamed, and collapsed sideways, his sword dropping from his lifeless hand. The other guard was quicker to respond, but as he turned towards Vernon, raising his sword above his head, John swung his long sword, Tegwen's Gift, in a powerful backhanded movement. The sharp blade cut deep into the back of the soldier's knee, where the leg armour was weakest, and the man collapsed to the ground, his sword just missing Vernon's head.

"Quickly!" John raced for his horse. Vernon stopped and gazed in horror at the second soldier, who was writhing in pain. He knew he had made an error of judgment, escaping death by a hair's breadth. But for John, he would be just another lifeless body. The noble calling he had longed for all his life was reduced to this: no honour, no glory, just a messy fight where people died, were maimed or escaped by chance. There had been no chivalry, no great display of skill and bravery, merely a bloody, and unpleasant encounter. Even the death of the Giant was an anti-climax: it had been a clash of powers beyond his understanding, like a strange, frightening dream in which his role had been unclear, and the result incomprehensible.

"Vernon! Quickly!" He was snapped out of his daze by the urgency in the voice. John was cantering over on Celestial, pulling Vernon's horse behind him. He staggered forward and clambered into his saddle. Vernon could see the crowd around the Giant beginning to rally. Already, soldiers were running towards them, silhouetted like black imps against the red glow. They turned the horses and galloped off towards the darkness, as the first spear embedded itself a few paces away.

In the wide ramifications of the camp, the guards were concerned with keeping the enemy out, not questioning the host within. It was this factor that John was relying on to save their lives. "Put your sword away. Make sure your helmet stays on!" He was yelling his loudest as they raced for the perimeter. "We can't hope to fight our way out. We must try to look as though we are on a mission!"

There was no sign of any pursuit, and although uncountable campfires lit up the area to their right, in front there was only a handful of small guard lights, well separated, still some distance away. Glancing behind, seeing the glow around the large wagons where the Giant had died, he wondered what would happen to this vast army. Would they act like a chicken without its head? Or were there other generals who could take on the mantel?

He realized he was feeling happy. It was unlike anything he had ever experienced. It was a heady mixture of relief, excitement, coupled with a remarkable sensation of power. He had faced his demon and survived. Earlier, he feared he might be unworthy of the trial he was to face, and yet when it happened he had felt confident, with no sense of fear. Now it was over; a new life was ahead of him. He let out an exultant cry, his voice loud and youthful in the darkness. Next to him, in contrast, Vernon crouched in his saddle, his face grim and impassive, waiting for the nightmare to end.

CHAPTER 20

THE WEATHER WAS PERFECT: cloudless blue skies, gentle breezes at night, and constant warmth. The countryside around the villa was an attractive mix of small farms, untended forests and bare hills dotted with sheep and goats. They had spent a restful week exploring the area on foot and on horseback, and enjoying the comforts of the De Bois estate, whose servants had quickly accommodated to their new guests. Throughout this period, they had both consciously avoided any overt physical contact, enjoying rather the gradual unfolding of each other's characters. Gwen had tried in vain to get Ralph to swim, but paddling was as far as he would venture. "If God wished me to swim he would have given me fins," he said. "Besides, too much water is unnatural." He failed to mention that he was a fine swimmer and from early childhood had practised in the family lake. In truth, he knew that swimming with Gwen would have destroyed his pretence of being physically reserved.

So, every day, he would exercise the horses, while Gwen swam in the sea. Ralph had banned any servants from venturing near Gwen's favourite cove, and she was at liberty to swim naked, enjoying, once again, the complete freedom of the exercise. "You have no idea how wonderful it is," she said.

"I have a very vivid imagination," he said ambiguously. "Also I can't swim..." In his mind he added, "...with you. It's too much temptation for any mortal man to bear."

"I could teach you."

Ralph looked at her wistfully. "I don't think I would be able to concentrate."

Gwen pretended not to understand. Every day he seemed more

desirable. She found him not only physically attractive, but also mentally stimulating. They were able to discuss philosophy and esthetics on an equal footing; at no time did he infer she was lesser person being a woman. She had expected him to be more demonstrative: to take her hand, to steal a kiss, perhaps to… but at this point, she always closed her mind, unwilling to stir those emotions bubbling just below the surface of her control. In one way, she was grateful he did not take advantage of their situation, but his very restraint added to his attraction.

"How long do you think we should stay here?" Gwen was sitting near the fountain in the courtyard, dangling her long fingers in the cool water. After an early breakfast, they had wandered outside to enjoy the warmth of the rising sun.

"I imagine we could stay for months. The members of the Order are not going to worry about their property rights while the High Lord is wrapped up with his Jerusalem project."

"Of which I appear to have been an essential part."

"Yes." Ralph studied her closely. She was a most remarkable woman. Her beauty was enhanced by her energy and intelligence, and he could see why the Order might wish to promote her, for she would fit naturally into the highest social order. At first, he had assumed that it was Gwen's physical attractions that had encouraged the Order to take such an active interest in her. He suspected she came from a powerful family, of which she was unaware; and this would be another important consideration for the Order, but there was more to it. There had to be. The Order was a fanatical, secret society of powerful men who would not have put so much time and effort into promoting a mere marriage. It must involve the seizure of considerable power to make it worthwhile. In recent days he had come to the conclusion that the importance of Jerusalem indicated the Order's intention to remove King Baldwin and replace him with the High Lord, but where did Gwen fit in? Sir Raymond de Wulfric had tried to reach Jerusalem with her, before the others of his Order, as though their entry into the city was going to signal some earth-shaking event. There was Lord William Longsword, who had deliberately provoked a battle with the Giant in the belief that he was guaranteed victory, merely by having Gwen with him. What was it all about? He stared up at a flock of small birds that raced across the sky. "Why do you think the Order wants to get you to Jerusalem?"

"They seem to think I will have some profound effect on their fortunes." She examined her fingers. "They believe I am somehow linked to an important family, with links to Jerusalem. In other words, they want to use me for their own advantage. I owe them nothing. They have controlled me throughout my life: they decided who my stepfather would be; they educated me as a child, then as a woman, and have prevented me from being myself. They have never told me the truth as to who I really am." She was beating her fists on her knees. "I will not be beholden to them any more." She stood up, and stared into the fountain. "Some of the Order believed John was my protector; they called him the Keeper of the Grail."

"And they think you are the Grail?"

She raised her eyebrows, and shrugged her shoulders. "It's silly what some people will believe. I don't feel special, nor do I want to be. I'm not even religious." She paused. "Spiritual maybe, but not religious. I have no magic. For a short time I had visions; I knew when the Giant was near, and I had a constant dream of the battle with the red painted cross on the hillside. But that's all. Many people have such experiences. I have no ability to change anything, and I have no desire to be rich and powerful." Tears formed in her eyes. "Thank God, I have been protected by my friends: first, John, then Martin, and now you. And you, Ralph, are the only one left alive." She sniffed.

Ralph placed a strong arm around her and drew her close. Without warning she began sobbing against his neck, her body racked with an explosion of hiccupping shudders, and he was reminded how tall she was. He could feel her full breasts pulsating against his chest and his body reacted to her closeness. Her warm arms closed around him like a vice. For the first time, he could sense her physical yearning. Their lips touched and she did not draw away, but increased their mutual pressure. Their mouths opened, allowing their tongues to inflame the sensuality of their embrace, their emotions erupting like the breaking of a dam.

Both were breathing hard, their passions uncontrolled. She did not resist or interrupt her intense kissing when he lifted her and carried her, effortlessly, up the broad stairs to her bedroom.

Throughout the morning, the building echoed with their lovemaking. At times, there were periods of unrestrained laughter and wild shrieks, and longer periods of amorous moans and whispered endearments. The younger servants grinned broadly as they crossed the courtyard beneath Gwen's window; the older women attempted to portray themselves as shocked, but not always successfully.

Lunch was left untouched in the main hall. It was not until the early evening the two lovers appeared; they were wonderfully relaxed, and unable to keep any distance between them. After eating a large meal, they wandered hand in hand down to Gwen's cove, where they sat on a rock and watched as small waves explored the beach, while the sun sank behind the mountains to their right. In the dusky light they embraced gently, occasionally staring wonderingly into each other's eyes, as though eager to discover ever more hidden secrets.

"I would like to get back to England as soon as we can," Gwen whispered. She ran her hand down his face, caressing his beard. "Ralph, my darling, let's get on with our lives. We've waited long enough."

"I'll travel to Limassol tomorrow, and see what shipping is available," Ralph agreed contentedly. "On one condition, of course."

"Anything."

"Anything?" He chewed her ear.

"There is nothing I wouldn't do for you."

"Will you marry me?"

"Of course. I couldn't do anything else." She was breathing deeply. "I love you, Ralph. I want to get back to England and become your wife."

"And we'll have an army of children."

"Of course."

As the darkness thickened, and she lay in his arms, Gwen smiled as she heard the reassuring call of an owl.

. . .

THROUGHOUT THE MORNING, CAVALRY patrols from both sides were engaged in fierce, bloody skirmishes, while the desert heat increased. The Crusader forces had formed up in battle order, facing south on mainly level ground some miles to the east of Tripoli. On their left was a riverbed with shallow, sluggish water, but its steep banks provided a natural defence from a possible flanking attack by enemy cavalry.

The High Lord and his senior officers sat stoically on their strong battle horses, waiting for the promised attack. They were positioned on a low hill, with a clear view of the empty plain ahead, their army columns spread out below them. In the front were the platoons of foot soldiers, their shields forming solid, seemingly impregnable ranks, each man armed with a spear or a sword. Behind them were rows of archers, mostly equipped with long bows that could rapidly unleash a hailstorm of arrows on an advancing enemy. However, such arrows, though numerous, were relatively inaccurate, having a limited effect on well-armed soldiers, whose armour and solid shields could withstand such attacks. For this reason, sections of crossbows were positioned among the archers. These weapons, while slow to load, and most useful at close quarters, were able to fire metal bolts capable of piercing any armour. Their weakness was their inability to reload quickly. When opposed to a furious cavalry charge, the bowmen might only have time to fire once. A combination of both bows provided a more solid defence, especially when protected by shields and swords.

On each wing of the army, strong sections of cavalry were drawn up their lances decorated with bright pennants, their squires bearing the larger banners and the heavy escutcheons. Behind the low hill, other knights and horse soldiers, a tactical reserve, peered anxiously into the sun, willing the enemy to appear. Far back, over a mile away, a small force of foot soldiers and a handful of horsemen under the command of Sir Payen de Montdidier, prepared to defend the rear of the army and the cumbersome supply wagons.

"What news?" De Warron demanded angrily. He and his officers had been ready for the predicted battle for hours, and the weight and heat of his armour was tiring him.

"No news of any advance, my Lord." The officer fought to control his impatient horse, while flies tormented it constantly. "The scouts' reports indicate the main body of the enemy is formed up more than two hours' march away. Much of their camp remains standing." The officer's voice indicated his confusion. "There are also reports of large bodies of irregulars fleeing the camp, and returning back towards Damascus."

Over the next hour, more reports arrived indicating further signs of the enemy's retreat and disorganization. The High Lord ordered his officers to oversee a controlled stand down of the army's preparations for battle. "Ensure the men get water and food. Double the scout patrols. Make sure there is a continuous watch on the enemy movements. We will camp here, but I want constant vigilance in case this is a trap."

"Could we not attack them, my Lord?" a junior knight suggested.

"No." The High Lord stared around imperiously. He was not unhappy with the suggestion, for it gave him the chance to demonstrate his leadership. "This is a strong defensive position. As you know, they outnumber us at least five to one. We have wasted today, and the heat has exhausted the army. It would be bad policy to leave this position and expose ourselves to possible attack on ground we have not chosen." The officers nodded their agreement. "Furthermore, our intention is to relieve Tripoli. If, for some reason, the enemy retreats, it makes it easier for us to achieve our goal: the advance towards Jerusalem."

Later, having discarded his armour, he relaxed in his tent with his senior officers. Outside, around the makeshift camp, tired men cursed the enemy they had prepared themselves to fight. None considered he might have died if battle had been joined that day; all were focused on the chance of loot, and a relief from the boredom of marching.

"There is no doubt, the enemy has lost heart," an officer announced. "I have just received a report that large formations of crack troops are returning to Damascus. Small cavalry units are still active, but even these appear to be mostly concerned with a defensive role."

Sir Raoul drank deeply; the wine was heavy, but lacked the flavour of his French wines. This unexpected retreat by the enemy was a pleasant relief, and the wine was acceptable. "Tomorrow we will advance on Tripoli. There may be some minor opposition, but I expect to relieve the city almost immediately." He frowned. "We still don't know the reason for the Giant's change of heart, so I intend to leave sufficient forces to monitor his withdrawal."

"Could we not inflict some retribution on the insolent scum?" a young knight suggested; it was understood he was merely flexing his muscles in older, more experienced company. "While the main body of our army is marching towards Tripoli, couldn't our cavalry turn the Arab withdrawal into a rout?"

"No. Today, we've had a bloodless victory. None of our Order has been lost, and I need to maintain our numbers. Remember, the enemy has infinite resources of manpower to fall back on, while we must treasure each of our knights, for they are almost irreplaceable in the short term. We will thank God for an easy victory. We'll set our sights on the accomplishment of our holy destiny." His mood changed. "I wish you all a good night. I want only the most senior members of our Order to remain."

After the younger members had left, Raoul looked around the small circle of battle-hardened knights, recognizing in each the ambition, ruthlessness and arrogance that he recognized in himself. "Have we heard from Sir Godfrey de Montbard?"

There was silence, and the eyes of the High Lord flashed dangerously. "What is the latest report from Antioch?"

"We have heard nothing since Sir Godfrey's report from Marqab. There is no news of the Maid," a knight replied.

"We are now so close to achieving our rightful position in the Holy Land, yet our most vital element has gone astray. Without Mistress Gwen, we have nothing." De Warren tightened his grip on his flagon, wanting to crush it in his manicured hand. "It is impossible to believe that de Wulfric could allow this to happen."

"How did he die?"

"Lord d'Escosse killed him," another knight replied. "That also is almost impossible to believe. Unless, Sir Raymond was murdered?"

"This gets us nowhere," Raoul snarled. "D'Escosse will be dealt with in due course. Our concern, our only concern, is for the welfare of Mistress Gwen. She must be found." There was a tense silence. The High Lord spoke decisively: "All of you will take sufficient forces, and acting independently, will search the area between Marqab and Antioch. Appoint your own substitutes; decide among yourselves which areas you will cover, and use any methods you think appropriate to draw out the truth. Meet up in Antioch. It is possible she may have reached there by now. When you find her, send me news immediately."

"And if we don't find her either here or in Antioch?"

"Then, we will look for her in Jerusalem."

"If she is not in Jerusalem? If we don't find her?"

"That is an unacceptable conclusion. It could mean the end of our Order as we know it."

· · ·

WHEN THEY WERE CERTAIN they were not being followed, they slowed their horses to a safe walk, and drew their swords, checking the darkness for any sign of life. At first light, they knew which direction they were going in and turned west, hoping to cross the path of their own advancing army. "Assuming of course our army is still advancing," Vernon said. He was still withdrawn and depressed, and this was his longest contribution for a while.

"We must assume they're still aiming for Tripoli. Unless they've formed up on some defensive hill, awaiting the Moslem attack."

Although not wishing to be identified by the Christian forces, it was safer to move towards them, until they discovered the state of the Arab army. Now it was daylight, it was possible to travel faster, but both were close to exhaustion, agreeing to stop as soon as they were able to find a suitable place to rest and find water.

"How many are there?" Vernon eased himself off his tired mount to join John, who was staring down at a small Arab encampment around a watering hole. The nomads were about half a mile away in a shallow valley. They seemed well established: there was a cluster of small tents, washing was drying on bushes, and beyond were camels and goats.

"Hard to say. I can see only a handful of men, but there are plenty of women and children." Although thirsty, John glowed with a wonderful sense of wellbeing. In spite of the ache in his tired limbs, he was free of the awful responsibility that had dogged him for years; his mind was clear, and he felt supremely optimistic.

Vernon licked his dry lips. They had been out of water for hours. Like his horse, he desperately needed to drink. "Let's chase them off. They don't look like fighters to me." He drew his sword. In his mind all Arabs were enemies.

"Put your sword away. We won't fight them unless we have to." John removed Vernon's helmet, and taking the bloody bandage that hung loose around his neck, he retied the material to cover one eye, then replaced the helmet. "Once again, you will play the injured hero who can't speak. I will do my best to avoid bloodshed." He smiled at Vernon's disgruntled expression. "All will be well. Trust me." They climbed back onto their horses and approached the camp at walking pace.

The children saw them first, jumping up and down, shouting a warning. Immediately, the women grabbed their infants and moved behind the camels. The men, numbering fewer than a score, bunched up, preparing to defend their families. They were poorly armed, relying mainly on strong staves, slings and the odd bow. None of them appeared to own a sword. There was a fearful hubbub from the women and children, until an old man with a long beard called for silence. He moved slowly forward to meet the two strange riders.

John called out a greeting, and dismounting from Celestial, bowed. The old man stared at the horse, obviously amazed by its size. He turned his attention to Vernon, with his bloody bandages, his odd mix of armour and peasant's robe. When John explained how they had both been involved in a fight with the invaders, and were in need of water and food, the old man nodded solemnly, leading the way into the camp, where they received the customary politeness and generosity of those who travel in the desert.

After a sustaining meal with many cupfuls of water, John was able to repay the nomads' hospitality by carefully answering their questions about Celestial, and demonstrating the use of his long sword. Vernon, who had recovered his good spirits, amused the children by revealing his bandaged eye, while making hideous faces.

When the horses were well watered and somewhat rested, John and Vernon prepared to leave, much to the protests of their hosts, who were immensely interested in John's news, his strange accent and his mysterious friend, whose wounds were not as serious as they had first been led to believe.

"Decent people," Vernon murmured as they replaced their saddles.

"You must be glad you didn't cut them to pieces," John replied softly, and quickly mounted.

Vernon sniffed loudly. Around him, the children giggled and made faces. Before getting on his horse, he did an impersonation of a monster, much to the delight of the young ones who ran off screaming.

John smiled down at the assembled people, who stood in a dignified group. They had been generous and welcoming. He was just beginning his final speech of thanks when a movement at the edge of his vision caught his attention. He turned to his left where the land sloped up to a ridge, and saw beyond the area where the camels were confined, a dark line of armed men had appeared. The sun was behind them. They advanced, menacing silhouettes, with their helmets and swords clearly outlined. There was a moment of heart-stopping incredulity, followed by chaos. The camels were already bellowing a warning, even as John yelled and pointed at the advancing soldiers. Instantly, the men of the camp were rushing for their limited weapons. The women began to ululate, a wild, fearful sound; gathering their weeping children around them, they raced for the doubtful security of their tents.

The soldiers came out of the sun in a wide formation; it was a few heartbeats before John realized they were soldiers from Christendom. They began to run fast towards the camp, their swords drawn, screaming horribly. Panic-stricken goats raced away in front of them, and nearer, the pinioned camels roared, fighting their restraints. The rapidly advancing men lashed out at any goat, unfortunate enough to be in their way. By the time John urged Celestial towards them, they were only a few hundred paces from the terrified nomads. He removed his turban. With his sword held high he cantered towards the charging mass of frenzied soldiers, confident in his ability to prevent a massacre.

But the blood lust was upon them. After days of marching and suffering in the unforgiving desert each man, encouraged by his companions, was eager to revenge himself on the enemy, which meant anyone who was not part of their army. Now, in a violent hysteria, they raced towards their prey like wolves attacking deer. They wanted to kill, rape and plunder; regardless of the innocence of their victims. They would feel justified: it was the way soldiers acted in such a war. Suddenly, unexpectedly, a bearded warrior on a Christian warhorse was waving a Norman long sword and confronting them. It did not matter; he would die too, the killing could not be prevented. The wave of battle-hardened troops rushed forward.

"Stop! I command you to stop!" John bellowed in the Saxon-part-Norman language that was English at that time. The distance between them was closing quickly. "I am an English officer! I command you to stop!"

The centre of the front was forced to hesitate as Celestial reared up in front of them. One soldier was stupid enough to ignore the danger, or unable to stop running. He fell senseless to the earth as the deadly hooves crashed down on him. There was a momentary pause in the centre of the column, but on each side the tide of blood-crazed soldiers pushed on, like a wave rushing round the sides of an impregnable rock.

John had glimpsed their faces; there was something different about them They did not look like English soldiers: they were too sallow; there was something about their eyes. "Stop!" he yelled. This time in French. "I'm an officer. I order you to stop!"

The excitement faded from the eyes of those soldiers who faced John, to be replaced by confusion: they needed to find a leader who would tell them what to do.

"Return to your officer!" John yelled. "I will kill any man who advances." The men were like punctured bladders, suddenly windless and without purpose. They stopped running, looking about, confused and uncertain as though coming awake from a bad dream.

He turned Celestial to his left, racing after a large group of screaming soldiers who were within fifty paces of the camp. He caught them just before they reached the camels, which were rearing up in terror. With the flat of his sword he knocked a handful to the ground as they ran, panting and roaring like individual nightmares towards the makeshift tents. He was in front of them, yelling at them in French, using Celestial's naked power to force them to stop. "Get back, you trash! I'm an officer. I will kill the first man who disobeys me!"

To the right the surge of charging soldiers was met by a determined group of nomads, prepared to fight for their families, regardless of the odds. But the soldiers' onrush pushed them back as if they were mere dross on a beach facing an advancing wave. Staves, slingshot and knives were no opposition to swords, shields and armour, no matter how brave the nomads were. They quickly fell to the overwhelming strength of the advancing soldiers.

The first soldier to force his way past the opposition was a big man who stank of weeks of sweat and bad wine. He rushed for the nearest tent; his mind focused on rape and murder. Dropping his shield, he slashed wildly at the flimsy material that separated him from the terrified women and children. He raised his sword to destroy the tent's doomed occupants, laughing maniacally. Everything changed: his eyes stared, his mouth opened in a soundless scream of pain, and he stopped as though suspended by an invisible thread. A sword had cut deep into his neck. With a deep groan, his heavy body collapsed lifeless on the ground. The horrified occupants of the ruined tent fled in panic.

Vernon raised his bloody sword, gave a satisfied grunt and turned to face the advancing soldiers. It had taken him a few moments to understand what was happening, as he had been enjoying himself, playing the fool with the children. The unexpected attack had caught him completely off-guard. He had eventually mounted his horse, watching in amazement as John, single-handedly, had taken on the advancing army of about a hundred men. He had witnessed the way the centre of the attack had been stopped, and how John had raced to intercept those on one side, allowing the other side to break through. The nomads had tried their best, but by the time Vernon was galloping to help, some of the soldiers had fought their way past the men folk, intent on murdering the innocent families.

Following John's tactics, Vernon pulled hard on the reins of his horse, causing the animal to rise up on its back legs, forcing many of the advancing soldiers to give way. Unlike John, his second language was French, and he yelled foul expletives at the soldiers in an accent they understood. After he had killed the leader of the group the rest ceased yelling, standing in awkward groups, panting like dogs, unsure what to do next. The surviving nomads had regrouped behind Vernon. When John trotted over, the mindless savagery of the soldiers had been replaced by bewilderment, as they tried to understand how their officers could be part of an Arab camp that they had almost destroyed.

It was at this point, that a lone rider came galloping over the hill followed, a distance behind, by a cluster of other mounted men. The rider careered down to the camp, scattering soldiers in his wake, roaring expletives and lashing out at any soldier who came within reach. He came to an abrupt stop in front of John, who was sitting on Celestial, with Vernon a few paces behind.

"I am Sir Payen de Montdidier," he gasped, "and I apologize for the unforgivable behaviour of my troops." He bowed his head quickly. Turning smartly in his saddle, he ordered the hostile soldiers to retire to the top of the slope. "I will kill the last man to move!" There was an angry murmur from the rabble, and for a moment it seemed they might defy him. However, with no natural leader among them, the mob paused, unsure how to act. When a group of junior officers galloped up, waving their swords, the men retreated reluctantly back up the hill.

Soon, there were no soldiers near the camp. The Arab women gradually emerged, their eyes wide with fear, and stood in small groups, hands to their faces, looking around for their men folk, their cries loud and anguished. Many rushed forward to embrace their injured relatives, grateful for their survival, but for others there was no such consolation. Their tragic voices wailed above the still bodies of their loved ones.

"I'm so sorry this happened," Payen said, as he surveyed the grim scene. "These are not my soldiers. I have taken command of them only recently. I was dealing with a series of reports from the main army, when I realized they had advanced beyond my orders."

"We're glad you arrived when you did. You may call me John," he said, trying to control his breathing, "and this is Sir Vernon de Kari. We are both on our way back to the main army." He was aware of the young knight's confusion. "I have been missing for a while."

"You have indeed." Payen gazed at John's thick beard. "Should I call you John, or Gilles de Plantard? I've heard of you, and you too, Sir Vernon." Payen dismounted and advanced towards the cluster of surviving men. The old man with the long beard bowed his head, as he listened to Payen's apology and his attempts at reaching some sort of restitution. After a short discussion, the young knight returned to where John and Vernon were standing.

"They lost three men, including one of his sons, and six injured. He has accepted the armour and weapons of my dead and injured soldiers, together with a small payment of gold." Payen shrugged his shoulders. "He's very philosophical. He says if God had not directed you two to his poor camp, all of them would have been slaughtered." He looked around at the weeping women, the frightened eyes of the children, and the excited faces of their men folk, who were holding swords, perhaps for the first time in their lives. "I think it's time we left."

• • •

LATER, OVER A BASIC supper, they sat around a fire and reviewed their situation. Payen and his officers, with the help of John and Vernon, had reinstated the necessary discipline among the surly French troops. A sergeant, who had encouraged the attack on the nomads, was stripped of his rank, his armour and his weapons, and was placed in leg irons, before a full parade of the other men. "By the time we eventually reach the main army, he will have suffered enough, marching in those chains," Payen remarked dryly. "Other officers might have executed him, but I refuse to take another man's life unless it is unavoidable."

Guards had been posted. The junior officers, aware of the mutinous feeling among some of the men, were on constant alert. Slowly, a sense of calm and order returned to the camp.

"Thank goodness the enemy did not continue his advance, we would have been easily destroyed this afternoon." Payen threw some dried camel dung on the fire. The tangy smell was something all desert travellers became accustomed to.

"So, the Arab army has retreated?" John gave Vernon a knowing glance.

"Indeed. I have reports that after failing to engage our forces, who were in a defensive position between the enemy and Tripoli, the army from Damascus suddenly disintegrated, retreating back in disarray." Payen rubbed his eyes as the fire smoked with a breeze, missing the excitement in John's eyes. "It is very strange, as they were thought to outnumber us by at least five to one."

John hesitated. He was about to explain how, with Vernon's help, he had defeated the Giant. But when he considered the unbelievable aspects of his story, a warning bell rang in his mind. If Vernon, who had been present, had been unable to believe what he had seen, how would Payen receive it? The young knight appeared to have strong religious views. How would he react to such a story? "Perhaps, something happened to their leader?" John said tentatively.

"I've heard nothing about that. There have been some outrageous stories about a giant and some magic swords." Payen laughed. "If that were the case, he and his swords were not that amazing. There again, soldiers will believe anything."

"Giants and magic swords! Those make for a good story." Vernon looked across at John with a straight face. "Well, I for one am glad we're not going to have a pitched battle. I'm getting thoroughly fed up with the desert and its smelly occupants."

"I hate to tell you this," Payen said, "but you smell worse than they do."

Vernon sniffed himself, looked vaguely uncomfortable, and stood up. "I think I'll just check on these unpredictable Frenchmen." He wandered away occasionally sniffing the air.

John and Payen sat together around the fire exchanging stories. John began by describing how he had been captured after the battle. He left out any reference to the Giant, or how he had come to understand and respect the local people.

"You speak remarkably good Arabic in such a short time in captivity," Payen said. "It has taken me nearly two years." He went on to explain how he had come to be in charge of the castle of Marqab. "It was there that I met your friend Lord d'Escosse."

"Ralph? He was at your castle?" John was astonished. "Vernon told me he'd travelled to Jerusalem!"

"That had been his intent."

"Was there a young woman with him?"

Payen gazed at the powerful young man in front of him, and noted the wild look in his eye. There was no doubt that Gwen, with her astonishing beauty, had conquered another heart. "Mistress Gwen? She arrived before him, in the company of a Knight of the Order, called Sir Raymond de Wulfric."

"Where is he now?"

"Dead. Buried outside the walls of the castle. Lord d'Escosse killed him in a sword fight." Once again, he felt the need to be accurate and formal. "De Wulfric drew first."

John looked quite amazed at this disclosure. "And Mistress Gwen?"

"They left together. Lord d'Escosse was eager to leave before other Knights of the Order came to investigate de Wulfric's death."

There was a pause as John digested this information. "Where did they go?"

Payen stared into the red embers of the fire, unsure what to say. Ralph had extracted a promise not to reveal his destination to anyone. But more importantly, what would Gwen have wanted? He imagined himself on his knees in front of her, and clenched his teeth. When he had behaved badly, she had treated him with kindness and sensitivity, not mocking him or flinging his childish protestations back in his face. He loved and admired her; he would not cause her further problems. She had seemed happy with Ralph.

"Payen. Where did they go?"

"Sorry. I must have dozed off." He affected a yawn. "Um. I don't know." He took a deep breath, and asked God for forgiveness. "He mentioned he was going to Jerusalem when he first arrived."

"I thought so," John said slowly. "There is something that has to be settled in Jerusalem. Both Gwen and I have questions that need to be finally put to rest. Gwen must have persuaded him to travel there. I imagine she needs to know the truth, as much as I do." He smiled broadly. "Perhaps, they hope to meet me there?" He clapped the solemn Payen on the back. "Vernon and I will be travelling to Jerusalem. We'll leave first thing in the morning."

"Then, why not travel with me?" Payen liked this young man, who although without title, showed outstanding qualities of leadership. Also, he was interested to see how John would react when he arrived in Jerusalem. How would he cope with his disappointment when he discovered Ralph and Gwen had never arrived? "Once I have delivered this mutinous gang of cutthroats to Sir Raoul de Warren in Tripoli, I am free to join King Baldwin in Jerusalem. It would be safer if we travelled together."

"Thank you, Payen, but I need to travel fast," John said. "I would hate to miss them in Jerusalem. Also, they might need my help."

"You will get there quicker if you travel with me. I have a scout who has visited the Holy City before. You have no idea how easy it is for you to get lost and attacked. Even with your gift for the language, you could take weeks to get there." Payen was pleased with his argument, and was not surprised when John eventually agreed.

"I, also, have reasons for needing to reach Jerusalem," he confided. "Reasons that could be of immense importance to our Church."

CHAPTER 21

"So, THIS IS THE much-famed Holy City." Vernon spoke with awe, as he gazed at the high walls of Jerusalem. He was dressed, once again, as befitted a knight, thanks to the generosity of Sir Payen. Now, with a sword, chain mail vest and new tunic, he had regained much of his former confidence and knightly pretensions.

It had taken them more than three weeks to travel down from Tripoli, during which time they had experienced extremes of weather and the rigours of the terrain. On a number of occasions, John was thankful he and Vernon had agreed to travel with Payen and his guide, avoiding the dangers of getting lost in an unforgiving country. On their journey, they were joined by a motley collection of merchants and pilgrims, each afraid of the robber bands operating along the main routes, grateful for the safety provided by the two armed knights and their servants.

John was content to remain in his Arab garments. He kept Tegwen's sword wrapped in a cloak, acting out the part of being Vernon's guide, unwilling to be drawn back into the Crusader ranks. His mind was focused on finding Gwen and Ralph, determined, once and for all, on discovering the truth about his ancestry and Gwen's importance in the Order's plans.

Celestial was clearly the largest horse in the group, causing some of the travellers to wonder how a mere Arab guide could afford such an animal; Vernon had hinted darkly at John's powerful and dangerous friends, silencing the envious questions. John's obvious strength and assurance prevented any of them from seeking to take advantage of this strange infidel; in their presence he spoke only Arabic, reinforcing his anonymity.

As soon as they came in sight of the City, the merchants and pilgrims quickly departed, some without even a word of thanks, keen to avoid having to make any payment for the security they had enjoyed over the past days. "Can't say I found them good company," Vernon observed, "not a noble hair among them."

"I have waited a long time for this moment," Payen spoke with a dramatic intensity. His eyes were fixed on the great stone battlements, which had been carefully repaired since the Crusader forces had breached them in 1099. "So much to do, and so little time to do it." Sitting proudly on his warhorse, he appeared to Vernon, who was perched on his small Arab horse, to have gained an aura of authority. He was like a man who knew exactly what he would do, and how he would do it.

"Yes, here at last," Vernon agreed, unsure what Payen was meaning. He looked up at the monk turned soldier. "Will you be staying long?"

"Perhaps for years. I have a lot to accomplish."

"Quite right." Vernon nodded sagely. Now that he had arrived, he was unsure what he was going to do, but felt confident that John would sort something out.

John turned to Payen. "I think it best if I entered the City by myself. You and Vernon will quickly be noticed. I will be able to move around more easily in these rags." He moved his horse forward, giving Vernon a thoughtful stare. "I want to trust you with my horse."

Vernon was visibly shaken. "Your horse?"

"Yes. It is obvious I will not be able to move freely around the city with such an animal." He dismounted. "We will swap horses until it is time for me to leave the City." John went to the front of the horse, and gently rubbed Celestial's muzzle. "He will allow you to ride him, Vernon, if I make it clear that I have given you the right to do so."

"You mean you want to find Gwen and Ralph by yourself?" he spluttered. What he really wanted to say was: "What about me?" But he didn't want to appear childish. There were bound to be plenty of people who spoke French or English; eventually he might meet up with his squire and his armourer again.

"It's something I must do by myself." John indicated the horse, and held out the reins.

With a mixture of reluctance and anticipation, Vernon dismounted and took Celestial's reins. The horse looked at him curiously, and sniffed his hand. Vernon had a lifetime of experience with animals, but knew he had never owned a horse as strong as Celestial. He spoke quietly, breathing into the huge nostrils, until he felt certain he had communicated with the intelligent creature. John watched silently as Vernon swung himself easily into the saddle. Celestial stood quietly, as if adapting to the knight's weight and posture.

"Well done." John patted Vernon's knee. "There are very few men who can ride Celestial, and even fewer that he will allow." He removed his cloak from behind the saddle, taking out the sword. Tegwen's sword glinted brightly in the hot sun. "I want you to look after my sword, as well. There is no way a mere peasant could own a weapon like this in such a cosmopolitan city." He handed it to Vernon, conscious of a great reluctance; it was as though he was parting with the only two solid reminders of his past life. "Take care of this," he said. "It's called Tegwen's Gift, and I want it back." He wondered why he had mentioned the name. "I want them both back."

Vernon licked his lips. "I'll guard them with my life. You can count on me."

John almost smiled. As usual, Vernon had managed to change the atmosphere without knowing he had done so. "I'll borrow your dagger, if I may. I promise to return it."

"Think nothing of it, old fellow." He felt very noble on John's horse. "Where and when shall we meet up?"

Throughout the exchange, Payen and Ishmael had sat quietly observing the action, noting the ebb and flow of emotions. Before John could answer, Payen addressed Vernon. "After I have presented myself to King Baldwin, I intend to set up camp in a ruined area of the Temple Mount, where the royal stables used to be. I am certain the King will allow me and some others I know to reside there." He turned to Vernon. "You may stay with me, if you wish, Sir Vernon, and we can both keep an eye on these valuable possessions."

. . .

JOHN FOUND A SMALL inn near the centre of the City, and thanks to Payen's further generosity, was able to rent a room and obtain a basic meal. He deliberately avoided eye contact with other customers, and apart from being a stranger, he attracted little interest. Once installed, he immediately set out to find Gwen and Ralph, but after two weeks of exploring the city, became convinced they had not yet arrived.

"I have no choice but to wait for them," John said, when he met up again with Payen. The knight nodded, but made no comment. Payen was standing before some ancient stone buildings, which at one time had served as the royal stables, but had long remained unused. It was clear that some considerable effort was being made to clean up the ruins, and John could see other figures toiling away inside. In spite of the apparent decay in the front, the space behind seemed dry and secure.

"Where's Sir Vernon?" John could not resist smiling when he said the name.

"He's gained a position with King Baldwin. Apparently the King was impressed with his horse and the quality of his sword." Payen grinned. "He's been welcomed into the King's personal guard. It looks like a long term appointment, unless he gets too involved with the women of the King's family."

"Amazing," John shook his head in disbelief. "Vernon has a remarkable way of concealing his abilities!" He smiled knowingly at Payen. "And what about you?"

"My meeting with the King went well. I, and my friends have agreed to help King Baldwin keep the roads free of brigands. The pilgrims who come from Christendom bring much needed money with them. There's been considerable lawlessness between the ports and Jerusalem; many get robbed, even more end up cancelling their intended visits. As you know, I am a knight and a monk, as are my brothers, who you see labouring in there." He indicated a small group of muscular men, who were busy moving piles of rock. "The King has given us permission to establish our religious order in these buildings, which are really caves that have been bricked up in the past. He has agreed that we can dig out an adequate space for ourselves, and our horses. Once we have the permission and blessing of the Archbishop, we will become a fighting order of monks, the first of our kind.

"I thought the Knights of the Hospital defended the pilgrims?"

'They provide care and medical help for the sick. They are too stretched to defend the roads as well."

"Do you have a name?"

"Of course. We will be known as the Poor Fellow Soldiers of Jesus Christ."

John sat down in a shady part of the ruins, and Payen joined him. "Why do you have to get the permission of the Archbishop?"

"Remember your ten commandments? Thou shalt not kill? We will need the Archbishop to allow us to become soldiers of God, both in word and deed."

"Soldiers have always killed people. That's what soldiers do. Knights are trained from their earliest youth to kill people. How does the commandment affect them?" John found himself personally involved in this discussion.

"Priests forgive sins on behalf of God. In this case, we are holy brothers. We will be fighting to preserve the Holy City for Christianity. The Archbishop is the only person who can grant us God's blessing on our endeavours."

"You make it sound very logical." John looked around at the broken stones, and the dark cave entrances set into the Temple Mount. It seemed a huge undertaking to excavate this area while attempting to guard the roads at the same time. He sensed there was something else that Payen had not mentioned.

"Why here? Why go to all this effort? There are other buildings the King could allot to you, allowing you more time to protect the pilgrims."

Payen did not respond immediately. He stared at John, as if seeing him for the first time. "I can't give you a full answer, but as I feel I can trust you, I will try to answer your question, at least in part." He looked about him, checking they were completely alone.

"You have had dealings with The Knights of the Order; what do you think they believe in?"

"They're men who believe in power. They come from rich and influential families," John said, struggling to organize his thoughts. "They believe Gwen is special. Their aim seems to have been to educate her, and bring her to Jerusalem. Once here, they seem to expect something amazing to happen." Payen nodded, but kept silent. "I have discovered that both of us were rescued from this city when we were very young, at the time it fell to the Crusaders. I believe we might both have come from important families. But I have no idea how the Order intends to use Gwen, or why some of their Knights have attempted to kill me. Certainly, they have tried to keep us apart."

Payen's eyes bored into John's. "The Order has lost sight of its destiny. Somewhere along its development as a secret society, its members took a great leap of faith, and lost their way. They came to believe that Gwen was a sacred being, without any proof. I and my brothers, who make up The Poor Fellow Soldiers of Jesus Christ, are searching for that proof."

"Do you think Gwen is special?"

Payen stood up, and brushed dirt off his stained tunic. "I have no reason to believe so."

John took a deep breath; another load seemed to have been lifted from him. "What happens when the Knights of the Order arrive here?"

"I believe the Order will gradually fall apart, for without Gwen, it has nothing. Many of its members will continue to search for her. She will become their Holy Grail. But many will lose heart and turn to other groups and beliefs to satisfy their need for power and excitement." He began to walk back to the stables.

"But why here? You haven't told me." John stood up, but did not follow him.

Payen returned slowly, almost unwillingly. "Because we believe that somewhere beneath this mountain of rock is the written proof of our beliefs. Ancient writings that could shake the foundations of the Christian Church as we know it today." He gripped John's hands. "Good luck in your search for your friends." He started to move away, then turned quickly. "I would not wait too long for them. It could be that Gwen has no intention of coming here. I hope, for her sake, she never does."

Before John could respond, Payen walked rapidly towards the entrance of the old stables, disappearing into the shadowy interior. He stood alone in the bright sunlight, feeling like a man who has arrived late at a celebration, unable to comprehend the fact that everyone has gone home. He was convinced Payen had given him a powerful message regarding Gwen, yet was unwilling to accept such advice. Without looking back, he walked away, knowing he would never see Payen again.

For another week, John continued his fruitless search of the city, gradually beginning to recognize the truth of Payen's last statements. His money was running out; he would either have to offer his services as a trained officer to King Baldwin, and risk being recognized by members of the Order, or work his way back to England. Late one afternoon, he climbed up to the Temple Mount to see the Al-Aqsa Mosque, revered by the Moslems as the third most important holy site in their religion. It was a beautiful building. He sat and contemplated it as the sun began to sink in the sky. To avoid the glare in his eyes, he moved round the building to an area of large, finished stones left over from a previous building. As he gazed up at the dome of the mosque, he became aware of an old man sitting on a low stone, close by. The man was busily eating a piece of unleavened bread; a wide cowl covered his head.

"You're late again," a familiar voice chuckled. "What a good job I had some food with me."

John shook his head in disbelief. "Owl. I had not expected to see you here."

"Why not? This is, like the standing stones, another of the world's important spiritual places. There have been a number of temples here over the past millennia, and this is just the latest, rebuilt by the Moslems in 1040. It was last destroyed 70 years after the recorded death of Christ by the Roman Emperor Titus." He indicated that John should sit next to him.

"I'm looking for Gwen," John said abruptly.

"Of course you are. Whenever I meet you, you're looking for Gwen." He broke off a large piece of the flat bread, and handed it to John. "Eat up. When you need to think, you need to eat. Thinking makes you hungry." He produced a small basket of olives, and a jar of water.

"Why can I never find Gwen?"

"Perhaps the hour is not right?" He laughed gently. "Do not take offence, my young friend. It is not yet in the stars."

"But when I met her in Cyprus, I thought she was my sister. If I had known the truth, if you had told me earlier, I might have married her. I know she loves me." He chewed angrily, unaware that he was eating.

"Exactly. What does that tell you?"

"What?" John stared at Owl in alarm, as the truth gradually dawned on him. "You mean I was not meant to marry her?"

"You are the Keeper of the Grail."

"But she loves me. What could be wrong in that?"

"If she was your sister, you would not think of marrying her."

"Of course not."

"You should see your role as her guardian, not her lover." Owl spoke as if it was not particularly important. "It is a fact of life, like having green eyes or being short or tall. It does you no good wishing it were otherwise." He passed the water to John.

There was a long silence as John wrestled with this revelation. "Do you know where she is now?"

"I know she's not in Jerusalem. But she is in no danger. In fact, I believe she is quite happy."

"Is she still with Ralph?" There was a trace of panic in his voice. If she was not in Jerusalem, then she could be travelling back to England with Ralph. What did Owl mean, when he said she was happy? "Is Ralph protecting her?"

"Ralph? Ah yes, your friend who has changed your life. You have met some fine people in the brief time since you first met Old Mary. I understand your latest friend has been of value to you also?"

"Vernon? Yes, he was invaluable in my final confrontation with the Giant," John said thoughtfully, seemingly unaware how Owl had passed over his question. "At least, that part of my life is over."

"It is over. You have made a major contribution to the preservation and development of the song. You remember the song?"

John nodded, absent-mindedly helping himself to some olives. He had so much to review. "So, that was my role, to kill the Giant?"

"You have still much to do with your life, but at least you won't be bothered by magic any longer."

"How can I escape it?" He held out his hand, palm up, towards Owl, while staring discontentedly at the gathering shadows around the mosque. "This is with me always, constantly reminding me I have no control over its power. I am branded, like a magician with a third eye."

"What am I supposed to be looking at?" Owl giggled. "It is a strong hand, rather grubby, but finely formed."

"With the sign of…" He stopped in mid sentence, and his eyes widened. There was no trace of the runes on his palm. Nothing to indicate he had ever had such a mark. He tried to remember when he had last seen it. Having carried the design for years, mostly unnoticed, on his right palm, it had become as familiar as the nails on his fingers. He stood up and rubbed the palm with his left thumb; there was no pain or sensitivity. It was as though it had never been. "It's gone!" The disbelief was strong in his voice. "When did I lose it?"

"You sound disappointed. I thought you were done with magical swords and signs of power?"

"I am. It's just…" He did not know how to react. Loss and celebration were at odds with each other; he felt strangely emotional. "So, now I must rely entirely on myself?" He sat down heavily. The shock was even greater than the relief he had felt after defeating the Giant. "It's as though it never happened."

"Exactly. You had a job to do, and you were given the tools to complete it. You were very successful." Owl nodded as though agreeing with himself. "You have no further need of such a gift." He packed up the remains of his small meal. "I imagine you have one more question?"

It was pointless to ask how Owl knew, and after a further examination of his hand, John looked into Owl's deep, dark eyes. "Will I... will Gwen be free of the Order?"

"The Knights of the Order are no longer relevant. The organization will soon fragment, reforming around a more successful and cautious body of men, whose initial formation is already achieved."

"Sir Payen and his Poor Fellow Soldiers of Jesus Christ?"

Owl did not appear to hear the question. He stood up and walked slowly towards a small, decorated stone, a remnant of a previous building. It was lying close by; it seemed to have a distinctive brightness. "I need you to move this. There is something beneath it that has been buried for too long." John narrowed his eyes. He sensed Owl was telling him something important. Without questioning, he approached the stone, but was unable to lift it.

"I think it's only necessary to push it aside," Owl chuckled.

John applied all his strength to the stone. It moved relatively easily, as though released from some restraint. Beneath it was a small hole, about twice the width of his hand. He knelt down, prodded around with Vernon's dagger, fearful there might be a scorpion or a snake in its dark interior; he could tell it was a shallow hole. When he was satisfied there was nothing dangerous, he reached in. After a brief exploration, his hand touched a small leather bag. "Is this it?" he asked, as he pulled it into the light. There was no answer. There was an empty space where Owl had been standing. He stood up and shook his head. It was as though, like the sign on his hand, Owl had not existed.

When he opened the leather bag, he was not too surprised to find it contained a small fortune in gold pieces. "The final problem is solved," he said aloud. "Now, I have no reason to stay." He walked briskly away from the temple, determined to say goodbye to Vernon and reclaim his horse and sword.

· · ·

IT WAS EARLY SUMMER when John eventually reached England. The journey had taken many months, during which he had lost track of time, often finding himself in places he had not intended to visit. His main problems had resulted from his attempts to avoid the stress of a long sea voyage on Celestial. It was for this reason he had first travelled from Jaffa to Limassol on Cyprus, and from the port, to the De Bois estate. Breaking the long journey across the Mediterranean was good for the horse. John nursed the faint hope that Gwen and Ralph had returned by this route, with the even fainter hope that they might still be there.

He arrived at the estate in the early morning, no longer dressed as an Arab, but as a rich traveller, riding a powerful horse and carrying a fine sword. He had a clear memory of the time when he and Ralph had first arrived at the grand old mansion: it had been alive with activity. This time it was empty, with all the signs of neglect and disuse. Without the supervision of their foreign overlords, the servants had quickly resorted to their customary inactivity. Eventually, he found a servant who spoke Arabic.

"Did an English lord and a young woman stay here recently?"

"Oh yes, Sir." The woman smiled at the memory. "They were much in love."

John turned quickly away, unwilling for her to see the emotion in his face. "Please get me some food. Find the stable boy to look after my horse."

The woman noted his change of manner. With a knowing look, she curtseyed and left the room. "That beautiful woman attracts men like wasps to a honey pot," she said to the cook, who was bustling around, tidying up the kitchen. "What should I tell him?"

"Tell him the truth. Tell him they left weeks ago. I heard they were going back to England." He helped himself to a cup of wine. "With luck, he won't stay long."

Within days, he secured a passage in a big merchant ship bound for Messina on the northeast tip of Sicily. From there, after an interminable wait, the ship eventually continued to Cagliari on Sardinia, where bad weather forced the ship to stay in port. It was weeks before he reached the busy city of Marseille and joined a heavily guarded band of merchants travelling to Paris. The journey was slow, the muddy roads and the inferior inns making it a tedious and uncomfortable experience. He disliked the stench of Paris with its immense crowds, and quickly hired a boat to take him slowly down the winding River Seine to the bustling port of Le Havre. Although there were a number of small ships and fishing boats in harbour, it took both gold and persuasion to get a Captain to take him to the small port at Christchurch.

The sky was blue and birds were loud in the trees as he made his way along the little-used roads to Woodford. He felt certain Gwen would have wanted to check on her stepfather, and was eager to get some confirmation of her arrival back home. During the long journey from the Outremer back to England, he had studiously refused to ponder Owl's declaration that he was not meant to marry Gwen. There had been the initial shock, in Cyprus, of the servant's confirmation that Gwen and Ralph were lovers, but like the memory of a violent hailstorm, he avoided dwelling on it. He was driven by a strong need to see her again, despite the warnings he had received, and regardless of the consequences of his actions.

He rode alone, along roads he dimly recognized. Occasionally, travellers had slowed or even followed him for a short while, attracted by his rich clothing, and the unusual quality of his horse. On such occasions, he had drawn his sword. Realizing he was a warrior, they had quickly departed. John was well equipped for travelling, and as the nights were pleasant he enjoyed sleeping out doors.

It was a dry, cloudy day when he came to the Flower Meadows: the long fields, where grass competed with wild flowers, was the place where he had first seen Gwen. He moved on down the rough path that ran along one side, wondering if Old Mary was still living in the area, and whether she was still alive. Somehow, it seemed to be like wondering if water was still flowing in the Avon.

A short while later he approached Woodford. On the outskirts of the village, was Tom's old forge where John had learned the skills of the blacksmith. It seemed smaller and cleaner than he remembered it. He rode slowly towards a young man who was concentrating on beating out a bar of hot metal.

"I'm looking for Old Tom," he called out, remaining in his saddle.

"Old Tom's dead," the muscular youth said truculently. "Me an' me wife live 'ere now." A young woman, with an infant in her arms, appeared beside him. They stared wonderingly at the tall, bearded man in front of them; they had never seen such a richly dressed person in their poor village. Their eyes strayed to his sword, then to Celestial.

"When did he die?"

The young couple looked at each other for assurance. "Maybe three, perhaps four years ago," the woman answered. "It were not too long after his daughter disappeared. Then 'is wife left. Old Tom weren't well."

"Has his daughter been back in the village recently?"

They shook their heads.

"Has anybody asked about Tom in the last few months?"

The blacksmith shook his head again, looking meaningfully at his forge. The woman touched his arm. "Remember that right tall man what come? The one what made a joke about 'is name being Little?" She turned to John, "I were outside when 'e come. Wanted to know about Old Tom. Didn't stay long, once I tells him Tom be dead."

"Was there a woman with him?"

"No." She was definite. "Just 'im. We'd know if there'd been other strangers. Not much 'appens round 'ere."

"Thank you." He leaned down and handed her a coin. "For your child." He trotted on through the village, heading north towards the Henge, leaving the two young people staring wide-eyed at the gold coin, the first they had ever seen.

It was mid-morning as he cantered across the great plain. Ahead of him, in the distance, was the Henge, its huge stones standing proud on the bleak landscape. He remembered his first sight of this amazing temple, how he had been unable to comprehend its immense size and grandeur, believing it impossible for mere men to have built such a place. It was here that he had met Owl for the second time, and where he had first met Ralph. He felt a lump in his throat and his eyes burned. He would not think about Ralph, his best friend, who had taken the woman John yearned for. As he rubbed his eyes, he saw, away to his left, a lone rider galloping towards the Henge.

His first reaction was of irritation. The rider was much closer to the stones than he was, and would arrive before him, depriving him of the solitary communion he craved. It was possible the man had not seen him, but either way, he was annoyed he would have to share the experience with a stranger.

He refused to hurry, slowing Celestial down to a walk, hoping the rider might continue past the Henge. It was possible, if he were a local person, that the stones no longer held for him the mystique and wonder John felt. The rider might gallop past. The horseman disappeared behind the monument; John was unable to tell if he had continued on, or entered the circles. The first time he had been here, Celestial had refused to enter the main circle, and he thought it unlikely that the rider had taken his horse among those forbidding stones. As he approached, he kept to the right of the Henge, and although he stood up in his stirrups, was unable to see any sign of the man. John made his way to the Avenue, scanning the plain in all directions. The horseman had vanished.

Cautiously, he advanced down the Avenue, dismounting by the Hele Stone. Celestial's large brown eyes were showing fear, and John stood holding its reins, while he carefully checked the site for any sign of the mysterious horseman. There was none. Feeling confident enough to leave Celestial untethered, he advanced slowly towards the Alter Stone. It was cloudy; wind moaned around the huge granite pillars, like the murmuring of a discontented herd of cows. He stopped by the thick flat stone, claimed by some to have been a sacrificial altar used by the early people, remembering his meeting with Owl. There was something comforting being surrounded by these massive stones; they were, as Owl had said, seemingly indestructible. John climbed onto the flat stone and lay back with his eyes closed. He forgot about the rider. His mind refused to focus on his intended journey to Ralph's estate, and he relaxed, sensing he was among friends. Owl had said invisible friends surrounded him when he was at the Greek temple; once again, he was aware of friendly support beyond his understanding. He breathed out deeply.

"It's quite a man you've developed into, isn't it?" There was a gentle mocking quality in the musical voice.

He sat bolt upright, as if stung by a bee. "Tegwen?" He knew he would remember that voice anywhere.

"Looking for me, were you?"

He slipped quickly off the side of the stone, facing the beautiful woman who had been his first lover. "I knew we'd meet again, some day," he whispered.

She was dressed in men's brown trousers fitted into knee-high boots of soft brown leather, and wore a pale green shirt, inside a brown leather jerkin. Around her waist was a thick leather belt with a short sword and a dagger, on her back was a quiver of arrows. In one hand she carried a long bow and in her other she held the reins of her horse, Gomar.

John stared at her, conscious of a pulse thudding in his neck. He had lied; he had never expected to see her again. She was exactly the same as he remembered her: short, buxom, with long, black hair, the colour of jet, and wondrous blue eyes that set him on fire. Remembering her broad, generous mouth, her full lips and her perfect teeth, he wanted to move closer to her to enjoy her sweet breath. He was suddenly aware of a feeling in his loins he had not known for a long time.

"There's a liar." She was laughing at him. "You never thought you would see me again." She advanced, dropping her bow, and letting go of Gomar's reins. Placing her hands on each side of his face, she looked up at him and studied him closely. "But glad I am you're back, even if you look like a wild man with that silly beard."

It was as though they had never been apart, that the years of separation were unimportant. His arms entwined her, and he drew her close. "I've always loved you," he muttered hoarsely. "You are the most amazing woman in the world."

"You say that to all the girls, don't you?" She laughed; it was an endearing, musical sound, full of joy and sexual arousal.

Their lips met, and they knew there could be no restraint. They kept their lips together as they dropped their weapons, their clothing, and all inhibitions. It was much later they spoke, when their initial passion was spent. They lay side by side, looking up at the clouds, with the huge stones standing like sentinels around them.

"I've a camp near here. We must go back and eat, yes?"

"Eat?" John raised himself on one arm, looking down at her. "You're all I want. Nothing else is important."

"There's silly you are. You need food to give you strength, isn't it?" She giggled as her hand explored his body. "And you're going to need lots of strength, cariad, I promise you."

•　•　•

BY THE NEXT MORNING, their seemingly unrelenting passion was exhausted. After bathing in a small, cold stream, they sat around a fire in comfortable companionship, well hidden from any traveller.

"Did you know I was coming?" He sipped a fragrant hot drink that Tegwen had prepared.

"How could I know?" She snuggled up closer to him, enjoying his scent.

"Perhaps it was in the stars?"

She embraced him tightly. "Perhaps it was, cariad. Does it matter?"

"No." He smiled at her and gently kissed her eyes. "I want to tell you everything that has happened to me since we last met. Unless, you already know?"

"Don't be silly. Just because I can read the stars, doesn't mean I know everything that's going on." She pinched him. "There's a gwirion boy you are."

"I don't speak Welsh," he responded, tickling her unmercifully.

"All right," she screamed with enjoyment. "Tell me your story. But no more tickling, yes?"

She covered them both with a fleece, and for the next few hours listened with rapt attention, as John recounted the complex, almost unbelievable tale of his past years. He found himself being frugal concerning his details of Ralph's sister, only later remembering that Tegwen, as a pagan priestess, knew all about Aelfreda.

"And you loved her?"

John sniffed. "Eventually. Um. At the time."

"Don't be embarrassed, John, cariad. She knew all about us, yes? When she made love to you at the Henge, the day Ralph and I celebrated the pagan festival, she knew all about you, look you." She smiled broadly. "I told her."

"What?" John felt overwhelmed by the disclosure.

"Why is it, now, that men can discuss their conquests, but think that women don't. Oh, there's a silly."

"Did you mind?"

"Why should I, then? I haven't given you any promises. Nor you to me. Free we are, and free with each other, yes?"

"Have you seen her since?"

"Of course, we're part of the old religion, aren't we?"

John took a deep breath. "How do you feel about Ralph and Gwen?"

"They'll be very happy, cariad." She stared into his eyes. "Ralph knew I was never going to marry him. It's in the stars, isn't it?"

"What about Aelfreda?"

"She's married."

"Married?" John was astonished. He felt both relieved and betrayed. His passion for Gwen had relegated Aelfreda to an embarrassing memory, made more so by the fact she was Ralph's sister. It was another aspect of his life he had refused to face up to. But at the same time, he felt abandoned. The irony of the situation was, at first, lost on him. "Who did she marry?"

"Some local Lord, isn't it? Saxon too." Tegwen nibbled his ear. "Jealous, are you?"

"Of course not!" He frowned. But gradually, the humour of the situation occurred to him. He began to laugh. It was a combination of relief and hysteria; soon he was shaking with mirth, tears pouring down his cheeks, while Tegwen laughed with him.

Eventually, he stopped, lying still, exhausted by the emotion. "What about Ralph and Gwen?" he murmured.

"Married as well." Tegwen said contentedly. "As soon as they came back, didn't they?" She giggled. "They had to, in the circumstances. Baby's due in a few months, isn't it?"

John stared up at the darkening sky, trying to digest the

information. "I suppose I should travel to their estate and congratulate them?"

Tegwen rose up, reaching for his right hand. "You no longer have the sign of power, cariad, yet you're still the Keeper of the Grail." Her voice had lost its playful quality. She spoke with a serious intensity, gripping John's attention. "Gwen and Ralph think you're dead. It is better they continue to do so. They will be happier, don't you think?"

"Why? Why does it matter if I once had a strange title? Sir Payen said the Knights of the Order were finished and that Gwen was unimportant. It's all over. It's in the past."

"No, cariad. Important things always continue. Sir Payen and his Poor Fellow Soldiers of Jesus Christ have not forgotten. Soon they will be powerful." Her eyes glazed over for a moment. "They will eventually be called the Knights Templar, and they will want to find Gwen." She shook her head as if getting rid of a fly. "You're the Keeper of the Grail, it is your role in life to protect her, yes?"

John sat up, his face creased with anger. "It's over! The sign of power, the Giant brothers, the Swords of Power, even Owl. It's all over. I'm just who I am. Nothing more; nothing special. No magic! It's over!"

"Yes, that part is all over." Her voice was gentle, and her sweet breath embraced him. "But you are still the Keeper of the Grail. Gwen is still the Grail. She will need protecting from a distance. That is your role in life, isn't it?" She slipped her arm around his shoulders. "Our role in life, cariad."

"You said we could not be together when we last met." He felt suddenly vulnerable.

"I said you had a journey to make." She smiled. "I said I would always be waiting for you, yes?"

"Yes," he said wondering at her beauty, "you did say that. But that was years ago. Why have we waited so long?"

She kissed him. "It was in the stars. We could not be together before you completed your journey. You have become a fine man." She paused, "Now, the hour is right."

As if to crown the moment, an owl called close by. Away in the twilight forest, another owl answered.

CPSIA information can be obtained at www.ICGtesting.com
Printed in the USA
LVOW12s0535180714

394658LV00001B/6/P

9 781897 435151